BAI

Angela Willans was educated at a Hertfordshire boarding-school from the age of seven and read English at the Universities of Cambridge and London. After working as a teacher, a tutor of handicapped children and a canteen waitress, she entered journalism on the *Daily Express* and went on to write for the *Daily Mirror* and the *Daily Herald*. For the past twenty-five years she has been the 'agony aunt' of *Woman's Own*. She has broadcast frequently on TV and radio and has also served on numerous boards and councils, ranging from Marriage Guidance and Brook Advisory Centres to the British Humanist Association and Cranborne Chase School. *Ballads* is her first novel. Her three previous non-fiction books are *Conflict in Marriage*, *Breakaway* and *Divorce and Separation*. She was married for twenty-one years to test parachutist 'Dumbo' Willans, has two daughters and lives in Henley-on-Thames.

ANGELA WILLANS

BALLADS

PENGUIN BOOKS

PENGUIN BOOKS

Published by the Penguin Group
27 Wrights Lane, London w8 5tz England
Viking Penguin Inc., 40 West 23rd Street, New York, New York 10010, USA
Penguin Books Australia Ltd, Ringwood, Victoria, Australia
Penguin Books Canada Ltd, 2801 John Street, Markham, Ontario, Canada l3r 1b4
Penguin Books (NZ) Ltd, 182–190 Wairau Road, Auckland 10, New Zealand

Penguin Books Ltd, Registered Offices: Harmondsworth, Middlesex, England

First published by Viking 1988
Published in Penguin Books 1989
1 3 5 7 9 10 8 6 4 2

Made and printed in Great Britain by
Richard Clay Ltd, Bungay, Suffolk
Filmset in Monophoto Sabon

CONTENTS

For Judy

BOOK ONE

I

HOUSE FOR SALE

The grapes were going to be unusually good that year, Martha was sure of it. She stood in the middle of the glasshouse and peered up at the vine. Its fruit, as yet barely the size of peas, was flushed pink in the light of the early-morning sun and looked full of promise.

Yes, she told herself, we'll remember 1966 as a good year, perhaps better than any other, and we'll store one bottle away, never to be opened.

She took a deep breath. It was partly to inhale the glory of the coming day. It was also to check on the state of the haddock poaching on top of the cooker in the kitchen nearby.

I wish, she thought, that Phoebe weren't so fond of haddock for breakfast. The sight of that pale-yellow flesh floating in milk almost put her off the morning. But it was one of the penalties of having her twin sister home at last. Haddock, Phoebe had said in that authoritative way of hers, was nourishment for the brain. And since Martha was not going to give up her tenure of every householder's basic territory – the kitchen – it was she who gingerly slid the fish into the worn poacher every morning, slammed the battered lid on top of it and ran out to the glasshouse to take the pulse of the day before getting dressed.

Today, however, she was aware of unease. For some reason the familiar routine of breakfast, gardening, painting, maybe a walk to the village, was going to be upset. But why? She turned anxiously from contemplation of the vine and ran upstairs to her sister's bedroom.

She took the wide, shallow stairs one at a time, resisting

3

another of Phoebe's maxims – that two at a time kept the body supple. She paused for a moment at the bedroom door. The sisters had a tacit rule not to meet before breakfast. But the mystery about the source of her unease overcame her reluctance to break the rule. She heard music and thought, well, anyway, she's up. In one move, she knocked at the door and went in.

Phoebe was doing her limbering-up. She wore a bright red leotard, which Martha thought somewhat comical, but brave, for a woman of 41, and was swaying her slim, broad-shouldered body from side to side, her arms above her head. There was the tinkly thump-thump of a ragtime number coming from a scuffed wind-up gramophone on a low table. Phoebe nodded at Martha and continued her swaying movements.

Martha stared at her affectionately. It's funny, she thought, how Fee can never pass up an opportunity to show how quick-moving and lean she is compared with me. In truth, the contrast was so slight as to be scarcely noticeable to anyone but themselves. They were far from identical but very alike, both tall, clear-skinned and brown-eyed, with straight backs and long, patrician feet and hands, and short, shining hair that softly followed the shape of the head. But, to Martha, Fee was quicksilver. And, to Phoebe, Mart had the serenity of a calm sea. For these particular qualities, each envied the other more than they could admit.

'Why am I edgy today?' Martha shouted.

Fee paused before ducking her head to meet her knees.

'Because people are coming to see the house.'

She raised her head sharply and saw that this statement on its own was being given too much importance. Martha's hand had flown to her mouth as if to stem a cry of pain or protest.

'There's a postcard from Alice today – on the dressing-table,' Phoebe added quickly.

Martha waved towards the record-player.

'Are you nearly finished? That noise – I can't hear a thing you're saying . . .'

4

But Phoebe knew she had heard and that nothing was going to divert her from milking today's events of every ounce of sorrow and alarm.

She straightened, walked slowly to the gramophone and switched it off abruptly without raising the needle from the disc, so that the bright, sweet notes tailed off into a sour groan. She kept her back to Martha as she turned and gazed out of the window at the garden.

'You know it has to happen,' she said quietly.

'Yes, but they might not be suitable. We ought to be told more about them first. Ballads isn't for just anyone. Supposing they want to put Formica everywhere, or get rid of the Aga, or put a horse in the orchard? They're bound to have a silly teenage daughter . . .'

'Whose name will be Pandora or Amaryllis or even something completely invented like Pandoryllis . . .' Phoebe turned as she spoke and smiled, hoping for a more successful diversion than the postcard.

For a moment Martha was caught off-guard by Phoebe's invitation to play one of their habitual games.

'Or maybe one of those American-style, stuck-together names like Amyjanemarie or Bobbysuejo . . .' Martha stopped suddenly and pulled her dressing-gown more tightly about her, as if to shut her sister out.

Phoebe looked at her with both irritation and sympathy.

'Well, if they do anything like that, it won't bother us, will it? We won't be here. Besides, no one would be suitable really, would they? Not in the way that anyone can ever feel about this place. They can't have the same feelings as we . . . as you have . . .'

Martha stared helplessly at the floor for a moment, searching for a counter-argument.

'You're no help,' she said at length. 'Why are you being so hard? You don't have to say things like that.'

'It's true though, isn't it? This house is you. You are this place. No one will have the same feelings about it. Not even me. You take those feelings away with you and have them

5

with you always, wherever you are. You don't have to be here to know it and love it.'

'Oh God, Fee,' Martha's expression became anxious and petulant. 'Why do you talk like that, making things so complicated? It's right out of one of your bloody psychology books. You know I won't understand. It's simple. I want to stay here and, in the end, die here. I don't want anyone else putting their pictures on these walls and talking in these rooms. You know how it is. We owe that to Papa, at least. These people mustn't come. And if they do come, you must tell them to go away.'

Phoebe knew that at this point she should have taken Martha in her arms and soothed away her awful approaching loss. I'm failing her again, she thought. But no, not me – it's life that's failing her again. But why does she always sink so heavily, almost drown, under her sorrows? Why can't she just take the slings and arrows, the way other people do? The way I have to? How can she still expect happy endings after all that's gone on in this house? All the evidence is that there are never happy endings, only a constant succession of beginnings and then what you make of them.

'Look, Mart,' she said in a gentler tone of voice. 'Don't make it worse. I do know how it is. And so do you, really. You know it's all about money and how long we can go on heaving fuel hods about and borrowing to mend the roof and getting the Land Rover up and down from the village. And seeing the rates go sky-high. And watching it all fall round our ears. Look how empty the place is! I mean, seven bedrooms for two people! We're rattling round in it. The kitchen and the glasshouse is all we use in the summer, plus our bedrooms, and there's only the breakfast-room in winter.'

'Yes, exactly, the glasshouse,' Martha said firmly, as if she had hit on the clinching point. 'I'm surprised you can think of letting that out of the family's hands. Especially after all that's happened there. You know what it meant to Papa. Doesn't it mean anything to you?'

'What? Are you crazy?' Phoebe could no longer keep up

6

her attitude of gentle understanding and the words came out harshly now. 'What on earth has history got to do with it? Do you want to slice the glasshouse away from the rest of Ballads and put it up somewhere else? As a shrine or something? For God's sake, Mart, let's try and keep all this emotion out of it . . .'

'How can we? You sound just like Alice . . .'

'No I don't. It's just that this is reality, all this mess, this shambles. It's wolf-at-the-door stuff, honestly, Mart. In a couple of years there wouldn't be anything left of Ballads, just a ruin . . .'

'I wouldn't mind being here, whatever it was like. I'd rather be hard up here than comfortably off anywhere else.' Martha spoke triumphantly, as if she had produced an open-and-shut argument.

Phoebe was now waving her arms about and punching the air for emphasis, a sure sign to her sister that she was struggling to be objective in the teeth of Martha's overwhelming subjectivity.

'Not just hard up,' Phoebe said. 'Do you mind? Poverty-stricken, that's what we'd be. Crawling into middle age and beyond in ghastly old clothes. The place tumbling down. Everything getting smellier, including us. We wouldn't know anyone, and no one would want to know us. Rain in the bedrooms and rats in the scullery and the Aga out and very likely no electricity either. The last bill's still over there . . .' She waved towards a table in the corner, neatly piled with papers and letters. 'But Mart, we've been through all this a hundred times before. Please see reason. Nothing can make it any different.'

Martha tightened her lips and the cord on her gown. She felt that surge of irritation, almost of hostility, towards her sister with which she was painfully familiar. Through the years she had experienced it again and again as she encountered what she thought of as Fee's hardness. It was more than irritation, she realized. It was a granite brand of frustration. Through the thumps and hair-pulling in childhood, Phoebe had always emerged as the moral victor, no matter how many bruises she incurred. Not for her the physical retaliation, or the Pyrrhic victory of more blows inflicted than suffered. Words were her weapon and they always prevailed. She knew how to choose them and place them where they would hurt most. And when they had outgrown the kicks and thumps, there had not seemed to Martha to be any other way in which she could express her own anger. The way of words was forbidden. Phoebe had made it her own. Besides, she knew perfectly well that she didn't have Phoebe's verbal skills.

Following on her feeling of frustration came its usual accompaniment, a mood of depression. She crumpled in a heap on to Phoebe's bed and let the tears come.

'I can't bear it, Fee. I just can't bear it. We have to go. I know that. But I can't bear it . . .'

Phoebe sat beside her, not quite touching.

'It's all right to be angry with me,' she said. 'It's all right.'

Martha jerked her head up.

'Oh, your analyst's talk. Don't give me that. I'm not angry. I'm very depressed.'

'Same thing.'

Martha wiped fiercely at her eyes with her fist and gave Phoebe a sharp push. She stood up and spoke without looking at her sister.

'O K then – what about this postcard from Alice? What's Mother got to say about selling the house? That's if she gives a bean . . .'

'No-o,' said Phoebe slowly, wary of being too confident that the storm was over. 'I don't think she cares more than she ever did, no. Anyway, what did you expect from a mere postcard? Her postcards, at any rate?'

She picked up the postcard from the dressing-table and peered at the picture side of it.

'It's from Brazil. She's in Rio de Janeiro. Not with Francis this time, I take it. Didn't she say his wife was dying or something equally grim? It's just a picture of streets and buildings, the usual thing. It might be anywhere.'

She flipped the card over to re-read the message.

'No meat here either,' she said. 'Do you want to read it?'

'Of course I do. You're always so hard on her.'

'Yes, I know you think so.'

Phoebe handed the card to her sister.

'Read it out loud,' she said. 'Alice would like that.'

Martha frowned but started to read in a level voice.

' "My darling twins . . ." ' she began.

'Oh yes?' interrupted Phoebe mockingly. 'Since when? And how come she's never said that to our faces?'

'Oh I don't know, Fee. What does it matter? All right if I carry on? "Have taken Rio to my heart. Can get Lizzie Arden stuff here and there's a marvellous masseuse in the hotel. Guess what? Someone on board took me for a fifty-year-old. Cup runneth over. All love, Alice." '

Martha remained staring at the writing, as if searching it for a deeper significance.

'See what I mean?' asked Phoebe flatly. There was no note of triumph in her voice but Martha heard it.

'All right then. She doesn't care about Ballads – or about me. And nor do you. And that's the whole trouble. Take it, take it.'

She flung the postcard at Phoebe's feet and stumbled from the room.

Phoebe stood still, gazing at the card on the floor. You with your overweening self-regard, she addressed it bitterly. I can take it, but look what you do to Mart. She still longs for what you were never able to give. The loving arms. The unconditional approval. Even common or garden liking would have been welcome, or just a few looks that said, 'You matter.' Or, indeed, any looks at all of any kind, thought Phoebe, struggling, as she often did, to remember one single occasion when their mother could be said to be actually seeing them. There was always something else in her eyes – a distant look, a flicker of boredom, a difficulty, it seemed, in focusing outwards rather than inwards. She wondered if Alice would be able to answer if she were asked what colour eyes her children had. They say you don't really love someone unless you can say that straight away. Alice couldn't, Phoebe was sure of that. She'd have to look it up in my passport. She's never really seen either of us. Looked when she had to, but never seen. And never will.

She glanced towards the door which Martha had left ajar. The air was still and quiet and the morning chill was not quite gone. She listened to the house for a moment, as she often did. It was strange that, on such a fair and motionless morning, Ballads was nevertheless full of movement, shrugging its roof-tiles and eaves, testing its joists and floorboards, calling forth tiny sighs and creaks from doors, window-frames and stairs. No one in the world could stand like this and hear it all, thought Phoebe. No one except me – and Martha, of course.

She could also hear distant, unidentifiable sounds from her sister. She knew that Martha would be busying herself somehow, her anger released by the open conflict between them. She would be deciding what to wear for the visitors, or eagerly setting up her easel in the glasshouse, or even perhaps humming as she set the table for breakfast.

If only, she thought, I could love her in the way she needs to be loved – to be held warmly and protected and have her whole world bathed in sweetness and light. It's what she has needed from our parents and from every lover she has ever had and, all the time, from me. To have it and be made strong, and then to be free of this want. And I've needed it too but soon realized it wasn't available, from her or any-one.

I intellectualize too much, of course. People keep saying so. And it's true. I'm doing it now, standing apart with my damned internal tape recorder and camera. I should have hugged her and said we'd work out ways of staying here. But we can't. There is no way.

She walked to the window and looked towards the northern sky, dropping her gaze gradually until it rested on the circular drive in front of the house. In her mind's eye she saw Papa – silly word, she thought, but it was his choice and so now it was Martha's and couldn't be changed – she saw the misty outline of his body, lean and tall like hers, bent backwards to peer up at the window of his and Alice's bedroom. His shotgun was tucked under his arm, its muzzle pointing to the ground and the butt settling easily in the crook of his elbow. He was not looking towards the window where she now stood. He never did. His eyes were fixed intently to the left of her and he was calling 'Alice, Al, can you hear me? Come to the window, Al. I'm just going. Alice! Alice!' He bent further and further backwards, almost as if, by so doing, he could see through the blank stare of the window and rouse his wife with the strength of his longing to say goodbye.

Why did he always insist on trying to say goodbye? She stared at her vision of Colin, trying to wrest the truth from him. Was he always afraid that he might not come back? That there would be an accident? Or that, when he did come back, she might not be there?

Her imagination could not conjure up an answer to his calls, for there had seldom been one in real life. Often he had forgotten, Phoebe supposed, that Alice was in London for the day, or even for a couple of days and nights, or perhaps for a whole week. He called and called, his voice rising higher and more urgently. Then he stopped abruptly and straightened and shrugged. Without looking for Alice anywhere else, no matter what time of the day it was, he would walk purposefully down the drive with his soldier's upright bearing. She saw him do that now and watched him until he was out of sight and the space in front of the house became empty again.

Soon there will be other people there, climbing out of their car with that awful predatory look of house-hunters and subjecting the whole of our lives to cash-register scrutiny. If only Alice had loved Ballads as the rest of us loved it! Then she would have devoted her money to keeping it safe and beautiful instead of splurging it all on cruises and high living and clothes and massages. If only, if only – I sound like Martha, Phoebe thought ruefully. She pulled her mind away from the window and went downstairs to soothe Martha and enjoy the haddock.

The woman in the back of the small car fidgeted impatiently as it bumped and groaned at a snail's pace up the narrow unmade road towards Ballads. She kept her eyes rigidly on the driver's neck, noting that it was rough and reddened. A tendency to boils, she reflected. That's what comes of shirts worn more than once before washing. But the state of Mr Coleherne's neck and shirt-collars was no surprise to her. Estate agents were a long way down in her pecking order, ranked with the poor and, by definition, feckless, art students, door-to-door salesmen and socialists. The horror of it was that the 1960s seemed to be producing a surfeit of members of all these groups.

She willed herself not to look at the hedges and trees bordering the lane. They represented the uncontrolled, haphazard element which she was continually striving to keep out of the Endicott family life at Bishop's Court in what she always referred to as the 'hub of London'. There, thank goodness, the rubbish was always collected, the street lamps worked unfailingly and the lime trees which lined her road were satisfyingly robbed every March of their wild, spear-like branches and transformed into impotent clenched fists at the top of bare trunks.

She sometimes wished a similar fate could befall her husband, Charles. This was not to say that she did not love him in her own fashion – which is the only way anyone can love, in any case – but merely that she wished he loved her in a different fashion from the one that caused him occasionally to feel aggrieved at the lack of what she teasingly called his 'bedroom comforts'.

She shuddered and drew back as a wayward branch of may scratched against the car window.

'Is it far now?' she asked.

'Just a jiff,' said Mr Coleherne, who was struggling against irritation too, for a different reason. Why on earth, he thought, hadn't these vendors had their lane made up years ago? The flintstones and pot-holes must be playing havoc with my suspension and tyres. He winced at the sound of the exhaust-pipe meeting a rocky prominence with some force. Out of the corner of his eye he saw Charles Endicott wince in empathy and he felt better.

'That's another attractive feature of this property,' he said cheerfully. 'With an approach road like this you don't get every Tom, Dick and Harry dropping in on you or roaring along outside on their motor bikes. Not that far from the madding crowd but all the privacy and peace you could want, eh?'

'Oh God!' said Sue Endicott, who wanted peace and privacy only marginally less than she wanted anyone else to have them. In her view they both came under the heading of self-indulgence.

'Well, that's certainly a point,' said Charles Endicott. He felt extraordinarily weary. In some ways this viewing was a high point in his life. He had long ago admitted to himself that he had acquired almost everything he had ever desired, including a very attractive, competent wife who adored him and tended all his needs except one. All that then remained was a house in the country, a desire that dated from his early life in a tight little suburb of London that almost, but not quite, sucked the ambition and hope out of him.

Three years ago his fortunes had reached a stage where this antidote to the grey conformity of suburbia and, indeed, the high claustrophobic walls of his present London home and office, was within his grasp. He had begun a secret game of anticipation which he well understood had to be prolonged for as long as possible in order to be enjoyed to the full. So he had taken his time and had been able to draw out the process of choosing a new home far beyond the realistic limits of the actual search.

He had first gathered particulars from all the leading property agents in London. He was quite clear about what he wanted – a large period house of some character and grace. Nevertheless, in the way of salesmen of all kinds, the agents sent him particulars of new houses, pre-war houses, houses with no grace or character whatsoever and the odd folly, castle and pretentious bungalow pumped up with sufficient additions and embellishments to be called 'a single-storey dwelling of charm and spaciousness', 'a veritable sun-trap' or 'a ranch-style home that invites immediate inspection'.

He had time enough to view some of these oddities, as well as property that more closely matched what he wanted, and had ended up with a deep interest in the Englishman's home, a sound formula for de-coding estate-agent-ese, and not a jot of respect for estate agents themselves. After exhausting the London agents he had progressed to advertisements in the Sunday papers and national glossy journals, then to the Home Counties local papers, then to outlying estate agents and hence to Mr Coleherne, whose cramped two-man office plied its desultory trade in the village two miles from Ballads.

This gradualism had effectively lulled his wife into the false hope that he did not truly intend to move house at all. Professing uninterest, she had nevertheless made occasional protests as they viewed – 'Surely you don't expect us to live out here – not a trunk road in sight. We'd lose all our friends,' or 'I couldn't possibly take on a kitchen that size.'

Lately she had begun to refer to the search as 'milord's hobby', with the clear inference that nothing serious was likely to come of it.

This time it seemed different, at least for Charles. Ballads had caught his interest straight away. He had felt a near-panic reaction as he read the details, pin-pointed its site on his well-studded map and began to list all the pros and cons in his thick file marked 'Property'. The feeling was almost sexual. It was a mixture of triumph at perceiving the possible end to his search and of a strange sadness that the dream he had cherished all these years was about to be realized and therefore lost for ever. Love, Plato wrote, was in essence a desiring. When you had what you desired, there was no more need for desiring. Except perhaps for something else. Ah, the tragedy of achieving your desire – greater, someone had said, than the tragedy of failing to achieve it. Perhaps, Charles mused, that's why marriages go wrong.

The car jolted round the last tight bend, worn to such a steep camber that the occupants of the car were flung to one side in disarray like rag dolls.

'I'll be black and blue tomorrow,' muttered Sue Endicott and then, more loudly, 'Charles, don't you get the feeling that this is a non-starter? I mean . . .'

Charles motioned his wife to silence. His eyes narrowed at the prospect ahead as they came out of the bend. There, stroked by the midday sunlight, was the house.

Mr Coleherne stopped the car at the entrance to the short, wide drive. Once there had plainly been stone pillars here. Blocks of pale sandstone, worn smooth by time and weather, lay in heaps on either side of the entrance. Ivy had woven its tendrils around them and over them. One large stone manorial ball lay at one side, sliced in two halves as neatly as if it had been a hard-boiled egg. Grass and weeds had colonized what was once a gravelled route to the front door, and a circular bed in the middle was roofed with the swaying umbrellas of cow parsley over a carpet of ground elder.

Mr Coleherne cleared his throat nervously.

'I must make the point that this property has not been well maintained – not by your standards, I'm sure . . .'

'Not exactly in impeccable order, as you might say,' said Charles with a teasing laugh.

Mr Coleherne laughed far more enthusiastically than this wry comment deserved. He was sweating and he did not at all like this house.

'The vendors,' he went on 'are – ahem – unusual. Twin sisters. Artistic, I believe. County folk with a difference. It's their old family home, handed down for two or three generations, that kind of thing. One of them has lived here all her life. The other comes and goes. No one around here knows them very well. The village has changed, new people, housing estates, second homes, you know the scene. It's happening all over now, with everyone being more prosperous – well, most people anyway.'

He gave a hollow laugh, reflecting on his overdraft and the sluggish market for this vast type of family house. They were mostly going for nursing homes and management colleges now. He couldn't think why anyone would want to use a place like this to live in.

'But there's no question about the quality of the place,' he said. 'You could do wonders with it. Just thought I'd warn you not to expect kitchen units, every mod. con., that kind of thing.'

He tailed off and the others remained silent, except for a long sigh from Charles Endicott. He was not looking at the neglected drive or pondering on the interior of the house. Here before him was the embodiment of his fantasy and he drank in the scene like a man coming up for air after a long submersion.

Ballads was surfaced in pale-brown, almost honey-coloured stone. It was of no particularly recognizable style. It had the air of having grown from the ground where it stood rather than of having been designed. Its sides were straight with no bay windows or pediments or porticos such as he had expected to find on a house of that date. It had an honest air about it, he thought. It seemed squat because it was of two storeys only and was spread out from the central part into two single-storey wings, one to the east and one to the west. The one on the west had been further extended with another wing of sorts, slightly lower in height than the other additions and looking more like garages, potting sheds and so on than living quarters. The whole curved away from him in an arc, enclosing who knew what land and gardens behind.

From one end of the building, again on the west side, a brick wall about eight feet high ran alongside the drive, taking a right angle away from the approach road to skirt the property and join up with the other end of the curve at the eastern end of the house. A walled garden was one of the magical ingredients of his fantasy and he gazed at this wall with deep satisfaction.

Away to his left could be seen a neglected orchard, with

heavy, tangled, unpruned branches drooping on to the long, wispy grass. Beyond that was the blue haze of a wood with tall pines and sturdy beech trees rising from a mass of tangled briars and ferns.

His wife tapped him on the shoulder lightly.

'Aren't we going to view it then?' Her tone of voice told him that she hoped he was also overwhelmed by all the signs of ruin and decay and that he had changed his mind about seeing inside.

'It's rather much, darling,' she added. 'I'm sure they wouldn't mind if we just turned round and rang them from Mr Coleherne's office. Taken suddenly ill or something. Actually, I *am* beginning to feel a bit nauseous, Charles.'

Mr Coleherne's neck reddened and his grip tightened on the steering wheel. Oh no, he begged silently, don't turn around now. Not after all this palaver and hard work. He saw his commission melting before his eyes, and also had a sudden visual flash of his hands tightening round Mrs Endicott's neck instead of the steering-wheel. His other fear was that she would be sick in his car. He quickly turned on the ignition and looked at Mr Endicott in what he hoped was an encouraging, take-it-for-granted kind of way that meant 'OK to press on?'

Mr Endicott nodded.

'Of course we're going to have a look,' he said. 'Press on.'

Mr Coleherne put the car into gear and drove slowly up to the front door. For all his relief that they were going to see over the house, his heart was heavy with anticipated failure. He couldn't think of an occasion when he had managed to sell a house to any couple who hadn't been united in their enthusiasm before they even passed through the front door. There was plenty of time and opportunity, once they were inside, for either of them to come up with all sorts of justified objections, he was quite realistic about that. But he had not lost hope yet.

'Just you wait until you see the Victorian glasshouse,' he said in the manner of someone coaxing children through a dull first course with the promise of jelly for afters. 'It's a later addition, quite amazing. There's nothing like it in this county, at any rate. Or anywhere else in Great Britain for that matter. Not as part of a private house, at least. Of course, there's always Kew . . .'

He guffawed loudly. He felt himself growing almost hysterical with the longing for some sign of approval from Mrs Endicott. He had no similar uncertainties about her husband. He sensed that he was in the bag.

He put the brake on with such a hopeful, hearty jerk that Mrs Endicott was thrown against the back of her seat. She yelped in protest.

Mistaking the reason for it, Charles Endicott turned full-face towards her and spoke in tones of the utmost sweetness and reason.

'Peeing on my chips again, my love? Well, let's see if it makes any difference, shall we?'

2

THE VIEWING

'Just look at that guttering,' said Sue Endicott as she stepped reluctantly out of the car and straightened up, poised to find fault.

She was feeling very uneasy, which was a rare experience for her. She liked nice things about her, nice things that were also clean, and she had so far managed to avoid places, things, events and people that did not harmonize with her idea of niceness. And if anything jagged, bizarre, not nice, or ugly loomed on her horizon she had developed a smooth skill at straightening it out or annihilating it.

This house-viewing, however, had an uncomfortable mixture about it that would not fit into one or other of the moulds labelled 'all right' or 'won't do'. On the one hand she felt a deep antipathy to all the signs of neglect and age around her and saw nothing of the beauty or grace of the house itself and its surroundings. On the other hand she was not completely insensitive and was aware that her husband had a longing to own this house, even before he had seen inside it. As she put it to herself, he had set his heart on it. So, frantically torn between his desire and her loathing, she thrashed about in an effort to seize on concrete, practical little details that would, she hoped, convince her husband that Ballads was one of those things that simply 'won't do'.

What she had immediately picked on to express her foreboding about the entire venture was a feature that also summed up the owners' ambivalent attitude to Ballads.

At one corner of the front of the house there was a down-pipe to take rainwater from the gutter that ran along the roof-edge of the main part of the building. This pipe had recently been painted a soft olive green. The brave, shining paint had not succeeded in hiding the pits and rusted patches in its surface; nor did it entirely conceal the black coat of paint that had previously covered it.

Moreover, it did not in the least draw attention away from the fact that the section of gutter above it was suspended uselessly from a broken bracket, allowing rainwater to pour freely from the roofing slates and fall in sheets down the surface of the windows below. To Sue Endicott the new paint was therefore an offensive, pathetic gesture. To her husband, however, it was a signal of confidence in the house's permanence, a protest, almost, against the slow destruction all around it.

'That's great,' he said. 'I think I'd stick with that colour for the rest of the guttering, eh Sue?'

His wife turned to the estate agent, searching his face for signs of an ally. Mr Coleherne was scuffing the weed-filled gravel with the toe of his shoe. He was used to the edgy behaviour of clients who were afraid of being talked into a purchase. It was noticeable how the ones who were against a place pitched straight in with pettifogging objections. One woman, viewing 'an immaculate bijou residence' which accorded exactly with her demands, except for the price, had said with her first breath as the car drew up at the entrance, 'I'm not going to stand for the colour of that front door,' as if, on becoming the new owner, she would be forced to embalm the property in its present state in every particular. He recognized that Mrs Endicott similarly liked resistance for its own sake and foresaw a gritty hour ahead.

He arranged his face into an understanding smile.

'Well, they do say that you can't judge a house at all from the outside. I do most warmly recommend an internal in-spection. You might get a few surprises. Shall we proceed?'

'Surprises?' queried Mrs Endicott sharply. 'Spare us those . . .'

She strode confidently up to the front door and yanked at the iron bell-pull that hung beside it. It came away in her hand.

'That's a good start,' muttered Charles Endicott. 'Now what do we do?'

Mr Coleherne picked up the jagged length of iron that had dropped to the ground. He felt like hitting Mrs Endicott with it. He arranged his smile again.

'I suggest I knock hard at the door. They may be right at the back of the house anyway' – and he could not resist adding mischievously – 'perhaps in the glasshouse . . .'

Phoebe and Martha were neither at the back of the house nor in the glasshouse. Standing at the ground-floor window beside the front door, only just rendered invisible by the worn lace curtains, they had silently observed the approach of the estate agent and his clients.

They saw a very pretty dark-haired woman with a slight frame and small features. She wore a tight velvet suit in a shade of purple known as 'grape' and matching high-heeled shoes with ankle-straps. She walked with little mincing steps and her small head, covered with a cap-like hat made of black and purple feathers, pecked forward in tiny jerks as she took each step. 'She looks like a bird searching for food,' Phoebe remarked.

Martha drew back from the window as they came nearer to the front door.

'Why is she got up like a dog's dinner?' she said.

'Perhaps she always dresses like that. D'you think they're happy? The man looks nice. Sort of relaxed. He could be hurt, wouldn't you say?'

'Yes.'

They had speculated together but silently for a while about Mr Endicott, noting the slow, quiet, weary way of him and yet the suppressed, boyish eagerness.

'Bet you she won't like us,' said Martha indifferently. She giggled as she glanced at her sister. 'You shouldn't have worn that daft outfit, honestly, Fee.'

Phoebe shrugged and grinned. She was wearing a dark blue boiler-suit, not the kind that was just then coming into Carnaby Street fashion under the title of 'leisure wear' but the kind that can be found – and indeed Phoebe had found –

hanging on a nail in a long-neglected outhouse and in which someone had actually constructed, repaired or stoked boilers. Or, in this case, had worn it to crawl under cars, for it was streaked with oil.

'Well,' she had said, 'this is going to be hard work . . .'

Martha had not seen this visit as an occasion for hard toil but as an unwelcome social event and had put on a voluminous, full-sleeved robe in a pattern not unlike William Morris-designed wallpaper.

'Anyway, let's go,' said Phoebe. She moved quickly to the door and flung it wide open.

'It wasn't locked,' she said calmly. 'You could have walked straight in.'

She was quite gratified to see all three of them taken aback and confused. She couldn't have borne it if they had been thoroughly composed and confident. Phoebe always liked to be the one holding the reins.

'But we wouldn't have done that,' said Mr Coleherne and Mr Endicott in unison.

The estate agent proffered the piece of rusty black iron that had come apart from the bell-pull.

'I'm afraid I was a bit too fierce . . .' he stammered. 'Many apologies. Will pay for repair, naturally.'

'Why? When you didn't do it?' Phoebe gave Mr Coleherne one of her wide-eyed, sweet smiles that always made people feel curiously guilty, perhaps because it caused them to doubt their initial judgement of her as cold and brusque.

Phoebe stepped back into the hall and waved a hand towards her sister.

'We welcome you,' she said with a slight bow, further confusing the visitors with her mixture of formality and directness. 'This is my sister, Mrs Martha Frayn and I am Miss Phoebe Whittaker.'

'And twins, I believe,' said Sue Endicott brightly, her head tilted to one side and her eyes narrowed. 'Not identical, I take it?'

Phoebe sighed with the weight of a long history of exactly the same question, posed in exactly the same way.

'No. Two-egg.'

Sue Endicott flinched slightly at this answer, more clinical than she fully understood or had wished for. She turned to her husband with a vacant expression.

Mr Coleherne stepped forward and went hurriedly through the introductions, attempting now to take the initiative and glide into his sales patter. He fervently wished he could have shown the Endicotts round without the sisters being present. He sensed their reluctance and incipient hostility. He fingered his clip-board nervously and swayed ingratiatingly towards Phoebe.

'Shall I do the honours? Save you and your sister the trouble? It's all written down here, right down to the last light-switch and item of door-furniture.'

Phoebe had already turned to lead the way from the hall into the room on the right of it. She called back over her shoulder.

'So good of you. But the honours shall be ours, do you agree, Martha?'

'Absolutely,' said Martha and they both swept through the heavy panelled door into the room which Mr Coleherne had dubbed 'generously proportioned lounge' but which the twins had always known as the drawing-room.

The three visitors were now reduced to a state of vague apprehension. Sue Endicott had taken in the damp, musty air of the hall, its unvarnished, uncarpeted floorboards, the dust on every window-ledge, the absence of furniture except for a motley collection of pictures on the walls, the cobwebs between the carved uprights of the vast oak staircase, and it filled her with uncontrollable inner revulsion. 'Not nice', however, was certainly not enough to describe the agents of all this displeasure. Mentally, she labelled the sisters 'impossible', and her contempt was more than she could bear alone.

She held back from going through the door until her husband was close on her heels. Over her shoulder she hissed 'My God, Charles! What are we doing here? Are they mad or are you?'

'Hush,' he said, and looked around him, his head on one side as if to hear as well as see what the hall could tell him. He hardly noticed the signs of neglect. He was much more interested in the catholic collection of pictures on the walls.

Some were prints of Old Masters and Impressionists, that much he recognized. Others were oil paintings of foreign landscapes – hot Eastern skies, Mediterranean beaches, white-washed villas clinging to the slopes of a harbour in the harsh southern sunlight. There were also charcoal line-drawings, pencil sketches and water-colours of English woods, houses, trees, fields and river scenes.

There were several portraits too – one of a beautiful, pensive child with coal-black eyes, another of a baby bent in smiling concentration over a shiny red ball. All had been carefully framed in a variety of styles appropriate to each picture. There seemed to be no rhyme or reason to the hanging of them. They were not placed with any desire to set them off, as in an exhibition. It seemed that they had simply been put up on the wall as a record of people and places important to the family – a kind of scrap-book rather than a presentation of the painters' art.

The wall was also a photo album. Mixed up with the oil paintings, water-colours and sketches were framed photographs, some fairly recent, mostly of foreign places and buildings – he thought he recognized the interior of the Blue Mosque in Istanbul – and others, in faded sepia, of a beautiful woman in the clothes of the 1920s sitting in front of a potted palm, of two small near-identical girls dressed in their party best and dropping a curtsy to the camera, and several of a strikingly handsome man in army uniform, posed with one shoulder, and his officer's insignia upon it, thrust foremost at the camera.

He couldn't tell whether he liked or disliked what these pictures told him about the house and its owners. He only knew that the excitement he had felt on the journey, and at first sight of the house, was now heightened. Like his wife, he inwardly trembled. It was not with disgust but with the frisson of the explorer who comes to the last few paces before the goal that has led him on is to be fully and finally revealed.

He patted his wife's shoulder and urged her into the room. 'Let's wait and see,' he said.

As for Mr Coleherne, he accepted the dust and gloom and disrepair, the jumble of pictures and the twins' bizarre clothes as vague background features in the total picture of a house that he knew was going to be difficult to sell. I wonder, he thought, as they entered the drawing-room, if they've done it up at all since I was last here. Most people go raving mad with paint and wallpaper when they're selling their house – silly really, because the buyers nearly always change it all again. But he saw straight away that these vendors had made no changes at all.

A piano stood proudly at one end on a semi-circular raised platform. It had the flawless patina of a museum exhibit. Sheet music, books, papers and periodicals were stacked in untidy heaps around the edge of the dais and on several small bamboo tables nearby. Scattered round the room were sheet-shrouded mounds of unidentifiable furniture. Here too were numerous pictures hanging from the moulded picture-rail at varying heights, mercifully concealing all but a few patches of the fading wallpaper in green and cream stripes.

The large sash-windows on one wall and the French windows on the south side were uncurtained and the glass in all of them was covered in a thin film of dust, gentling the midday sun that shone on to the dust-sheets and huge glass-fronted bookcases and scattered Indian rugs.

The piano, Charles Endicott thought, looked utterly out of place in this setting. It seemed cared for, whereas everything else he had seen so far spoke of a careless indifference – except, of course, for that freshly painted drain-pipe.

'Do either of you play?' He waved towards the piano and smiled at Martha.

She smiled back, wide-eyed and friendly.

'Play what?' She glanced at her sister for approval.

'That – er – lovely instrument . . .' He was beginning to

wish he'd stayed silent or merely asked something impersonal like how they kept the room warm. Apart from the empty fireplace, he saw no sign of central or any other kind of heating.

'Forgive us,' said Phoebe. 'But we can't think what else one would do with a piano, can you?'

He was about to speculate a while on her curious use of 'us' and 'we'. It came out so naturally that there was nothing 'royal' or pompous about it. Perhaps they really did speak with one voice? But was this from intuition or because they'd talked about most things together and come to agree on all of them?

His musings were interrupted by an astonishingly free, warm laugh from Phoebe. He found himself joining in as if he had somehow been liberated. Now he was beginning to understand. The twins had some perpetual game, perhaps even a conspiracy, and its main purpose seemed to be to keep up their defences against any threat from outside. They used mockery, it seemed, and a silent, mutual understanding. He relaxed and released all his responses to behave as they wished.

Spontaneity, however, was unknown to Mrs Endicott. She had pursed her lips at Phoebe's laugh, puzzled by its un-expected warmth. She was now pacing tensely from one end of the room to the other, glancing up and down the walls and from side to side.

In an instant Martha was at her elbow, inclining her head upwards too, intent on sharing Mrs Endicott's viewpoint.

'If you're measuring, I can tell you that it's ten feet high between floor and ceiling. I got the ladder out and our father's long tape and measured it . . .'

'How kind of you.' Mrs Endicott had, as usual, imagined this task to be done entirely for her benefit. 'But actually I was wondering about power-points. I can't place them . . .'

Martha simulated anguish and clapped one hand to her forehead.

'Oh dear! Them? You said "them". You're looking for several sockets, are you? Some people do have a great number,

I suppose. We've never felt drawn ourselves. Never wanted all that upheaval again, in any case. Our mother was always very acid about the mess it made when they first had the electricity put in. That was before we were born, of course. We've always found things called adaptors very useful. That is, if you want gramophones, lamps, fires – that kind of thing . . .' Martha glanced towards her sister, apparently for help.

Phoebe could not possibly have heard the conversation but she came across the room and spoke as if she'd been party to it.

'There's a point just above the skirting on the east wall,' she said briskly and steered her sister towards the door.

Sue Endicott was left floundering among memories of whatever lessons at school might have featured the points of the compass. She decided she had had enough of being made to look foolish by these incredible women and was about to drop the subject of power-points when Martha called across to her in a friendly voice.

'We're so lucky to have the garden facing south, aren't we? And the sun coming across right from the moment it rises over there in the east' – pointing towards the windowless wall on her left where the fireplace stood.

'Thank you – too kind,' said Mrs Endicott, not caring now whether Ballads had been wired up in every room for sixty sockets or none at all. But she hurried to the east wall and bent down, as far as her tight skirt would allow, to peer at the skirting. She straightened up with a cry of triumph.

'It's broken!'

'That's true,' said Phoebe. 'And now, shall we go to the dining-room?'

In the dining-room, which, in shape and size, resembled the room they had just seen, the viewing was much as before. In contrast to the drawing-room, however, this one was suffocatingly over-furnished. A large oval table, with an empty tarnished silver fruit-bowl in the middle, was surrounded by eight matching chairs with tapestry seats and high, straight backs. At either end of the room were two massive, identical sideboards with bow fronts and brass handles to their numerous cupboards and drawers. There was a lingering smell of spices and sauces in the room, as if the very walls had caught the flavour of countless heavy meals through the generations.

Phoebe ushered them on to the breakfast-room next door, which was smaller and completely empty, then upstairs to the first floor. She sprang lightly about with her hands thrust into the pockets of her boiler-suit and now and then issued protective directions. 'Mind that stair – it's loose. Keep to the left edge of it.' 'Watch this low beam.' 'Don't touch that door-knob – it comes off. Here, I'll open the door.'

Mr Coleherne had retreated a few steps to the rear of the party, sighing frequently and referring resignedly to his clip-board. He had nearly given up. Mrs Endicott's dislike of the place completely dominated the couple's response and he was unaware of the quiet, growing conviction in her husband that he wanted it more than anything he had ever wanted in his life.

'Look,' said Phoebe as they went through a stained glass door into the short, da.k passage leading to the kitchen. 'You'll find some damp here – quite natural in a house without a damp course.' Mr Coleherne groaned silently, wishing he had briefed the vendors on not drawing attention to anything unless they were asked about it.

They were in the kitchen now, a large sunny room with a quarry-tiled floor, a solid fuel cooker with four ovens and a vast scrubbed deal table in the middle.

Up on one wall was a glass-fronted box containing two rows of bells, each neatly labelled with the name of the room in which a touch of a bell-push caused it to jangle and summon service. High on the ceiling was a clothes-airer, of wooden slats in a metal frame, which could be lowered and raised by a rope stretched across to a cleat on the wall.

Suddenly anxious to make a contribution before he could be thought to have lost his grip, Mr Coleherne jumped in with both feet.

'Oh, just look at those period features!' he shouted. 'You could get a fortune for those in one of those nostalgia shops for Victoriana . . .'

'Ye-e-e-s,' breathed Mrs Endicott longingly, her eyes lighting up. Then she lowered her head as she caught sight of Phoebe's aghast expression.

Phoebe stared at the floor and the atmosphere went tense.

'Oh yes, of course,' she said, speaking very deliberately. 'You could dismantle the whole place if you liked. Take the glasshouse down, pane by pane, and sell it in California . . .'

There was silence for several seconds. Mr Coleherne shuffled his feet sheepishly and everyone avoided everyone else's eyes.

'Shall we look at it then?' Martha stood with her hand on the brass knob of the kitchen door. She looked questioningly at Phoebe, received some unspoken message from her sister and then nodded happily and looked towards the visitors.

Charles Endicott had for some time stopped looking more than cursorily at the rooms, noting only that all of them would take massive heating, rehabilitation and furnishing. He was waiting to see the gardens and land surrounding the house and, above all, the glasshouse. Through the many windows they had passed as they toured the house, he had had tantalizing glimpses, though from none was it possible to view the entire area of walled garden, lawns, flower-beds, borders, fountain, woodland and orchard. The many additions to the house jutted south of the property, enclosing terraces and vine-roofed areas, each concealed from the others by the extensions themselves or by shrubbery. From every window at the back, however, it was possible to see a part of the enormous glasshouse attached to the back wall.

It was semi-circular in shape and jutted from the south-facing, back wall of the house like the prow of a mighty ship. Its gently sloping roof was capped at the apex with another structure which echoed the shape of the building below it and was an average-sized glasshouse in itself. Its roof, as shallow and gently sloping as the one beneath, was crowned with a row of decorative wrought-iron loops and curls.

He registered the large size of the glass panes, quite impossible to replace, he guessed, with the panes one could normally order from the local garden centre to fit a standard greenhouse. But he instantly brushed aside any considerations of cost and inconvenience. If, in its entirety, it fulfilled the promise of his limited glimpses and of the churnings inside him, he would have it – anachronism, folly, white elephant or whatever it was.

The sisters and their visitors went out of the kitchen, turned left into a short gloomy corridor and went through a multi-coloured glazed door into the Victorian glasshouse.

It was immediately apparent that it was here, in contrast to the sparse, echoing, dead rooms they had seen so far, that the life of the house was focused. There was an easel and artists' paraphernalia in one corner, fighting for space with tubs of avocado plants and trailing gourds. The black and white tiled floor was covered here and there with Numdah rugs, goatskins and home-made tufted woollen mats in bright oranges and reds. Roughly folded newspapers and open books lay on tables of white-painted metal, or of polished wood or covered in brilliant red and gold lacquer in Chinese-style designs of dragons and fantastic birds. There was a faded, chintz-covered, roomy settee with a tortoiseshell cat asleep in a nest of cushions, a radio, rows of packed shelves against the house wall, white supporting pillars studded with hooks on all sides, from which hung miniature pictures, plant-filled baskets and small gardening tools, a torch, a storm-lamp, a panama hat and several dolls from foreign lands, dressed in their native costumes.

The slightly curved, glazed sides of the building rested on a wall of bricks, about two feet in height and deep enough to provide a useful ledge all around the inside perimeter. On this ledge were more signs of life – potted plants at various stages of growth, pieces of pottery, bottles of wine, cups, mugs, scissors, string, pencils, notebooks.

The impression was that the sisters' entire daily lives took place here – eating, drinking, planning, reading, writing, paint-ing and relaxing. Charles Endicott was reminded of the detailed drawings in children's story-books where all the life of a family is portrayed in one cosy room. Sue Endicott wondered anxiously where the sisters' lives went in the winter and Mr Coleherne was trying not to notice the large number of cracked panes just visible beyond the vine branches and tendrils that snaked across the inside of the roof.

Martha had hurried to the far end where some geraniums and tomato plants grew in pots on a raised slatted shelf by the double doors to the garden. She turned her back on the others and began fiddling with the plants, caressing the as yet small trusses of tiny, hard, green tomatoes and tweaking out the little fern-like shoots that imprudently sprang between stem and leaf. She found her eyes were misting over and she shook her head vigorously to clear them.

To the watchful Phoebe, Martha's shaking shoulders were a sure sign of her sister's distress. And why not? she thought. For she too heard the voices crowding in from the past and resented the visitors' intrusion in this most seminal of places where all the joys had been celebrated, all the wounds nursed.

She sat down in a canvas chair with wooden arms. Along the strip of canvas supporting her back was printed in faded black capital letters the name 'COLIN'. She looked ex-pectantly at Mr Coleherne and his clients who were standing in the middle of the glasshouse, seeming at a loss for words. They peered up through the vine leaves to the glass above and the sky beyond. Their faces were bathed in the cool green light, making them look sickly, and drops of conden-sation splattered on their shoulders or on to the floor. She noticed that some of the feathers on Mrs Endicott's hat were shiny-wet, their fluffiness turned to aggressive little spikes.

At length Charles Endicott murmured 'magnificent, magnificent' and spread his arms wide in a kind of helpless gesture.

His wife turned towards him, in profile to Phoebe, and

mouthed 'cup of coffee', miming the raising of a cup to her lips. This was not lost on Phoebe. She struggled not to remember all the times she had been called 'pokey nose' as a child and all the occasions when she had caught glances or whispered remarks passing between the adults and had bluntly asked, 'What did you say? What did that look mean? What's happening?' Always she had wanted to know what was happening, to be in the know, to share in and, if possible, control the chancy, secretive affair that life seemed to be.

She sprang up quickly.

'I would offer you coffee,' she said, 'only we haven't any.' She paused long enough to take in Mrs Endicott's startled embarrassment. 'But perhaps you'd like a glass of our own wine? Last year's, of course,' she added waving towards the vine above them and its cluster of infant grapes.

'How delightful . . .' Mr Endicott started to say.

'I don't think . . . a little early for us,' interrupted his wife, who drank nothing except dry martini and an hourly fix of coffee. It was plain that she was now straining to leave.

'Well,' said Mr Coleherne, 'we've troubled you enough. I'm sure we've seen all we need of the house. Perhaps you'd allow us to make our way back to the car via the grounds? I noticed a gate in the wall. Could we wander a bit and then go out that way?'

He obviously wanted what was left of the viewing to be without the sisters' company. Phoebe thought for a moment of balking him. Then she suddenly felt tired and dispirited, with no taste for further sparring.

She was aware also of Martha's shaking hands and bowed shoulders as she moved along the length of the shelves, still with her back to the room. We've both had enough, she thought.

'That sounds like a good idea,' she said. 'If you go out of these doors, you can walk all round the walled garden – Mr Coleherne knows what to show you – and then if you go through that little iron gate in the wall, where the peach trees are, you could have a look at the woods on the other side of the house, in the front. There's a pond, too, and the orchard.'

Martha turned round quickly, undecided whether to stand her ground until the visitors had gone or make a run for it straight away. She felt crumpled and rigid at the same time. Her fingers were curled tightly round a bunch of discarded tomato shoots and she looked down and saw that they had stained her hands green. Someone will say something jokingly about 'green fingers' she thought, but it won't be Phoebe.

'You really do have green fingers, I see,' said Charles Endicott kindly. 'All these healthy plants, the lovely things growing in the garden – they must take a lot of work. But you have the touch obviously.'

Martha beamed at him, took a hesitant step forward and then broke into a run across the glasshouse and to the house-door. She could be heard going down the passage to the kitchen, her footsteps mingled with little moaning noises.

'Is she all right?' asked Mrs Endicott without seeming to care one way or another.

Phoebe glanced at her without answering.

Mr Endicott gazed up at the vines, searching for something bland to say. Nothing would come. His soft suede shoes were splashed with drops of condensation from the vine. One tear-shaped drop hovered at the point of a leaf above his head and then, in slow motion, fell on to his thick, greying hair. He put his hand up to his head and smiled at Phoebe.

'Such a beautiful, unusual place,' he said softly. 'You must be sorry to be leaving it.'

'Ah,' said Phoebe, wanting very much to let it all tumble out. You can't know how much, she thought. No one can. What could you or anyone, except Martha and me, know of the summer evenings here under the vine, with Father, that magical man, playing the violin as if he were paying for his life with his music, with Mother twining her fingers through her soft auburn hair and gazing dreamily through the glass at the fountain and at the children playing there, three of them

33

then, and all of them making distant, noisy bids for the attention of their parents?

But that attention, she had always imagined, was offered exclusively to each other and had never extended to the twins, though perhaps there had been room there for their brother Jack. Truly, the children of lovers are orphans, she thought with a sigh. But I wish it had stayed like that, with them apparently wrapped up in each other, rather than turn into the chilling years that followed. She saw, for the hundredth time or more, the vivid picture of their father stumbling towards their mother, his arms outstretched and stiff, like someone who had dropped something precious, his face distraught with grief. And she saw their mother, standing there by the doors to the garden, her expression as still and cold as stone, draw slowly away from his pain and step out into the night air.

Had that ever happened? If it had, did she really witness it? Or was it a fleshing-out of the little she knew about the feelings that passed between her parents? And all the changes in those feelings she had been made aware of as she and Martha grew, and noticed, and speculated?

Martha had never believed that Phoebe had watched that particular scene in the glasshouse. She swore that they were always upstairs before dark anyway. What would Phoebe have been doing lurking in the garden and peering into the glasshouse late on a summer's night? Phoebe had no answer. But the picture kept coming back and it never lost any of its vividness and shock. Even now, with Mr Endicott standing in front of her and the murmurings of his wife and the estate agent in the background, she felt her body tense up with the pain she saw on their father's face and the terrible sense of loss in the air.

She shut her mind against the picture and smiled warmly at Mr Endicott.

'That,' she said cheerfully, 'is the understatement of the year.'

The others came across to shake hands. 'Tell your sister many thanks too,' said Mr Endicott, and his wife nodded vigorously.

As they left the glasshouse Phoebe sat back in her father's chair again and gripped the arms. If they take it, she thought, Martha will die.

She sat there for some time, absorbing the impressions left by the visitors. Mrs Endicott, she thought, is all that I hate in a woman. Self-absorbed, cold and totally oblivious to other people's needs and feelings. Why do I hate that so much? Is it because our mother is like that? Is our mother really like that, in any case? Do we see her as she is, or is it a distorted view? Do all children get a hopelessly untrue picture of their parents?

Or do I perhaps hate Mrs Endicott because she's like me? And I hate myself? Just a straight case of projection? Phoebe groaned aloud and slumped further down in the chair, turned her head wearily and saw Martha at her shoulder.

'She's rather awful, isn't she?' Martha said sympathetically.

'Yes, she is. But does that make you hate her?'

Martha moved round to face Phoebe and said calmly 'No. I just think she's awful – no feeling in her. But I don't hate her. You do, though?'

'Yes. Why do I? Why can't I just tolerate people like her, the way you do?' She frowned and added, 'Am I a bit like her?'

'In some ways, yes. Little ways. You have your brittle moments . . . But you're full of good things too. And I don't think she is. Well, anyway, if she is, she doesn't use them. So you've no need to hate her.'

Phoebe touched her forehead briefly in a kind of salute.

'Oh Mart,' she said. 'Thanks.'

'You were worried?'

'Yes. Nothing unusual, you know that.'

'I should give up this self-analysis, if I were you.'

'I wish I could.'

Phoebe got up from the chair with a heavy sigh and walked by Martha to stand looking out of the glasshouse at the fountain. It wasn't working now, hadn't done so since Martha's husband left. She remembered Donald mending it, time after time, his cheerful, broad face creased in concentration as he skewered some kind of instrument into the nozzle at the top.

'*He* was all right though, wasn't he?' she said eventually. She did not have to consider, then or ever, whether or not Martha would know who she was referring to. She always knew.

'Yes. He's very all right,' Martha said cheerfully. 'Makes you wonder how he chose to marry her, doesn't it? Did you fancy him?'

'I did rather. Very bland sort of person. I like that. Very perceptive too, I think. In a way, I hope he buys the house. But not with her. He'll have to get a divorce first . . .' She was laughing now and turned to see whether Martha's mood had brightened too. She was regretting that she had referred to the sale of the house. I should shut up about that for a while, she thought. Mart's had enough of it for one day.

Martha was standing stiffly by one of the round iron tables, one hand tracing the outline of the patterned ridge around its edge. Phoebe sighed and thought no, she's still miserable. How am I going to deal with this all over again – and again, and yet again, and maybe for ever? She'll always grieve for Ballads, long after we've left it. If only there were someone else to hold her sadness for her as well as me. A mother, for instance.

Martha looked up, caught her sister's expression and shook her head.

'No,' she said. 'I'm not keening over Ballads. It's not that.'

'What then?'

'It's the other big thing. You know.' Uncharacteristically, she stared hard at Phoebe, willing her to pick up the reason for her anxiety without her having to put it into words.

'You know what it is, don't you? You must know . . .'

Phoebe thought for a split second of pretending not to understand – and knew Martha would see through it.

'If it's about our father,' she said, 'what's brought all that on? We agreed, didn't we? You don't really want to know the truth. And I'm not worried about it. We agreed, remember?'

'You agreed. I didn't.' Martha's tone was surly.

'Oh, Mart, come on! There'll be lots of time before the house goes. We can have a go at everything in the attic and . . .'

'No, I still don't want that. I just want to talk about it. Just see if we can work something out. I can't stand the uncertainty. But I don't want it ended either. Don't expect me to explain – I can't.'

She brushed a hand across her forehead, looking confused and close to tears.

It was too late to avoid the memories now. Colin was there, his boyish face dark and drawn, one hand on the banister at the foot of the stairs, one foot on the first step. He was being pulled upstairs to his study by an urgent despair that they knew to be tragically more important than anything he had felt before. And they were delaying him, soothing him, diverting him, their impulses just as urgent, their emotions equally despairing.

They were seventeen – how young we were for our age! Phoebe thought. We knew little then about Alice's secret life or Colin's solitary wretchedness. We were still naive, though never trusting. We were even dressed alike, not yet confident enough to make our own choices. Those awful shapeless wartime slacks and heavy sweaters, and our hair lank and long, held curled on to our necks by net snoods. No wonder his eyes wouldn't rest on us.

She saw him glance up the stairs longingly and heard herself and Martha trying to coax him out of his black mood. Then he said something she could never recall because it was utterly lost in the shock of his next words.

'. . . That's if I'm your father, of course.'

If, if, if, if . . .

The picture was gone. The word 'if' was circling explosively in her head, like a Catherine wheel, sending out spluttering sparks and making her blink. She looked up and saw that Martha's eyes were tightly shut and her lips were forming 'if, if, if,' again and again.

She took the few steps that brought her to Martha's side.

They stood for a moment, nearly touching, their eyes drawn to Colin's chair.

'It'll be all right,' Phoebe said at length.

'Yes, I know.'

'We'll find out when you're ready.'

'Yes, when I'm ready.'

BOOK TWO

3
1917 ALICE

The girl with the long auburn hair was standing as she had
stood at seven o'clock in the morning every day of her life
since she had left school. At the front door of her stepfather's
hotel she gazed yearningly down the wide, tree-lined street as
if Eldorado or a crock of gold lay at the far end. She wore a
faded blue apron over her ankle-length full skirt and she held
a bright yellow duster in her hand. She swung her arms
lightly from side to side, more as if the wind had blown them
than as if she had willed them to move. Her bones were so
slight, her skin so pale, her movements so dream-like, that a
passer-by might have mistaken her for a barely animated
clockwork doll going through the motions of a slow pavane.

She turned her gaze from the street and on to the large
brass knob in the centre of the panelled front door. Slowly,
the hand holding the duster came to rest on the knob and
started to caress it in mechanical circular movements. This
was Alice's regular early-morning task, the polishing of the
door-knob.

'It must shine, shine, shine,' her stepfather had said in his
breezy way. 'Brighter than the sun, brighter than your hair,
O Alice of the crowning glory! It's the first thing that
everybody sees. Coming down the street, they will say, "Ah,
there's the Clarendon! I can see the door-knob shining." By
our door-knob shall they know us, eh Alice? Make it shine
and blind the whole of London.' He should have been an
actor, she often thought. She smiled to herself and flicked her
duster in the air to hear it rustle and swish.

It could not be said that she either enjoyed the task or
disliked it. She was as neutral about this as about almost

41

everything else in her uneventful life. Inside her head, however, there was more life and colour, tragedy and romance than was packed into the lives of all the inhabitants of that long street. She was seventeen and all her dreams were, for the moment, fresh and untested.

Suddenly, there was a tap on the window to the right of the door. In the silent morning street it snapped like the crack of a whip. Her head jerked up sharply. A thin, pinched face, with a surprised expression, could be seen behind the net curtain. It was Alice's mother. The look of surprise was permanent, at least for as long as Alice could remember. She supposed it had something to do with her. And it was certainly true that her mother had never fully recovered from her shock at producing a daughter who was as pale and passive as she herself was dark and active.

She tapped again on the window and shouted against the glass.

'Come inside. Leave that. Come in now.'

Alice took a last look down the road. A baker's boy came clattering by on his bicycle. He was leaning back nonchalantly, his hands in his pockets, skilfully steering the bike and the loaded basket on the front of it by tipping the crossbar gently one way and then the other with his knees. Steam from the fresh loaves seeped through the white cloth on top of the basket.

He called to her 'Hullo, Miss Carrots,' and she waved shyly.

A soldier approached, looking up the stone steps towards her and slowing his steps as he came closer. She turned away from him with a sigh. Soldiers were not part of her dreams. Not private soldiers anyway, with no buttons and pips anywhere to be seen and with soft-topped hats flopping over their bristly hair.

If he had been an officer, especially a cavalry officer, with puttees and shiny boots, a firm, taut cap, a leather belt, and brass buttons all over his jacket – that would have been different. He would have been given one of her rare half-smiles.

The soldier stopped at the foot of the steps, open-mouthed and expectant. Alice turned away and walked into the hotel, shutting the heavy front door behind her. Inside, she sensed at once that something different and important had happened or was about to happen.

Her mother came bustling out of the front room with an unaccustomed air of drama.

'There you are,' she said. 'I should have told you last night, of course, but you went up early . . .'

'Told me? Told me what?'

'Why I have to call you in . . . Now, Alice, don't fluster me. Just pay attention. There's someone calling later. I didn't want it. But your stepfather and I thought it might be best if we allowed it . . . if we allowed him, this – er – man to come just the once.'

Her voice tailed off. It was plain to Alice, who never normally made any judgements, or had any opinions, about people's moods or feelings, that her mother was embarrassed and searching for words.

'What man? Why is he coming?'

Her mother waved her hand vaguely as if to move aside a barrier between them. She appeared more hesitant and awkward than Alice had ever known her to be.

'Oh Lord, Alice,' she said. 'You'd better come here into the front room. Did you finish the door-knob?' She switched on to safe ground and was able to look Alice in the face. 'Is it a good shine, the way he likes?'

'Of course, yes. But Mother, what's this all about? Why can't you say?'

Her mother hurried into the room in front of her and stood by the fireplace, muttering distractedly to herself. 'So strange of him. Why does he want to come after all this time? I don't know what to think. "Just to have a picture I can carry in my mind," he says. Still the crazy artist. But perhaps this will be the beginning and the end of it . . .'

Alice stood just inside the doorway. Never one to start a conversation, to probe or pry or respond unless asked, she simply waited until the reason for the strange charge in the atmosphere and her mother's odd behaviour was made clear.

Mrs Meadows palmed an imaginary line of dust from the chimney-piece and ran her hand down the side of her apron. She kept her gaze fixed on the red, pleated, shiny paper fan which filled the fireplace.

'We've not talked much about your . . . your . . . the man who was your father.'

Was? Was her father? Alice's immediate thought was that this man she had never seen, who was never spoken of and whom she only knew as 'the artist', was now dead.

'You mean he's died then?' She spoke as if she had been asking, 'Is that all?'

Her mother flushed with irritation.

'Why ever should you think that?'

'You said "was". As if I don't have a father any more . . .'

'Yes, you have. You certainly have. You have Mr Meadows. And a very kind, generous father he is too. Far more than . . . than . . . the artist.'

'Yes, Mother, I know that, but . . .' Alice was losing hope of getting her mother to stick to the point.

'I won't be flummoxed like this. Just be patient. I said "was" because he gave up his entitlement to that name – father – long before you were born. We won't rake over old coals but that's a fact he can't alter. He fathered you in the physical sense, yes' – and Mrs Meadows faltered awkwardly on the word 'physical' – 'but that was all. He's been no more of a real father to you than, well, some of the regular visitors here who take a kindly interest in you, for my sake, and talk to you and bring you ribbons. And that's a great deal less than Mr Meadows has done for you. If anyone's to be called Father . . .'

She smoothed her apron again and stared into the fireplace. The fingers of one hand were drumming nervously on the chimney-piece. Alice had never seen her so distracted and at a loss.

'Well?' she said. 'So he's not dead.'

'He might just as well have been. All these seventeen years, and not a word. But no . . .' She drew a deep breath. 'He's coming here. I suppose it's to see how you . . . how we're getting on . . .'

She fell silent again. No, she thought, there wasn't a jot of concern for her welfare in his letter. It was only the child he was interested in. How could he upset them all like this? The letter had come by the afternoon post, just in that busy time between getting the tea-things cleared and preparations put in hand for dinner. Since the envelope looked official and grim and was in a strange hand, she had sat down here in the front room for a moment to read it. Just as well, she thought, for otherwise she might have passed out with the shock when she saw the signature at the end – 'Edwin Foster' – and read what he had to say.

'I'm not well,' he'd written. 'I want to see the girl and have a picture of her I can carry in my mind. I trust it will not be inconvenient for you and your family if I come to your residence at noon on Tuesday, having reason to travel up from the West Country the previous day and to stay in London overnight. I regret that I'm not in a position to offer any recompense for her sustentation' – all these long words, she thought irritably, what does he mean? It's been dictated by a solicitor, that's plain. He wants to make sure I'm not going to dun him for anything – 'but I trust', the letter went on, 'that she's now in a position to provide you with domestic services in return for the care you have devoted to her without, alas, any help from me. I'd be obliged if you would acquaint her with the news of who will be calling on her on Tuesday next. Yours truly, Edwin Foster.'

How strange, she thought. This cold, stilted letter came from the same hand that had fondled her that hot summer's night on Parker's Piece. And, worse, it came from the same heart that had praised her beauty and promised her love, respect, and her portrait in oils. She, poor innocent – she blushed as she thought of it – had thought he was enamoured of her body in a painter's way, as a model for his art, and that all of Cambridge, both town and gown, would soon know Mary Thorne, who helped in the café in King's Parade, as the favourite sitter of Edwin Foster, that talented artist who would one day be famous.

There was no reason, then, to deny him the walk along the Backs at dusk nor, when it grew dark, the rest on that grassy expanse, so spacious that there was privacy there, however many other young couples had chosen it for their embraces too. When they were lying down and he kissed her so long and warmly that she felt as if the sun was inside her, and stroked her arms, and then her breasts and then her thighs, she grew soft and yielding and could no more have cried 'stop', and put an end to her dreams of future romance and cherishing, than fly to the moon.

So Alice was the result. There had been no modelling sessions in his rooms in Wordsworth Grove, only a growing chill between them as her pregnancy became more obvious, and he had never again looked at her with any love or tenderness, only with guilt and resentment.

Finally, his father had come to the back-street terraced house she shared with her mother and given her a handsome sum 'to forget about the silly boy'. He had filled the doorway with his loud presence, his thick fur-collared coat and the smell of cigar-smoke. 'He has an artistic temperament, my dear, and will be no good for you or your child, not ever, and it would be unwise if you ever thought of him again.'

So Mary Thorne had become wise and had put out of her mind the pale-blue eyes and the sandy hair and the flying green scarf round his throat and all the wild endearments he'd shouted on Parker's Piece. They had not been for her, as she had supposed, but for the whole world that lay in wait for his conquering, with his charm, his talent for deception and his father's money.

She looked at Alice and was forced to admit what she'd always been able to deny up to now – that she resembled her father in many ways. Still, she thought, I'm not one to hold that against her. Nor against him either, for that matter. Things have turned out very comfortably, considering. I only wish her father had stayed in the past, where he belongs, that's all.

'Well, there it is,' she said. 'He's coming here. Just this once. There's no need to make too much of it. We shan't be asking him to stay to luncheon. No doubt you'll tell him what a good father Mr Meadows has been. I think he ought to know that.'

Alice was almost dizzy with the effort to take in what was happening. Her mother, she realized, had no idea how many of her thoughts and day-dreams were devoted to speculations about 'the artist'. She did not, even now, know his name or where he lived or anything about him. When she had asked, her mother had dismissed her questions with 'That's all in the past,' or 'It's a closed chapter.'

And yet, in fantasy, she knew everything about him. Her musings had drawn his face, with laughter lines round the vivid blue eyes, and had coloured his skin pale gold and his hair as richly auburn as her own. She was familiar with his artist's long, flexible hands, his protective arms, his commanding height and the tilt of his head as he bent earnestly to listen to her. No one ever listened. She was certain that he would.

She knew too, so well, the way he walked with a jaunty air, not caring what people thought of him, and how he wore clothes she had only seen in picture books – a black velvet cloak lined with red silk and a big floppy hat with a large brim and a silk scarf knotted carelessly round his neck. She saw that very clearly, even felt the texture of the scarf in her hand.

His voice was low and strong. He did not smell of hair-oil, like so many of the visitors to the Clarendon, nor of whisky like her stepfather, nor of antiseptic soap like her mother. He had his own aroma of man, warmth and love – the aroma of 'father'. And as she lay in bed at nights and dreamed of him, she smelt the grass and trees and wild flowers of the fields he'd painted, and the salty tang of his seascapes.

And now it was all going to be here, in this room in her home – all that colour and life that had been the subject of her longings for so long. If only, she thought, the girls at school could see him. How they'd mocked her about the father that had never appeared, and never sent a birthday card or even a prayer-book for her confirmation. They would be sorry now, seeing that all that she had told them was true. But she would forgive them. He would want her to.

Her mother was still distractedly patting the furniture and tweaking the curtains as Alice came out of her reverie.

'Lord knows what he'll think,' she was muttering to herself. 'My residence indeed! He'll have a residence all right, down there in Cornwall. But what does it matter what he thinks? He has no right to think anything ... Oh come on now, Alice, get on with you. He won't be here until twelve o'clock. And there's the dining-room to see to – there are three gentlemen to breakfast. We can't neglect them for the sake of an artist up from Penzance to look us over ...'

'But shall I put on the white dress?'

'My dear girl, that's for occasions.'

'And this isn't an occasion?'

'Look, don't go getting ideas. He'll be in and out of here before you know it. He's got nothing to give us and we've nothing to offer him. He's a stranger, child, a stranger who's calling as one and going as one. It's just a whim of his, a touch of curiosity more than likely. Stay as you are. But take off that apron. When you've done the dining-room, of course ...'

Her mother went to plump up a hard, unyielding cushion in the armchair by the window and then walked quickly from the room.

From the hall she shouted 'Use that duster here, if you will. The table in the hall is far from cleanly.'

She always said 'cleanly', as if clean were a dirty word. I wonder, Alice thought, if she'd be so fussy if this were a real home instead of a hotel. I dare say she would. It seems to be her whole life, having things cleanly and 'to rights'. She knew her mother would now be hurrying along to the kitchen, almost tripping over her own feet in her eagerness to 'put things to rights' there before breakfast. So she had time to think a little longer about her father. She sat in the armchair by the window, curling her legs under her on the seat and, as always when she wanted to think, she put her thumb in her mouth and began slowly twisting a strand of her long, fine hair.

Would he take her away, perhaps? Was that what it was really all about? Was he lonely, painting all by himself in that big house by the sea, and needing a companion for his later years? Like all filial fantasies, hers was one of a man alone, world-weary and sad. Why else would he come visiting now, never having written or acknowledged her existence before – not in all her seventeen years? Of course, he hadn't been very interested in a mere child. But now that she was an adult – well, he had plainly been waiting for her to grow up and now he was going to claim his own and plead with her mother to let her go with him.

The thought of leaving this narrow, gloomy house with its knobbly green wallpaper and dark curtains, the perpetual smell of cabbage, and the noise of comings and goings, of fireplaces being scraped of ash and bells ringing and nowhere a hint that it was also a home – the thought of a change made her tremble with excitement.

I could make him take me away, she thought. She already knew the power of her looks to make men do as she wished, and she was also aware that women did not seem to be so easily influenced. The young salesmen, the officers on leave, the middle-aged men up for the London theatres and clubs, the elderly men from Manchester or Bradford coming to see their bankers, brokers and solicitors – the ever-changing male inhabitants of the cold rooms on the three floors above where she sat – they all turned to stare and yearn as she passed by. And soon they'd contrive to engage her in conversation in the drawing-room, or on the stairs, gazing in surmise at the thin material of her blouse or the gap between skirt and shoe.

She knew well why they looked, and breathed more heavily, and either blushed or swaggered according to their natures. She knew why they brought her ribbons and combs for her hair, cheap little pieces of jewellery, tiny lace-edged handkerchiefs and bottles of eau de cologne or ashes of violets. She knew why her mother smiled indulgently as these gifts were proffered and nudged her and said, 'It's all right, Alice, you may have it. The gentleman's only being kind. He wants to show how much he likes being here and having us attend to him, isn't that right now, sir?'

The gentlemen would smile sheepishly, daring occasionally to take Alice's pale hand in their damp, red ones as they pressed their gifts on to her. 'A lovely girl, Mrs Meadows. She'll break a few hearts, you'll see . . .' And they would take another pull at their whisky or ale and their eyes would go moist with the memories of the things they had done in their youth or with regrets for the things they had not done.

'Oh, thank you,' Alice would say, with a modest dip of her head. She would draw back lest, as happened once or twice, the donor should so far presume on her gratitude as to plant a wet, alcoholic kiss on her cheek.

The trophies stayed unused on her bedside table. She fingered them sometimes, smiling to herself. They were, to her, promises of greater gifts, once she was free to use her power to the full. She craved far more than jewellery and scent and ribbons. She wanted more than anything else to be out there in the theatres and restaurants and big private houses, with one tall, devoted man at her side and all other men in tormented rivalry for her favours. But how was she to get there? It needed the tall, devoted man to start with. She was sure of that. He had to be a man who was already part of that world and who would sweep her into it.

Surely, there was a chance that this man, the visitor, the artist, would open the first door? If he too was moved by her beauty and she told him how she suffered here, wouldn't he, an artist, rich, and of her very flesh and blood, see at once that she must be rescued? He would say, 'Come with me. I will take you where you belong.' Then he would move to London, away from his lonely big house, and they would go about in society. The sort of man she knew him to be couldn't possibly have anything else in mind except rescue.

Alice felt full of hope and excitement as she uncurled herself from the chair and went to the window. The street was coming to life with the sounds of horses' hooves and carriage wheels, pedal bikes and motor cycles. Schoolchildren and office-workers scurried along the pavement, some alone and some in chattering groups. In the distance, she could just hear the clank of a tram as it reached its terminus at the Edgware Road on its first journey of the day from Sudbury. On the opposite side of the road a man in a flat cap repeatedly cranked the starting-handle of a large, dignified motor car, spitting on his hands between each manic burst of energy. For the first time in her life she felt that change was possible. The air was full of it.

She went out into the hall and languidly passed the duster over the heavy mahogany table, deftly skirting the silver tray for the post and a brass vase containing a fern-like plant.

As she turned towards the stairs, her stepfather came out of the study to her left – a large man with a gold chain straining across his stomach from pocket to pocket, linking his hunter watch with a heavy fob. He always looked jovial. Even at this hour, before breakfast, he wore the ruddy colour and the faint sweat of the bar-room joker.

'Ah! Our little Abigail,' he shouted. 'All ready for the visitation, are we? What a turn-up for the book, eh? Wouldn't I like to be a fly on the wall when the artist greets his long-lost fledgeling . . . except, of course, I'd fall off, wouldn't I?'

'Yes, Papa.' Alice could hardly raise a smile. The word 'Papa' seemed suddenly curious and wrong. What, she wondered, would she call this man when her real father had established himself in her life? That's if she were ever to see her mother and her stepfather again, once she had left the Clarendon. She did not find that prospect at all unpleasing. They had each other, after all, and she had always felt an outsider. They would probably feel as relieved as she would when the parting came.

For an instant, she thought of saying something about not wanting to call him 'Papa' any more. He had never showed her any unkindness. He simply treated her as if she were a pretty kitten of no importance to him. If she said, 'I don't want to call you "Papa" now. I have a real father and that's his name,' he would probably have patted her head and said vaguely, 'Yes, yes, quite right. Must get things tickety-boo, mustn't we?' and would have waddled back into his smoke-filled study.

So she said nothing and went up the red-carpeted stairs to her bedroom on the third floor. It was not an attic room, which she would have preferred, that being more in harmony with her being an artist's daughter. But it was light and pleasant and, even if it didn't have the dormer windows and sloping ceiling of the room above her, which was occupied by the two maids, at least it had more space than they had and was thankfully further away from the wheezing and banging of the hotel's plumbing.

Alice went straight to her wardrobe, a heavy, dark piece of ornate furniture with room enough, she had often thought, to hold the entire outfitting of a complete family as well as all the goblins and monsters she had, as a child, been certain were spending their nights there. Her own few garments looked, in its vast interior, like the clothes of someone who had just arrived from her native land by boat with all that she could carry.

Mr and Mrs Meadows did not think clothes important. Their attitude to anything of a covering nature was that it should be practical, sombre and respectable. Hence the dark, hard-wearing and plain furnishings of the hotel. This policy, when transferred to the matter of dress, ensured that the three members of the family wore the kinds of clothes that were suitable for their daily tasks, and each had one item for use on high days and holidays.

In Alice's case, this one festive garment was her white dress. She wore it for her birthday tea, and for Christmas dinner, and on visits with her mother to friends or to spy out the 'cleanliness' of a rival hotel. She had also worn it on one unforgettable night out at the Crystal Palace with her mother, her aunt and her cousin Arthur. It was from Arthur's open-mouthed admiration that she knew this dress had some special magic about it and suited her to a T. She would have dearly liked to have worn it today.

She opened the door of the wardrobe and separated the

dress from the thick plaid skirt that hung beside it. She laid her cheek against its silky folds and thought of her father again. Her mental vision of the tall, auburn-haired man was slightly marred by the smell of camphor wafting from the wardrobe. On each of the half-dozen hangers hung a little muslin pouch with two or three mothballs inside. Alice often wondered about these and why they were there. She had never seen a moth in her life. Were they kept away by these throat-catching, strong-smelling bags? Did they hate the smell as much as she did and keep their distance, flying somewhere away over the roof of Paddington Station to houses where there were no little bags on hangers? Or was their purpose to poison and kill?

She sometimes wished a moth would venture into the wardrobe, just so that she could see what happened. But none did. Her room was barren of all life except her own. She always thought of the room as empty of hope too – but not now, only four hours before what she was certain was to be the most momentous day of her life. After twelve o'clock today nothing would ever be the same again. And still she wished she could wear the white dress, as a mark of the day's importance and all that it promised.

It was now a little after eight o'clock. She could hear the distant clatter of crockery from the kitchen as breakfast for the hotel guests got under way. In the rooms around her on the third floor and in those below, she was aware of the stirrings of people readying themselves for the day. Bedroom doors squeaked and banged. The geyser in the nearby bathroom rattled and hissed as Mr Evans, up from Cardiff to meet his son on leave, took his morning bath.

There was the noise of china meeting marble as another guest emptied the water jug into the hand-basin and plonked it back on the washstand. Her stepfather had talked of having running water in every bedroom but it was plain that this piece of progress was not going to be made until his luck on the horses changed.

Every improvement at the hotel depended on Mr Meadows's varying fortunes at the race-track – or rather, not at the course itself, but in his dealings with Mr Butterwick, the bookmaker in the next street. He, as Mr Meadows kept remarking, had made enough money out of her stepfather to furnish and decorate three or four first-class hotels. Alice also benefited from Mr Meadows's gambling habit. For it was she who was invariably asked to 'take this note to Mr Butterwick', and who thoroughly enjoyed the quick sprint round the corner and the short wait outside the bookie's firmly closed door until one of the regular gamblers came along and took the note inside for her. She had never been inside. It was as mysterious as a public house. She imagined both of these forbidden places to be full of uncouth men swearing and spitting for all they were worth.

Oh heavens, Alice thought, why must life be so daily and dull and practical? If she had to live in a hotel, why not one of such grandeur that it had music and flowers everywhere, and people dressed in the height of fashion sweeping down grand staircases, and telephones, and uniformed porters? All the Clarendon had was one old man in a grey cotton jacket sighing and complaining as he humped the guests' rather shabby luggage upstairs or shuffled on the pavement outside while he reluctantly tried to catch the eye of a passing cabbie. But soon none of that would matter.

She tied the sides of her long hair back into a wide blue ribbon on the crown of her head, put a buckram belt around her narrow waist and went downstairs to help with the serving of breakfast.

The hours went by so slowly that Alice thought the day had died on her. She tried to hurry time along by chopping each hour into quarters – fifteen minutes to help clear the breakfast tables, then fifteen minutes to re-set them for lunch. Next she had to check the list of incoming and departing guests in the big blue book in her stepfather's study. But that did not take more than two minutes, so she spread out the allotted time by a long gaze out of the window from one end of the street to the other.

He might be early. Artists are not good time-keepers, she knew that. He could come at ten as easily as at twelve. But it had started to rain and the street was full of unartistic-looking people huddled under large umbrellas and, here and there, an unprotected figure loping through the downpour with bowed head and hunched shoulders. The heavy raindrops danced up from the pavement like tiny globes of glass and the gutters at the roadside were already running headlong with water with a noise like a train in a tunnel. Rain makes dreams, she was discovering. She had reached Paddington Station, her father's hand in hers, when her stepfather came into the room behind her and, as was his irritating ritual, approached her and tapped her on the bottom.

'Penny on the drum, penny on the bum,' he said mechanically and turned to the open register on his desk. He rubbed his hands briskly. 'Right! How many in today?'

Alice turned reluctantly from the window and shook her hair back from her shoulders.

'Only two. Mr Henson. And Miss Arkwright, the one with the dress shop in Oxford.'

'Oh Lordy me! She always has something to moan about. Last time it was damp sheets, or so she said. Though how damp sheets could possibly get past your mother's eagle eye beats me. Have you done the bed yet?'

'No, just going to. But it's all right. I'll make sure her bedding's aired . . .'

'Let Mr Henson get damp instead, eh?' He roared with laughter.

Alice made no reply, her mind far away again. She turned once more to the window, made a quick checking glance up and down the street and then walked slowly to the door.

As she reached the door and paused, her stepfather placed his chubby hands flat on his desk and stared down at them.

'Funny girl,' he said gruffly. 'I'll never make you out . . .'

Alice smiled and was pleased. She much preferred to think of herself as a mystery than an open book. But she was already preparing to open the pages for the one person to whom she felt they belonged. In just over two hours, she thought, there'll be an end to a lot of mysteries and, to Mr

Meadows's surprise, she started humming as she walked to the kitchen for her next task.

Alice began her final vigil at ten minutes to twelve. She stood between the window and the back of the armchair in the drawing-room. From there she could see out of the bay window straight along the street in both directions. Ahead of her was a clear view along the side street that led to the park. Only if her father came to the back door of the hotel, which was reached from the side street to her right, would she fail to see him before he arrived at the front steps. Alice immediately dismissed that possibility. She was quite sure that he was not a back-door man.

The rain had stopped about an hour earlier and soon afterwards the sun had come out in full strength, turning the wet pavements into steam and the umbrellas into parasols. Alice almost wished it were still raining so that the streets would be as bare of people as before and she could be sure of seeing her father as soon as he turned into the road. Then she could watch him as he approached the hotel.

As it was, the sun had brought out the prams and nannies and strollers, so that she had to keep craning this way and that to discern every figure that was half-hidden by another, or that was too far behind a group of people to be seen at all, except as a moving blob in the distance. But any blob could be him. So she ducked and weaved behind the net curtain, unseen but seeing all, and searching all the time for the tall man with the auburn hair and the striking eyes and the dramatic, flowing cape.

That is how she came to overlook the slightly built man with the bald patch in his sandy-coloured hair and the drawn grey face who walked cautiously up the stone steps and rang the front door-bell.

As the bell jangled in the kitchen Alice jumped away from the window as if struck, ran forward to peer through the net curtain again and then drew back once more. Who was that annoying visitor on the doorstep? What bad luck that he should turn up just as her father was due! She stood stock-still in the middle of the room, daring to go neither back to the window nor out of the room to answer the door.

Supposing her father, having seen someone already on the door-step, went round to the back? Supposing no one was there to go to the back door and supposing he said, 'Oh dear, I'm not expected today,' and turned away to go home? And supposing that he was so disappointed and cross that he never ever tried to see her again or wrote to her mother or anything?

In her panic she was dimly aware of someone answering the front door and she thought, that's all right then, I can go to the back door and make sure I don't miss him. As she turned to run out of the room the door opened and her mother, looking strangely at ease and almost smug, ushered in the small man with the sandy hair and the bald patch and said, 'Alice, dear, this is your father.'

'No,' Alice said. 'No, no.'

She reeled back, as if from the force of a strong wind. Her face, already pale, was drained of all colour. She was aware of her mother tutting anxiously and putting a hand out to steady her. But she drew away from her and backed to the far side of the room. Her eyes were fixed in naked shock and disappointment on the stranger.

There had to be some mistake. This could not be 'the artist'. He was small and ordinary, and he looked empty. The arms that should have been ready to hold her and sweep her off hung limply at his sides. His thin wrists protruded from the kind of mackintosh worn by any passer-by in the street and his eyes, not a vivid blue but pale and watery, flickered hesitantly round the room. She felt a great chill coming over her.

Why had everyone pretended all these years? She tried desperately to recall what she'd been told about this man that was so different from the reality. Then she was forced to realize that, in fact, she had been told nothing. And the chill turned to a fiery embarrassment and shame at the picture she had conjured up from her own hopes and imaginings. She had been betrayed, by him and by her own dreams. She looked at her mother and then at the quiet nothing-man. If only one of them would speak – the silence was becoming unbearable.

He turned to her mother and raised his eyebrows, not shocked but mildly surprised.

'Would you leave us alone, please?' he said. His voice was low and strong. It sounded as if he was used to commanding people and being obeyed. Alice almost jumped as he spoke – his voice was one thing, perhaps the only thing, she thought, that she had got right. But the rest was so wrong that she grasped at the wild possibility that he might be a servant or a messenger of some sort, sent to fetch her, so that her father would not have to see her mother or explain things. The artist himself was waiting round the corner, or in another hotel nearby, and would come later, when this man had cleared the way. He was a kind of John the Baptist, that was it.

When her mother had left the room, Alice turned to the man impatiently.

'When is he coming then?'

'Who?' He looked steadily at her, without smiling.

'My father . . . the artist . . . him . . .'

'You thought he was still an artist? And tall, perhaps? With flowing hair, the same colour as yours?' Now it was just noticeable that he was smiling.

'Yes, yes, he's like that. That's him, yes. Where is he?'

'What sort of a man is he, this man, your father?'

Alice found his gentle questioning infuriating. What she wanted was answers. Her anger overwhelmed her normal passive acceptance and all that she had been keeping inside her came tumbling out.

'I don't know. I don't know. I know nothing, don't you understand? No one has told me anything. I just want him to know me. And keep me. He might love me too. It's not much to ask, is it? I've done without him all this time. I could help him now. He must need someone, the same as I do . . .'

She felt frightened by the strength of her own feelings. It was the first time they had ever been voiced and they seemed far more painful now than they had ever been while kept secret.

The man looked away from her with a sad expression. He sighed.

'*I* am your father,' he said simply. 'May I sit down?'

Alice motioned him to a stiff-backed chair in the corner by the fireplace and stood at the other end of the room, her back to the window. She seemed dazed. As far apart as they could possibly be in such a small, furniture-crowded room, they stared at each other in silence.

Edwin Foster was in the middle of one of his bouts of depression. It was ironic, he thought, that this strange, subdued girl, so unlike her anxious, bird-like mother, had thought him to be a romantic artist – no doubt the kind who painted beautiful, long-haired girls like her in his attic studio and was rich and famous.

For he too had had that fantasy in his undergraduate days. He winced at the memories of the hours spent with his sketch-book by the river and out in the fields, of the jug full of paint-brushes in his digs and the pile of canvases that lay against the walls. He had taken to wearing smocks and bright scarves and was astonished to find how eager the local girls were to seek his company and drape themselves on his couch in attitudes of abandon.

But then, it was not so ironic. This girl was a product of those times and those fantasies. How could she or her mother know that Mr Foster senior, having taken control of his son's unfortunate lapse into fatherhood, at once decided to take control of his whole life and steer him far away from smocks, oil-paint and willing models and into the grey, dusty world of commerce?

Edwin recognized that to some people this world was one of high adventure and excitement, with its own kind of romance. Mr Foster senior's business was haulage – 'We carry the world' was his boast and his firm's slogan – and he would come alight at the mention of the far-away places listed in his order-books and at the sight of an upward curve in the graph of the annual cash turnover. But compared with Edwin's hopes for the Bohemian life among kindred spirits in Chelsea, it was like being consigned to hell.

59

It was from that change in his life that he dated the depressions that dogged him for the rest of his days. His sunny personality darkened, his shoulders rounded and his hands lost their extravagant flexibility. He wore dark suits with sombre cravats and wing-collars. All his movements became tamed and cautious. No longer was he offered the alabaster bodies of adoring girls. He met only the young people whose parents knew his parents. He played tennis with them and danced with them at balls and coming-out parties, but he never touched their bodies. He discovered that he had no wish to. Although he tried often to get back to his painting, he found that nothing would come to his mind or his hand and he would stand in front of an empty canvas for hours of torment, with tears running down his face for the talent and hope he had lost. He blamed his father entirely. He had driven the life and vigour out of him with his insensitive, domineering hold on his life.

There seemed no hope of shaking off this influence. Not even his father's death, for which Edwin passionately longed, would, he imagined, make any difference to the outsize conscience and load of guilt his father had bludgeoned into him. Try as he might, he could not break away from the idea that he had to win his father's approval. It was, or seemed to be, a matter of life or death, of survival.

So he had to surrender his autonomy, such little as he had had in those few years in Cambridge away from his father's surveillance. Nothing he did after that was ever spontaneous or of his own volition. Always it was measured first against his father's views or attitudes. At every corner and turn of his life, Edwin would ponder, what would Father do? Will Father approve? What will he say? His subsequent actions were determined by what he was quite certain would be the answers to these questions. For he knew his jailer well, as all prisoners do.

His conscience had counselled him not to make this visit to the Clarendon, which was why it was causing him such great anguish to be sitting here in front of his daughter and seeing her whole body radiate anger and accusation against him. But he had been frightened by his last bout of depression, which had seemed never-ending, and had decided to find out what had become of the child he'd fathered when he was young and happy. His depression had lifted slightly as soon as he had made this decision and had found a way to make the visit without his father's knowledge. But the blackness was still there and the visit itself was no relief from it.

As he stared at Alice he could scarcely believe that she was indeed his child. But he thought he saw something of his own mother in her colouring – that rich auburn hair, neither red nor sandy but a pleasing marriage of the two – and in the milky smoothness of her pale skin. What he had never seen in anyone before was the still, calm surrendering air about her. Except for that emotional outburst, which had stung him to pity, she gave no sign of her thoughts or her wants. She seemed to be utterly passive, ready to go where the wind blew. He shivered at the thought of how easily she could be led if she truly had no more will of her own than he had.

At length he asked, 'What were you expecting? Tell me.'

'Nothing. No, nothing really. Why did you come?'

'I wanted to know . . . whether . . . well, what you were like.'

'And then go again?'

'Yes.'

'Why?'

'Why come or why go?'

'Both.'

He found himself admiring the directness but appalled at her seeming lack of concern for him. For a girl, she was astonishingly hard. Did she know he was ill? Wasn't it obvious? He glanced down at his hands and saw they were shaking. Did she care?

'Now, Alice,' he said. 'What a nice name that is, by the way. This is just an indulgence. I'm not well and I wanted to see how good a job your mother and stepfather had done.' He wondered if that sounded patronizing and searched for something more personal and concerned to say. He felt more and more awkward, made worse by the knowledge that she was not going to help him out of it in any way.

'Are you happy?' He leant forward, trying to appear interested. 'Do you know what you want to do with your life? Is there anything you want in the way of education or training?'

'I've been to school. I left two years ago . . .'

'Yes, I know. But college perhaps? Even university, if you're at all academic?'

'I don't think so.'

Her heart sank further with every word he spoke. I can't believe it's true, she thought. This isn't my father. There's still some kind of pretence. And yet something very strong told her that it was her father and such a wave of loathing came over her that she could no longer stand up. She sat in the chair by the window, painfully recalling how she had sat there only a few hours before, dreaming of his coming and all that would follow.

'I've finished with education,' she said. 'I know enough. I thought . . . had thought . . . that I, that we . . . would . . .' She bent her head.

'Would be together?' he asked gently.

For a moment it seemed that she would nod in agreement. But she raised her head and spoke angrily.

'No, no, certainly not. Not us. Not you and me. I and the real one, the artist, the father . . . I know he'd have wanted me to go with him. Leave all this and be with him. He does want that. I know he does. He must want it . . .'

'But I'm the real one. I'm your father. The other isn't real. It's what you dreamed of. I'm real. Look, you can touch me.' He put out his hand limply, without getting up from his chair, and was not surprised when she stared at him scornfully. Neither of them wanted to touch, he thought resignedly.

'I can't take you with me,' he went on, 'because I'm ill most of the time and I live in this huge house in Cornwall with my sister and her family. I'm not married but I'm not alone.' He sighed heavily. 'It's cold and dull there. You wouldn't like it.'

'You don't come to London much then?'

'Hardly ever. This is the first time in ten years and I fancy it will be the last.'

'No theatres? No meals in restaurants? Don't you go to the opera or Ascot or the Derby? Don't you ever go abroad, on boats, and stay in Cannes or anywhere like that? I mean, when there's no war on?'

'No, never. And I don't read the *Tatler* or the *Illustrated London News* or the society news, which you obviously do.'

'Oh yes,' she said almost cheerfully. 'I read them a lot. I always have. They're always here for the guests. I like the people they talk about. They're having fun and they've got money. I'd like to be like that . . .'

'Well, I don't have fun and I don't have money.' He made an effort to sound cheerful too. 'So there we are. I'm not much use to you, am I?'

Alice flinched at this and was silent for a while.

'Don't you even paint pictures any more?' She felt that there was still the chance that inside this grey, clerkly little man was the soul and skill of an artist, waiting only for the right spur to be famous and rich. But he dashed this one last hope with his laconic answer.

'No, I never paint now. I don't do anything, actually.'

He stood up and turned towards the fireplace. He was struggling with tears of melancholy. Why had he come? This girl was far away from his world. On reflection, everybody was. What had he hoped for? That somehow this consequence of his dog-days could lead him out of his dark tunnel and back into creative life again? How could she do that? She was herself hungry for colour and life and had expected these things to come from him. The blind leading the blind, he thought bitterly. She will not care for me and I cannot care for her.

His bitterness was hugely surpassed by Alice's own. Her dreams had collapsed into this small grey reality. He shouldn't have come. How could he be so cruel? If he'd stayed away, she could have thought of him for ever as she had been used to. And then the added cruelty of turning her down. 'I'm not much use to you, am I?' – and he had actually smiled as he said it.

She was surprised, all the same, that he, of all people, seemed to be unaffected by the power that she knew she had over men. She had certainly not expected that. She had imagined him warming to her beauty, softening to her unhappiness and, in the end, surrendering to all that she wanted. Yet perhaps she had known this right at the start. For she recalled that she had not tried any of her lowered eyes and shy, seductive smiles. She must have felt that they'd be no use. In fact, she hadn't felt that he was really interested in her at all. He must have taken one look and decided she was not worth bothering about. All the time they'd been in the room together, she'd felt terribly alone. He had dismissed her at once and for ever.

'Well?' she said, with unaccustomed bluntness. 'I expect you'd like to go now? You've seen all you want to see?'

He winced. If that was a counter-rejection, he supposed he deserved it – but it hurt.

'I'm sorry. But yes, I should be going now. Isn't there anything that you'd like to tell me about yourself, though? Like what you'd like to be when you're older?'

'Oh, don't worry. That's easy. I'm going to be Alice, that's all. And you'll see, there will be people who'll want me . . .'

'Yes, yes, there will. I'm sure there will . . .' His voice tailed away and he sighed as Alice turned her face away, dismissing him.

'I would have been something to you, you know, if I'd had the chance.' He felt quite unable to let go of his shame and sense of failure.

'Would you?' said Alice in a tone of disbelief.

Edwin Foster put his hand out a few inches and then withdrew it slowly. He couldn't tell whether or not she would have responded to a handshake – but he felt unwilling to take the risk. He knew that in a few minutes, when he was outside and alone, he would be back in his blackest of black moods.

He backed towards the door.

'I'll need to have a few words with your mother,' he said. 'And then I'll go. So goodbye, Alice . . . goodbye.'

Her lips moved in the shape of goodbye but no sound came. She waved faintly – a child's wave that wasn't certain of its purpose. As soon as her father had left the room she lowered her arm and stood stock-still for a few seconds, staring blankly towards the half-open door. Then she flung herself into the armchair and curled up into a foetal ball. Her thumb slid into her mouth and her head came gently to rest on top of her knees.

She heard low voices in the hall, and then the front door opening. He's going, she thought, and fought against the urge to catch a last look at him. She was so successful that she remained staring into the dark space made by the curve of her body while his footsteps died away past the hotel and down the street.

4

LOOKING FOR LOVE

August 1917 was not the best of times for Alice to begin her trawl for men who would admire, love and cherish her. Although she was unaware of it, the day of her father's dismal visit to the Clarendon was the third anniversary of Britain's declaration of war on Germany and the country was weary and dispirited by the years of bloody, muddy, costly conflict.

For her, the war was merely a reason for such minor inconveniences as a shortage of French millinery items and of certain foods. In the hotel there were two meatless days every week – Tuesdays and Thursdays – when the guests sat at the dining-tables with an air of cheerful sacrifice and were served with what her mother described as 'country loaf' and which no one was impolite enough to categorize truthfully as a baked mash of carrot, cabbage and breadcrumbs with a great deal too much gravy browning added.

However, now that her eyes were directed more to the world outside the hotel, she became aware of the dearth of young men in everyday life. There would be many days when she would see no one but children, women and old men from the hotel windows and on her excursions to the shops or the park. On other days she would occasionally see a serviceman on leave, perhaps with a girl on his arm, or a one-legged young man hobbling along on crutches, or a pair of them, one bandaged around the head, the other carefully guiding his companion up and down the kerbs.

She noticed that if the streets were crowded people drew away from the wounded and flattened themselves against the railings of the houses or the trees that lined the road, with a kind of reverent respect, so that the young, maimed men walked along a path cleared for them as if they were untouchable. There was a quietness surrounding them, caused perhaps by a pity that could not speak, perhaps by an awkwardness that dare not. Mothers and nannies drew their children to their sides and caught their pointing fingers with a mild slap. Cries of 'Look! What's wrong with that man?' were hushed with disapproving frowns and the offending child pulled back against the adult's side.

If Alice had been older and more worldly, she might have wondered why this was so – this strange, collective desire to put a decent distance between the onlookers and the participants in the war. She might have concluded that it arose from a tremendous feeling of guilt and hopelessness that so many men were being sacrificed for, as they were told, home and country. If she had been standing in an East End of London street, however, or in the market square of a provincial town, she would not have had to wonder at all. For there the wounded serving men and the ex-soldiers were greeted with warmth and friendliness. It was not unusual for them to be asked in off the streets into strangers' homes, so that civilians were able to express their sorrow and shrive their guilt at surviving the massacre.

Nor did Alice have any idea that, after the war was over, it was the middle and governing classes who would have their way with the promised 'rehabilitation' of the country and of the returning heroes. Many of those who survived would soon come to feel that they were indeed shunned and untouchable. For they were, in the main, left to deal with what was left of their lives as best they could, while the scene was set in the wider world for the rise of dictators and yet another culling of the nation's young men.

In the hotel, Alice now had a greater interest in the guests and what they talked about. No longer did she duck her head demurely as they complimented her or turn away with a shy smile. She began to size up the male guests as to their possible wealth, freedom from ties, and attractiveness. It was the beginning of her life-long pragmatic interest in the age, income and marital status of anyone who came to her notice or into her life.

From six o'clock every evening she helped in the bar, which was a small, doorless room opening out from the dining-room. Mr Meadows had made it as much like a gentlemen's private club as possible and it was a dark, cosy haven of crimson plush furniture, its walls closely covered with pictures of racehorses, trainers, owners and jockeys. Alice liked its atmosphere of gentlemen at ease and was pleased that few women came into it. Occasionally a married couple who were staying at the hotel would take a sherry here before dinner, or, more rarely, a man on his way to the station would bring his female companion in. Alice was quick to notice that any man accompanied by a woman was careful not to be seen staring at her – but stare he did, all the same, as he came up to the bar alone to refill their glasses.

She had been used to taking no notice of the men's conversation as they lolled at the bar in front of her. But now, wishing to feel more a part of their world, she would move nearer to the bar as they talked and look for an opportunity to join in. At first she had thought her mother would disapprove of this new habit. But she had underestimated Mrs Meadows's enthusiasm for any course that might lead to Alice's indepen-dence – which, in her terms, meant marriage. So Alice had been pleasantly surprised when her mother, squeezing past her in the bar as she made small talk with two guests, had nodded approvingly and hissed in her ear, 'That's right, dear. Keep them happy . . .'

It was extremely hard, however, to keep herself happy. She was poised for adventure and excitement while all around her there was nothing but despondency and sighs of 'When will it end?' Again and again she heard them reassure each other with 'Surely it can't be long now that the Yanks are with us.' The men who had given her ribbons and chucked her under the chin now stared gloomily into their glasses or drew crumpled newspapers out of their coat pockets to check and share the numbers of dead and wounded. Mr Thomas, the bald, plump, kindly man who came to stay once a week, was more fearful than ever for the welfare of his nineteen-year-old son, who, in an eager flush of patriotism and comradeship, had joined the Pals battalion in their home town in the Midlands.

'You see, lass,' he said one evening as they faced each other across the bar, 'they've just started another battle at Ypres. The third one in that area – a place called Passchendaele. I shouldn't bother you with my worries, I know that. But you're only a young thing yourself, he's not much older than you. Why, if he were here, he'd be eyeing you up no end. "Crikey, Dad," he'd say to me in that cheeky way of his, "what a beauty!"' His eyes went misty and he blew his nose fiercely. 'And he says it does nothing but rain there. If it stops at all, it's never long enough for the mud to dry out. And this is the summer. Think, lass, what they'll have to put up with in the winter. But there, I expect it'll all be over by then.'

Alice made an effort to sound hopeful. She put her hand on Mr Thomas's arm as it rested on the bar.

'I'm sure he'll be all right,' she said. 'Don't fret.'

In the event, they were both wrong. The fighting at Passchendaele went on for a further three and a half months, until mid-November. Young Frank Thomas was among the 400,000 British soldiers who died there. And the war continued for another year.

As the summer months of 1917 turned into autumn, Alice continued her campaign to grow up, gain independence and get out in the world. On the first of September she put her hair up and never again, except at bedtimes, wore it loose, plaited or tied with a ribbon on the nape of her neck. Her family and the hotel regulars were downcast at this change.

'Your best feature and you want to hide it,' was her mother's irritated comment. Her stepfather teased her with mock deference. 'Oh pardon me, Madam,' he would say, bowing low and humbly, 'I didn't realize a lady was passing by . . .' and he would chortle as he walked on while Alice tried, and always failed, to think of some quick retort that would maintain her dignity as well as putting an end to his tedious jokes.

The trouble was that she felt she was on the point of blossoming but all around her were people who were fading into greyness, dull habit and no hope. Daily she studied herself in the full-length mirror on the door of her wardrobe and sang inside with pleasure at the narrowness of her waist and at her long, slim legs and firm, small breasts. She had no desire to move about as she gazed at herself. She did not think it in the least necessary to practise moving gracefully or to try out different expressions, or, indeed, to show any animation whatsoever. To her mind, it was enough for beauty simply to be there, to exist in a state of suspension, ready to be stared at, admired, even touched. One did not expect a beautiful picture to respond to admiration or to say, 'How good of you to look at me and admire me. What can I do for you in return?'

In the same way, she felt, she was to be the calm, neutral focus for men's eyes and they would be privileged if allowed to display her to the gaze of others, much as a proud picture-owner would get satisfaction from putting his treasured possession on show. As for being possessed by a man, far from being an unwelcome thought, it was all she wanted, to escape from the unappreciative people around her into a world where beautiful things were owned and admired and where she would eventually come to belong – to that world and to one person in it.

There was one person in Alice's life who shared her fantasies with glee and complete understanding. Daisy Lawson had been at school with her and lived only a street away, overlooking the park. She was on the plump side and shorter than Alice, but carried herself with such confidence and vivacity that she gave the appearance of much more maturity and poise. She had a strong face, with dark eyes and a full mouth. Her hair, like Alice's, was long and she had put it up a good year before her friend had come out of plaits and ribbons. But, in contrast with Alice's coppery auburn hair, Daisy's was almost black and glistened like sealskin.

Mrs Meadows frequently remarked that Daisy seemed to

be 'very experienced'. She never elaborated on this but Alice had no doubt that she did not mean it as a compliment.

In their schooldays Daisy had been a foil for Alice in every way – her expression always lively and her cheeks high-coloured in contrast with Alice's pale serenity, her movements dramatic and bold against Alice's shy timidity. Separately, they were certainly noticeable. But together they had something extra, something later known as glamour and later still as charisma. Alice, her mother noted, became more positive and defiant when she was in Daisy's company, and for that reason she was never too happy when the girls were together.

They were allowed to go to nearby shops on errands for the hotel, and now and then Daisy came to tea at the Claren-don or Alice called at Daisy's home for a game of ludo or draughts. At least, that was their intention but the friends always began and ended by speculating on their future loves and lives and poring over copies of the *Queen* and *Fashions for All*, subsiding into giggles over the advertisements for Reduso corsets, liberty bodices, and shoulder braces 'for the correction of narrow chests and weak backs'.

They inspected their shapes and complexions endlessly. Now and then they would toy with the idea of sending up for trial boxes of 'a permanent and harmless remedy to improve the figure', but always agreed in the end that a shilling was too much to pay just to solve the mystery of what the box contained. Daisy, however, was much more tempted by the promise of Oatine cream to give a 'dainty charm' to her complexion – 'You're dainty enough as it is,' she told Alice enviously – and dragged Alice to the local chemist to buy a small jar at one shilling and three halfpence. Whenever they met after this purchase, Daisy would proffer her cheek to Alice's touch and exclaim, 'Just feel! Pure velvet!', and Alice would agree, 'Yes, such daintiness and charm!', though secretly quite unable to detect any difference.

The subject of Alice's envy, however, was not any detail of her friend's appearance but Daisy's whole life. It seemed to be far freer and more exciting than her own. Her large home was always full to bursting with two brothers, three sisters, visiting cousins, aunts, uncles and grandparents, not to mention parents who doted on all their children with such a warmth and fulsome pride that it made Alice ache with a feeling of loss. Everyone shouted at each other and teased, cried and laughed at full spate. Alice longed for all this easy emotion to be the currency at home instead of the constant injunctions – 'Be quiet,' 'Don't cry,' 'Keep your laughter low, dear,' and 'It's not nice to mock.'

What was to be envied most of all was the fact that long ago a distant relation from the Highgate branch of the sprawling Lawson family had been earmarked as Daisy's future husband. She and Julian had already exchanged kisses, rings and clumsy embraces. So Daisy had nothing of the uncertainty about finding love, marriage and family which dogged Alice's search, and that of most girls of her age.

However, this certainty seemed to have its drawbacks. Daisy often complained that she had had no time to 'find out about men' and to 'have fun'. Perhaps this was why she vicariously enjoyed pushing Alice into minor adventures. On their trips to the shops she was quite shameless about nudging her when a good-looking youth went by and making loud remarks about him. Alice would cringe with embarrassment, which made Daisy talk all the louder and occasionally give Alice a push towards some poor, pink-faced boy so that they collided and he had to retreat with mumbled 'excuse me's' and 'I beg your pardons' while Daisy doubled up with laughter in the background, one hand on the crown of her hat to stop it flying off and the other swinging her dolly-bag round and round like a lariat.

The highlight of Alice's week, however, was not with Daisy. It was the regular outing with her mother to Hyde Park on Sunday evenings.

Sometimes, if the hotel was not too busy and there was one of the staff to take charge, her stepfather would come too. She did not enjoy those occasions quite so much. Mr Meadows would want to play the part of the jaunty man of the world and swing his cane about and raise his hat to every female they passed, be it a small girl bowling her hoop ahead of her parents or two very old ladies clutching at each other for support, and bent so double that they failed to see if Mr Meadows or anyone else was behaving in a courtly fashion or not.

Then, when they reached the bandstand, he would not sit down beside Alice or his wife but would stand behind them, one hand on the back of his wife's seat in a proud, protective pose, and would beat his other hand up and down in the air in time with the band. Worst of all, when there was a tune he thought he knew, he would sing in a way that approximated to the tune only enough to show that it failed to close on it entirely. Alice felt shamed by the way people turned round to look at him and put their hands over their ears. She would shift her chair a little way from her mother's and the bellowing noise behind it, hoping people would think she was nothing to do with this coarse man and his whisky voice.

It was better when Mr Meadows had to stay at the hotel and she and her mother went to the park together without him. There were a lot of sideways looks then that she did not mind at all. Sometimes, in a family group that strolled by, there would be a prosperous-looking father with a handsome moustache and bright eyes skimming over the crowds. His glance would fall on her and she would note how it stayed there for a while so that he had to turn his head as he passed. And the look said, as loud as words, 'Oh my lovely! I wish you were mine!'

Her mother would always notice too. Her whole attention was fixed on the impression Alice made on the people who passed them. She had eyes for nothing else. A large part of this close attention was devoted to dividing the general public, or, at least the male portion of it, into those who were entitled to admire her daughter and those who were not. When she intercepted the glance of the well-dressed family man, all was good humour and nudges and 'He'll know you next time he sees you, won't he?' Or, if it was an obvious gentleman and he was alone, 'It's all right to nod a greeting, dear. If he's alone, it's perfectly polite. But not if he has a lady with him. Just look the other way or pretend not to see him.'

If, on the other hand, it was a rough young lad, with thick boots, and red wrists sticking out of his jacket sleeves, who gawped at Alice and ventured a wink or a whistle, Mrs Meadows would grip her daughter's elbow tightly and steer her at right angles across the path and on to the grass as if the devil were behind them. It was not that she was a snob in the real sense of being prejudiced against the working classes. It was simply that, having come from them, she wanted to deny their very existence as well as any place for them in her own life or in Alice's future. Like many a climber, she was afraid of looking downwards.

Mrs Meadows always came back from these excursions satisfied and triumphant. 'It was a good thing I was with you,' she would say. 'Several of them would have approached you, I'm sure, if I hadn't been there. That wouldn't do, of course. Still, it's all good practice, getting stared at. You must learn to carry it off. And you did very well.'

Alice was half glad that they would not dare approach. She was not sure she was ready to deal with the mysterious world of men yet, face to face. But it was a disappointment also. She would have liked some of those distant admirers to come a little nearer and say the words that were in their glances. She was getting rather tired of waiting for love. She felt she'd be certain to die if something exciting and romantic did not happen soon.

Romance and excitement, however, were already beginning their journey towards Alice. Far away from Hyde Park, in a gracious terraced house in Bath, Colonel Frederick Arthur Whittaker (retired) was reading a short, reassuring letter from his nephew, Lieutenant Colin Whittaker of the Royal Warwickshire Regiment, who was on active service on the Western Front. In his letter he reported to his uncle, his only living male relative, that he had been wounded – 'just a scratch', he wrote – and would be coming on leave in two weeks' time.

Colonel Whittaker decided that he would make the journey to London, meet his nephew off the boat-train at Charing Cross and stay up for a few days to show the boy the town.

He also decided that he would book rooms for them at the only hotel he knew of that charged neither too much nor filled its rooms with *nouveau riche* munitions barons.

His choice was the Clarendon Hotel.

The Colonel worried a great deal about his nephew. He could not imagine how his younger brother, Colin's father, could possibly have brought up his son in the right way. Peter was so very unlike any of the generations of Whittakers who had preceded him in the army. Not for him the bluff, open, uncomplicated ways of Frederick himself and their father. He had always been a secret sort of chap, unhealthily given to sitting by himself in corners and wryly observing the rest of the family and their visitors.

Frederick thought he detected some of the same introversion and complexity in young Colin and often remarked to his docile wife, Clarice, that he considered it his duty to 'bring the boy out of himself'. He was not insensitive to the blow it had been to Colin when his parents died within a few months of each other when the boy was only fourteen. A rum business, he thought, the way first one and then the other had just given up.

Perhaps Ballads, that ramshackle but oddly beautiful house, had something to do with it. He had never felt at home there, although it was his birthplace and his father's pride and joy. He had been surprised and delighted when Peter offered to buy him out after their father's death. He had agreed at once and taken himself and Clarice off to a neat, orderly life in Bath that suited them both down to the ground.

He had seen very little of his brother after that. Peter seemed to have withdrawn more and more into himself, spurning almost all contact with his elder brother or, indeed, with anyone else until, in the end, it seemed that he simply ran out of the will to live, as if he had reached the end of his journey inward and found only death waiting there. I suppose, thought Frederick, it was probably cancer or some other incurable illness, but one had to admit that Peter had

75

somehow invited his early grave by turning his back on life and, what is more, had encouraged his wife in the same melancholy opinion of the world.

In all conscience he had done his best, and so had Clarice, to rouse Colin from too prolonged a mourning for his dead parents. They had been careful not to breathe a word about the probable cause of his mother's death, never completely confirmed, but plain enough to anyone who called at Ballads during the six months after Peter died.

Maud had always, the family agreed, been a little too fond of fortified wines. There had been an amazing amount of bottles of sherry and port stacked in that cold little room they called 'the dairy' between the kitchen and the glasshouse. A dignified woman, as squarely built as a Norman tower, she moved through the gardens and the rooms of Ballads with such awe-inspiring stateliness that no one could have guessed that for a greater part of the day and for all the evening hours she was as drunk as a lord. Clarice never believed it to this day.

However, the family doctor confided to Frederick that 'the poor lady had a liver like a colander. It was a miracle she didn't go before her husband did. I just hope the boy hasn't caught any of his parents' weakness. I've never known two people with such a determination to destroy themselves. Can't account for it, Colonel, I'm afraid . . .'

Nor could Frederick explain it, seeing that he himself was as strong and as little given to introspection as an ox. In any event, he was determined that if Colin had any tendencies of this unhealthy kind, they were going to be quickly nipped in the bud.

What gave Frederick both the opportunity and also the inclination to take on responsibility for Colin was the fact that he and Clarice had not themselves been blessed with any children. He had no wish to look for any reason for this beyond telling himself that it was probably due to some deficiency in his wife. The conception and bearing of children was a woman's business, after all, and he had done his part in the bedroom at regular, well-spaced intervals throughout their married life.

Nor was Clarice encouraged to speculate on their childlessness, not even when all her brothers and sisters reproduced themselves with such a high degree of fertility that none of them had fewer than five in the family and one sister had no less than twelve children in as many years. Secretly, Clarice had doubted that her body could be so unlike those of her siblings as to be completely barren. But, since it was unheard of for any man, especially a Whittaker, to be incapable of fathering children, unless, of course, he was damaged in that part of the body which was required to be whole and healthy in order to procreate, she dismissed any thought of Frederick's possible incapacity as soon as it entered her head. They did not talk about it, and no one would have dreamed of raising the subject with them. Thus they were able to convince themselves that their childlessness was an intended blessing. It allowed them to play an active part in the life of the Church and the town, to follow closely the lives of Clarice's sisters and brothers and, most important of all, to step into the breach when Frederick's brother and then his sister-in-law died, leaving Colin an orphan in a great melancholy house with only a handful of servants for company.

They were much relieved when Colin, at eighteen, decided that he would join the regular army. But Frederick was still left with some anxiety about whether the boy was ever truly going to fit into the Whittaker mould. Like his father, he had some decidedly maverick qualities. He played the piano, and played it well. And he was what Frederick termed 'a scribbler', which meant that he wrote a lot. He had seen evidence of this in Colin's study at Ballads. It was plain that he wrote letters, notes and lists, drew maps and plans – the room was full of papers and exercise books and ledgers. He suspected Colin might even keep a diary and wouldn't have been at all surprised if some of his 'scribblings' were in verse. He had a poet's look in his eye – questing, romantic and troubled.

Nevertheless, Frederick hoped that these soft edges would be squared off satisfactorily once Colin was in the army. In the event, this process was accelerated more than Frederick could possibly have wished. For in the year that Colin received his commission in the Royal Warwickshire Regiment, the Great War broke out and for the next four years he was to be batted between England and the battlefields of Belgium and France like a shuttlecock. His uncle was quite certain that this experience would very quickly knock the poetry out of him.

Unfortunately, there was no way of telling, just by the look of him. The boy seemed well-mannered, upright, honourable, brave and modest. He avoided any discussion of his personal feelings about service at the front, which was right and proper, and showed no tendency, as in former days, to question the realities of life or ponder on the meaning of things.

Frederick had been considerably put out, he remembered, when Colin, a month after his mother's death, had asked his uncle, 'Why do I have to go back to school? What is school for?'

'To learn things, of course.'

'But I can learn things here . . .' Colin swept his arm round to embrace Ballads, its grounds and the fields and woods beyond. 'Things that are lots more important than any of the stuff they try and cram into us at school. This is all alive . . .' He faltered as he said 'alive' and Frederick felt a stab of pain for the boy who had seen death come so close. 'This is all I want to know. I love this place, Uncle. It's my duty to learn about it and look after it. How can I do that if I go back to school?'

Frederick stretched his rather meagre reasoning abilities to locate an answer. He thought it possibly was more important that Colin kept Ballads going, with its kitchen garden, the well-run shoot and all the staff who were dependent on the place for their living. It would, he judged, have been more useful if Colin were learning how to manage Ballads than learning Latin and Greek, or being encouraged in music-making and writing. Besides, Peter had neglected the place abominably and it needed some enthusiastic attention. But not from a fourteen-year-old boy, that was just absurd.

Then he hit on a logical point.

'But you'll never be able to look after it well unless you can earn some money at a useful career. It won't pay for itself, you know. Your parents' money left you very comfortable but it won't last for ever. You'll want to marry and have a family . . .' – he noticed Colin grimacing in embarrassment – '. . . of course you will, and you'll need to have some sort of income to keep them here at Ballads. So just you soldier on and see what happens, eh? All the staff here love your home. It's their home too, remember. They'll look after it well.'

So Colin had soldiered on, spending his school holidays partly at Ballads, under the wing of the nanny-cum-housekeeper who had been there all his life, and partly with his uncle and aunt at Bath. He had no close friends among the other boys at school. He was well-liked but not popular. He was good at the kind of sports that offered a challenge to him alone – like running and swimming – but he hated team-games. He was never invited to the homes of the other boys and never thought of asking any of them to Ballads. By the time he went on active service in 1914, he was, to all outward appearances, a model young Englishman of the middle class, and what went on under the surface was, his uncle decided, no business of anyone but Colin. Moreover, he keenly hoped that it was no business of Colin's either and that the moody, deep-thinking strain which had been apparent in his father was now happily laid to rest in the cemetery of Westknoll parish church just two miles from Ballads.

During the long battle of Passchendaele, Colin had taken two leaves in France and had been wounded once, in the shoulder, seriously enough to keep him in a field hospital behind the lines for two weeks. So it was not until November, as the battle drew to a humiliating deadlock, that his uncle came up from Bath to settle himself into the Clarendon Hotel ready to meet him at Charing Cross Station the following morning.

He was greeted at the door by Mrs Meadows.

'Welcome, Colonel Whittaker,' she said. 'If you'd kindly sign the register and then you'll be shown to your room.

Your nephew will have the one next to it. I understand he's not arriving until tomorrow?'

'Quite right, thank you. That's the drill . . .'

He was about to put his case down when a young girl came out of the room to his right and went to take it from his hand. She was of such an astonishing beauty, with a mass of auburn hair piled in thick coils on top of her head, that he was taken aback for a moment and gripped his case more tightly.

'Oh no, surely you have a porter . . . This young lady, I couldn't burden her . . .'

Mrs Meadows tutted kindly and waved Alice forward to take the case.

'Quite all right, Colonel. This is my daughter, Alice. A strong girl. The porter is otherwise engaged.' Down at the bookie's shop, she guessed silently. But that was for her husband to deal with.

Frederick removed his hat, smiled at Alice and let go of his case. He stared after her as she went upstairs.

'Extraordinary!' he muttered. The girl had not spoken and yet he was conscious of some sort of entreaty in her attitude. She seemed so out of place in this businesslike, hushed establishment that, if he had met her alone in the hall, he would have taken her for a guest whose choice of hotel had been made for her. Don't be surprised, she seemed to say. I am only passing through.

For her part, Alice had marked Colonel Whittaker as a nice but stuffy old gentleman who would be giving her second-class attention – polite but distant interest. She expected little more from the Colonel's nephew, in spite of his youth and army commission. Daisy, who had more experience in these matters, said that all the young officers that she'd come across were only interested in their mothers and horses. She added that, having met one or two of the mothers in question, this seemed to amount to much the same thing.

All the same, any young man staying in the hotel was an unusual event that needed every bit of help she could give it. It was definitely what her mother called 'good practice'. How was she going to net a big fish, after all, if she did not have some experience of netting smaller ones?

So Alice spent some time on her appearance on that misty November morning when Colin was expected at the Clarendon. She put on her long green serge skirt that swung around her ankles as she walked and a plain white georgette blouse with a wide, floppy collar, pinned at the throat with a cameo brooch. At the top of her piled-up hair she carefully placed a green petersham bow, so that its ends hung down almost to the nape of her neck, and secured it with hair-pins. She wondered momentarily if she was going to be too cold without her long woollen jacket but, gazing at it hanging on the chair beside her bed, she decided it looked unbearably middle-aged and domestic and that she was prepared to suffer a few shivers in order to look quite the opposite.

Downstairs, the work of the hotel was going on as usual. An elderly couple were taking mid-morning tea in the drawing-room, where the fire crackled merrily. From the kitchen came the clatter of pots and pans, crockery and cutlery, as preparations were made for luncheon. There was a smell of boiled beef in the hall and Alice wrinkled her nose in disgust. She looked in the mirror behind the hall-table and was well pleased.

Then, with something as ordinary as a clatter at the front door and Colonel Whittaker's deep voice saying, 'Here we are then,' Alice's life started on its course of long-awaited change.

As the Colonel stepped into the hall, Alice saw a slim man just a little taller than herself hesitating shyly behind him. It was his eyes she noticed first. They were dark and fringed with long, black lashes. The brows above were dark too and as straight as lines drawn with a ruler. As she looked, there seemed no end to the depth of his eyes and she felt helpless and excited at the same time, like a swimmer caught in a strong current.

'Ah! And here's Alice!' boomed the Colonel. 'Alice, my nephew Lieutenant Whittaker. Come in, boy, so's we can shut the door. It's freezing out there. And here we are, all set for one of your delicious luncheons.' He walked purposefully into the drawing-room, expecting Colin to follow him.

Colin had lost his shyness, however, and stood in front of Alice, smiling broadly, his cap and stick clasped in both hands behind his back.

'He told me your hair was ... was ... like it is ... glorious!'

Alice showed no sign of her usual shyness either. She moved towards him.

'He told me nothing about you,' she said, laughing.

'Well, you shall learn about me.' He looked past her up the hall and towards the stairs as if he expected to be pounced on for his forwardness.

'That is, of course,' he added, 'if your people will allow me? You look so young. Perhaps it's not allowed? I mean ... I'll ask my uncle if we can all have a jolly evening together. We'll ask your mother too. Would that be a good idea?'

He knew he was gabbling and getting muddled. He felt as he had so often done lately, as if time were against him, that if he didn't seize on every experience that presented itself, it might be lost to him for ever. But he knew nothing of love or courtship. There had been just one girl, a long time ago when he was seventeen and before the war broke out. She came to play tennis at Ballads with her brother and a friend. She and Colin had sneaked off into the orchard where she suddenly and surprisingly flung herself on the grass.

'Oh Colin!' she cried dramatically. 'My ankle has given way.'

She lay there looking up at him invitingly, with her long white skirt caught around her knees and her freckled arms spread out beside her in an attitude of surrender. He went on his knees beside her and, with grave attention, began to stroke one of her ankles.

'Not that one, silly.'

As he placed his hands gingerly round the other ankle, she giggled.

'Not that one either. Here, this is where it hurts.' She grasped his hand and placed it on her breast. She began to moan so alarmingly that Colin feared he was hurting the soft, warm flesh that lay under his hand.

He saw a money-spider making its way through her tumbled hair, shut his eyes tightly and bent his head down to hers. They pressed their lips together and writhed and fumbled at each other's clothing for a few minutes until, with as much speed as she had pitched herself on to the grass, she wriggled from under him and was on her feet, smoothing her skirt down and frowning at the grass stains on her white shoes.

'I'd better go now,' she said airily. 'The others will be wondering what's up.'

'But ... but ...' Colin was still sprawled on the ground and was feeling inexplicably angry.

'Oh, don't worry,' she said impatiently. 'That was very nice. You'd be all right if you just learned a bit more about kissing.' She narrowed her eyes as she stared down at him.

'You're very good-looking. Did anyone ever, you know ... any other girl ... have you ever actually known a girl, you know what I mean?'

'Oh yes, lots.' Colin surprised himself with the quickness of his lie and got to his feet in one move, avoiding her eyes.

'Oh really?' she said. 'I wouldn't have thought so. I'm extremely experienced myself. I expect you could tell ...'

'Oh yes, of course.' He felt certain she was lying too and he brightened. 'Then perhaps we could come here again? You could teach me to kiss if you like.'

'I shouldn't think so. My fiancé wouldn't have that. Did you know I'm engaged to be married?'

'No.' Colin spoke flatly, beginning to dislike her. He had an awful ache in every part of his body. It was a hunger and a crossness and he felt like grabbing this smug girl and shutting her stupid mouth with his mouth until it grew dark in the orchard and all his ache was gone. He couldn't remember her name now. He had not had the chance to get closer to her, or to any other girl, and he had assumed that, until he had a wife, further explorations would have to wait.

Here, in the hall with Alice, he could not explain why he

should be troubled by memories of the girl in the orchard. He tried to picture this serene girl with the auburn hair throwing herself on the grass at his feet and the picture would not form clearly. She was different, quite different, and he knew at once that he needed her.

What he could not know was that he needed her as lover, mother, wife, friend, nurse, comforter and goddess all rolled into one. Deep down, beyond conscious thought, he saw her as the answer to all his needs. And Alice's needs were as great as his – for lover, protector, father, guide, husband and friend. But a seventeen-year-old girl in an England that was just emerging from Victorian and Edwardian conventions was not expected to have wants, let alone pursue them. Alice's role was to wait until her white knight in shining armour came to sweep her away, not to run halfway to meet him. However, she knew there was much she could do to make her white knight wish to pursue her and she was in no doubt that she would do it.

So they smiled at each other in the hall of the Clarendon and knew that, at last, this was the beginning of something exciting and important.

5

COURTSHIP

Everyone concerned had good reason to encourage the courtship of Alice and Colin, and to make it a speedy one. For the Colonel, it looked like the answer to a nagging worry – how Colin was going to settle down to life at Ballads on his own when the war was over. If he stayed in the army he would often be overseas and unable to look after the place, and if he left the army he would be there all the time, living like a hermit. A young, adoring wife was the only answer, he felt, and if Colin's choice was to be this quiet, auburn-haired beauty he was going to give him his full support.

Mrs Meadows had no hesitation in accepting the Colonel's invitation to her and Alice to dine out with him and his nephew that evening. She knew what it meant and she thanked her lucky stars for the perfect timing of Colin's visit to the Clarendon. Alice's life at the hotel was coming to its natural end. She had no training for anything, was too young to go into war-work of any kind and had outgrown her use-fulness and her enthusiasm for the menial tasks in the hotel. What's more, she was restless and might prove troublesome before long. How else could she move to another life unless it was via marriage? And what better husband than this lonely young man with a house of his own and apparently no worries about where the next guinea was coming from?

Mrs Meadows was not the sort to dance with joy, but as she dressed for the outing and swathed her best and biggest hat with a length of grey tulle, her heart did a little jig. And when she went downstairs to foregather with the others in the hall she had the high colour in her cheeks that was normally seen only when she staggered into the dining-room with the

Christmas goose after several hours of personal responsibility for the roaring kitchen range.

I always knew, she thought as they trundled up Piccadilly in a spluttering taxi-cab, that Alice could turn anyone's head if she put her mind to it. And as they sat at their table amid the bright lights and clatter of the Trocadero restaurant, she was thankful to see that Alice was indeed putting her mind to it. She was wearing her white dress, with the wide sash tied in a large bow at the back, and her hair was pinned up and decorated at each side, just above her ears, with clusters of tiny, white artificial flowers. Mrs Meadows had never seen her daughter offer so many shy smiles, so many expressions of rapt attention, so many charming little dips of the head and waves of the hand, all of which gained Colin's open-mouthed admiration. Her eyes were unusually bright, but apart from that she was as calm and reserved as ever and her mother marvelled once more at whatever strange quirk of heredity had produced this swan from what she always thought of as 'the shame of the past'.

Oh Edwin, Edwin, she mused after her third glass of wine, it all held more ruin for you than for me, as it turns out. She felt a moment of pity for the man she had loved and then drew herself up in an effort to quell a regrettable bout of sentimentality. Well, it's his loss, silly man, that he's not here to share this evening of triumph. She beamed at the Colonel and successfully swallowed a hiccup.

Colonel Whittaker was enjoying himself too. Being in London was rather like playing truant from school. He felt *en fête* and unbuttoned. He drew the young people out to talk about themselves. He complimented Mrs Meadows at length on the excellence of the Clarendon and, in his booming voice, he praised every lady in his line of vision and, by twisting and tilting his chair alarmingly, many who were not. To all four of them it felt like a celebration, and the war, the dead and the wounded were all forgotten.

However, it was precisely the war that both generated and also permitted the rapid pace of the young people's courtship.

There is nothing as powerful as the fear of death or mutilation to accelerate the course of human passions. Colin, like all men on active service, had experienced more terror and physical discomfort than he would ever feel for the rest of his life. At the same time he had longings for exactly the opposite – for comfort and security – that he would never feel so strongly again. So it was no wonder that his meeting with Alice, like almost every promising little encounter between a serviceman on leave and a nubile girl, imploded into a feeling of deep commitment in a matter of days, whereas in normal times it would have progressed slowly through the appropriate rituals and been spun out for a year or more.

It was not only the fighting men who felt this pressure to love and be loved while there was still time. The women felt it too. For it was a rare family that escaped the loss, the wounding or the imprisonment of a relative or friend.

Everywhere, for Alice and everyone else to see, there were touches of black, symbols of nationwide loss. Black armbands, black dresses, black hats ringed with black ribbons, swathes of black draped across shop-fronts and windows, black bows tied on to door-knobs, black frames around young men's portraits and black borders to the letters in which the bereaved spread the word of their grief.

It all meant far more than present grief, however. It meant that thousands of women of Alice's generation had no hope of the only future that was open to many of them – marriage. They would never have a lover or a husband or children. The men they could have loved had been savagely culled – nearly a million were dead by the end of the war; over two million were wounded or taken prisoner. Of those who came back there were thousands who were physically or mentally maimed by their experiences and whose womenfolk were to spend the rest of their lives tending their damaged bodies and minds.

It was no wonder, then, that Alice and Colin seized on each other's youth and longing and believed it was love. Both were emotionally deprived, both looking to be held and wanted, both ripe for a radical change in their lives. To themselves and to those around them, it was obvious that they were 'made for each other'.

As Alice lay in her bed that night, she did not feel the November chill in her unheated room. She curled her toes round the stone hot-water bottle and the rest of her, under the thin quilted cover, was warmed by hope and by love for the dark-eyed soldier.

Colin's uncle went home to Bath the day after their evening at the Trocadero. Colin had intended to go to his home at the same time for a week there before returning to France. Instead, he stayed on at the Clarendon and set about wooing Alice to such good effect that, two days before he was due to leave England, he was able to press Mr and Mrs Meadows for permission to ask for Alice's hand in marriage. In the event, no pressing was needed, either of them or of Alice. So it was as Colin's fiancée that she went with him to Ballads for the day just before he was due to go back to the front line.

The train journey to Westknoll was the first time that Colin and Alice had been alone together. Neither of them could believe or contain their astonishing good fortune in finding each other. They constantly turned back from looking out of the window to stare at each other with wide smiles of triumph and discovery.

Alice had been outfitted, thanks to her stepfather's burst of generosity, with clothes she had only dreamed about before – a serge skirt which narrowed at the ankles and a matching jacket which flared out from the waist and was trimmed at the neck with a narrow band of fur. On her head was a fur toque, edged with satin. Even without Colin's ardent attention, which never wavered, she felt cherished by the unaccustomed softness and luxury of her clothes and by the train journey itself, so like being cocooned in a small, intimate room on the threshold of adventure.

There had been much speculation at the Clarendon about the wisdom of this journey entirely alone with Colin. Mrs Meadows had been quite flustered about it.

'I think,' she said to Alice, 'we had better at least suggest that someone comes with you as chaperon.'

'Oh Mother! You're not thinking of coming along, surely?' Alice's usual submissiveness was starting to wear thin.

'Well, dear, we have to think of how it will look to his family at home. A young girl going there who only just met him a week ago. It might be considered very forward. They'd wonder what sort of a mother you had who would allow it.'

'But there isn't any family there – only his old nanny and the servants.'

'That's just it, Alice. No other person to keep an eye on things. An adult from our side of the family, that's who should be there . . .'

'But we're adult. At least, Colin is. He's been twenty-one for ages. And we're engaged. Doesn't that make a difference? Anyway, if you think someone should come with us I think it ought to be Daisy.'

Mrs Meadows shuddered.

'Oh no,' she said briskly. 'Quite unsuitable. She may be engaged too but she has no idea, no idea at all, of how people like Colin behave. Whereas you, goodness knows how, seem to fit in quite well with their ways. I hope you keep it up.'

'Good then, it's all right if we go together, just us.' Alice congratulated herself on bringing Daisy into the conversation. She knew that her mother would rather she went un-chaperoned altogether than went accompanied by Daisy. She turned away as if the matter was settled and Mrs Meadows was left wondering how she had come to be bested by a girl who had always, up to now, behaved so timidly.

Alice has found a new confidence, she thought, and the tears stung her eyes at the loss she suddenly felt and the certain knowledge that, from now on, she would mean less and less to Alice. That's if, she wondered, she had ever meant anything to her at all. Who could tell with such a remote girl?

Colin did not find her at all remote. On their journey they had the carriage to themselves and she returned his touches and his kisses with puppy-like eagerness. Yet she managed, as they stepped from the train at Westknoll Station, to walk with such suitable dignity by his side along the platform that he felt his pride might burst out of him. And that was precisely the impression that struck the station-master as he came up to greet them. My word, he thought, Mr Colin has found himself a treasure and doesn't he know it!

'Good morning, sir,' he said, touching his cap. 'The car's waiting for you in front. And good morning, madam.'

'Not "madam" yet, station-master. This is my fiancée, Miss Meadows.'

Just in time, Alice drew back the hand she was going to extend to the station-master and inclined her head a little instead.

'Good morning, miss, it is then, and welcome.' The station-master tipped his cap again and thought how touchingly young she was. Only a child, but with all the calm in the world and that shining coppery hair enough to blind a man.

He walked with them across the station yard to the car parked on the far side. Barratt, the driver, who was also the gardener at Ballads, was standing erect beside the bonnet, his cap held over his heart, his high boots shining like glass and his moustache waxed to an astonishing stiffness.

The car was a Rolls-Royce Silver Ghost Tourer which Colin's father had bought only a year after the model was first produced. He lived to enjoy it for three years and bequeathed to Colin, alongside the car itself, his great fondness for it. This was equalled by Barratt's pride and tender, loving care for the vehicle. It still looked brand new. There was a spray of winter jasmine in the silver flask attached to the inside and facing the back seat.

Alice's hand flew to her mouth at the sight of the car. She restrained herself from running towards it and allowed Colin to take her gently by the elbow and hold her steady as she stepped on to the running-board and seated herself on the far side at the back. The seats were high and well upholstered and behind her head the top of the car was folded back like a fan. A half-hearted November sun had come out, but the air was raw and she snuggled into her fur collar and drew the tartan rug across her knees. She held herself stiffly, half through awe at the majesty of their ride, half through cold, and now and again she looked sideways at Colin without turning her head.

'It's all right,' he shouted, mistaking her stillness for fright. 'You can't fall out. Have you never been in a car before?'

She shook her head.

'Only a bus. And the taxi-cabs, with you. Nothing like this . . .'

He patted her hand under the rug. But his thoughts were on Ballads. He leant forward to talk with Barratt, and Alice heard only shouted snatches of their conversation – 'dogs in fine form, sir', 'no luck with the Bramleys this year, I'm afraid', 'yes, all the staff are well, I believe . . .'

Alice felt a surge of love for Colin. The car, the deference of the station-master, the respectful waves from a few people in the village as they passed through, the promise of a big house and servants, the ease with which Colin laid claim to her and brought about this visit to Ballads – all of this fitted exactly with the images of high living that she had held for so long.

Colin sat back in his seat and turned towards her.

'Wait until you see the glasshouse,' he said. 'Just wait.'

'The what?'

'The glasshouse. I bet it's the biggest you'll ever see. Except at Kew. My grandfather had it built, just before he died. It was the first in the county. Now everyone's got one. Only much smaller.' He waited for her response, his eyes shining.

'What's it for?' Alice had to shout as Barratt put the car into bottom gear for a steep part of the hill ahead of them.

Colin turned away from her, not knowing what to reply. It wasn't for anything, he thought. What a strange question! It was just there, part of his past, part of his heritage, part of him. He pretended he hadn't heard her question. He put his arm across her shoulders and squeezed her gently. Such a child, he thought happily. I will have to teach her everything, lead her everywhere. He found the thought very agreeable and patted her in a proprietorial sort of way.

'One more bend, then up the lane and you'll see Ballads.'

Alice leant forward and soon, across Barratt's right

shoulder, the slate roof and pale stone walls of her future home emerged into sight from the surrounding trees.

Her first impression was that the house was staring at her. Its huge windows, those on the lower floor almost reaching to the ground, had none of the lace curtains she was used to seeing in London, and looked like unblinking, critical eyes. Even the smaller dormer windows in the roof stared out in the same way, with no welcome in them. The heavy front door, with massive iron fittings on it and beside it, was firmly closed, not a staring eye but a sleeping, indifferent one.

There was not a sign of life to be seen. Where, Alice wondered, were the bright lights streaming from windows and doors? Where were the servants rushing out to greet their master and new mistress? Where were the colour and magic all the magazines and books about grand houses had promised her? The November chill was on everything, including her dreams.

She sighed. Colin mistook it for wonder and took her hand. 'Isn't it wonderful? Don't you love it?'

'Oh yes,' Alice murmured, 'I'm sure I shall . . .' She was finding it hard not to shiver. There was a brooding silence all around them that made London and the Clarendon and the train journey, even the village they had just passed through and all the people in it, seem like another world.

'Isn't it quiet?' she said as she stepped out of the car.

Colin turned towards her, his face bright and grateful.

'Yes, exactly! Isn't it marvellous? I knew you'd feel it. I don't think there's this kind of peace anywhere else on earth. Honestly I don't, Alice. The world won't bother us here, I promise you.'

This was so far from the kind of promise she wanted Colin to keep that her spirits sank even lower. She followed Colin up to the front door. To her surprise he gave a strong tug at the heavy bell-pull.

Alice touched his arm timidly.

'Why isn't it open? And don't you have a key?'

He laughed with what she thought was a trace of bitterness.

'Oh no. It's always been kept shut and bolted on the inside. My parents always thought . . . I think they wanted it that way. We all got used to it. And then my nanny, she's still here, you know that . . . She keeps up all the old ways. I'm sure she wouldn't want it kept open. I see no reason to change it. But . . .'

He peered impatiently into the window to the right of the door and when he turned back he was frowning.

'But she must be here. Or Cook. Or someone. This is too bad of them. They know we're coming. Uncle arranged it all. My dear, I'm so sorry. What a welcome for you . . .'

His words sounded kind but he spoke over his shoulder, without looking at her, and she noticed that his hands were clenched tightly, as if he wanted to strike out.

The chill was really in her bones now and she felt close to tears. When I'm living here, she told herself, I'll have the front door unlocked and unbolted all the time and in the summer it will be wide open. There'll be no tugging at bell-pulls or people kept shuffling out here in the cold.

Just then, the door opened and it was Barratt who stood there smiling.

'Here we are,' he said. 'I just nipped through the back from the garage, Mr Colin. I reckon Mrs Gray is not too well. And Cook sends her apologies but she and Ethel are busy with the meal.'

'Quite all right,' said Colin merrily. 'Good of you to let us in, Barratt. Many thanks.' There was no sign now of his anger or impatience. Alice somehow knew that he wasn't going to complain or tell anyone off about the lack of welcome and the wait in the cold. I'd like to see the servants at the Clarendon get away with half as much laziness and cheek, she thought. My parents would never allow it. It was her first encounter with that particular brand of middle-class courtesy and masculine honour which puts the avoidance of ill-feeling or the likelihood of 'a scene' before considerations of practicality or plain justice.

Colin ushered her in, explaining, 'Mrs Gray is what we call Nanny. Here, let me take your coat. She's not a Mrs really. Never married, of course. Too busy looking after other people's families, mostly ours. But she's always been called Mrs . . . makes her feel better I suppose. Still, you can meet her next time you come here. Look,' he waved his hand towards e dark passage leading from the back of the hall, 'there's a place for . . . er . . . washing your hands, just there on the left. Then we'll have luncheon straight away. I hope it's in the drawing-room and that there's a fire. I'll wait for you here.'

When she joined him again in the hall, he was standing with his eyes shut, breathing deeply. He kept them shut as, hearing her approach, he put his arm out to touch her.

'Listen, listen,' he said. 'Can you hear it talking to you?'

'Hear what talking to me?' She was feeling numb from the iciness of the cloakroom and from the alarming clamour of the pipes after she'd flushed the W C, even more ear-splitting and threatening than the plumbing at home.

'The house, the house,' Colin said cheerfully. 'It talks, you know . . .'

He opened his eyes and saw her bewildered expression.

'Oh well, it doesn't matter. Another time, perhaps. You'll hear it though . . . I promise.'

Another promise, Alice thought dismally, and followed him into the room on the right of the hall. Both of them were thankful to see a generous wood fire in the large marble fireplace. Inside the marble surround, and bordering the iron grate, was a frame of glazed tiles depicting cream lilies on a brown background. They looked funereal, even beside the warm blaze of the logs, and Alice was conscious again of the clammy hand that seemed to have touched this house.

Colin stood with his back to the fire, rubbing his hands behind him.

'Now, you stay here and get warm for a bit. I've just got to run up to my room and see to a few things. Soon we'll eat and then you can see all the rest of the house. And the glasshouse.'

As he walked towards the door, he waved towards the piano.

'You can play something, if you like. Do you play?

'No, I don't. Do you?'

'Yes, actually. Well, never mind. You could read a journal or something. There are lots over there, on that table by the window.'

'But, but, Colin . . .'

Alice was aghast at the prospect of being left alone. She clutched at the only way she could think of to hold him there.

'Don't I get a goodbye kiss?' she said and offered her cheek towards him, remembering his ardour on the train journey.

He laughed awkwardly and moved nearer towards the door.

'No, not here, old thing. Someone might come in . . . I'll be back in a tick . . .' and he was gone.

It was funny, Alice thought, how different he was from the Colin she'd known during the past week at the Clarendon. There, he didn't seem much older than her and he was happy and laughed a lot. Here, he seemed to be weighed down with – well, what? Worries and duties? Or were there sad memories here?

She picked up one of the journals from the tables, saw that it was five months old and had few pictures in it but a great deal of very small print, and put it down again. She looked out of the window and saw a fountain in the distance, half-shrouded by the slowly gathering fog. To the left, just visible beyond the jutting edge of a part of the house, she could see a towering curved wall, formed entirely of panes of glass. The glasshouse. That must be it. She shivered again and moved to the fireside and sat down, clutching her knees and rocking pensively to and fro, waiting for Colin.

Up in his study, Colin went straight to the bureau between the two windows looking on to the drive. He noted with delight that his papers and books were all as he had left them the last time he was home and he patted them fondly. Then he took from his pocket a small bunch of keys and unlocked the bottom drawer on the right of the bureau. He took out a thick book, bound in marbled paper like a ledger, and put it on the top of the bureau. He took out a pencil and opened the book at the first unused page, about halfway through. He put the date at the top. He sucked the end of the pencil and stared out of the window at the woods stretching into the distance from the east side of the house.

Among the tall beech trees, gaunt and leafless now, he saw, in a blur which was part fog and part the mist of memories, the outline of his father. His back was towards Colin. He was stoking up a bonfire with that concentrated angle of his body which meant that he wanted no one near.

In his mind's eyes, however, Colin was near, walking hesitantly up to his father, drawn by the glow of the flames, the crackle of the burning twigs and the warm, woody smell of the smoke. He saw clearly that he was about seven and was wearing his garden clothes – a tweedy suit of knicker-bockers and jacket, with stout leather boots and a flat cap. He held a stick in one hand and with the other he held closely against his side a toy dog whose furry skin had been worn smooth from constant clutching. Colin kept it with him as much as possible these last few months. He did not want anyone to get the idea that he was not taking it with him when he went off to boarding school after his next birthday. The dog went with him, now and for ever.

'Can I throw this stick in?' he heard himself say.

'You mean may I throw this stick in. You are able to throw it in, aren't you? So don't ask me if you can or can't. But I say you may not. Which means that I do not allow you to. Do you see the difference, Colin?'

He did not turn round or seem to expect an answer. So Colin waited a while, watching his father's face get redder as he bent to the ground for more wood and then hurled in into the flames.

'May I throw this stick in?' he asked at length.

'No. Just go and fetch some more wood. Over there, by the shed. And then put it right here.' He swung his foot up and brought the heel of his boot down again on to the ground with a mighty thump, making a dent in the turf a few feet from the bonfire.

'And don't come any nearer than that. You could be burned alive, you know that?'

Colin shrank back, as much from his father's coldness as from the horrors he presented as the result of disobedience. But it was always like that. 'Don't you dare climb that ladder – you'll split your head open.' 'If you touch that dog, he'll have your hand off.' 'Keep away from the village children. Who knows what diseases they're cooking up in those unwashed bodies?'

So there was danger in the everyday world. It meant injury, death and destruction if you tampered with it. People too. Get close and they'll have you, in one way or another. And yet, the adult Colin reflected, his father had not said anything about the real dangers. Nothing, for instance, about war. Nothing about shells and snipers' bullets that tore people apart. Nothing about being wet, cold, hungry, tired and afraid in a narrow trench, a coffin for the barely living. Nothing about the stench of blood, excreta and death. Nothing about the pictures in your head that would not go away. He'd said nothing about any of that.

Colin thumped his fist on the blank page of his diary. He leant towards the window and glared angrily at the spot where he had conjured up the figure of his father shutting him out from the shimmering, sparking excitement of the bonfire.

'You were wrong! You were wrong!' he shouted. 'I'll never forgive you. Never.'

Then, more quietly, he muttered, 'When I have children, I will love them and set them free . . .'

He sat down abruptly, puzzled by his own resentment. There had been times when his father was tender. When he was ill or plainly unhappy, there was nothing he would not do then in the way of questioning and talking – 'Tell me, old chap, what the trouble is. I can't help if you won't say what it is . . .' And when he had haltingly told of his pain, there would be long, rambling, philosophical explanations about why he ought not to feel hurt or unhappy. Colin would nod and smile and be grateful and eventually his father would put on his louder voice and say, 'That's all right then,' and leave him – still with the pain or unhappiness and with the additional anxiety of wondering if he had sufficiently pleased his father by his response. But it all added up to the conviction that it was better not to let on if you were troubled. People never listened or understood.

He picked up the pencil and under the date on the fresh page he wrote, 'I'm engaged to Alice. Next time I'm at home I'll write about her.'

He shut the diary with a bang and put it back in the drawer.

'I'll show her the glasshouse soon,' he said soothingly to himself and hurried down to the drawing-room.

When he went into the room, he saw that a meal of cold cuts and boiled potatoes had been laid on a small table by the fire, with two chairs drawn up to it.

'Let's eat then,' he said, 'then you shall see the glasshouse. The rest of the house can wait until next time. We haven't a lot of time.'

He smiled at Alice and thought how pale and pinched she looked.

'Were you lonely here, all by yourself?'

'Yes, a bit. I should have come with you. Why didn't I?'

He looked at her with a puzzled frown.

'I have to be by myself sometimes, you know. All men do. You'll get used to it. But I will always look after you. You can count on me for that.'

He was reminded of his feelings of responsibility and affection when his favourite dog came into his possession as a puppy. He drew himself up with pride and stabbed his fork into a potato.

'Yes, I'll get used to it, of course,' Alice said calmly. She thought to herself, it would be better if I don't have to, all the same. This house is no place to be alone in. By hook or by crook, I'll have people around me.

Alice ate in silence while Colin talked about Ballads and his plans for its future and his own.

'I've finished with the army,' he said. 'I was never cut out for it anyway. Uncle Frederick says he can get me into the

City. Would you like that, to be married to a City gent? I'd only have to go up to London now and then, maybe once a week or something. There's lots of things for you to do here while I'm away.'

'What sort of things?' asked Alice in her practical tone of voice.

But she saw at once that Colin was not used to practical questions and had no ready answers. He waved his fork in the air and laughed.

'Funny girl with your feet on the ground . . . I don't know what girls like to do. Perhaps you'll sew or knit. Or paint, like my mother did. There's all her stuff here. I think it's still in the glasshouse. Or there are marvellous walks in the woods, and across behind them, in the fields. There are two dogs, you know, lovely beasts. They'll adore you. You could take them for walks. And there'll be the house to run – at least, Nanny runs it but you'll be able to choose what we're going to eat. And you can shop in the village. Everyone there will want to see you. We could open up the tennis court. Would you like that?'

'I've never played tennis. But, of course, I'd like to learn if . . . if . . . you'd teach me . . .'

'Oh my sweet girl, I shan't have time for that. There's a lot for Barratt and me to do here. But someone will. We'll find out. Some of the other wives around here are bound to be hot stuff at it. One of them will take you in hand. Then you and I could play in the summer evenings. My mother used to do that.'

He looked out of the window and sighed.

Alice cleared her throat nervously, feeling it was necessary to make some sort of stand straight away.

'I don't think, Colin, that I'll be able to be like your mother, not at all, not in any way . . .'

'Of course not. Whatever made you think I would want that? Besides, she was a big lady. And you, my sweet, are more like a racehorse, a real thoroughbred. And just right for me.'

He grinned at her and blew her a kiss across the table.

Alice felt the magic returning. Perhaps it was foolish of her to think that Colin wanted to mould her to Ballads and to his life here. He loved her enough, surely, to let her be herself and to make changes in his life and home to suit her?

'Well,' she said. 'I've eaten all I can, thank you. What about the glasshouse?'

Colin led her out of the room, through the hall and along a corridor which passed the doors to the cloakroom, the kitchen, the scullery and the 'dairy'.

'Shut your eyes,' he said, 'and don't open them until I say.'

Alice did not merely close her eyes. She screwed them tight shut, like a child playing hide-and-seek. In the darkness she was aware of scuffling and whispering to her left. There was the smell of food, far richer and more interesting than anything she had just been offered for luncheon, wafting from an open door.

'Good afternoon, Mr Colin,' came in a soft chorus of two, or was it three voices, one gruff and fat, the other, or others, on a high, giggly note.

'Afternoon,' Colin said, then, to Alice, 'keep them shut. We're nearly there.'

He opened a door and guided her down a shallow step which was evidently at the threshold of the glasshouse, for she was immediately assailed by a chilling blast of air smelling of earth and foliage. She shuffled further along, one hand held in front of her to ward off any obstacles, and then Colin put his hands on her shoulders and said, 'Open sesame'.

Her first sight was of Colin, who had scampered a short distance away and was standing in the manner of a circus ring-master, his arms spread wide and a beaming, welcoming smile on his face. Then her eyes moved above and beyond him, taking in the vast expanse of glass, the soaring iron arches, and the bare, snaking branches of the vine that canopied the whole room. Lower down, on shelves and on the floor, were several potted plants in their winter dress of skimpy leaves or naked stems.

It felt to Alice like out of doors and yet there were Indian rugs on the tiled floor, and scattered pieces of well-worn furniture, two heavy wrought-iron tables of intricate design and painted white, a collection of wrought-iron chairs, and over all an oppressive feel of abandonment and long-ago life that had suddenly been brought to an end.

She looked sideways at Colin as she turned this way and that, wanting him to know that she was really looking and taking it all in. She could not deny her impression that he loved this place and thought it was beautiful. But she was quite unable to guess why he loved it and admired it so. And it was not something she felt she could ask him.

She walked gravely towards him.

'I've never seen anything like it. It's so huge, Colin, and . . . well . . . I don't know . . . it just takes my breath away . . .'

He raised both arms above his head as if saluting a champion.

'I knew it! I knew it! I knew you'd fall in love with it.' He whirled round in a circle and came to rest beside Alice.

'Ah, but I love you better,' Alice said teasingly and turned away from him to sit down on one of the iron chairs. She winced at its hardness and decided to test his willingness to change anything about his adored glasshouse.

'These chairs are rather hard, aren't they? Shall we have something more comfy one day?'

'Darling, you shall have anything you like, anything that will make you happy. It's wonderful in the summer. The sun gets here nearly all day. Look, it rises over there by the kitchen garden and comes right the way round over the top of us and then, in the evening, it comes in this side, across the road to the village, and if you wanted shade, there's masses of it under the vine. We'll make it a paradise for us, you'll see.'

'Oh Colin! A paradise!' Alice echoed and hoped that her sigh of despair sounded like one of appreciation.

Evidently it did, for Colin strode up to her and raised her from her chair into his arms and kissed her hard and firmly on the mouth. It was a different kiss from the shy, gentle ones in the railway carriage and she did not enjoy it as much. Somehow it felt as if it was not for her but for what Colin thought was her whole-hearted delight in Ballads and the glasshouse. Her eyes were wide open as he embraced her, his own tight-shut, and as she gazed upwards at the endless vista of glass and vine, she wondered how long it would take to breathe some life and comfort into her beloved's idea of paradise.

6

MARRIAGE

As soon as Colin had taken Alice home to the Clarendon, he left for Dover and the Channel crossing to the Western Front. It was agreed that the wedding would take place when Colin next came back to England.

Life for Alice went on much as before. She helped out in the kitchen and dining-room at the Clarendon and served drinks at the bar. Twice a week she went with Daisy to a dingy hall in Shepherd's Bush to roll bandages for the wounded and wrap up parcels of cigarettes, books and chocolate to be sent to the base camps in France and Belgium. During the long evenings she made clothes for herself and wrote short, stilted letters to Colin in a childish hand.

'Dear Colin,' she wrote for his birthday in March, 'I write to you with my fondest wishes for your anniversary. I trust you are in good health, as I am at present. I hope you will be home soon. With loving greetings, your fiancée, Alice.'

There were two important changes in Alice's life, however. One was that she was driven to take more interest in the course of the war, not because she expected to have any comprehension of what was going on, but because everyone at the Clarendon, and many of its guests, now felt they had a personal stake in the victories and defeats of the armed forces and were constantly questioning Alice and discussing among themselves where Colin might be fighting, how he was faring and when he was likely to be coming home.

Sometimes she wondered if, like so many young women, she might be bereaved before she was even married. But that fear did not make it any easier to understand the constant advances and reversals of each side on a small patch of the border between two far-away countries. Daisy had tried to help by bicycling all the way to Fleet Street one crisp March morning and buying a sixpenny copy of the *Daily Mail*'s *Bird's-Eye Map of the British Front*. The girls pored over it together for hours with Daisy pointing out the towns and the rivers which featured in the news, irritating Alice with her impeccable French accent and quite failing to replace Alice's romantic dreams of her soldier-fiancé with any informed wider view of the fortunes of war.

Those who did follow the news closely and with understanding were finding it difficult to obey the government's exhortations to keep their hopes high. These hopes plummeted as news came of the surprise German offensive from St Quentin in March 1918 and how it had rapidly penetrated the British lines to a depth of forty miles; sank even lower when it was known that a second heavy onslaught in the area of the River Lys in April widely breached the British front; rose when the Americans made their presence felt at Château-Thierry in June; rose still more as the Allies achieved the upper hand both at sea and in the air during the spring and summer of 1918. But they said nothing to Alice except the anodyne words used on all sides to keep unpatriotic pessimism at bay – 'It won't be long now.'

The second change in Alice's life was that she now had standing. She was betrothed, and moreover the betrothal was to an army officer serving at the front. This accorded her a great deal of respect from family, friends, hotel staff and guests. Even Daisy, who was now married to her Julian, did not rank as high, since her husband was serving in comparative safety as an intelligence officer somewhere in London. Daisy could protest all she liked that he too was in danger from the Zeppelin and aeroplane bombing raids on London, but Alice did not consider that equal to being shot at on the field of battle, and said so.

In accordance with her new status, Alice was no longer the subject of teasings and sly propositions from the gentlemen guests. Even the japes and jollities of her stepfather were things of the past. She was still only eighteen but her hair was up, her skirts were long and there was a diamond on her finger. By the rites of post-Victorian England she had become spoken for, respectable, settled and virtually middle-aged. Her life as a young girl was over, if indeed it had ever begun.

She could not help envying Daisy, all the same. She had always been on the wild, tomboyish side and showed no sign of adopting the dignity of a married lady. When she and Alice were out in the parks and streets together she still jumped over the hoops lining the flower-beds, made rude remarks about passers-by in a stage whisper and threw her hat up at the lamp-posts.

'Come on, Al,' she'd say, waving her arms about like a windmill, 'let yourself go! Don't be so niminy-piminy!' She would tug at Alice's arm or snatch her friend's hat off her head and run into the distance, limping with laughter.

When Daisy came panting back, Alice would try to explain.

'You see, Daisy, Mother says Colin wouldn't approve. She thinks you're a hoyden and that you don't care what Julian might think if he could see you. Anyway, I don't see there's much fun in prancing about like a gypsy. You look quite stupid sometimes. I don't want to look like that.'

Daisy never took umbrage. She would simply burst into laughter again and take Alice's arm and walk by her side for a while.

Alice sometimes wondered if Colin really would disapprove if she acted her age. She thought hard about this because she had a slight, disturbing suspicion that he might not be any good at having fun either. He laughed quite a lot but it was not a merry sort of laugh like Daisy's. It seemed that it was more often a laugh of relief or a way of hiding his serious feelings. Still, she was certain that this, like everything else, would all be different when the war was over. It was what everyone was saying about anything that didn't seem quite right. 'When the war's over' was the magic charm that was going to end everybody's doubts and worries, big and small.

Peace came at last and the Armistice was signed on 11 November in 1918. Alice and Daisy joined the celebrating crowds in the streets, linked arms with strangers, waved Union Jacks and promised each other a life of unending happiness from then on. Even among the seething, singing mass of people Alice maintained her dignity and her air of someone apart, but Daisy lifted her skirts and climbed on the bonnet of a bus with a group of sailors and allowed anyone to kiss her who had a mind to.

Colin went with his regiment to occupy Germany and finally sailed for home in early 1919. When he called at the Clarendon on his way to Ballads, Alice was astonished to see how much thinner and older he looked. There was a distant look in his eyes which she had not remembered noticing before. At any rate, he did not look like this in her dreams of his home-coming. There seemed, also, to be less of his dark, smooth hair and he had shaved off his moustache. And surely he had talked more quickly and eagerly before and had more of a spring in his step?

Mrs Meadows noted these things too and suggested to Alice that the wedding should wait until Colin had had a rest and a holiday. Both the young people pooh-poohed this idea. Colin wanted Alice to be with him, as his wife, when he settled back at Ballads. And Alice could wait no longer to leave the Clarendon behind and start her new life.

So, on a blustery day in March 1919, their marriage began.

There was no bright welcome for Alice at Ballads this time either. She met the staff only when she had unpacked her few belongings in the main bedroom she was to share with Colin and, noting the absence of flowers or any sign that there was a newcomer to the household, had come downstairs again and stood in the hall, wrapped in its silence and gloom.

After a while Colin appeared from the drawing-room, hugged her absent-mindedly and led her to the kitchen, where she was introduced to Cook, the house-maids, Peggy and Ethel, and Nanny. The two girls seemed as nonplussed and shy as Alice herself felt, but Nanny, an obviously no-nonsense kind of person, shook her hand briskly and turned at once to a discussion with Colin about household matters, leaving Alice to stare around her at the vast kitchen.

She was amazed at its size and at its lavish equipment. There were two black cooking stoves, numerous pots and pans ranged upside down on shelves, one large table in the middle and two smaller ones at the sides, cupboards on the walls and cupboards at floor level, and, on racks or on hooks in the ceiling, monstrous ladles, fish-kettles, stew cauldrons and fierce-looking butchers' knives in all sizes. So much to cater for five or six people! The kitchen at the Clarendon was decidedly smaller and barer and that had to serve twenty or thirty people with three good meals a day. Remembering the cold cuts and soggy potatoes of the luncheon on her first visit to Ballads, she wondered if all these oversized trappings were ever put to use.

When she and Colin sat down that night to a dinner of tepid mutton stew and carrots, she was quite certain that not only were all the utensils largely unused but so also was any imagination or thought in the preparation of the meals. I can do something about that, she thought cheerfully. But not yet. Not until I feel more at home here.

Feeling at home at Ballads proved to be more difficult than she imagined. The routine of the house seemed as solid as cement. Colin was so happy to be home that he simply sank into the life he had always known and plainly expected Alice to follow behind him – but at a considerable distance.

There were the everyday rituals of meals, walks in the grounds with the dogs, and evenings by the fire in the drawing-room. These, and little else, were shared with Colin. In between, Colin would go off by himself to see neighbours, or walk to the village, or simply disappear for an hour or so, leaving Alice to her own devices. When he was not out he shut himself in his study for hours on end, and what he did there Alice could only guess at. He had straight away made it clear that this room was for his use alone and he had simply hustled her past its imposing locked door when he showed her the rest of the house.

Her first morning at Ballads set the pattern for all the days to follow. When she woke up the place beside her in the large, creaking double bed was cold and empty. Colin was already halfway back from the village with the *Morning Post* under his arm, his every step bouncing with the excitement and pleasure of being home.

Alice found a cold cup of tea beside the bed and drew the sheets tightly around her, wondering which member of the household had been in the room earlier and caught sight of the rumpled bed and possibly even her very best night-dress in a heap on the floor. She blushed and smiled to herself. What her mother called 'intimate relations' was better than she had led her to believe but not as interesting as Daisy had made out. She hoped, however, that there would not be too much of it. If Colin's fierce embraces and silent, clenched-teeth kind of activity last night were a sign of his love for her, she could think of far more agreeable ways for him to give proof of it. Like some warmth in the bedroom, she thought with a shiver. And a bathroom that was not yards away down a draughty passage. And his company first thing in the morning.

She made her way to the breakfast-room. This was a small room, by Ballads standards, and was furnished simply, with a small round table at the window, two chairs drawn up to it, a sideboard, and one easy chair against the wall by the window.

As soon as Colin had breezed in, Ethel appeared with boiled eggs, toast and tea. Alice nibbled at some toast, watching Colin closely for any sign that he might want to talk. He grinned at her occasionally as he ate but he stayed silent too until, his breakfast finished, he pushed back his chair and flung himself into the armchair with a hearty cry of 'Right then, let's have a look at the paper.' And there he stayed for half an hour or so, rustling the pages occasionally or saying 'Hrrumph' with interest or irritation. Alice felt he would have been just as happy if she had not been there at all.

When he had finished with the paper he rose and stretched, said, 'Back in a while,' and strode from the room. She could hear his footsteps going up the stairs to his study and then the door closing softly, almost secretly, as if he were on a guilty mission. Perhaps, she thought, he can't get out of the habit yet of living alone. She began to dream about how life could be when and if he changed back into the Colin of those magic days in London when he was courting her.

She was startled out of her dreams by the door opening. Nanny walked in and came over to the table, her eyes flicking over the dishes and coming to rest on Alice with a look of surprise.

'Not banting, are we?' she said, noting the untouched egg and the half-full toast-rack. 'Aren't you thin enough as it is?'

Alice, who was used to unqualified admiration of her slenderness, immediately decided that some time, by some means, Nanny would have to go. How on earth, she wondered, could such a forbidding person have had anything to do with babies? She didn't look as if she had a lap at all and Alice shuddered inwardly at the thought of being held by those beefy arms and harsh hands. Nanny also had the faint beginnings of a moustache on her upper lip and smelled of wintergreen.

Alice smiled sweetly and shook her head.

'Oh no, of course not. I just didn't feel hungry today. I expect it's because everything is so . . . so strange.'

'We'll soon get over that,' Nanny said cheerfully, as if urging a child over a slight case of measles.

She flicked aside her starched white apron and drew a notebook and pencil from the side pocket of her dark blue skirt. She licked her thumb, a habit that Alice's mother had taught her to loathe, and turned a page.

'If you'd kindly approve the menu?'

Without waiting for a reply, she read out rapidly, 'Shepherd's pie with cabbage for luncheon, with stewed pears and custard for dessert. And for dinner, lamb cutlets – one of Mr Colin's favourites – mashed potatoes and carrots, trifle to follow. And Cook's made a seed cake for tea.'

She turned for the door and was halfway through it before Alice managed a quiet 'Thank you, Nanny. That will do very well.' She pulled a face at her departing back and, after making sure that Nanny had arrived back in the kitchen, made her way to Colin's 'paradise', the glasshouse.

She had meant to make it her custom to come here every morning, perhaps to read, to write letters to her mother and Daisy, or she might even do her sewing here, or take up knitting or painting as Colin had suggested. But, once through the door and down the small step from the passage, she felt again the intimidating, hard stare of that wide expanse of glass that she had experienced when she came with Colin more than a year ago.

It was an overcast day and the light outside was dim enough to turn the endless panes of glass into mirrors. As she strolled to the far end she saw her image reflected at every step like a walker in a dream. Here and there the glass was misted with condensation caused by the inadequate paraffin heaters at either side of the room, and her image then became even more dream-like. She turned this way and that to escape the tall, pale girl who mimicked all her movements, and finally sat down on one of the hard iron chairs with a twinge of recognition. There was a thin cushion on its seat which in no way prevented her bones from jarring as she shifted position in an effort to find comfort.

One day, she thought, I'll change all the furniture here, and I'll do away with all these ugly great plants and get some light, feathery ones to hang from the roof and sway in the air. She supposed there was not much she could do about the few gas-lights that stuck out from the walls on wrought-iron brackets and which, she could tell from their pitiful size, would only create dim circles of light a few feet around them. But Daisy's family already had electricity in their home and her stepfather had plans to install it at the Clarendon. So perhaps one day this place too could be flooded with light and warmth. And could have lots of people in it. That's what she needed most of all, Alice decided. People. Lots of people. Especially people noticing her and loving her and not treating her like a child.

Meanwhile the glasshouse was left empty every morning. As the weeks went by, Alice gradually lost her enthusiasm for making that or any other room in the house a scene of bustling activity. While Colin was shut in his study, or out in the neighbourhood, or gone to London to his new work, she would sit in the drawing-room and leaf through the *Illustrated London News* or the *Lady*, or sometimes, if she could keep it secret from the rest of the household, one of the fourpenny Fleetway Novels that kept alive her former dreams of romantic love.

One day she discovered that Ethel and Peggy obtained copies of *World's Pictorial News* from time to time, with all its engrossing society gossip and detailed reports of court cases of divorce, breach of promise and murder. She would borrow the newspaper whenever she could and curl up in an armchair for the morning, lost in longing for the kind of dramatic, talked-about lives led by actresses, duchesses, society ladies, friends of the Prince of Wales, the infamous and the famous, indeed by almost everyone, it seemed, who was not Alice Whittaker, aged nineteen and living at Ballads with only a too often absent husband for company.

Alice was puzzled by the change in Colin from the dashing soldier who had wooed her to the remote, unpredictable husband who neglected her so much. It did not occur to her that the man who was now something of a mystery to her was the real Colin and the ardent suitor only one facet of his nature, one which had served his need and hers at the time of their meeting. She had not thought of Colin as having a past that had helped to shape his present. For her, life had begun when she met him, and she had completely put behind her all that had gone before. She imagined that Colin had done the same. But then, like many people, Alice thought of life as a succession of several separate lives rather than a continuous moving stream. So she had no idea of all the feelings, fears and hopes that are gathered on the way and sent to the depths, out of sight but flowing so strongly that they score the course of the stream for the rest of its journey.

Alice's mother had in fact spoken often before the wedding of 'the terrible suffering of all these young men at the front'. Among the male guests at the Clarendon, whenever there were no servicemen on leave within earshot, there was often talk of 'the nightmare of the trenches' and incredulity at the wholesale massacre required to gain a mile of advance, a mile, moreover, that was often lost in retreat the very next day with a similarly horrifying number of dead and wounded.

Alice wanted to close her mind to it, thinking it preferable for her not to know and for Colin not to remember. As they had prepared for the wedding, however, her mother had tended to speak more of Colin's imagined state of mind than of the intimate side of married life, which Alice would much rather have heard about, and repeatedly pressed Alice to 'give the poor boy a chance to get it off his chest'. So Alice steeled herself to give him that opportunity, whilst fervently hoping that he would not need to take it.

As she lay in his arms in bed one night, a week after the wedding, she drew her head back a little from his and looked towards the ceiling, trying so hard to shape her words into a sympathetic tone that they came out in little more than a whisper.

'Was it awful, Col? While you were . . . while you were out there?'

He stiffened and held his breath. For a split second, he was so still that the silence in the room was as deep as the silence of the sleeping world outside. Alice ruffled the bedclothes gently to break the spell. Then he released his breath in a long, sad sigh, appeared to come to a decision and turned to her with forced jocularity.

'Grim enough, my sweet. But a closed book – that's the best thing. Here, what's that? There's a cold tiny foot in this bed. Whose can it be, I wonder? Shall I warm it?'

So she never referred to the war again. When his Uncle Frederick and Aunt Clarice came to stay at Ballads for the first time since the wedding, she greeted them in the hall with a whispered 'We don't talk about the war – not yet.' And what she meant was 'not ever'.

All the loneliness and secrets disappeared like magic in the evenings. These were Alice's favourite times. They would eat their meal at the big table in the dining-room, served by Ethel, he senior of the two maids, and Colin would talk easily about what he had done that day and how the dogs were and what progress he and Barratt were making in getting the gardens in good order. She accepted the fact that if he referred to the world outside Ballads at all, it was not to the scandals and gossip of London society, about which she longed to hear, but to how the Secretary of State for War, Winston Churchill, had bowed to pressure and speeded up the demobilization of the troops, or to Lloyd George, the 'Welsh Wizard', and whether he was going to lead the country back to prosperity. 'But how are they going to find jobs for all those servicemen?' he mused, half to himself and half to Alice across the dinner-table.

'I expect he'll find a way,' Alice said comfortingly, not knowing who Lloyd George was, or Winston Churchill, or how many ex-servicemen were looking for jobs. But she did know, thanks to some innate skill, how to find the right soothing words which made a man feel he had said something worthwhile and thoughtful. It was a skill she was to use to her advantage throughout her life.

After the meal they would go into the drawing-room, and here Colin was all hers and it was the best time of all. She would loll on the sofa while he searched through the music-sheets for love-songs and waltzes. Now and then he would exclaim, 'Ah! That's one of mother's,' or, 'No, I never liked that one.' The firelight would dance up the walls and flicker on the ceiling and Alice would feel enclosed by warmth and love.

When he had decided on a song or two, Colin would go to the piano, brushing her forehead with his lips as he passed, or trailing his hand along the length of her outstretched arm, and then settle himself on the piano stool. She would watch his thin brown fingers turn the knobs on either side until he was at a comfortable height and then her eyes would follow his hands on to the keys as he spread them to play.

She would then turn her attention to the vulnerable nape of his neck as the music drifted over her. 'Pale hands I loved, beside the Shalimar,' he sang in his clear, light voice, or 'The temple bells are ringing,' never faltering over the notes or the words and occasionally even turning to smile at Alice while he still continued to play and sing. All the dreams she had shared with Daisy of music and firelight and a loving man would crowd into her head and drive away the everyday disappointments and loneliness.

More often than not they would end up clinging to each other on the rug in front of the dying fire and sometimes, not so often, making love hastily as they lay there, listening out for any step in the hall or on the stairs in case a maid or, worse, Nanny, should come in and surprise them.

Next morning, however, it was just the same as the morning before and the morning before that – the cold space beside her in bed as she awoke, the silent breakfast, the rustling of the newspaper, Colin's departure to the study and Nanny's perfunctory consultation over the menu. Then there was the emptiness of the day ahead of her and the difficulty of filling it – and nothing else on the horizon until the evening.

Soon, however, Alice had her purpose and the perfect antidote to boredom. A few months after the wedding she found that she was pregnant.

Colin was overjoyed. For him, too, parenthood offered a new purpose. As an only child he had longed, not for brothers and sisters, for they might have made inroads into his privacy, but for children of his own who would be dependent on him for love and control and safe-keeping. He was certain that he had a strong parental, caring streak in him. He had always been good with pets, especially when they were very young and helpless. From the moment that Alice told him the news, the future of his whole life and of Ballads took on a new and brighter aspect.

He at once became tenderly solicitous towards Alice. In his limited experience, expectant mothers were semi-invalids, gathering their strength for the biggest ordeal known to woman. As a result, Alice found herself cherished and cosseted beyond all her hopes and passed the months of her pregnancy in a glorious state of passive contentment.

Jack was born on a mild, welcoming day in April 1920.

Alice might, perhaps, have taken it as a warning that Colin's tender care was, from the moment of the child's birth, switched from mother to son. He spent hours cooing over him and cuddling him and took to having the cradle by his desk in his study on occasions. Sometimes he would even bre k his routine to take Jack into the glasshouse for that short part of the morning when he was awake. Wrapped in several shawls, the baby would be cradled in Colin's arms, held high against his neck, while his father strode between the pillars and plants, murmuring softly about the vine and the grapes and the sunbeams.

But Alice was not warned. She was as starry-eyed about the role of wife-mother as she had been about the prospect of being Colin's wife. She took it for granted that, once the novelty of fatherhood had worn off, Colin would turn to her with far more devoted attention than he had ever shown before her pregnancy. That attention might even stretch to giving her some of the high life and good company she craved.

As yet she had no inkling that she was never again to know at Ballads the happiness and contentment she had felt during her pregnancy. Nor was she ever to get closer to Colin than she had been during those evenings when the *Indian Love Lyrics* had drifted through the fire-lit room. So she confidently embarked on the changes that she felt would improve their new life together as a family. The first of these changes was to get rid of Nanny.

It was a bright June morning when Alice took the bold step of interrupting Colin's study of the *Morning Post* after breakfast.

'I think,' she said in a matter-of-fact tone of voice, 'that it's time for Nanny to retire.'

He looked at her in disbelief and slowly put the newspaper down on the table.

'Are you serious? Just when there's Jack to look after?'

'That's why, Col. I mean, have you seen the way she tosses him about like a bundle of washing? Besides, she doesn't want either of us to have a say in his life at all. She's always giving me orders and . . .'

'You don't like her, do you? I've noticed that you don't get on with her.'

Alice had never spoken out so positively before and was pleased to see that it made Colin listen seriously, even though he seemed to want to reduce it to a personal level. Which is what it is, Alice thought to herself wryly.

'No, I've never taken to her. She treats me like a child. But that's not the point. It's just that she's not good for Jack. He's nearly three months now. He needs someone younger . . .'

'You're young. He's got you. You're his mother. Anyway, how can we boot her out after nearly forty years? She looked after me when I was a baby. My mother had no complaints, as far as I know. She let Nanny run things in her own way. How could we manage without her?'

'Easily, Colin, you'll see. I'll get someone else, of course. A young girl – which is what your mother did, after all, when she got Nanny. Anyway, Nanny needs a rest. Wouldn't your parents have thought so by now if they'd been alive?' She considered this last point to be something of a master-stroke and stayed silent to let it soak in.

Colin ruffled his hair and looked down at the floor. Then he picked up the paper again and waved it distractedly.

'I'll think about it,' he said. 'I can't make up my mind now. It's too sudden.' He paused and sat down in the armchair, shaking the paper out of its folds. 'But when it comes to it, I'd better explain to her and give the marching orders. All right?'

'Of course,' said Alice meekly, cheered by the fact that he had said 'when' and not 'if'. She felt the battle was won.

So it was that Colin had long talks with Nanny and, as a result, found her an ugly retirement villa on the South Coast to which she departed sullenly and in a state of shock one wet Saturday morning, her navy-blue pot hat clamped so severely over her bushy eyebrows that she was probably spared the sight of Alice dancing a little jig in the hall during Colin's solemn goodbyes.

Immediately she had gone, Alice made local inquiries for a

young, malleable country girl and, within a week, biddable, stolid Rose, one of the six children of the blacksmith in Westknoll, was installed at Ballads to take care of all but the interesting highlights in the upbringing of the newest member of the Whittaker family.

And now, Alice said to herself as she strolled through the blissfully Nanny-less rooms, I'll get some life into the house. The next thing I'm going to do is to ask Daisy to come and visit me.

This proved to be even easier than getting rid of Nanny. Colin was delighted when Alice suggested, towards the end of the summer, that she ask Daisy to Ballads for a few days.

'A great girl. She'll cheer you up all right. Why didn't we think of this before? You can have the car and Barratt if you like, and get about and see some of the countryside.'

Alice doubted if either she or Daisy would want to drive around looking at trees and hedges but was pleased at the chance of a certain kind of freedom offered by the use of the car. She hugged Colin warmly and, as they were preparing for bed at the time, he took this as a sign that, as he put it, she was in 'the right mood', and clasped her tightly in return. Wondering, as always, why she did not feel like melting into his arms in the manner of all romantic heroines truly in love, she nevertheless relaxed and yielded and was soon lying beneath him, feeling nothing and thinking happily about Daisy and the fun they would have.

It was early October by the time Daisy's visit was arranged. Alice waited at the hall window for her arrival. She had gone through her wardrobe with mounting dissatisfaction before choosing a cotton day-dress with a dropped waistline and a handkerchief-pointed hem which just revealed her ankles. She knew from reading the social and fashion journals that skirts were getting shorter and shorter. Already some daring 'bright young things' were displaying their knees, and the favoured materials were not the thick and heavy kind in her wardrobe, but thin and floating. Some of the frocks seemed little more than camisoles, with scooped necklines and no sleeves, and were often worn with a loose, matching jacket which hung unshaped from the shoulders and had full, straight sleeves with trimming at the cuff.

So she knew she was unlikely to look as fashionable as Daisy, who had an obsessive interest in clothes and all the money in the world to indulge her tastes, besides having all the smart London shops on her doorstep.

All the same, Alice was unprepared for Daisy's appearance as she stepped out of the taxi which brought her from the station. The shock was so great and so mortifying that she stood rooted in the hall for several seconds before running out to greet her friend.

Daisy's long dark hair had been cut to a severe bob, with cow-licks curving either side of her face on to her cheeks. She was heavily decorated with cosmetics, her eyebrows pencilled into high arches, her face powdered to an astonishing whiteness and her cheeks rouged faintly pink. Her mouth was shaped with a deep-red lipstick into a pouting Cupid's bow. Almost covering her hair, except for the cow-licks, was a close-fitting vivid green helmet which reminded Alice of the bathing-caps she had seen on a visit to Hayling Island. Daisy's coat was a tight sheath of black sealskin, rising to a stand-up collar framing her face, and under one arm she hugged a matching clutch-bag which was, it seemed to Alice, barely large enough to hold anything more than her friend's train ticket and possibly one handkerchief and a hair-comb.

As Daisy stood beside the taxi, looking towards the house, it was apparent that her coat, and whatever she was wearing underneath, reached only to her knees, and her short, plumpish legs were covered in pale, sheer stockings. On her surprisingly small feet, which Daisy constantly and mockingly used to compare with Alice's size sixes, she wore patent leather shoes with stubby heels and diamanté buckles across the instep.

Alice opened the front door and ran out.

'What's happened to your hair?' she shouted as she walked towards the taxi, where Daisy was still poised by the open door, as if for a photograph.

Daisy opened her arms wide and closed them round

Alice, then held her friend at arm's length, shaking her gently.

'Oh Al! Isn't it divine? Don't you madly love it? Anton did it. Everybody's going to him. You'll have to, darling. You can't wear your hair like that any more. No one has long hair now . . .'

'But Daisy, you look like a boy!' Alice had meant it to be a sort of reprimand but Daisy did a little leap in the air with joy.

'Oh good, you darling! You couldn't have said anything nicer. Come on, Al, let's go into this mansion of yours. Bit on the gloomy side, *n'est-ce pas*?'

Alice had forgotten Daisy's way of sprinkling her conversation with French phrases and at this reminder she felt a wave of affection for her and for their times together in London.

Daisy was prattling on as they walked towards the door.

'Don't you get rather blue mooning about here all day?' she asked.

'Yes, yes, that's just it.' Alice's eyes filled with tears of relief at being understood. 'Oh Daisy, come inside, quickly, quickly. There's so much to tell.'

Daisy hugged her when they reached the hall and said, 'Tell away then. But Al . . . you're crying. Is it as bad as that? Show me *le lavabo* and then I'll be all yours and all ears.'

When Daisy joined her by the fire in the drawing-room, Alice was surprised to see that her jade-green frock was even shorter than her coat and realized that this was the first time she had seen her friend's knees. She noted that they were plump and completely round.

'Daisy, those clothes . . . how long have you been wearing such short skirts? Does everyone in London? I thought it was just people in society, and actresses. And what does Julian think? I thought he was quite stuffy.'

Daisy rubbed her hands over her knees to warm them, and laughed.

'Jules? Well, at first it was a big shock. He said it was terribly unfunny and that I was to take the clothes back to Madame Eva right away. He said I was to come back with something more becoming to a banker's wife. You're right,

Al, he can be a stuffy old darling sometimes. But just imagine Madame Eva's face if I'd marched in and handed back over fifty guineas' worth of clothes specially made for me and said my husband didn't like them! She'd have told everyone in London and Julian would have been the town joke, I mean, the absolute laughing-stock. But I talked some sense into him. You know old Jules. All he thinks about is making money – that's why we're so gorgeously rich. But he wants me to be happy, so in the end he said actually I looked very interesting in this get-up and he thought it might be a good idea if he took me out now and again to enjoy ourselves. And that, my dear Al – to answer your other question – is how yours truly entered high society, right plonk in the middle of it, and why I'm having the most spiffing fun.'

Daisy paused and studied Alice's face with concern.

'Sorry, Al. It's obviously not a case of spiffing fun here. Does Colin still adore you? Does he want to make you happy? Is it great fun being a mother?'

'Yes . . . and no. Yes, I think he still adores me in his way. And no, I don't think he wants to make me happy. I don't think he would know how to, anyway. The funny thing is that he tries very hard with me if I'm not well or there's some crisis or other. He was bliss all the time I was pregnant with Jack. But if everything's just going along in an ordinary way, as it is for most of the time, I don't think he really notices much if I'm here or not. I don't think he even cares about the other way round, whether I make him happy or not. He has so many other things to make him happy. He loves this place. He dotes on Jack. He even loves all the people who work here and seem to go with the furniture. He loves his dogs and his guns and his garden. He quite likes going to the City now and then, and going to his club, though he never says what he does there . . .'

'Nothing, darling, if it's anything like Julian's club. They just sit in leather armchairs, as far as I can make out, and smoke and drink and gossip about other men. They eat a lot too, great mounds of beef and suety puddings, like they all had at school. I think it's just a place where they can be boys again and not have to think about their wives or their taxes or their work.'

Daisy settled herself more comfortably in her chair and looked mischievously at Alice.

'But is Colin, you know, loving to you? What about the bedroom side of things? Anything like we expected?'

Alice felt herself blushing, try as she might not to. She had lmost forgotten how easily Daisy used to coax her out of her shyness with that direct, bold air of hers.

'Well, to be honest, that's not exactly spiffing fun either. I suppose I was expecting something rather exciting . . . certainly warm and rather swoony and like . . . like . . . well the kind of thing we used to talk about, remember? About being swept off on horseback or in a carriage and pair or being kidnapped by brigands. I mean, just one brigand, the chief one, and how it always ended on soft cushions somewhere, in a golden tent or on board a beautiful ship or perhaps even in a grand house . . . though not like this one . . . and wherever it was, there was music and shaded lights . . .'

She paused as Daisy's hand flew to her mouth as if to stifle a laugh.

'But Al, we were so young then,' she said.

'It was only two or three years ago.'

'In time, yes. But we've done a lot since then, a lot of things, a lot of growing. Well anyway, I certainly have.'

'Exactly,' Alice said crossly. 'And I haven't, that's the trouble. What I didn't expect, and you needn't try to pretend you did either, was all the clenched teeth and heavy breathing, all that trying so hard. Shouldn't it be easy? I mean, it isn't a job of work, is it? Anyway, I never get at all excited myself, do you?'

'Yes, often.'

'I'd like to know how. I never seem to feel like it when he does. Well, not usually. There have been times. Here as a matter of fact, right on this hearth-rug . . .' and she smiled sheepishly.

'Oh you wanton! You evil-living woman!' Daisy was curled up in a fit of the giggles.

'It's all right for you to mock,' Alice said. 'But where's the romance and loving in it? That's what I want to know. We hardly ever hold hands or just hug or kiss. If we do, it's the start of all that clenched-teeth business again.'

Daisy was serious now and looked at Alice sympathetically for a few moments.

'Poor Al,' she said at length. 'I think the trouble is that you're just not happy at the moment. You may have a baby son – for which I envy you to the skies – but you don't seem to have much else. It stands to reason, in this house. It's like a mausoleum. I don't understand it. There's nothing about the place . . . you know . . . flowers, or music, or people.'

'Oh but Col does play the piano in the evenings . . .'

'Does he really? How can you stand the excitement? No, Al, I mean life in capital letters. That's what's missing. Things going on, making plans for the next day, getting out, having people in. Do you know, last week I went to the pony races at Ally Pally, the next evening I went to the "43 Club", Kate Meyrick's new place, and another day Julian and I went to a special kind of party in a friend's house where they served drinks called cocktails which are funny mixtures of things like gin and vermouth. And next week we're going to see some ballet at the Alhambra, and Julian, who's really turned into a "bright young thing" himself, is bent on us going to see Alice Delysia at the London Pavilion and then having a meal in Soho, and one of these days we're going to have a five-shilling flip in an aeroplane at Hendon. And there are lots of parties to go to, fancy dress or treasure hunts . . .'

'Oh Daisy, do stop.' Alice put her hands over her ears and bent her head almost to her knees. 'How can you? All those marvellous things and I haven't a hope of doing any of them. Colin doesn't want to go out, or have people in, or stay in London for a night, or stay anywhere except here. He thinks parties and treats are a waste of time and money. He says it's nice here, just us and Jack and the servants and his precious Ballads.'

She looked at Daisy thoughtfully.

'You see, Day, he doesn't want to see other people and he

doesn't want them to see him, or me. I don't think he likes people really. No one's called and I don't know anyone to call on, and I haven't the sort of clothes to do it in anyway. So how on earth do you think I'm ever going to see your Alysia de Whatnot or get a flip at Hendon or do anything or see anyone . . . It's so awful. I might just as well be in prison.'

Alice dropped her head on to her knees and wept.

Daisy let her sob for a spell. Then she suddenly leapt up, bright-eyed, and reached out to take Alice's hands in hers and swing her to her feet.

'Never fear, Daisy's here!' she exclaimed. 'Why on earth didn't I think of it before? There's someone here you do know. At least, I know her, which is the same thing. Or will be. Listen, Al, where's Deep Ditchling? Is that a place you've heard of? Isn't it round here somewhere?'

Alice was caught up in Daisy's eagerness and spoke in the same rush.

'Yes, yes, it's not far. Colin's mentioned it. He goes there to order something or . . . what is it? Just let me think for a sec . . . Yes, I know, he goes there to ride sometimes. There's a farmer there, with horses. And he gets manure from there, to use on the garden. I'm sure it's Deep Ditchling. But why? Who lives there?'

'None other than the famous Dorothy, or Madam Dot as everyone calls her, don't ask me why. She's frightfully rich and holds lots of parties and is mad to have everyone meet everyone else. I've only seen her in London. She's got another place there, a house in Park Lane. I've never been to the Deep Ditchling place but they say her parties there are wilder than the ones in London. She loves match-making. She'd adore to find friends for you. She knows an incredible number of men, all ages, and I'm sure . . .'

'But, Day, hold on. I couldn't meet men . . . could I? I'm married, and a mother. Colin wouldn't let . . .'

'. . . You're really killing me, darling. Why ever not? Just as friends. And lots of women too. Anyway, I've met a few men at her parties and had a bit of a flirt. Julian doesn't know. And if he did, he wouldn't throw a fit or anything. I'm not going to do anything dreadful. And nor are you. But think how nice it would be to be admired and have some laughs and go to a few places.'

In spite of her doubts, Alice's head was spinning with hope. She was about to ply Daisy with more questions when there was a knock on the door and, before she could say 'come in' or 'don't come in', the stringy figure of Cook entered, holding in front of her a loaded tray of tea-things. Behind her Peggy carried a tiered cake-stand piled high with scones, egg sandwiches and a cherry cake. Cook gave Daisy a startled glance and said, 'good afternoon' through pursed lips. At any rate, Alice thought, Cook must have been impressed by a previous stolen look at Daisy. She had never served a tea of such magnificence or taken the trouble to bring it in herself. Alice thanked her warmly. Not for the first time she marvelled that someone so starved-looking could be so interested in food and its preparation, even at the low level at which Cook operated. But perhaps Cook didn't eat much of it herself, Alice assumed, the way she could seldom face any of the meals she used to help prepare for the guests at the Clarendon.

'Tell me,' Alice said to Daisy in an in-front-of-the-servants tone of voice, 'Have you seen my mother lately?'

'*Pas du tout*. But I hear she's well. Why? Doesn't she come to see you here?'

The door closed behind Cook and Peggy, and Alice leant forward eagerly.

'It's all right. Forget Mother. That was just to fill in while Cook was here. We write to each other sometimes, not much. She's always too busy to get away. You know what she's like . . . Now, tell me more about Dot.'

By the time they had munched and sipped their way through the tea, it was arranged that Daisy would suggest to Colin that she and Alice take a drive in the country next day, and on that drive, according to Daisy's grand design, she would suddenly recall that one of her mother's friends lived at Deep Ditchling and would Barratt kindly go in that direction so that they could see if it was convenient to call on her? Barratt could hardly say no, Daisy pointed out. And Colin wouldn't be asked, so he couldn't say no either. All that remained was for Alice to say yes.

Alice saw the prison gates swinging wide open. She said yes, yes, and yes again. Dinner that evening passed in civilized conversation between herself, her husband and her friend, and Daisy skilfully arranged it that Colin repeated his offer of the car and Barratt for the following day. Everything was set fair and the girls said goodnight to each other with the hushed excitement of conspirators on the eve of battle.

7

ALICE STEPS OUT

Daisy had to steel herself to keep a straight face when she saw Alice come downstairs to the hall in a long, belted, dun-coloured coat and pudding-basin felt hat with a dark brown band round it. How killing, she thought. Alice looks like an ambulance driver. Madam Dot will wonder where I dug her up. Still, that could be altered in no time at all. What must obviously be done straight away was to get some sort of dress allowance for the poor girl out of her rather intense but startlingly attractive husband.

Daisy had woken up in the guest-room fully prepared to take charge of the day and, indeed, of Alice's entire life. She led the way out on to the drive and gave a delighted gasp when she saw the Rolls waiting for them, and Barratt in full fig beside it.

'Very nice,' she hissed to Alice. 'Your Colin has an eye for a car. What a beauty! And the chauffeur looks rather spiffing too, if a little rustic.'

She put out her hand to keep Alice a step behind her.

'You needn't do anything. I looked at the map in my bed-room and I know the rough direction. I'll tell the man where to go. Leave it to me.'

As they approached the car, Barratt went to open the door and took a startled step back as Daisy, in the sealskin coat and the cloche hat, her round knees on full display, breezed up to him and gave her orders.

'Go west, if you will. I'll let you know later where we'll be stopping.'

Barratt broke into a broad grin.

'You want to go along of the horses then, my ladies? Right you are. West we go, and hold tight.'

The girls scampered into the car. They looked at each other and burst out laughing, rocking to and fro on the leather seat, hugging themselves and gasping.

'I expect he thinks we want to order some dung,' Daisy said in a whisper. She put on an imperious expression and nudged Alice in the ribs. 'We'll have two tons, my good man, and kindly put it on the seat next to the driver.'

'Daisy, hush, he'll hear you . . .'

'Or perhaps you'd kindly back the horse up to the car and let him deliver it himself? Thank you. That would be splendid.'

They rocked helplessly for several miles, inventing more and more absurdities and slipping easily back into the infectious laughter of their schooldays, until they finally flopped back against the seat, breathless and exhausted.

'Do you think we're anywhere near Deep Ditchling yet?' Daisy was suddenly anxious that they might have missed it. She began to scan the road signs on their route and then leant forward and cupped her mouth in the direction of Barratt's left ear.

'Where are we?' she shouted.

Barratt drew the car to a sedate halt at the side of the road and turned a beaming red face towards his passengers.

'Had enough, have you? Want to turn for home?'

'I should think not,' said Daisy indignantly. 'The thing is that I just saw a sign-post to Deep Ditchling and I recall that I have a dear friend who lives there. Would you please take us there and we'll see if she's at home.'

'Oh yes, that would be Madam Dot, I suppose?'

'Suppose what you like. I'd like you to drive to Deep Ditchling to begin with and we'll then enquire as to where my friend lives.' Daisy's voice was sharp enough to make Alice cower back in her seat. But Barratt continued to beam knowingly at her.

'No need for that, dear lady,' he said calmly. 'If it's Madam Dot you want, I know where her house is. Everybody in these parts knows that house.'

He half turned back to the steering-wheel and added in a

mumble, 'Everyone, that is, except Mr Colin. Doubt if he knows where anyone is who doesn't live at Ballads.'

Daisy turned to Alice and jerked her head towards Barratt. 'Saucy devil,' she said. 'Anyway, we're getting there.'

Soon they were sweeping between white pillars set in a white wall and approaching a tall William and Mary house with a portico over the front door. Daisy tugged at Alice's arm and motioned towards three cars parked carelessly at the top of the drive.

'Look, we're in luck. She's here and there's company. That's George's Delage, I'd know it anywhere.'

As they neared the front door, they could hear music of a curiously rhythmic, foot-tapping kind.

'That's jazz,' Daisy said as she virtually hauled Alice out of the car. 'Just you wait till you hear it. Oh Al, come on. This is life all right.'

The front door was half-open and as they reached it a pretty girl, with short fair hair and a long rope of pearls swinging below her waist, passed through the hall and turned towards them.

'Oh, goody-goody,' she said, swaying up to the door. 'It's Daisy-Daisy. Come in, do. And who's this orphan you've got with you? What fantastic hair! Dot will want to make much of that, mark my words.'

'She's tipsy,' Alice murmured and pulled back. Daisy glanced at her impatiently.

'Don't be daft and spoil it all. It's only one of Dot's elevenses parties. Probably champagne. Come on . . .'

The fair-haired girl was standing in the doorway of a room to the left of the hall and shouting to someone inside.

'It's Bicycle-made-for-two. She's brought a copper-haired orphan with her, all done up in a VAD uniform. Darlings, surprise, surprise!'

From inside the room and fighting to be heard above the jazz record, came a gaggle of voices raised in a tuneless chant of 'Daisy, Daisy, give me your answer, do. I'm half-crazy all for the love of you,' and next there was a sea of bright faces in the doorway and from them emerged a fat woman with dark hair scraped back in a bun and jewels everywhere on her person where it was possible to pin them, hang them or clip them. Her plump hands, with short little fingers like miniature sausages, were covered in rings of various colours and designs. She waddled rather than walked towards them and spoke to Daisy in a deep, chuckling voice.

'So you've tracked me down to my country lair, have you? Hoping that George would be here, were you?'

Daisy reddened and said, 'Hush,' grimacing towards Alice. Madam Dot then swivelled her considerable bulk towards Alice and embraced her like an old friend.

'This is my best chum from school,' Daisy said. 'Alice Whittaker from over Westknoll way.'

'Of course, of course. You live at Ballads, don't you? With that gorgeous young soldier-hero. And a glasshouse like a cathedral, I'm told.'

Dot broke off her hug and drew back to look at Alice searchingly.

'I'm so glad you found me,' she said. 'And what beautiful hair. Beautiful everything, my dear. Such a calm face. Come along in and we'll celebrate your arrival.'

The next two hours passed in a happy haze for Alice. She soon found herself the centre of attention as some twenty men and women of varying ages took it in turns to flutter round her, asking questions and making comments and then drifting off to make way for others to do the same. Her hat was snatched from her head and a glass shaped like a Y was placed in her hand, bubbling with champagne. At one stage she found that someone had draped a peacock-blue shawl round her shoulders.

'Look, look everyone!' A girl's high-pitched voice sounded from behind her. 'Look at how well this suits her. Isn't it just the thing to set off her hair?'

'No, darling, quite wrong.' A man's voice came from by the window. 'Much too obvious. Aesthetically quite appalling, Bunty. Take it off and try that paler blue thing that Daphne's trailing about with her.'

From the corner of her eye, Alice could see Daisy and Dot

huddled in conversation by the door. From time to time one of them would glance her way and nod intently or appear to ask a question. A thin man with glasses stroked her hand and asked her, 'How can you be so calm? Doesn't this awful world repel you?'

Alice was trying to think of a reply when she saw Dot coming towards her, beckoning with one bejewelled hand.

'Come, child, and let's see what we can make of you,' she said and took hold of Alice's arm. She steered her through the groups of chattering people, collected Daisy with her other hand and marched the two girls upstairs to an ornate bedroom.

The furniture in it was all light and spindly and highly polished. The curtains at the windows and around the brass bedstead were of pale-blue silk and the walls were lined with mirrors and sunny landscape paintings. Alice marvelled at the contrast with the gloom and heaviness of the furnishings at home and realized with a shock that there was only one mirror in the whole of Ballads and that was a small, spotted, oval chevalier in the corner of her bedroom. No wonder, she thought, that I don't seem to care what I look like, the way I used to. I never see myself.

Daisy and Dot plumped themselves on the side of the bed, both of them being too short to keep their feet on the floor. Daisy swung her buckled shoes up and down against the bed and Dot crossed one leg over the other and pulled her full black skirt over her outstretched foot.

'Now Alice,' she said brusquely, 'just look in the mirrors. And tell us what you see.'

Alice strolled sheepishly round the room, looking this way and that into one mirror after another. In all directions her reflection came back to her as a shadowy, uninteresting figure, so unclear and timid that it seemed to melt into the background of pale walls and curtains. She stared at her feet and stammered awkwardly.

'I . . . I . . . don't really know. I suppose I see me, Alice. Yes, that's all. Me. In a dull skirt and blouse that I don't like . . .'

Dot tutted impatiently but her voice was kind.

'No, my love. That pale-brown mouse is not you. It's not Alice. The real Alice is somewhere underneath, full of colour and beauty. Would you like her to come alive?'

'Yes, oh yes, I would. But of course, it's not possible now. I'm married, you see, and Colin wouldn't . . . I'm sure he'd want me to stay as I am.'

Dot turned to Daisy and raised her eyes heavenwards.

'That's not a good reason for spending your whole life as a little brown mouse, now is it? All those people downstairs – they're all married, or have been. Some of them to each other, some of them to people who aren't here. You don't need to worry about Colin. He'd be pleased, wouldn't he, to have a lovely wife with friends and places to go. Why, he'd love you all the more, wouldn't he, Daisy?

Daisy leapt up from the bed and ran to stand beside Alice, one arm along her friend's shoulders.

'That's right,' she said in a soothing voice. 'Just think, Al, you could have just the life you've always wanted, just what you deserve too. And still have Colin, Ballads, the baby and everything else.'

Alice stared at them both for a while. She was feeling dazed by the brightness of the room, the champagne and the concentrated attention of Daisy and Dot. There was something mesmeric about those two raven heads bent questioningly towards her, those two pairs of dark, peering eyes pleading with her to listen and surrender to change. The room swam with images of a chic, willowy girl acknowledging blown kisses and cries of 'darling' in crowded places, a focus of admiration, someone to be courted and loved, to be asked to parties, photographed, written about – someone, in short, who was somebody. In the background was the equally hypnotic murmur of talk and laughter, the clink of glasses and the sweet, yearning sound of jazz, all of it coming from a group of people who seemed to have everything she longed for.

She shook herself and looked from Dot to Daisy and back again and nodded.

'Yes,' she said.

The word was hardly out of her mouth before Dot eased herself from her sitting position and clapped her hands together.

'Good girl,' she said. 'That's settled then. Pop over here again tomorrow, the pair of you. Come to luncheon and we'll see what we can do with you. Now, off you go, and tell that handsome husband of yours that you've met Daisy's nice friend and that you're going to see her again tomorrow. That's all that's necessary.'

In the car on the way back to Ballads, Alice was as near as she would ever get to being hysterical with hope and happiness. But outwardly she was calm and it was Daisy who bubbled away about Madam Dot's magical powers to transform her young friends and usher them into the warm, exciting country she ruled over.

'You'll see, Al. She'll give you lots of poise and confidence. No more of that glooming about whether you ought to do this or ought to wear that. You'll be the one who makes all the decisions. And quite right too. This is 1920, not the Middle Ages, and you're only twenty, not some frumpy matron.'

Under Daisy's enthusiasm, Alice's slight fears about how Colin would react to her having a life of her own barely struggled to the surface and then sank back defeated. By the time they reached Ballads, Alice felt that she was about to do everyone a favour by allowing herself to fall under Madam Dot's wing and dance to her tune.

Besides, she was well aware that, although she loved Colin in her fashion, she loved herself more and that this turn in her life was wholly in the direction that she had foreseen and wanted after her father's visit to the Clarendon. She was on the way to being Alice, just Alice, and not anyone's daughter or wife or mother.

When Colin joined them for dinner that evening he was all charm and high spirits after a good day's walking and shooting. Alice found it easy to tell him the bare details of their visit to Deep Ditchling, leaving out the fact that there was any other company at Madam Dot's house and playing down that lady's flamboyance and dominating ways. Colin was given the impression of a kindly middle-aged woman who welcomed the friendship of a young neighbour and who would get Alice involved in the social life of the neighbourhood at the respectable level of tea-parties, committee work and charitable affairs.

He smiled broadly at Alice across the table, and turned to Daisy.

'I'm so glad you came, Daisy. You're a real brick. I was starting to worry that Alice might get lonely here.'

Alice made a round 'oh' of disbelief and looked at Colin teasingly.

'But you never told me that!'

'You never asked . . .'

'What do you mean? I never asked you if I was lonely?'

'No. You never asked me if I was worried about you.'

'Oh, I see.' But Alice did not see and looked at Daisy in a puzzled way to see if she could enlighten her. Perhaps, as his wife, she ought to keep asking Colin what he was thinking? Would he answer anyway? It was funny that he only spoke personally about her, or himself, when there was someone else to hear it. She felt confused and searched Daisy's face for an answer.

But Daisy was looking at Colin with a frank, understanding smile and, not for the first time or the last, Alice wondered why it was that she seemed to miss a lot of the unsaid things that passed between people, including her and Colin. But it wouldn't do to accept the role of looker-on. She could at least give the impression of sharing the language and avoid feeling left-out.

So she smiled understandingly at Colin too.

'Don't worry about me,' she said. 'I'm going to be all right.'

The next day's visit to Dot was all that she had hoped. Again, there was a crowd of people there, of both sexes and mixed ages. One elderly man hovered at her elbow with a silent air of protection. Daphne, who had been there the day before, rushed up to her with the gift of the blue wrap that had so suited her. The thin man with glasses who hated the world tried again to engage her in conversation but was brushed aside by another young man who bore a drink for her and plied her with waspish comments about the other guests. She said very little. She discovered she had no need to. All these people appeared to be desperate for a listener. She was happy to sit back, fix her grey-blue eyes on their faces, nod and smile in the right places, and fulfil their need.

There was a man in the far corner who particularly caught her eye, perhaps because she was unable to catch his. He looked to be in the middle thirties, tall, fair and heavily built, with an aura of power and wealth about him. There were two young girls hanging on his words but he appeared not to notice them as he talked commandingly at a spot above their heads. Once, while he was talking and Alice was looking his way, his eyes glanced in her direction but passed over her as if she had not been there.

'Who's that?' she asked, pointing him out to the gossipy young man who was still slandering the rest of the company with huge enjoyment.

'The big fellow? The one who's spouting to those two girls? That's Francis Bourne. He owns coal-mines or something equally beyond the pale in Kent. Very rich. Travels a lot, shows off all the time. A terrible philistine. I don't know what Dot sees in him. But women go dizzy about him. Actually, my wife is. That's her on his right. But then she's dizzy about everyone, including me. We have no secrets . . .'

He continued to feed her with details of his married life, which Alice half wished he would have the sense to keep secret, while she put the information about the big fair-haired man to the back of her mind and thought to herself, one day people like him will look at me and stay looking.

She and Daisy and Dot went off to the bedroom again after the buffet lunch and for nearly an hour they talked about Alice's appearance, who should re-style her hair, where she could go for clothes, how it could be arranged that she made frequent trips to London, where she could stay overnight and how she could explain all this to Colin.

The other two women circled Alice repeatedly, tweaking at her hair and clothes, spinning her round with a push on her shoulder, until Alice began to feel like her mother's tailor's dummy and at length summoned up the courage to protest.

'Look, this is tiring me out. Haven't you finished yet, deciding what to do with me? Don't I get a say about it?'

Dot clapped her hands delightedly and gave Alice a pat on the back.

'That's better, my dear. That's the spirit we'd like to see. Of course you have a say in things. In everything that concerns you from now on. That's the whole idea. You're much too self-effacing at the moment – wouldn't say boo to a goose, would you? That's all going to be different. Now, let's all sit down and work out where we've got to.'

Where they had arrived was at a plan for Alice to establish a pattern of regular visits to her mother and stepfather in London, gradually increasing her overnight stays so that she could be free to go out in the evenings as well as visit shops, hairdressers and dressmakers in the day. Sometimes she would actually stay at the Clarendon. Other times, with the Clarendon as a cover, she would stay with Daisy or with Dot at her London house.

To every qualm or doubt that Alice expressed, Daisy and Dot had an answer. Perhaps Colin would miss her if she went out a lot and stayed away from home overnight? But, asked Daisy, how much time did they spend together now? Well, hardly any, Alice had been forced to admit. Only at mealtimes and then they hardly spoke. In fact, Alice had said, getting into her stride, Colin really led his own life inside himself most of the time. He spent hours in his study. It was just as if he was on his own already. And anyway, he had Jack now. He adored him, and when Rose, the new nurse-maid, wasn't playing with him and looking after him, Colin was.

'There you are then,' said Dot triumphantly. 'He won't miss you. He might even be glad to have Ballads to himself some of the time.'

'But I'm his wife. I ought to be there.'

Daisy laughed explosively.

'Darling Al, why? For goodness sake, why? You don't run the house. Cook and the maids and Barratt seem to be quite *au fait* with all that. Been doing it for years, haven't they?'

'Not really. There used to be Nanny – she did everything.'

'From what I can gather she did almost nothing except boss everyone else about and give the orders. I bet everything goes a lot more smoothly without her.'

'Well, yes, you're right. We're all happier without her. I don't know about Colin though. He does a lot about the house since she went . . .'

'. . . And loves it, I bet,' Daisy interrupted.

So it went on until finally all Alice's qualms were settled and, guilt-free, she and Daisy took their leave of Dot, with instructions to arrange a dress allowance for Alice and to lay their plans for her first visit to London.

When they returned to Ballads at teatime, she and Daisy talked over the details until the time came for Daisy to catch her train back to London. As the friends parted, Alice's only remaining doubt was how she was going to get from Colin the increased allowance she would need to finance her new style of life.

In the event, she discovered she had underestimated Colin's tremendous wish to please and to live up to his self-image as a generous, giving man. He hated meanness in others and went to great lengths to avoid it in himself. There had been clues to this, if Alice had been looking for them, in the way he always over-tipped, avoided confrontations about money, and tended to placate equals and servants when it looked as if he could be open to a charge of lack of generosity.

As luck would have it, he had also just made up his mind to buy a second car, a Renault tourer, and when Alice made her request he had already decided that, in all honour, he owed Alice a suitable gift at the same time. He had been considering giving her a dog of her own or paying for riding lessons. It was fortunate that he did not voice these generous impulses, for Alice would have been dismayed to realize how much he perceived her needs in terms of his own. Luckily, he had no time to mention them before Alice raised the question of a larger allowance as they took coffee in the glasshouse.

Watching her unusually animated face and the glow of the gas-light on her hair, he felt a surge of love for her and also a great sense of relief that she had expressed a want that he could meet without difficulty and without giving up any of his treasured privacy. In truth, as Dot had guessed, he rather looked forward to the times when he and Jack had Ballads to themselves, with Rose and the others to look after them, and he offered Alice a monthly sum that was comfortably in excess of the amount that Dot and Daisy had suggested would be needed.

Throughout the autumn of 1920 Alice and Daisy tried by letter to arrange their first day out in London. But first Christmas was upon them, and then Daisy wrote that her engagement book was so full there was no room for her friend's trip. Their letters became less frequent and Alice would have gone into a pessimistic decline if she had not had an ornate, utterly secular Christmas card and a few short notes from Madam Dot, each expressing the hope that they would soon meet again. At last, in April 1921, Daisy wrote that she was free for the day on the Tuesday of the week after next and if Alice could arrange to stay with her mother at the Clarendon, both the night before and also the night after, she would collect her from the hotel and they would go on their shopping and transformation spree.

Alice's mother and stepfather welcomed her warmly, but with a new note of deference. They had not seen Alice since the wedding, nor had they ever visited Ballads or seen their grandson. They were bemused by her air of excitement and confidence and disturbed by the fact that Colin was not with her.

'I know it's all different since the war, Alice, but I do think it's still improper for a young wife to travel about the country on her own.' Her mother spoke tentatively, unsure that she still had any right to chide Alice about anything. 'It's just not circumspect,' she finished lamely, equally unsure as to whether she had chosen the right word.

They were sitting in Mr Meadows's stuffy little office off the hall, each with a glass of sherry held awkwardly in front of her. Alice realized that she had never before been in the hotel as a visitor. She saw it with fresh eyes as unbearably cramped and her mother as someone with no more worldliness or appeal than the cook at Ballads. In fact, she and Cook were very similar in looks and manner, she thought. She stared at her mother with something like pity.

'Oh Mother! Still the same!' she said, with a feeble attempt at a laugh. 'And no telephone yet? Or the electricity? Colin's talking about both,' she lied. 'I wouldn't be surprised if we had them by this summer . . .'

'That's very nice. What sort of a life are you having then? You seem to be full of beans and look very well, I must say.'

'Oh no, I wouldn't say my life had started yet. You wouldn't believe how dull it can be at Ballads. That great greenhouse that Colin loves so much and is always empty. I'm almost dying of boredom and don't see anyone. But all that's going to be different now. Daisy and I are going to . . .'

'That scamp of a girl is about then . . .'

'Yes she is. And she's saving my life. We're going out tomorrow to get my hair done and to get me some new clothes.'

Her mother's voice rose.

'Hair done? What does that mean? Not cut, I hope?'

Alice sighed impatiently.

'Yes, Mother. Cut. Cut really short. It's the fashion now. You must have noticed.'

'Can't say I have. But that's as maybe. It's all right for girls with wispy hair of no particular colour, but there's no one with a head of hair like yours. It would be criminal to have it cut. Besides, what does Colin say?'

Alice smiled into her glass. The girl's getting a sly look about her, Mrs Meadows was thinking. What's she up to?

'I haven't asked him,' Alice said, looking up from the glass and straight at her mother. 'But it doesn't matter what he thinks. He's not my jailer. But I'm quite certain that he either won't notice or he'll be pleased . . .'

'Won't notice? Have you gone mad? He loves your hair. Anyone could see that when he was courting you.'

Alice emptied her glass and stood up.

'Yes, I know. But it's different now, quite different. I just don't know whether he loves me or not now. He's very . . . well . . . distant most of the time.'

'That's nothing to worry about. Husbands are like that. But he'll notice for sure if you cut your hair, believe me.'

Alice spoke half to herself, turning her back on her mother to pick up her coat and handbag.

'He notices Jack more than me now. Much more.'

'Well, you can do something about that, you know. That's up to the woman in a marriage, Alice. You have to keep up the er . . . love and interest . . . the bedroom is the place for that.'

Alice rounded on her mother almost angrily.

'That part of it is all right, thank you. You needn't go on about that.'

Mrs Meadows looked away. Alice noted that she was either blushing or was flushed from the sherry. She leaned down towards her mother and spoke more gently.

'Will you come and see your grandson soon?'

'Yes, of course. I want to see him. In the summer, I think, when the weather's nice and your stepfather has some more help.'

They were both silent, knowing that there was not going to be any visit to Ballads.

'I'll go upstairs now and settle in,' Alice said. 'It's going to be a busy day tomorrow.'

Her mother, red-faced and at a loss for words, put her hand out clumsily and just caught Alice's arm with a light touch.

'Lovely that you're here, after all this time,' she said. 'But you're different and I'm not used to it yet.'

'Never mind,' Alice said lightly. She was wondering how

long it would take her mother to get used to the even more different Alice who would emerge tomorrow.

She slept in her old room on the third floor. It was now one of the guest-rooms and it felt strange without any of her possessions in it. She looked out of the window at the familiar view of tall houses, small back gardens and, in the distance, the shiny, curved roof of Paddington Station. Not unlike the glasshouse, she thought, and shuddered. London had not had any enchantment for her in the old days. She knew nothing of it until Colin had given her a short glimpse of its pleasures when they first met. But now it was different. She was on the brink of being involved in its life, the shops, theatres, restaurants and homes. She felt at the hub of the world, from which point all things were possible.

Below her, in the evening streets, there were people walking and talking, hurrying to a show or a party or strolling towards the park, people hailing cabs or running down the steps of houses. People, she thought longingly. Compared with the silence and emptiness of Ballads, there were crowds of them within her reach. And behind her, out of sight, across the tree-tops of Hyde Park, there was Dot's London home. Before long she would be there, as much at ease as Daphne and Bunty and the young man who gossiped and the old man who gazed at her protectively and the tall, fair-haired man who had coal-mines in Kent.

But what about Dot herself? She was beginning to understand why they called her Madam Dot. It was quite plain that one of her social amusements was to pair up her friends of opposite sexes and not to worry in the least whether they had other partners in marriage or not. Alice's thoughts skirted round the subject warily. She scented danger there but also found it attractive. What if someone fell in love with her? She stared at herself in the long mirror on the door of the wardrobe. Even with her unfashionable hair and out-dated, dull clothes, she had to admit that it was more than a possibility. And what if it happened?

She saw herself in a scene with Colin in the glasshouse at Ballads. He was wringing his hands and pleading with her:

'No, no, Alice. Don't leave me.' She was responding coolly: 'I can't help it, Colin. He wants to take me away from all this . . .' – sweeping her arm round the vast, cold room and its odd collection of furniture – 'How can I stop him? He loves me and, yes, I love him. But I shall always be your friend, Colin . . .'

She checked her thoughts abruptly. No, she decided, if there was any other man, even if we loved each other to distraction, Colin will never know about it. No matter how he and I get on together, I'm better off as his wife, and mistress of Ballads, than out in the world on my own, or even divorced and remarried.

Having thus entertained the idea that her new adventure might encompass a lover, and being quite sure that she could handle it in such a way that she would have her cake and eat it, Alice went to bed contented.

The next day was spent in a bewildering whirl of activity with Daisy. Up and down Bond Street and the hushed back streets of Mayfair and Knightsbridge, in and out of taxis and discreet little shops looking like private houses, into Anton's with a weight of hair coiled on top of her head, out again light-headed with a mere cap of auburn silk reaching only to the tips of her ears, into an Aladdin's cave of beads, earrings, scarves and handbags, on next to Swan and Edgar's and out again with pots of cream, powder, lotions and lipsticks and finally to Gunter's for tea, where the girls looked at each other over the silver tea-pot and plates of pâtisserie with saucer eyes and an exhausted kind of glee.

Most of her purchases were to be delivered to Ballads by carrier next day. But Alice had chosen to wear some of them straight away.

Her tweed coat was in a similar style to Daisy's sealskin one and the collar rose behind her head to a fur-edged U-shape. Under this she wore a straight, waistless dress with no collar, elbow-length sleeves and a pleated skirt ending at the knee. As she was trying it on at Madame Eva's, Daisy had loudly drawn attention to the new unsuitability of Alice's bust.

'Now look,' she had said, 'you can't have a bosom with a dress like that. You'll either have to slim it down or wear a very tight camisole and no bust bodice. Or wind something round your top half to flatten it down. Bosoms are right out of fashion, Al, honestly. I'm all right because the rest of me goes in and out so much you don't notice mine. I've got no waist anyway, and a tum that comes out nearly as far as my bust. But you're more like an hour-glass and you'll just have to get rid of some of those curvy bits. You can't look right in a dress like that while you've got them.'

Alice had dared to grumble a little.

'I don't know. With short hair and no bust, aren't I going to look more like a chap? I can't see the sense in that.'

'That's exactly it. Looking like a chap and still being a girl is just what the idea is now.'

'And men . . . er, that is . . . people . . . will like me if that's how I look?'

'*Vraiment, ma petite*,' said Daisy confidently.

'And Colin?'

'Who knows?' Daisy's tone implied 'who cares?'

Nevertheless, Alice was far from reassured, and as she and Daisy stepped out of the taxi in front of the Clarendon, she had a moment of sheer fright at the enormity of what they had accomplished that day.

She clutched at Daisy's arm and looked anxiously up at the windows of the hotel.

'What do you think Mother will say? She'll likely have a fit. Oh Daisy, do you think I should have? I mean . . .' She patted her shorn hair. 'She was bad enough when I put it up. And last night she was already getting cross with me for having my hair done at all. What's she going to think about this? And Colin . . . I've never done anything like this before. He might get quite angry.'

Daisy shook Alice's hand away scornfully.

'Come on, Al. You're a big girl now. It doesn't matter what your Mama says, now does it? You're not her little girl any more. And Colin will just have to get used to you making decisions for yourself, won't he? Good Lord, he's not your keeper. Come on, race you up the steps.'

Daisy's scorn always worked. In the end, it was her approval that counted – and now, Madam Dot's as well. So the two girls scrambled up to the front door, their arms full of parcels and their gleaming caps of hair lifting in the breeze.

Alice had expected a skirmish with her mother straight away but the hall was empty and the hotel silent.

'Quiet,' she said, with her hand to her mouth. 'Everyone's getting ready for dinner. Let's make ourselves scarce.'

They went upstairs to Alice's old bedroom and started to sort out what they had bought, decking themselves in beads, twisting scarves round each other's necks and mincing up and down to show off their silk-clad legs. They could have been ten-year-olds dressing up in adults' finery, so great was their delight in the novelty of Alice's appearance and so great also was Alice's child-like fear of her mother's reaction to the change in her.

They had re-parcelled some of the goods and were just planning how to give Alice a flatter bust-line when there was the sound of the door from the kitchen banging shut and voices in the hall.

Alice stiffened and seemed to look round the room for somewhere to hide.

Daisy went up close to her and looked her squarely in the eyes.

'Now, don't get worked up,' she said. 'And don't say anything. Let her speak first. Call out to her that we're up here. Go on.'

Alice went out on to the landing and leant over the banisters.

'We're up here, if that's you, Mother. Up in my room.' Her voice was just loud enough to carry downstairs but it was shaking with apprehension.

After a few seconds, there was the sound of feet mounting the stairs and then Mrs Meadows pushed the bedroom door open and her beaming smile changed instantly to a look of horror. Alice was standing by the bed, bolt upright, with Daisy beside her in a similar strained attitude.

'Well!' Mrs Meadows exploded. 'You may well look guilty, my girl. What have you and Daisy been up to?'

'Isn't it grand?' said Daisy, with all the charm and cheerfulness she could muster. 'We've been shopping, don't you know.'

Mrs Meadows gave her a withering look and turned to Alice.

'One thing you certainly haven't been shopping for is hair. What's happened to it?'

'It's been cut off, Mother. And I sold it, actually.'

'What do you mean, sold it? Are you short of money or something?'

'No, I wanted it short. It's the fashion. And I didn't know what to do with all that stuff when it was cut. So Anton bought it from me, for wigs.'

Mrs Meadows turned towards the door in despair and then back again. Her hand came up as if she would strike Alice, who backed away and sat on the bed. Daisy immediately sat beside her.

The three women stared at each other, round the room, at the floor and towards the door for a minute or more. Alice was counting on the fact that her mother disliked any kind of scenes or show of emotion. She had always described that sort of behaviour as 'common'. All during her childhood, Alice had won battles with her mother by stolidly and silently holding her ground until her mother became trapped in her reluctance to express emotion at any temperature above cool. It worked once more, for her mother appeared to give up and a sad expression took the place of her angry one. She sat down on a chair facing the bed and looked down at the floor and sighed.

'I don't take to changes at all, that's the trouble. It was hard for me when you got married. I missed you. I don't know why but I always thought you'd marry a London man and we'd be seeing something of you – you know, once a week kind of thing when we'd have tea together . . .'

She was speaking in a monotone, her thin face held tightly against an admission of sadness. Alice felt embarrassed. Her mother seemed to be talking about her as if she were dead, or somehow lost for ever.

'Anyway,' Mrs Meadows went on, 'you're right away from me now, a different person. There's a grandson I've never seen and perhaps I never will . . .'

Alice tried to interrupt with an emphatic 'No, of course you will,' but her mother continued as if Alice had not spoken.

'No, you and Colin, and now Jack, are in a different world. And you, Daisy, you've helped her to go even further away. All this modern stuff. The short skirts and the bobbed hair. Well, if it's what you want, there it is. But' – and she drew a deep breath and looked at Alice – 'I don't think it would be right, not comfortable at all, I mean, if you came to stay here again. Not any more. I'll be here, of course, if you ever need me badly. But I don't think you will.'

She rose stiffly and made as if to put her hand on Alice's head and then withdrew it.

'It's best if you stay at Daisy's tonight. If that's convenient?'

She avoided looking at Daisy, who merely gasped, 'Yes,' and turned to Alice in bewilderment. What was going on? If this had all been happening in her family, she and her mother would have been hurling insults at each other by now, crying and wailing and calling on the gods, and ending up with tears and hugs, and love laid out for all to see. The coldness and awful resignation in the room chilled her to the bone.

But Mrs Meadows was already out of the door and walking across the landing and Alice had started to cram clothes and parcels into her travelling case.

She looked at Daisy with a wry grin and a shrug of the shoulders.

'Not what I expected,' she said. 'But then, I think she was really always waiting for me to be married so's she could stop being a mother. She never liked it, being a mother. And I'm not sure I do either.'

Daisy was uncharacteristically subdued. Alice seemed

lightened and liberated by her mother's strange attitude and that was hard to understand.

'But gosh, Al, she's turned you out, shown you the door. Don't you mind one bit?'

'Why should I? I'm free now, don't you see? I'll never have to worry again about what she thinks. And you did it all, you clever thing. If I didn't have you for a friend and hadn't met Dot I'd still be a prisoner at Ballads. Just the same as I used to be a prisoner here really.'

'But she's still your mother . . .'

Daisy saw the set, uncomprehending look on Alice's face and had the sudden intuition that it was Alice herself, and not her – the 'scamp of a friend' – who had somehow brought about this scene in the bedroom with Mrs Meadows and made the outcome inevitable. Alice had wanted this break from her family and accepted it with satisfaction. Her friend's kind of freedom, Daisy now realized, meant liberation from any bonds that did not directly serve her interests. She felt a shiver of alarm at the thought of how Alice might one day find Daisy herself of no further use.

'You're all right then?' she asked.

'Perfectly, thanks. I say, Daisy, what about all this?'

Alice pointed at the clothes she'd been wearing when they set out that morning. They lay in a crumpled heap on the bed. The 'ambulance driver's uniform', as Daisy and her friends had called it, looked empty and useless, like the cocoon discarded by an emerging butterfly.

Daisy brightened at this evidence of the change she had wrought in her friend. She began to look forward to showing her handiwork to Julian at home right away, and, later, to Dot.

'I should just leave it here,' she said. 'You're not going to need it now.'

'No, thank goodness. But . . .' Alice hesitated anxiously. 'Where will I stay, now I can't come here any more?'

'We'll put you up sometimes. So will Dot.' Daisy laughed and added mysteriously, 'And there'll be other places soon, don't you worry.'

8

FRANCIS

When Alice arrived back at Ballads after her shopping spree in London with Daisy, she was surprised to find Colin at the open front door of the house. As the Rolls came up the drive he turned abruptly to the side of the door and studied a conifer that grew there, tugging at its branches impatiently. Had he been waiting for her? Alice wondered. If so, he apparently did not want her to know that he had.

She had a tremor of fear about his reaction to her changed appearance, but decided to take the bull by the horns, leapt out of the car as soon as Barratt had brought it to a stop, and did a pirouette a few yards from where Colin stood.

'What luck you're here! Now you can be the first to see the new Alice.'

Colin still had his hand on the small tree and kept his eyes on it.

'Well, yes, I came out to have a look at this. Barratt said he thought it should be pruned . . .' When he raised his head it was not to look at Alice but to gaze above her at the distant trees. Alice's high spirits drooped at once.

'Was I too long away?' she said. 'Did you . . . was I missed?'

'Of course not.' He at last looked at her and smiled bleakly. 'It's just that I was about to go to the kennels. Bosun's a bit off colour. He wasn't well before you left actually but I don't expect you knew that.'

Alice had expected Colin to greet her either with anger or with delight, but not with this chilly indifference, laced, so she thought, with some kind of accusation.

'I'm sorry,' she said. 'No, I didn't know. But what do you

think of my hair, and these clothes? Notice anything different?'

Colin made an effort to look at her, his expression strained and wary.

'Ah yes, your hair seems to be shorter. Daisy's example there, I suppose. It looks well enough. But a pity. I can see your knees. Is that the fashion now? But you'd better go in. Here, I'll get your case from the car. Don't wait for me. I'll bring it in. I want a word with Barratt anyway.'

'And Bosun? Shall I come with you to the kennels?'

'No, it's all right. Barratt will. I'll see you at dinner.'

He walked past her towards the car, making a wide berth as if to be certain not to touch her.

Alice walked slowly into the house. It was almost, she thought, as if Colin knew what the day in London had meant to her, not just the change in her appearance, but all the plans she and Daisy had talked about, all the schemes that Dot was hatching for her, all the secret thoughts she had about meeting new people and perhaps even having a lover. She felt that his sadness was not about his favourite dog or the ragged conifer but about her. What did he know? And how could he know it?

I wish Daisy were here, she thought as she went upstairs. She knows how to handle people and their strange moods. She looked out of the bedroom window at the drive and saw Colin and Barratt standing close and saying little but looking comfortable with each other, like very old friends. Oh well, she mused, what Daisy would say is 'What are you mooning about now? Did you expect him to roll out the red carpet? Look, if he doesn't kick up a fuss about you being away and doesn't make a song and dance when you come back, that's all the better, isn't it? It's what you wanted, after all. Don't be so soppy, Al. It's the dog that's worrying him, not you . . .'

'Yes, Daisy, you're quite right, as always,' Alice said to herself and turned to the spotted mirror to see what her short hair looked like in the context of home.

At dinner Colin acted as if the incident in the drive had never taken place. He said, 'How pretty your hair is!' as he sat down, and they went on to talk about the dogs and the garden and their son as if they were two happily married people in perfect harmony.

Towards the end of the meal Colin leaned back in his chair and smiled at Alice, seeming to wait for her full attention.

'What do you think,' he said, 'of the idea of having a telephone here?'

For some reason Alice felt that she had better not appear too thrilled at the suggestion, though she was, in fact, almost delirious at the prospect of being more in touch with Daisy and Dot.

She kept her voice as casual as his.

'That seems a good idea to me. It would be nice if you were able to ring from London if you were going to be late or anything. And I could order things from the shops, couldn't I?'

Colin looked at her in what she thought was rather a knowing way. But he smiled with his old boyish charm.

'I'll see to it then. And now, would you like some music?'

During the next few weeks there was no word from either Daisy or Dot and Alice began to wonder if all the happenings in April and last autumn were just a teasing dream. She was worried too about the necessity to keep her hair constantly trimmed, being none too certain that anyone but Anton could do it justice. Nor had she any oppportunity to go out in her new clothes. After a while she concluded that if something was going to be done to make her new life a reality, it was she who would have to be doing it.

Her first venture was to change the furniture in the glass-house. She anticipated some difficulty with Colin about this. He had become very unpredictable lately. In his withdrawn moods he would either retire to his study or, if they were together, would be excessively watchful. When she spoke he ruminated on her words for several moments so that she began to have the feeling that he was trying to catch her out in some way. At length he would answer her cautiously, weighing his words and observing her closely for her reaction to what he said. In his opposite, expansive mood, he airily agreed with everything she said, not out of goodwill, it seemed to Alice, but out of complete indifference.

She therefore took care to raise the matter of the furniture when he was quite plainly in one of his 'don't care' moods and was not surprised by his response.

'Yes, of course. The stuff in there is rather old. Get what you like, within reason. The money's there. But don't ask me what to buy. I know nothing about furniture. But I'd like you to keep my canvas chair there, the one with my name on. And don't throw away any of the old stuff. It can go in one of the garages, or in the attic if it's not too big. Some of it might come in. You never know.'

In one trip to the Army and Navy Stores and the Times Furnishing Company, she managed to choose all that she needed and within two days the iron chairs and tables and the heavy, stiff-backed settees had been replaced by cane tables and chairs and well-upholstered armchairs and sofas. The monstrous, light-gobbling plants she banished outdoors to take their chances in the open air. She was amazed to see how, without their competition, the vine took on a new delicacy and grace and how the glasshouse itself appeared to spread out its arched walls and open up to the sky. This is more like a paradise now, she told herself. The next thing is to get electricity here and fill it with light. And after that I shall fill it with people.

That done, she turned her attention to the hall, which had always struck her as a depressing introduction to the house. It was bare of furniture and of decoration, except for the heavy maroon-coloured curtains at the windows and a carved oak table by the wall. She bought a large mirror to hang above the table, and a plant and silver tray to go on it, and failed to notice that she had reproduced the ambience of the front hall at the Clarendon. But still the hall looked less than welcoming. She then had the idea of putting on the wall by the stairs several of the pictures that were scattered about the house, hanging almost unnoticed in isolation on a wall here and a wall there.

Some of these pictures had been painted by Colin's mother, who had had a mild talent for oils. There was Colin as a three-year-old holding a red ball, another of the garden at Ballads, showing the fountain and the roses, and one miniature self-portrait depicting Maud in a large hat and a white blouse with a collar like the frills round the cutlets her mother often served at the hotel. All these, and more, she put on the staircase wall and stood back in admiration when it was done. The hall, she now felt, looked welcoming and interesting – a fitting place for friends to get their first impression of the inside of Ballads.

By far the most exciting change, however, was when the telephone was installed one day in July. Fortunately, there was no question of having the instrument in Colin's study – 'I don't want the interruption,' he told Alice, 'and anyway it's for your use more than mine.' So it was placed in the drawing-room, on the bureau by the wall facing the windows.

When the engineer had gone, Alice paced in front of the instrument and tried to decide if she would dare use it and who she would ring if she did. Not that there was a great deal of choice. Dot and Daisy were the only people she knew who had telephones too and she had kept their numbers in a slim, gilt-edged book in happy anticipation of this very moment.

Warily, she lifted the ear-piece from its hook at the side of the stalk. The whole thing, she thought, looked like a black daffodil with a baby one attached to its side. She put her mouth to the trumpet at the top of the stalk. She heard a click and then a homely female voice saying, 'What number, please?'

'Er, do you mean what number is this? Or what number do I want?'

The woman laughed in a kindly way.

'Ah, that would be Mrs Whittaker on Westknoll 16, wouldn't it? I know your number, dear. Just had the telephone put in, haven't you? And this is your first call, isn't it? Just you tell me the number you want and I'll plug you in. It's quite easy, really.'

Alice thanked her with relief and whispered the number of Dot's Park Lane house.

'You'll have to speak up a little more than that, dear,' the kindly voice said. 'Right we are then ... just hang on for a moment.'

In a few seconds Alice heard the burr-burr that signified Dot's telephone was ringing. When Dot answered in her gruff, no-nonsense voice she sounded so close that Alice jerked her head back from the mouthpiece.

'Hullo, hullo, who's that?' Dot was saying with increasing impatience.

Alice put her mouth against the black circle again and said, 'It's Alice Whittaker.'

She squirmed with pleasure when Dot launched at once into a fulsome welcome.

'Oh, my dear. I did so hope you'd ring me. I've heard such great things about you from Daisy. We're all dying to see what you've made of yourself. And we've all missed you. Are you coming to London? Why don't you come tomorrow? Daisy will be here so you'd be telling the truth if you said you were coming to see her. These little prevarications, Alice, so tiresome but so necessary. What do you say?'

'How kind of you!' Alice was taken aback by Dot's instant intimacy. 'I just rang you really to see how you are. Perhaps when you're next at Deep Ditchling?'

'Nonsense, my dear. I shan't be there for ages. There's too much going on here in London and round about. I shan't be budging until August. So I'll see you here tomorrow, drinkies and a bite at midday and then perhaps some jollity in the evening. You can stay here for the night, of course. Right then, that's all settled, isn't it?'

Dot did not wait for an answer and there was a click as the telephone went dead. Alice held the ear-piece against her cheek for a moment, a feeling of panic mounting at what her call might have set in train. This then was it. The double life had begun. She had been ready for it from the day that she and Daisy had first gone to Dot's house at Deep Ditchling. So there was no turning back.

She ran upstairs to sort out the clothes she would take with her and, of decidedly secondary importance, rehearse what she would say to Colin about being invited by Daisy to spend the day and night with her 'for old times' sake'.

Dot's house looked commandingly across Hyde Park. As Alice walked across Park Lane towards it, she began to take fright again and her pace slowed. All the downstairs windows were open, and so too were the French windows on to a first-floor balcony from which wistaria hung like a waterfall. On the balcony, and just inside the room behind it, she could see a crowd of bare-armed women and blazered men waving cigarette-holders and glasses about and throwing their heads back in laughter. A glass came crashing into the courtyard below and two or three of them leant over the rail of the balcony and chorused 'Whoops darling!' and turned back to their chattering.

If she had had anywhere else to go she would have turned tail and fled. She was conscious of the nearness of the Clarendon, just across on the other side of the park, but accepted that she had bolted the door for ever on that haven. Neither her thoroughly modern hair-style nor her smart silk suit could quite take away the feeling that, inside, she was still the 'brown mouse' in the dull, heavy coat and the out-of-date coils of hair. She slunk into the porch and waited for her courage to come back.

But Daisy had seen her from the balcony and was down at the front door in an instant. She put an arm round her and said, 'You look absolutely spiffing,' and all was well.

Daisy showed her to a pretty pink bedroom on the second floor, where Alice left her case and ran a comb through her hair.

'I say,' said Daisy, 'it's grown a bit, hasn't it? Anton's for you tomorrow, Al. But don't worry, it still looks grand.'

She led Alice back downstairs to the first-floor drawing-room. Alice saw that this was the room with the balcony and was amazed at its size. It stretched the depth of the house and had evidently once been two rooms, for in the middle was a wide, graceful arch and in each half of the room was a massive fireplace with an ornate mantel over it and a tasselled bell-pull beside it. Crystal chandeliers winked and tinkled overhead and everywhere there was softness – in the plump furniture, the heaped-up cushions, the scalloped-edged lampshades and the corded silk swags which held back the flower-patterned curtains.

There seemed to be no softness, however, about the people in the room. They, in contrast, appeared brittle and sharp. Their laughter was like the sound of the glass that had shattered on the courtyard, their movements were jerky and theatrical, their conversation in high-pitched italics. The women's shoes were pointed, their bodies angular, their made-up faces harsh and aggressive in the sunlight that poured into the room.

Alice felt threatened and would have backed away had not Dot then swept towards her, hugged her effusively, led her across the room to a group of people in one corner, made hasty introductions, snapped her fingers at a white-coated servant to bring Alice a drink and dived back again into the mêlée on the balcony.

Alice stood silently, smiling and listening to the people round her who had returned eagerly to their ragging of a gossip columnist. No one made any effort to include her in this and she was passing the time by wondering if and when Daisy might come to her rescue when she felt a touch on her elbow and heard a deep voice at her shoulder.

'You look scared stiff,' said the voice. 'Here. Come away from these harpies . . .' The hand gently turned her away from the group and she found herself looking at the tall fair-haired man she had seen at Dot's house in Deep Ditchling.

'I'm Francis Bourne,' he said, implying that she should know him. She smiled shyly and nodded.

'So you've heard of me?' He sounded teasing and amused.

'I suppose I should say yes . . .' Alice began.

The man frowned. 'Why should you say yes if you mean no?'

'I don't know. I mean, if everybody knows you, then I should . . . I've seen you before. And someone told me who you were, and that's all. I don't know you . . .'

Alice was shifting from one foot to another and her hands were shaking so uncontrollably that the liquid spilled from her untouched glass on to the carpet.

'Oh dear,' she said meekly. 'What should I do about that? Dot's lovely carpet . . . I ought to do something . . .'

He took the glass from her and put his other hand firmly on her shoulder.

'Now, look here. That's enough of all these "shoulds" and "oughts". I saw you coming in as if you wished the floor would open and swallow you up. What's all the fright for? None of these people can hold a candle to you, you know. Except the superb and unbeatable Dot.'

Alice put on the slightly simpering smile that had won the hearts of the guests at the Clarendon. 'Thank you, sir,' she said, looking gratefully into his startlingly pale-blue eyes.

'Oh Christ!' he said angrily. 'What a performance! Quite the Miss Winsome, aren't you? That wasn't a compliment. It was a statement of fact. I don't deal in compliments, as you'll soon find out.'

He held out Alice's glass.

'Here, take this. Now, stand up straight, hold your head up and tell me your name.'

'It's Alice Whittaker. And you've no need to bully me.'

He threw his head back and laughed loudly. The freedom and naturalness of his laugh astonished her. It made other people's laughter sound as if they were trying to smother a pain. It also engaged the whole of his face, so that it was not just a matter of an open mouth with a sound coming out but of laughter written all over him and sparkling from his eyes.

'That's better,' he said. 'I knew you had some spirit in there. So you're the brown mouse that Madam has been taking in hand. I think I see the hand of the ebullient Daisy too in that overgrown bob and those ridiculously fussy shoes. I think I could do better myself.'

'If I let you . . .' Alice felt this was somewhat daring of her, but he ignored it.

He looked her up and down appraisingly.

'With your colouring and carriage – when you stand up

properly, that is – you should wear plain, simple things, lots of white. And black too, you'd look good in black. And you don't need half that muck on your face. It makes you look like every other dolly in the room.'

'Like Daisy too?' Alice had a pleasing feeling of rivalry.

'Yes, especially her. You could chip it off with a chisel. But she doesn't have to care. She has a rich, doting husband and a rich, doting lover. As for you, if you're going to have short hair why not go the whole hog and have a shingle? Then we could all see that willowy neck of yours and what looks to me like a very nicely shaped head. Hang on there. I'm going to get myself a drink.'

He strode off, leaving Alice staring at a patch of cream wallpaper embossed with fleurs-de-lys and wondering what had hit her. She felt dazed by this man's concentrated interest in her. His eyes had not wandered from her face all the time he had been talking to her. But did he mean it? Was it just his party habit? Did he really want to 'do better himself' and join the large number of people who seemed to want to take her in hand? He plainly knew what he wanted and was used to getting it. He exuded power and authority. Not even Madam Dot had given her this feeling of wanting to follow wherever she was led, nor such a strong conviction that she was on the threshold of both safety and adventure.

She turned her head from the wallpaper to a mirror on her right and saw Francis Bourne making a path through the crush of people behind her, glass in hand, and thought 'It's all right then. He's come back. This is a beginning.'

At around half past two the guests started to drift away. By that time Francis had won from Alice almost the entire story of her life. Now and then he would say brusquely, 'No, skip that bit. It's boring,' or 'Tell me more about that.' He pressed her for details about Colin. 'I've heard he's a nervy lad with great charm,' he said. 'I dare say you're in love with him?' but in his usual fashion did not wait for an answer. He brushed aside any reference she made to Jack, the servants or the domestic life at Ballads by saying, 'That's of no interest to me. It's your business and no doubt you'll get on with it.'

As they talked, Alice gained the certain impression that this was not just a party encounter and that he intended to see her again. When he referred once or twice to 'my wife', her heart sank. Then she told herself she was married too and what had she really expected from any new friends? Not marriage, after all. Just some life and love and amusement. And, most of all, admiration and cherishing and a touch of luxury.

This man conjured up an image of precisely the style of life she wanted. He stood for furs, champagne, smoked salmon, warm, softly lit rooms, big cars that purred through the night to country inns and sea-ports, couture clothes with no thought to the price. This was the tall man with the strong arm and the commanding air who would take her where she could be seen. She would sit beside him in night clubs and fashionable restaurants and wear long, white, slinky dresses with diamanté shoulder-straps, and fly to Nice and St Jean de Luz and Le Touquet like the women in the society journals.

So when he came up to her after saying his goodbyes to Dot and said, 'I'm calling for you here at half past eight. Put your glad rags on,' she could do nothing, in her dream-like state, except nod her assent. He, however, had already turned for the door and was gone.

From that evening Alice's double life began and Francis Bourne became her keeper, her friend and her lover. She began to make regular visits to London twice a month, to which, outwardly at least, Colin made no objection. At first she spent the night on these occasions at the mews house off Sloane Street that Francis owned. But this, it soon became apparent, was also used by his wife on her rare trips from Kent to the London shops.

Alice had no desire to meet his wife or to come across any indications of her presence. Once she found a toothbrush in the bathroom that was neither Francis's property nor hers, and it gave her such a shiver of guilt that she repeated to Francis her wish to have a place of her own in London where he could visit her and stay whenever he wanted.

Since she seldom expressed any needs, chiefly because, in his well-organized way, he anticipated them all, he agreed and before long Alice became the owner of a smaller mews house nearby and the employer of a part-time housekeeper to keep it in good order between her visits.

It took Alice several months to lose her qualms about their *affaire*. What she was doing, she realized often, was committing adultery, and so was he. The word had sufficient ugly resonance from her reading of the *World's Pictorial News* to make her long for some sort of reassurance. And one day when she and Francis were returning to her house in a taxi after a night out, she raised the subject.

'This is adultery, isn't it, Francis? You're an adulterer and so am I. Your wife could divorce you for it. And Colin could divorce me. If they found out. Doesn't it worry you?'

He took his arm away from where it had been lying across her shoulders. In the flickering light from the windows she could see that his face was stern.

'Oh my God!' he said. 'Not feeling guilty, surely? Sometimes you have the inhibitions of a house-maid.'

His brutal honesty no longer wounded her or disturbed her in the least. On the contrary, she found she rather welcomed it. She knew where she stood and could drop all the guessing and searching for meanings that seemed to bedevil her relationship with Colin.

'That's probably because I *was* a sort of house-maid, when I was with my parents. So yes, of course I feel guilty.'

'All right then,' he said resignedly. 'We'll thrash this out when we get back. Don't expect a shriving from me in a taxi-cab, my sweet.'

When they were seated in her doll-like house, each with a glass of brandy and with the curtains drawn and the lamps lit, Francis lolled back in his chair, stared at the ceiling and said, 'Right! Are you listening?'

'Yes, I am.'

'Well, I must tell you that my wife is a good woman who does everything for me that a wife should. But she doesn't love me physically – and don't grin like that, you hussy – and she's a plain woman who doesn't look good at my side, as you do. She doesn't like dressing up and she dislikes London or anywhere else except home. She thinks this is a city of sin, and in some ways she may be right.'

He lowered his head and smiled at her, then went back to staring up at the ceiling.

'In case you should ever ask,' he continued, 'I love her and I shall never leave her, never. And in case you should ask about children, we have one, a daughter who's backward, physically, mentally and in every other way. My wife . . .'

'What's her name?'

'Come now, don't be silly. It's not important. After this I shan't speak of her. She, as I was saying, is devoted to the girl and cares for her completely, with the help of a nurse-maid. Her life is as full as she wants it. If she knew about you – and she may do, for all I know – she would not call it adultery but common sense, and might even give the *affaire* her blessing. No, don't gasp in that stupid way. There are, my dear Alice, many women who are as different from you and the women you know as it is possible to be. They speak a different moral language and they don't see wrong where there is none. Besides, kings and princes have had mistresses all through the ages and no one shouts "adulterer" at them.'

Alice sat silent while his words sank in. She knew she was naive, he was always telling her so. And how much he enjoyed educating her and trying to shake her out of it! But what would happen when the education was done and she was as sophisticated and mature as he evidently wanted her to be? Would he pass on to another naive twenty-two-year-old? It was a danger she had the wit to foresee and she resolved to hold back some of the youthful ingenuousness that he found so attractive and yet wanted to change.

'That's as maybe,' she said at length, and saw him scowl at the cliché. 'But what about me and Colin? That's adultery for sure. He doesn't know and would probably be outraged if he did. I do, after all,' she added primly, 'sleep with him as well, you know.'

Francis groaned.

'Oh do spare me the domestic details! If all that meant anything to you, you wouldn't be sitting here with me in this house with the double bed upstairs or revelling in the flesh-pots the way you do, you dissipated girl. If you truly think it's wrong, then hurry back to Ballads and stay there, mouldering away among the dogs and the guns, and take up your duties as a mother – yes, you protest, of course – that isn't what you want. You want me and the life we lead together from time to time. So have the courage of your desires and don't talk to me of wrong or adultery.'

'And if Colin found out?' Alice persisted.

'He mustn't, that's all. Hang on to him, if you can. There are hundreds of women all over Great Britain and the Empire, perhaps thousands, cheating their husbands. Ninety per cent of them have the nous to stay faithful in every way that matters. They're discreet, careful not to arouse suspicion or cause hurt. They never run their husbands down to lovers or friends. They offer their undivided attention when they're at home. They run a comfortable home and don't run up bills their husbands can't afford to pay. You get the size of it, Alice?'

'It's very clear, yes.'

'The remaining ten per cent, who are foolish enough to think that infidelity can be made acceptable by exposing it, make a big hoo-ha, beg in vain for their lovers to marry them, let their husbands lose face and then the balloon goes up. The result is divorce, which is ugly, costly and often ends in tears. You've seen some of the divorcées in Dot's crowd . . .'

'Yes, there's Poppy, and Lady Mary Something-or-Other, and Dot's niece, Jane.'

'Well, you know what they're like. I know lots more and they're all the same. Searching desperately for another man to stand between them and middle-aged loneliness. They'll have any man rather than none. They don't have any standing – they're just stuck in the world of the once-married. They can't make an ordinary friend of a man because of their hunger to make him their own. And they can't make a real friend of any woman because every one is a rival.'

He stretched and yawned and stood up.

'And that's enough of Uncle's curtain lecture for tonight. You can digest it all when you get back to your glasshouse.'

'I hate it,' said Alice bitterly. 'It's better than it was but it still needs people in it. It's such a brooding sort of place, so terribly Colin, in fact.'

She had hoped that Francis would now listen to her as intently as she had listened to him. She felt like talking about Colin and his mysterious ways. She still felt a curiously unbreakable bond with him. His attraction for her, though different in nature, was as strong as the magnetism of their first meeting and their courtship. What did she feel for him? Was it love, or being in love? She needed to tease this out and, in her naivety, somehow thought that Francis could help.

Her hopes were dashed, however, when Francis said curtly, 'Let's drop all this woe, shall we? You and that husband of yours, you've made your bed and I believe you've got the sense to lie on it, eh? Talking of bed . . . Look it's after midnight . . . Come on, sink that brandy and let's be on our way.'

9

COLIN

Alice took Francis's little lecture to heart and did what she considered to be all the right and dutiful things necessary to keep her marriage a going concern. But it was not easy. One of her difficulties was that she had no notion of what Colin expected or wanted from her.

He accepted her comings and goings between Ballads and London, and made no demands on her not to go, or to leave home later or return earlier. He never asked her what she did there, where she stayed or whom she saw. Yet there was his watchfulness and his wry, slow smile when she volunteered some information that would, she imagined, put his mind at rest.

'Daisy and I went to the flicks last night,' she might say, and Colin, after a pause, would murmur, 'How nice!' or 'Did you?' She had no way of knowing if he believed her or not. After a while she gave up referring to her London visits at all, believing that Colin had no interest in anything she did outside Ballads.

They were both aware of much dangerous ground between them. They avoided it by communicating in a light, casual way, never questioning or prying or in any other way risking an exchange of feelings.

But one thing Alice could not fail to notice was that Colin was becoming more eccentric and mysterious. To begin with, there were the long hours he spent in his study. Summer and winter, whenever he was at home, he would go there immediately after breakfast for two hours or more, again for a spell after lunch, and often he would be there for an hour before dinner and hurry upstairs immediately afterwards. Sometimes it was one o'clock or later before he came to bed.

What did he do there? His Uncle Frederick had told her that as a youth Colin had written poetry. Was that what he was doing now? Or was he writing a book, keeping a diary or just reading? Sometimes, as she passed the door, she would hear the rustle of paper or his footsteps across the room. As young Jack began to walk and then to talk, Colin would take him into his study with him occasionally, and even then she could hear only brief bursts of childish chatter and Colin's quiet, steady voice. Mostly there were the long, mysterious silences.

There was also the disturbing matter of Colin and his music. Almost as soon as she had started her visits to London he had shown a fidgety, disgruntled attitude to the piano. More often than not, when they were together in the drawing-room after dinner, he would leave it unopened and if she murmured, 'No piano tonight?' he would shrug and say, 'All right then,' and get up slowly from his chair and flick impatiently through the music-sheets.

When he eventually sat down at the piano it was seldom to play the haunting notes of a love-song. Instead he would bring his hands down fiercely on the strident chords of a military march or he would tinker with several different melodies until he slid into harsh discords and finally stood up and put the piano-lid down with a bang.

'Sorry, old girl,' he'd say, 'I'm going upstairs,' and he'd be gone.

His disenchantment with the piano came to a climax one day in the winter of 1923. It was a particularly raw evening with snow on the ground. They had finished dinner as usual at about half past eight. Colin got up from the table and, as he walked round to pull Alice's chair back, he waved towards the door.

'You can go in by the fire,' he said. 'I'm just going up to the attic.'

'What? In this cold? It'll be freezing up there.'

'I dare say,' he said. 'But I must go.'

Alice sat for about half an hour alone by the fire. She felt no curiosity about what he was doing in the attic. He was accustomed to going up there quite frequently without explanation. When he emerged he would invariably go straight to his study, so she had no idea if he went there to recover some possession that had been stored away or whether he merely went to survey the reminders of his past family life.

The door opened with a whoosh of cold air and Colin came in. He had a violin cradled in his arms. He walked across the room and stood in front of her without a word, his eyes hot and steely in the firelight.

At length, he thrust the violin away from his body towards her.

'You see this?' he said.

As so often happened, she mistook his mood and answered teasingly.

'Ah! Have you found something nice to play with? Does Col want to make squeakie-weakies then?'

He stiffened and clutched the violin tightly against his chest. She noticed the steady tic at his temple and turned her head abruptly away from him towards the fire.

'For pity's sake, Colin, what is it now?'

'This,' he said slowly, 'is what my father played. I shall play it. The piano is too slow. I can't move my fingers fast enough on it. This is faster, you understand? Listen . . .'

He put the violin to his shoulder and flourished the bow in his right hand. Flamboyantly, he brought it round in an arc, flashing in the firelight, and scraped it across the strings. Alice gazed at him in horror as he moved the bow back and forth uncontrollably. It made a wild, shrieking sound that grated on her whole body. The fingers of his left hand played a random dance on the strings. His foot tapped and his head nodded and he had a fixed grin on his face which failed to reach his eyes. There was no recognizable rhythm or melody in the sound. It was movement and noise he seemed to want and to want them fast and loud and free.

He stopped abruptly and swung the bow down by his side.

'What do you think?' he said.

'What do you mean? Think? How can I think anything with all that noise going on?'

164

'Yes, all right, it's just a noise now. But I could learn. I could play it better than the piano. It's more my style, don't you agree?'

Alice stared at her feet and moved her head slowly from side to side. She imagined she was exhibiting thought. She licked her finger and rubbed it on a spot on her green, patent leather shoe and then flopped back in the armchair, her arms spread wide over the sides. She looked relaxed but her fingers were clenched.

'No, I don't agree,' she said studiedly. 'You're not fast and loud like that. I don't know what's got into you. You're much more piano than that darned, scraping thing.'

'But I told you. I'm going to learn to play it. Sometimes it will be quiet and gentle. I want something I can play in the glasshouse – even in the garden, perhaps in the woods . . .'

'What? Are you serious?'

'Yes, deadly. In the woods, maybe, and in my study, or the nursery, or wherever I like. I can sit in the glasshouse and play, or stand up, or walk about. I can take it anywhere and that damned thing' – he waved the bow at the piano – 'can go for firewood for all I care.'

'But you used to love it. Remember those marvellous times before Jack was born? All those lovely tunes . . .'

'Tunes?' he said scornfully. 'What? All that sugary stuff? Do we want tunes? You may have loved it, Alice. I didn't. Never. But I'm going to like this. I'll play it as well as my father did. Or better. You'll see. You'll have more than tunes.'

He put the bow and violin carefully down on top of the piano. He kicked the piano stool until it rested under the keyboard and stood for a moment looking resignedly at the closed lid, like someone at the side of a grave.

He ran his hands through his hair and smiled to himself.

'I'm going to see if there's any fiddle music up there. I know he had lots,' he said, and walked purposefully to the door without looking at Alice.

She sat in the quiet room and felt certain he was going mad.

What's happening to him? she thought. Why this sudden hatred for the piano? His playing of it was, she felt, the only link with the carefree days when there was warmth and love between them and none of these prickly moods of his. Sometimes she felt as if he hated her, and himself and his whole life. But why? He had Jack now and complete freedom to do as he wanted. Admittedly she had changed, but she was naively confident that, by following Francis's advice to the letter, she was managing to keep her double life from having any effect on Colin. He never complained. It wasn't an important issue between them. If anything was eating away at him, then it must be something quite separate from their relationship, something from the past.

Reluctantly, Alice started to ponder on her mother's warning about the 'terrible suffering' of the young men who had gone to war. But that was all finished with five years ago and surely he would have got over it by now? Beside, these things were best forgotten. That had always been her attitude and she felt it ought to be Colin's too.

But occasionally in the past, especially after they had made love, Colin had surprised her by not falling asleep straight away. Instead he would start to talk in a dreamy voice, his head turned away from her towards the wall or half buried in his pillow.

'I thought of you, you know, in the war, when you were waiting for me . . .' Or, 'My friends, the chaps, I wonder about them. Are they making love to their wives at this very moment? The lucky ones, like me, who came back? They used to rag me, you know. The virgin lieutenant, they called me. Can you imagine?'

He would continue to murmur sleepily, but then it would grow louder and she would feel the bed shaking with his restrained tremors until, like a no-nonsense nurse, she would pull the sheet back across him and pat him briskly and say, 'Now, Col, no need to rake over old coals. Go to sleep. It was lovely and I had a thrilling time . . . no need to talk like that . . .'

She would flop back on to her pillow, frowning mildly at the ceiling and longing for sleep.

All she knew of his inner struggles was what could be seen. There was the tic at his temple which appeared every time they had a disagreement. Also he was now in the habit of clenching his jaw so that the muscles tightened at the side of his face, giving him a harsh, grim expression. Another thing that made her turn her head away with a sigh was the way that the pupils in his normally limpid dark eyes would contract into pin-heads and pierce the space between them for all the world as if he wished her dead. Yet from his mouth would come the usual bland phrases – 'Care for a walk in the woods?' 'Shall we give the dogs a run?' 'Fancy a drink?' or 'Let's have our coffee in the glasshouse.'

Alice's double life continued throughout the spring and early summer of 1924. Lulled by what she saw as Colin's indifference, she became bolder and sometimes spent two or more consecutive nights in London with Francis. Her face began to appear now and again in the society journals – 'Mr Francis Bourne and Mrs Colin Whittaker enjoying the races at Ascot', 'Among the spectators at Wimbledon were Mr Francis Bourne and Mrs Colin Whittaker', 'Mr Francis Bourne and Mrs Colin Whittaker in the Stewards' Enclosure at Henley', 'Mr Francis Bourne and Mrs Colin Whittaker share a table with friends at the Charity Ball for St Dunstan's'.

As the pace of her life speeded up and her bond with Francis became stronger, Alice felt more and more obliged to humour Colin in his moods and in the one need she was capable of perceiving, his sporadic and apparently urgent desire to make love. These occasions usually followed one of their talks about nothing in particular which hovered all the time on the edge of abrasiveness but never quite tipped over. There was never any slow build-up of physical closeness or of affection. One moment they would be talking warily, their eyes never quite meeting, both striving to keep the hostile undercurrents well out of sight and speech, and the next moment they would be clasped together on the sofa in the drawing-room, or on a rug in the glasshouse or, more rarely, in bed, and thankfully sink into release and oblivion.

At these times they spoke little. When they did, they spoke more truthfully than they knew, of want rather than of love. Alice invariably ended with the feeling of a duty well done. Colin, who could not stop himself from hoping that one day, in one such liberating embrace, he would recover the seventeen-year-old Alice who had loved him, always emerged from these encounters with a bigger burden of loneliness and frustration than he had carried before.

In June 1924 Alice accompanied Francis for the first time on one of his trips abroad. She was away for three days in Paris and, fearing that this exceptionally long absence from Ballads might be pushing her luck too far, she hurried home straight from the Golden Arrow's arrival at Victoria Station. She was at Ballads in time to have dinner with Colin that evening, during which she did her utmost to give the impression that she had just returned from an arduous series of dress-fittings in London.

In the glasshouse later, however, they were both sufficiently on edge to start one of their circular arguments that ended in sexual release. And two months later Alice knew for certain that she was pregnant.

Her first reaction was joyful. She had enjoyed being pregnant before and looked on this second time as an opportunity to be passive and cherished again – a holiday, as it were, from the demands of her hectic double life. And she had no doubts about how Colin would react. He had often referred wistfully to her first pregnancy as a time when 'Ballads was a real home', so when she told him, she read nothing but pleasure in his guarded smile and the remark, 'Good. Then perhaps we'll be seeing you here more often.'

Then she began to worry about the effect on Francis. Would he want to end their *affaire*? He would hardly relish the idea of escorting a pregnant woman around the social high-spots. And, if he agreed to a temporary parting, who could say that this would not turn out to be permanent?

She told Francis the news on a visit to London in early September. They had been to a show at the Alhambra, dined afterwards at Hatchett's, and were debating over a drink at her house about whether to go out again for an hour or two at a night club.

'Well, actually, Francis,' Alice said, in that little-girl voice that made him know she was anxious, 'I feel rather too tired to go on anywhere else.'

'That's unusual.' He was looking at her attentively and half smiling.

'Yes. But there's a reason . . .'

'And that is?'

'I'm going to have another baby.'

'Pregnant, you mean? How much?'

'About two and a half months, I think. It's due next spring.'

He paused and did a rapid calculation in his head.

'So you slept with Colin soon after our trip to Paris?'

He shrugged and turned away as if he had lost interest.

'But, Francis, what about us? What shall we do?'

He sat down, thrust his legs out and stretched his arms sideways. He leaned his head back and laughed.

'My dear girl, what can you do but go on and have the baby? And what I do is go about my life just the same without you until the spring.'

'You mean, you'll wait . . .'

'Look here,' he said, still relaxed and slightly amused, 'you don't think that a six-month gap is going to mean curtains for you, do you? Surely you know what we have together is worth more than that. Or perhaps you think I may be on the look-out straight away for someone else?'

'No, no, of course not . . .'

'So you do think so! Well, I can't blame you. I've never promised you life-long fidelity after all. We both have other . . . other partners. As your condition so amply proves . . .' He laughed again, but harshly this time, and stood up.

'Well, let's turn in then. You'll go on coming here sometimes, won't you? For as long as you're able. But I won't be here. I've a lot to do this winter, in any case. I've got my share of unrest and strikes at the mines – you won't have heard, of course – the men have never settled down since the war. They seem to have turned against private mine-owners. Some say we deserve it. But you may well look blank. I won't bore you with all that . . .'

He came close and looked at her with an unusually tender expression.

'Look, Alice, just you let Dot or Daisy or someone know when it's all over. And we'll celebrate and take up where we left off. A bargain?'

Alice took his outstretched hand.

'I'll miss you though,' she said.

He gripped her hand tightly.

'No, you won't. You'll be too busy getting ready for another Whittaker. And I'll be too busy to moon over you, I assure you.'

He walked slowly across the room and waited by the door for her to follow. He spoke over his shoulder.

'That nervy lad of yours will reap some benefit anyway. A second child, eh? It's good news for him, isn't it?'

He sounded envious.

This time Alice was extremely large. Colin's Aunt Clarice predicted that, of course, it would be another boy.

'The size of it, my dear,' she said. 'You can tell it's male. And look how low he's carried – that's a certain sign.'

Rose, Jack's nurse-maid, also claimed to know about these things.

'Another lovely little boy like Master Jack,' she cooed. 'Oh, madam, won't it be marvellous? Mr Colin will be that thrilled.'

In the final months Alice had been aghast at the size of her swollen belly. She had nightmares of producing some kind of monster, or a child with the maturity of a six-month-old. She questioned her doctor querulously.

'Surely there's something wrong? I didn't have to carry this great weight last time. It's too much. How do you know it's all right? You've never had a baby. And nor has Colin,' she added bitterly, thinking of his cheerfully dismissive attitude to her complaints. All he wanted to do, it seemed, was stalk her round the house and garden with his wretched violin or escape to his study. Nowadays there wasn't even silence from that quarter. When he was up there, either by himself or with Jack, the violin could often be heard all over the house. And by the scraping, scratching sounds that sometimes emerged, she had an idea that he was attempting to teach Jack to play the instrument as well.

'Och now,' Dr MacBean would say, 'you're only a slip of a thing. That's why it seems so big. I dare say you have a lot of water. It's nothing to worry about. I've not a doubt that you'll have a fine baby.'

On 28 March 1925, two weeks before Jack's fifth birthday, Alice went into labour at two o'clock in the morning. Summoned by telephone, Dr MacBean strode into the bedroom with tousled hair, sleepy eyes and the collar of his pyjama jacket sticking out from the neck of his pullover.

'Don't you worry,' he said briskly. 'The second one's like shelling peas. Not a bit of trouble, you'll see. Out you go, laddie, and get the brandy ready for us. And you, lass, just do as I say and you'll be a mother again before you know it.'

Alice offered herself passively to the rhythmic waves that took hold of her body. When Doctor MacBean said 'push', she pushed. And when he said 'hold on', she held on. At length she had a feeling of release that surprised her by its gentleness.

'You have a wee girl,' said the doctor in a puzzled tone of voice. 'My word, you certainly took us all in with that fat tummy. I wouldn't say she was more than four pounds or so ... But, wait a minute, there's another. A little more work to do yet, Alice. Well, well. Twins it is!' And about ten minutes later he was holding up a second baby girl.

Alice had an instant feeling of revulsion. It's like rabbits, she thought, or cats, or servant-girls, having more than one baby at a time. How dare they invade my body like this, in pairs? And why do they both have to be girls?

As she slipped into sleep she reflected that there were now five in the family and the males were outnumbered. My life is ruined, she thought, by all these damned females around me.

10

THE TWINS

When Rose first came to Ballads as nurse-maid to Jack, she thought to herself how soppy they were, these two idle, story-book people who spoke so little but who watched each other so much. And what an unnaturally thin, quiet child they had!

Compared to the brothers and sisters who followed her into the family at home, he looked like a miniature adult. He had no dimples and creases, no soft rolls of pink flesh. Instead there were those pale, smooth limbs, skin as waxen and fair as his mother's, dark, wise eyes and a reedy little voice, more like a bird's call than a lusty baby's cry.

He'd never been a baby like those at home, cooing and gurgling in an improvised cot in the corner of the crammed living-room, crawling unregarded under her feet like puppies, banging their heads on the kitchen table and staggering on to their soft, plump feet in their own good time so that, before you knew it, they were swaying from one piece of furniture to another and grasping at your skirt for dear life.

'Look at that now, he's walking,' Mama would say on her way through the kitchen to the washing-line. She'd dump the basket of clothes on the floor and take the sticky, beaming child up on to the cushion of her chest and nuzzle him.

'Clever boy, my angel,' she'd say and, putting him down, give him a pat on the bottom towards the next level of healthy neglect.

Madam, however, had no chest to speak of, let alone a cushiony one and, in any case, Rose had never seen her hug or hold young Jack. This was amply made up for by the intense interest lavished on the boy by his handsome father with the sad eyes. She had never known a man spend so much time with a child. He was always carrying him in his arms or on his shoulders round and round the glasshouse, up and down the garden paths, in and out of his secret room up there on the first floor.

The strange thing was that his father's devoted attention did not seem to put any more life into the child. When he was not in his father's company, he would lie in his cot in the nursery in splendid isolation and all Rose's efforts to talk and play with him had no response. And she was hampered, to say the least, by Madam's objection to baby-talk.

'Use proper words to him,' she had said. 'We don't want him saying "ta" or "moo-moo" or anything like that. And I'd rather you didn't tickle him as I've sometimes noticed you doing. It over-stimulates him. He'll learn to laugh when something amuses him, not otherwise.' But Rose never did find that there was anything which amused young Jack.

Often she longed to take him into her arms and give him a real, warm, motherly cuddle, something quite unlike the fervent, manly clutches he had from his father. Just once she had tried it, with a wary listening-out for any noise on the stairs, but Jack had squirmed and pulled away as if her arms were an unwelcome restraint, so she had laid him back in his cot with a sad sigh. A baby who did not like cuddles was an unhappy mystery to Rose.

He would sleep for an hour or two in the mornings but it was never the deep, serene sleep she was used to with her younger brothers and sisters. How marvellous it was when they lay flat on their backs, their arms flung out and their pudgy hands spread open like tiny starfish, their bodies limp and relaxed but somehow still warm and lively from the chattering and games that had gone before the swift collapse into sleep.

Jack waved his arms about while he was sleeping almost more than when he was awake. He made little whimpering noises like an animal in distress. His straight, dark eyebrows would tense and his fists clench and unclench. It disturbed Rose so much that sometimes she would wake him and prepare him early for his outing before lunch.

The walks in the coach-built, glossy blue pram were his only form of exercise – and that was scarcely exercise as she knew it. He would be propped up like a doll among the frilly pillows and coverlets, turning his head slowly towards the trees or the noises of the outside world, and thus they would make their slow, dignified way down the drive, out on to the bumpy cart-track and down the gentle hill to the village.

They would encircle the shop-bordered green and then turn for home by the same route they had come. Sometimes, when a dog barked, Rose would catch herself saying 'woof-woof' quietly, from habit, and then she would look round guiltily in case one of Madam's acquaintances might be passing by and would report her disobedience. She knew that Madam herself would not be anywhere near to hear her. She seemed to spend more time in London than at home. And when she was at home she spent most of the day on the telephone or flipping through books about the doings of society people. Mr Whittaker, who, she guessed, would not have cared how many times she said 'woof-woof' in his son's hearing, spent most of his time in his study, or out with his guns in the fields and woods, or walking round the garden with Barratt. That was another mystery to Rose, how the family managed to live so well, seeing that Mr Whittaker never seemed to do more than half a day's work in a whole week.

So Jack had grown in the quiet, stilted way she had come to accept. At four years old, dressed in grey flannel shorts and Fair Isle jumpers, he walked gravely round the house, either alone or two steps behind his father, asking for nothing and having nothing demanded of him except that he should look clean, speak clearly and politely and smile for his parents, whether there was anything to smile about or not. No doubt his life would have continued in this way, and his parents' lives in their way too, had not Madam surprised everyone by getting pregnant again.

The twins were much more like Rose's idea of what babies should be. It was true that Phoebe, the one born first, was on the weedy side and had that anxious look of the potentially troubled and troublesome child. But Martha came fully up to expectations.

At six months she had a full head of gently curling fair hair, and dimples in her cheeks, wrists and elbows. Out in the pram she sat erect and waved her arms slowly as if acknowledging the homage of inferiors. Rose secretly called her 'Princess' and hugged her often without a thought of what Madam might say. Not that Madam seemed to have a mind to say anything about either of the twins or their upbringing. She was now away from Ballads more often and for longer periods than before they were born.

Rose herself was inclined to be tolerant of Alice's indifference to home and family. This slim, smartly dressed, beautiful woman was of a different world from hers. None of the usual rules applied. But Rose's mother could not contain her contempt when told of the strange way of things at Ballads.

'Why did she marry and have children at all, Rose? Tell me that. A woman of that kind, she ought to be on the stage or living in London among all those smart people. What's going to happen to those kiddies? Who's going to care about them when you leave? A father's all very well but no one can get far without a mother's love, can they? You're all that stands between them and the fate of orphans, Rose. The poor little mites . . .'

'It's all right,' said Rose stolidly. 'I'll never leave them . . .'

'Well, for your sake, I hope you will one day. Marriage and family is what you're cut out for. Of your own, I mean. But, for their sakes, well, I don't know. I just don't know.'

'You don't need to worry,' Rose said comfortingly. 'I really do love them like they were my own. I'm not going to leave them until they're ready, no matter what. Jack's got his daddy, after all. And I expect Mr Whittaker will take an interest in the twins when they're older. For now, they're happy with me, they really are. You should just see how they laugh when we play peek-a-boo . . .'

'I only wish I could!' her mother exclaimed. It had always rankled with her that, although she was only a couple of miles from Ballads, none of the Whittaker children had ever been allowed in her house. Rose had shyly suggested one day that she take Jack to her parents' home on her afternoon off and had been met with an ill-concealed look of horror on Alice's usually calm face.

It was obvious that Madam was struggling to find an excuse to say no and eventually she had looked away and said, 'No, Rose, that won't do.'

So Rose's mother had only her daughter's accounts to go on for her picture of the Whittaker family, a picture she embellished with her own lively imagination and her un-flattering opinion of the ways of the upper classes.

'Well, anyway,' she added heatedly, 'I dread to think what the future holds for them, with a mother who doesn't know they're born. I just wish the poor little things were mine.'

It was true that the twins' birth had made very little difference to Alice's life. When they were two weeks old she had rung Daisy to announce that she was back in circulation again and before another week was out she was celebrating her reunion with Francis Bourne at a rowdy fancy-dress party at Dot's Park Lane house.

None of her crowd of friends referred to the twins at all and even Francis merely said, 'I hear it was twins – what a surprise for you! But you don't look in the least ravaged by it all – far from it. Are you fit enough, do you think, to come to Deauville for a week next month? Better say yes. Bourne doesn't give second chances.'

He laughed heartily and hugged her. She felt enormous relief that their bargain had been kept and that nothing had changed. It was just as if she had merely slipped away for a month's holiday and, in her absence, time had stood still.

She went to Deauville with Francis and soon similar trips and outings were regular events. Throughout 1925 and 1926 there were few fashionable places in England or abroad where Mr Francis Bourne and Mrs Colin Whittaker were not seen enjoying the sun, or the sea, or the races, or a stroll on deck, or the nursery slopes, or their luck at the casino.

Whatever the social, sporting or theatrical occasion – the

first night of a Noël Coward play, one of Lady Londonderry's fancy-dress balls, Cowes Week, the first showing of a silent movie starring Charles Chaplin or Mary Pickford, the first express run of the luxurious Golden Arrow Pullman from Calais to Paris, a cruise aboard the *Berengaria*, the *Leviathan* or the *Aquitania*, a night out at the Kit-Kat club or at Rosa Lewis's Cavendish Hotel – wherever it was fashionable for the bright young things – and the wealthy but not so bright or so young things – to be seen, there Francis and Alice would be, laughing, dancing, drinking, eating, spectating and chattering and, best of all in Alice's view, being noticed and talked about and admired.

Life at Ballads came to be an enjoyable respite from Alice's frantic other life and she was thankful that, since the day that Madam Dot first took her in hand, she had been able to keep her home quite free from any influence or visits by her London circle of friends. So she was alarmed by a telephone call from Dot, one summer day in 1927, which signalled the end of this happy state of affairs.

In her usual way, Dot simply announced her intentions, with no thought of asking if Alice agreed to them.

'We're coming to see you, dear, Eugene and I. Don't do a thing. We love you as you are. We won't stay to luncheon. Just a cocktail at noon. All right?'

No, it's not all right, Alice thought, and panic rose in her. For Dot, everything would have to be just perfect. She had always been curious about Ballads, and Alice knew her visit would be reported to Bunty and Daphne, Adrian and Bertie, Jane and Polly – the whole crowd of Dot's hangers-on. Why doesn't she just quiz Daisy about Ballads and leave me alone? The whole lot of them would lounge in Dot's over-stuffed sofas and shriek with laughter. She could hear them now. 'Sounds a shambles, darling, how could you bear it? The poor dear hasn't an earthly idea of running a home. Not brought up to cope with servants, of course. Do tell about the glasshouse. Sounds like the Crystal Palace. How killing! Any sign of the neurotic husband? Or any of the young?' And they would collapse into girlish shrieks, men and women alike, and gossip about her maliciously until the next figure of fun or scandal caught their attention.

'All right,' she said resignedly into the telephone. 'I'll see you in a couple of hours.'

But Dot had already rung off. Alice held the receiver for a moment, frowning at the buzzing noise. Oh God, she thought, I wish Francis were here. He's the only person who can stand up to Dot when she's in one of her Boadicea moods. Then she realized with horror that it was Rose's half-day off, which meant that the children would be brought down for an early lunch in the kitchen with Cook and the maids. Not only that, it was not one of Colin's London days, nor was he out visiting locally. He was busy with Barratt in the grounds and would be expecting luncheon with her in the glasshouse. So possibly all three children and their father would be appearing on the scene while Dot and her companion were still there.

Alice had difficulty in imagining how the two sides of her life would react to each other. Bloody, bloody Dot! Why did she have to be so terribly overbearing?

But perhaps Dot would be in her usual hurry, dashing off to the races at Kempton, or wanting to get back home to prepare for one of her parties. Alice decided that she'd offer them cocktails straight away, so that after less than an hour, with nothing else to do, Dot and Eugene would go, leaving no chance of a clash with Colin and the children.

She called out to Ethel in the kitchen as she ran to the glasshouse.

'Drinks in the glasshouse, Ethel. Three glasses, all the bits and pieces, gin, martini, some whisky, bitters, a lemon – fast as you can.'

In the glasshouse she saw that all looked orderly and right. She took two ashtrays from the cupboard by the door – Dot smoked like a chimney and no doubt her new squire, like all the others, shared her taste for black Balkan Sobranie. She put them on two of the new cane tables and then ran her eye over the vases of flowers that were scattered round the room. She made a *moue* of distaste at the one that held giant lilies and irises – they were the sort of flowers her mother had liked to have in profusion in the gloomy rooms of the Clarendon. They reminded her of illness and death. She would have liked roses everywhere. But who was she to argue with Barratt's twice-weekly delivery of flowers from the garden? Perhaps a word with Colin would get results? No, all he would say, she knew, was, 'Yes, yes, of course, I'll ask him for roses.' And nothing would happen. She wondered if Colin actually heard anything she said, he was now so much in a world of his own where only Jack could sometimes reach him.

She hurried upstairs to change from her linen house-dress to a sleeveless frock in French-blue chiffon. Most of her favourite clothes were kept at Knightsbridge, but this one she had tired of and brought home. Since Francis had always liked it she felt confident in it, for all that it was not the latest fashion.

She went along to the day nursery and paused at the door. She heard Rose's slow country voice against a background of light knocking, wood against wood. She walked in.

Rose looked up placidly and then her face lit up.

'Oh madam,' she said. 'What a lovely frock! You do look grand.'

'Really, Rose? Do you like it?'

Alice welcomed a compliment from any quarter, which Rose knew well. The nurse-maid was sitting on the floor, an open book on her lap, with the twins kneeling close against her, one either side. They stared at their mother without making any move towards her or any acknowledgement of her presence.

Seven-year-old Jack was in the far corner of the room, seated at a small table on which there was a block of wood with holes in it. He had been banging pegs into these holes with a miniature mallet, but as his mother came into the room he put the mallet carefully down on the table and stared pensively at it, his hands lying limply in his lap.

Alice skirted Rose and the twins and stooped over Jack, taking care to hold the floating pleats of her dress away from the scored and possibly splintered legs of the table.

'That looks like a heavy job of work. My, you're strong!'
she said.

Jack turned his head towards the window and sighed.

'It's not hard,' he said flatly. 'I expect you could do it.'

He turned abruptly towards her, though without looking
directly at her.

'Would you like to try?' He picked up the mallet and
offered it to her.

'Oh yes, I would, I would. But not now. Mummy's busy,
you see. Some people are coming to see me. That's why
Mummy's got this pretty frock on. Do you like it, Jack? Does
Mummy look pretty in it?'

Behind her, Rose suppressed a 'tut' of irritation. Even from
children, she thought, Madam wanted flattery. If only she
would, just once, do something for them, something they
wanted. Why couldn't she bang one of the pegs in, for goodness sake? She watched for Jack's reaction and saw him get
up from his chair, still not looking at his mother. He stood in
front of a bookcase by the wall and spoke with his back to
the room.

'What a lovely frock! You do look grand!' he said, par-
roting Rose's words.

Strange child, Alice thought. So much of Colin in him,
without any of his charm. Why hadn't Colin himself, with all
the time he spent with his son, yet managed to teach him to
appreciate women and be gracious and polite to them? Even
Rose could do a lot better than this, surely?

'Is he well?' she said to Rose in a half-whispered aside.

Rose scrambled to her feet and helped the twins to theirs.

'Yes, madam, I think so. We've been having a nice time
here this morning. But I think Jack would probably rather be
outside . . . out with his father. The twins aren't company for
him really, are they?'

'I'd rather you didn't put that idea into his head. His father
can't look after him just whenever the boy wants. That's
what we pay you for, Rose. He doesn't have to play with the
twins. He has his own toys. And he needs a bit of time spent
on his manners. See what you can do about that.'

Alice glanced towards Jack, whose back was still stiff and unresponsive, and turned to the twins. They were standing close against each other, leaning inwards, shoulder to shoulder, their heads inclined fractionally towards each other.

Alice smiled at them, thinking how delightful they looked, so alike and so seemingly ready to be made much of, as females should be. She put her hand out towards them. Martha, whom she thought of as the prettier one, leaned forward as if to touch it. But without leaving her sister's side she could not quite reach it, so she leaned back again close to Phoebe. Alice saw that their hands were clasped together between them, and as Martha drew back their grip on each other tightened.

'Do they always hang together like that?' she asked.

Rose looked at the twins and smiled. Without thinking she said, 'Oh no, madam, only when they're frightened or at a loss . . .'

Alice was feeling more and more cross. Like all her visits to the nursery, this was turning out to be a disaster.

'I really don't think they could possibly be frightened of their own mother, Rose. We'll hear no more of that. Look, the reason I came up was that visitors are coming quite soon. I know it's your half-day and I can't ask you to keep the children up here after twelve o'clock. But I want you to keep them up here until then. You can then bring them down to the kitchen on your way out. Cook, Ethel and Peggy will be there, with luncheon ready. They can stay in the kitchen until my guests have gone. Please explain that carefully to Ethel. I don't want the children among my guests, is that understood?'

'Yes, perfectly.'

As Alice left the room, Rose anticipated telling her mother, with great glee and the certainty of receiving much indignant sympathy, about the latest evidence of Madam's strange aloofness from her children. Or was it, she wondered, their aloofness from her?

Alice was just outside the nursery door when she heard

Jack shout out in an excited voice, 'Look, Rose, a car, a big black car!'

She ran down to the hall, checked her appearance in the mirror, drew a deep breath and stood at the bottom of the staircase as Ethel came to open the front door. She remained stock still, her confidence ebbing, and felt quite unable to walk out on to the drive as her guests stepped out of the car.

All too soon they were there in the hall, Dot in one of her tight-fitting helmet-like hats in black silk, dangling jet earrings swinging as she walked, and her plump body hidden under a loose edge-to-edge coat of black satin. Alice had the impression of a black beetle, and even more so when she was clutched by Dot's arms in a tight embrace – so very like being squeezed by the pincers of a greedy insect.

'Darling girl,' Dot was saying, 'lovely of you to have us. We've been saying all the way along how excited we are to be coming to your charming home.' Then, in a changed tone bordering on sharp, 'Is the lord and master about?'

'Er, not yet. But I think he may be later.'

'Good, good. He's not to be missed. Now, darling, this is Eugene, who takes wonderful photos and will very likely want to capture you in his little black box.'

She waved towards the short, slight man who was still hesitating just inside the front door. Alice stared in disbelief. If Dot was a beetle, this was the butterfly. He was a riot of colour, from the straw-like peroxided hair and the cerise cravat down to the yellow jacket, emerald green trousers and shiny matching pumps. In his hand was a far from little black box with 'Eugene' stencilled on it in white. He put it down and advanced on Alice with both arms aloft.

'For any friend of Dot, a large hug is the order of the day,' he said, and before Alice could either retreat or step forward, she found herself drawn against his yellow jacket, with a strong smell of patchouli in her nostrils and his coarse, clownish hair against her cheek.

'And the next thing I want to see,' he said as he relaxed his grip on Alice, 'is your famous Victorian glasshouse. That, my darlings, I must capture for posterity – and possibly for a few pennies from *Country Life* as well.'

'Commercial little beast,' Dot said and gathered them both to her side as she turned towards the drawing-room.

'In here for the drinkies?'

Alice had not checked the drawing-room for tidiness and steered the other two firmly away from its door.

'No, not there. Why not the glasshouse straight away?'

'Ooh yes, how delicious!' Eugene was gurgling with anticipation. 'I've heard all about it. Quite the place for orgies, you naughty girl.'

Alice gave him a faint, bewildered smile and led the way through the kitchen corridor to the glasshouse. As she opened the door, she was taken aback to see Jack sitting bolt upright on one of the bent-wood chairs, his legs swinging about a foot from the ground, his arms crossed against his chest. He looked, she thought, like someone sitting in judgement.

'What on earth are you doing here? Where's Rose? How did you get in here? I only left you a moment ago.'

He stared at the table and seemed to be deciding which question to answer.

'We came down the back stairs,' he said. 'The twins are in the kitchen having a meal, which I don't want because it's a dark brown stew with lumps in. Rose has gone home. The clock said twelve ages ago.'

He leant sideways to peer into the dark corridor behind Alice.

'Is my father there?'

Alice turned to Dot and Eugene helplessly.

'I'm sorry. He shouldn't be here. Such a nuisance. It was all arranged differently.' She turned back to Jack impatiently. 'No, your father is not here. And if he was, he'd be as cross as I am.'

'Would he?' Jack narrowed his eyes in doubt and smiled a small, secret smile to himself.

Dot lunged forward and put up her hand to silence Alice.

'Not another word, my dear. Such a handsome little boy. He shall help hand round the drinks. Would you like that?'

She swayed towards Jack in a bizarre seductive manner.

Alice noticed that the child had the unattractive habit of looking at people only when they weren't looking at him. When they looked, he turned away or lowered his eyes. Now that Dot was gazing pleadingly at him, he wriggled down from the chair and walked past her to where the glasses, bottles and decanters stood on a table against the wall.

'All right,' he said. 'Come on, Mama . . .' and he began to drum his fingers on the table, making the glasses clink and rattle.

Dot seemed irked by her failure to charm the boy and was looking round for a chance to impose her will in some other direction.

'Well, now,' she said brightly. 'Since Jack is here, what about the heavenly twins? Why aren't they here too?'

'But, Dot, they're only two years old, for goodness sake. I mean, we're here to have a drink and talkies . . .' She felt everything getting out of control and going wrong. 'Anyway, Colin won't approve if he finds them here . . .'

Jack's voice piped up from the drinks table.

'He won't mind . . . my father likes children.'

It was Eugene who came to the rescue.

'It's piccies time,' he shouted cheerfully and leapt into the middle of the glasshouse with his camera held out in front of him. 'Let's get a drink in our hands, all of us – you do it, Dot, my love, you know what we all like – and then you can all be my models. And you, young lad,' he said to Jack with surprising firmness, 'can go over there by that big plant in the corner and be seen and not heard.'

He then flung himself into an energetic performance with his camera. He darted this way and that, the camera hugged to his chest, to try one subject after another, putting the plates in and pulling them out with tremendous flourishes and cries of '*olé!*' Now he was framing Dot and Alice against a rubber-plant, now Dot alone leaning against a pillar, now Alice alone looking up towards the vine. The sun streamed in and on to the far side of her head, making a soft halo round her hair and throwing her face and body into shadow.

'Aha! *Contre jour!* Just the shot I wanted. Stay quite still, my lovely, until I say you can move.'

Alice froze unnaturally, her eyes glazed and her mouth stiff with a nervous smile. This, she decided, was a lot more difficult than flashing a bright smile for the press cameras at the races, with Francis by her side for support.

The shutter clicked and Eugene called out '*Olé!* Done. You can move now.' He strode importantly to his black bag and carefully put the slide in it.

At the same moment, Ethel came to the open door and tapped on it gently.

'Madam, the twins are in the kitchen. They've had their meal. Seeing that Master Jack is in here ... we wondered if ...'

Alice's heart sank. Now they were all three of them going to be in here, turning the place into a nursery and no doubt staring at her guests in their awful silent way.

'Thank you, Ethel, but Jack can go into the kitchen too now. Or they can all three go into the garden with you.'

'Yes, madam. But that isn't so easy. Cook and Peggy and I have ... er ... our other duties and, as you've often said, the kitchen is not the best place for the children.'

Cheeky lump, Alice thought. She wants them to come in here, and she knows I don't.

Dot rose from her chair in a swirl of black silk.

'Come on, Alice. We're all dying to see the twins.' She looked commandingly at Ethel. 'Let them in. We'll take care of them. We could all go into the garden if that's what Madam wants.'

Ethel needed no further excuse to back rapidly out of the glasshouse and return in a few seconds with the twins. She ushered them through the door and down the step, and was gone. The two girls stood close together where she had left them and looked slowly round the room in some confusion.

Eugene was the first to break the silence.

'The little things! They're quite frightened, Alice. But so beautiful. Oh I do love pairs of things. I shall take their picture ... I must.'

He went to busy himself with the black bag again. Neither Dot nor Alice made any move towards the twins, Dot because she did not know how, and Alice because she was waiting for the gratifying moment when they would run to her.

Jack too was waiting. He had been sitting cross-legged on the floor to one side of the glasshouse, palming a large glass marble between his hands and following every word of the adults' conversation. He dropped the marble as the twins came in and let it roll away from him under a table. He looked round at the adults, one by one, with a solemn, testing look on his face. But, unlike them, he knew that it was to him that his sisters would turn.

Simultaneously, the twins saw him. Still holding hands, they ran unsteadily towards him. Within a few feet of him they stopped and looked down at him.

'Jack,' Martha said softly, turning to look into her sister's face.

'Jack,' Phoebe echoed, nodding and smiling.

They bent down and squatted on their heels in front of him. And there the three of them stayed in satisfied, motionless silence as if the twins' whole purpose in coming into the glasshouse was to make this rendezvous with their brother.

Eugene tiptoed up to Alice as if they were in church and whispered in her ear.

'What a charming tableau! They really are enchanting.' He raised his voice and turned towards the children. 'You really are a lucky boy, Jack, to have two such delightful sisters.'

It broke the spell. Jack scowled and rose quickly to his feet. Carefully, he brushed himself down with his hands. Then he retrieved the marble and put it in his pocket. He turned to the garden door and said, over his shoulder, 'Going into the garden.'

The twins made as if to follow him but Eugene ran to the door and stood in front of it. He looked at Alice pleadingly.

'Just keep them here for five minutes. No more, I promise you. I must get a few pictures. Just for me, please, Alice.'

Dot chimed in with 'It will only be five minutes, dear boy.

I have to be home by a quarter past one at the latest. So just get on with it.'

Alice could see that Dot was none too pleased with the way the morning was turning out. I expect she's miffed that she hasn't met Colin yet, she thought. But thank the Lord that awkwardness had been avoided. She began to place the twins in various positions, as commanded by Eugene, and was thankful to find them as docile as dolls. When she turned their heads in one direction, they stayed there. When she said 'Smile!' and bared her teeth at them as an example, they followed suit and smiled. But they never lost their hold on each other the whole time.

Eugene was just strapping up his bag for the last time and Dot was taking her final beady-eyed look round the glass-house and through its panes to the grounds outside, when suddenly the door to the garden opened and Colin was standing there looking quizzically at Alice.

At once she ran to his side and took his arm.

'Such a pity you've only just come in. Dot and Eugene are on their way home now. But there's time for you all to meet.'

She gabbled through the introductions anxiously, wondering if Dot, out of sheer curiosity, might postpone her urgent departure and linger on for further chats and drinks.

Mercifully, however, Colin had taken his cue from her and as he shook their hands he said with what sounded like genuine regret, 'I'm so sorry this is hullo and goodbye. I would like to have seen more of you and perhaps shown you round Ballads. But another time? I do hope so.'

As he spoke, he walked slowly towards the door to the corridor, forcing them to keep pace with him as he talked, and gently guided them along towards the front hall. Alice stayed in the glasshouse with the twins and watched Colin and her guests until they were out of sight. She heard Colin's voice continue while they were in the hall. Then it faded as they evidently walked together out to the drive and to Dot's car.

She felt overwhelming relief that Colin was being so charming and relaxed. He could, after all, have strongly disapproved of beetly Dot and the butterfly Eugene. He can't have seen anyone like them before. Three cheers, she told herself happily, for the English gentleman, and she waited with the silent twins for Colin to come back and receive her gratitude.

But he did not come back into the glasshouse. After the noise of the departing car, and the sound of the front door gently closing, there was no sign of Colin or of any movement or noise from the front part of the house. Alice could hear Cook and the maids serving up lunch in the kitchen. Spoons scraped round saucepans and a knife thumped up and down on a wooden board, chopping parsley to sprinkle, as always, on the mashed potato. The twins were sitting dreamily on a sofa, watching the flickering shadow of the vine dance on the floor.

So he was not going to have any lunch. He was not going to ask her anything about Dot and Eugene. He was not going to hear her well-prepared explanations of how she knew them and why they were visiting her. And he was throwing away one of their rare chances to talk together when both were in a friendly, relaxed mood. The strain of Dot's sudden visit, the children's intrusion and the demands of Eugene and his camera were now compounded by disappointment and frustration at Colin's unexpected withdrawal. She put her head in her hands and, dry-eyed, cursed him bitterly while the twins curled up against each other and dropped off to sleep.

Alice was determined to draw Colin out during dinner that evening about his encounter with Dot and Eugene. She had her opportunity when he remarked casually, 'The glasshouse looked very nice this morning, don't you think? I liked the lilies – Barratt's good at those.'

'Yes, lovely lilies. I tidied it up a bit, of course, for the visitors. What did you think of them?'

'Who?'

'The people you met this morning. You know, in the glasshouse.'

He grunted amiably and looked down at his plate.

'Quite grotesque, if you want to know. Still, it takes all sorts. But I was sorry to find that Jack had been there with them. He was in the garden, you know, very unsettled.'

So that's where Colin had gone after Dot had left, to Jack in the garden. And I wonder just what sort of a picture the boy gave of my friends and their behaviour? Not a very pleasing one, she guessed.

'The twins were there too, actually,' she said, thinking this would dilute his anxieties about Jack.

'Yes, I know. I saw them. But they're too young to worry about grotesque people.'

'Was Jack worried then?'

'Not after we'd talked, no. So there was no harm done in the end.'

Colin picked up his glass in a deliberate way as if that action closed the conversation.

'Harm?' Alice said, her voice rising. 'What harm could there be for him in meeting my . . . my visitors? They're not dangerous, Col.'

He drank from his glass and studied her seriously over the rim. Then he put the glass down, again with a deliberation that seemed to signify the subject was closed.

'If you say so, Alice. If you say so. But I'd rather Jack was kept away from strangers. He's a sensitive chap. You don't know how much he broods on things. But I know.'

He stood up and Alice looked up into his face. She felt chilled by the intensity of his feelings for Jack. But surely they were wrong? The boy was quite normal and ordinary. And meeting strangers and learning to get along with them wasn't dangerous, was it? In fact, the boy needed more of that, not less. How else could he become well-mannered and sociable? She opened her mouth to speak again but Colin shook his head to silence her.

'No more of this,' he said. 'Don't fret. I know what I'm doing. If you'll excuse me, there's something I must finish attending to upstairs. No coffee for me, thank you.'

He walked out of the room with a light step and she could hear him whistling as he went upstairs to his study.

Alone in the glasshouse, she mused on the fact that Colin seemed well pleased with their conversation at the table. But it had disturbed and confused her. It had been a way of dismissing her friends, she knew that. But there was also a subtle warning there about Jack and some nameless harm that threatened him.

A breeze had risen in the dark garden and it pressed the hollyhocks against the glass with sinister scratching noises, like fingers trying to force an entry to the glasshouse. Alice shuddered, pushed her untouched cup of coffee aside and stood by the garden door for a while, peering into the moonlit garden. The fountain was just visible in the distance. In daylight it always looked inviting and friendly with its jet of water fanning out into a mushroom-shaped shower of droplets which pattered into the pool beneath. But now, bathed in the silvery half-light and without its cascades of water, it looked forbidding and implacable, like a stone sentry at the gates of an enemy camp.

Alice was no more accustomed to listen to her own feelings than to anyone else's. Now, however, she could not ignore the powerful sensation of impending tragedy which emanated from the fountain. She tried to shake it off by turning this way and that to look at other areas of the garden. But always her eyes were pulled back to the fountain. It was not terror that gripped her, more a gentle feeling of hopelessness and inevitability, a tragedy to come – perhaps tomorrow, perhaps years ahead – that could not be stopped, that had to be.

At length her practical, self-regarding nature asserted itself and she told herself she'd be in no fit state for her trip to London the next day if she didn't get a good night's sleep. She turned her back on the garden and her mind to the treats in store tomorrow. There was to be a visit to the Adelphi Theatre and supper with Daisy and Julian at Hatchett's afterwards, and she had a new glittering sheath of a dress to wear. She shook a fist at the fountain and, practising a few Charleston steps on her way, she went to bed.

II

LOSS

Alice was half relieved that she heard nothing and saw nothing of Dot, or her friend Eugene, for the rest of the summer. During August everyone seemed to be away, in any case. Even Francis was somewhere at the seaside with his wife and daughter. She whiled away the hot days at Ballads by reading and attending to her clothes and sitting under a sunshade in a deck-chair on one of the terraces looking on to the garden.

She had thought about the whole family getting away to a seaside resort too. But Colin was not enthusiastic.

'It would be madness,' he said, 'to go away just when the gardens are at their best. Who would eat all those wonderful fresh vegetables? And use all the cut flowers? We just can't do that to Barratt when he works so hard all the year . . .'

Since Colin himself spent most of his time in the garden and grounds during the summer, Alice felt that perhaps it was more for his own sake that they stayed at home to reap its harvest. But it did not worry her. She was not over-fond of sun on her skin and sand in her hair.

It was nearly the end of August, on a sunny day with a slight chill in the air, when Alice sat in the glasshouse after luncheon feeling particularly contented. Colin had shared the meal. He looked bronzed and fit and was in a comparatively light-hearted mood that she played up to. They teased each other a little and she led him on to talk about his work in the garden. He had gone off again after the meal to ride with a neighbouring farmer, but as he went he had said gaily, 'See you at dinner tonight – and some music afterwards, what do you say?'

She had a Dornford Yates book open on her lap. She had read a few pages and decided that she liked its tone of high adventure and romance and its cast of well-born men and women, but she tired very easily of the descriptive passages and often turned her gaze from the page to the garden.

It was Jack's last holiday before he started boarding school. She could see him standing at the rim of the big, deep bowl of the fountain. He always seemed to be standing and staring at something, she thought. Why was that? Surely, boys of seven were more inclined to fling themselves about in vigorous activity? Shouldn't he have a bat and ball or something? Or be learning to ride a bike? That would be a lot more jolly than learning to play the violin or lolling about in his father's stuffy study.

She was distracted by the sight of the twins climbing carefully on to the low brick wall that divided the terrace from the expanse of lawn below it. Rose was smiling down at them as they stood proudly on top of the wall, their arms outstretched like wire-walkers. Phoebe was in the lead as they began to walk cautiously along the top towards where Alice was sitting just inside the glasshouse.

A cloud came in front of the sun and the light changed to that strange brightness that comes before a storm. Suddenly the air felt threatening and Alice's thoughts flew instinctively to the night when the fountain had loomed so menacingly from the shadows of the moonlit garden. She glanced at Jack and saw that he was looking yearningly towards the house, or was it at the twins, or was it towards her? From this distance she could not tell, but there was something so un-childlike about his deep, brooding stare that she felt a flicker of alarm and walked to the door of the glasshouse.

She had only just reached it and put her hand on the knob when she heard Rose cry out.

'No, Jack, no. Get back.'

The garden was full of menace now. The twins still walked along the wall. But their giggles were now sounding un-naturally high-pitched, like a record played too fast. The roses nodded in the slight breeze with a weird, rhythmic insistence; a flight of rooks, stirred by Rose's shout, wheeled and cawed overhead as if echoing her warning.

Then Rose was running, running full-pelt across the lawn, her apron flying high around her throat, her hands out-stretched. The twins tumbled in disarray on to the grass below the wall and Alice stood rooted to the step outside the glasshouse, one hand still on the knob of the door.

She saw Jack seated on the rim of the fountain's bowl. In painfully slow motion, he slid into the water. He was looking down into the pool as if mesmerized and he was smiling joyfully, as at a playmate who had been away and had come back.

Rose was still some fifty yards away from the fountain and turned her head towards Alice as she ran. Her mouth was opening and shutting with words Alice could not hear. At last Alice herself moved forward, but with nothing of her usual lightness. She felt herself putting one foot in front of the other with the heavy deliberation of a sleepwalker.

She saw Jack's head go under the water and thought, it will bob up again in a moment. A second later, Rose reached the fountain and flung herself on the ground at the rim of the pool. Both arms went in and she stirred the water frantically like someone at a wash-tub. There was a look of horror on her face as she called out to the approaching Alice.

'Oh, madam. It's all the weeds. Clumps of them down there. He'll be caught in them. But I can't swim. I can't swim . . . Where's Barratt, madam? Please, please, oh Jack, you poor mite, please, come up for Rose. It's so murky. I can't see him. He hates the dark. Oh Jack, Jack . . .'

'Get him! Get him!' Alice felt anger rising hot in her throat, at Jack for going into the water, at Rose for not being able to swim, at Barratt for not clearing the weeds from the pool, at Colin for not foreseeing the dangers. He saw so many dangers that weren't there, why not this one that was?

Yet she still could not believe that it was anything except an untidy, foolish incident. Soon, she was sure, Jack's head would break the surface, the smile washed from his face. Or, any moment now, Rose would pull her threshing arms out of the water with a cry of triumph and Jack would be held fast in her hands. Rose would say, 'There you are, madam, he's safe and sound,' and bundle him up to the nursery to be dried and changed.

But Rose was now in the water. Alice was amazed to see that it came up to her chin. The pool when empty had never looked as deep as that. Now she was badly frightened and found the strength to kneel at the edge and reach one hand towards Rose. Behind her, she heard the twins still chattering and laughing as they tumbled over and over on the grass as if nothing was happening.

Rose was taking deep breaths and pinching her nose between her fingers before repeatedly bending down into the water, sweeping her strong brown arms from side to side and gasping as she raised her head above the surface.

'Get him!' Alice said again. 'He went in just there, where you're standing. Rose, you must be able to touch him. What can we do? Barratt's nowhere about. There's only you, Rose. Get him out!'

Rose suddenly stiffened as her hands moved through the water.

'He's here. He's caught. Wait . . .'

It was raining now and no one noticed. Rose appeared to tug upwards and Jack's limp body was in her arms, just below the surface of the water. She turned slowly and, lifting him high above her head, as if she were about to don a large hat, she turned and placed him gently on the ground at the edge of the pool. She waded to the rim and clambered out, pulling the dead weight of her long, soaked skirt after her. As Rose went on her knees beside Jack, Alice was astonished to hear a loud wail and realized it came from her own throat.

Rose stared at Jack in disbelief and turned towards Alice. Her hair was plastered in wet streaks across her ashen face.

'Oh, madam. I'm sorry. He's gone. We'd better get the master.'

Alice wanted to say, 'Don't be so silly. He can't have gone. It's just a pool. He was only in it for a few seconds. Things like this don't happen.' Then she remembered her sense of foreboding that night she had seen the fountain in the moon-light, and she knew that it had happened. She looked forlornly at Rose and saw that she was weeping quietly.

'Isn't there anything we can do? Can't you make him breathe again?'

Rose did not answer. She had seen death before and recognized it. She stared again at Jack who no longer looked like Jack. He seemed smaller, and so grey. The worst thing of all was that she was quite certain that he had wanted to go deep into the pool and to stay there.

It was fortunate for Alice that her relationship with her son had been almost non-existent. There were not any of the wrenching gaps in life without Jack which most mothers would have experienced at the loss of a child.

There were no games and talking and sharing, no family jokes or rituals to be missed, no confidences to be remembered with pain or remorse. She did not have to bear with his vacant seat at the table, for he had never shared a meal with his parents. There was no keening over his neglected toys, his unused clothes, the signs of his boyhood that had been left behind.

For one thing, these had never been a part of Alice's life. Jack had spent all his waking hours with Rose and his sisters, with his father, or out by himself in the grounds. For another thing, Colin had, within two days of Jack's death, gathered up all the sparse evidence of his son's life that lay about the house, and had bundled it into a cupboard in his study.

There was the red ball he himself had played with as a child and had given to Jack, a half-sized cricket bat, properly fashioned in willow, two exercise books found among the journals in the drawing-room, one with hesitant drawings of pond life and flowers, the second with lines of copper-plate writing which Jack had clumsily copied in splodged, spidery loops of black ink. He snatched the child's wellington boots from beside the garden door to the east of the glasshouse, and his muffler from the hook above it. He had seldom gone into the day nursery or into Jack's bedroom while his son was alive. After his death he did not go into either room again. He instructed Rose to remove all Jack's clothes and possessions from these rooms and dispose of them in whatever way she wished.

'But Mr Whittaker,' she had protested, 'some of his things . . . it would be nice for the twins to have them. Couldn't they keep his toys? The little engine you made him. We mustn't get rid of that, surely? The twins are so fond of it . . .'

'No, Rose. It wouldn't be nice for the twins to have any of it. I want it out of the house. Be a good girl now and see to it.'

He smiled at her wanly and Rose felt a strong urge to comfort him with some kind words and a cuddle. How like Jack he was in this sad, wasting sort of mood and how she wished she'd been able to comfort the boy too. There had been something so doomed about him. She saw the same message now in his father's red-eyed, pale face and the mournful sounds from his solitary violin-playing in his study. If he were to become sick from grief, she thought, there'd be nobody but me to nurse him back to health. Madam would hardly notice there was anything amiss. This proud feeling of responsibility emboldened her to put her hand on Colin's arm and look with concern into his face.

'It's very hard,' she said softly. 'I lost a young brother once. It gets better, it really does get better.'

To her surprise he allowed her hand to stay there on his arm for several seconds. He made a slight choking noise and his eyes filled with tears. Then he patted her hand gently, took it up, placed it down by her side and slowly let it drop. He stared for a moment at the place on his arm where her hand had lain and then he looked at her directly.

'You really are a good girl, Rose. Such a big heart. Thank you. And now I must make quite sure that there's nothing left . . . there's still the glasshouse to check.'

Months later, he had a moment of horror when he put his hand idly down one of the settees in the glasshouse, between arm and seat-cushion, and came up with a well-worn domino.

He remembered at once how Jack had lamented its loss and, in a fit of pique, had pushed the rest of the dominoes across the table and on to the floor.

'Papa, it's no use. It won't come out right. There's one missing. Look, the circle won't join up. The double two isn't here . . .'

Alice had just at that moment come in through the open door to the garden.

'What a pity!' she said in a theatrically woeful voice. 'But it doesn't matter. We can soon buy another set.'

Colin had jumped up angrily.

'That's not the same. Can't you see it won't do? The boy wants the one that's missing, and he wants it now. Don't worry, old chap. We'll find it, you and I.'

Thus dismissed, Alice had left them to their search. But they had no success. Jack had never played with his dominoes again. Colin took the piece he had found too late and put it at the back of a bookshelf in his study, so that it was there but not there. And all the time and thought and stilted affection he had spent on his son he now turned on to Ballads and its grounds and on to the feverish records of all that took place within its boundaries.

What he was surprised to find, as he pored over diary, papers and maps in his study, was a rising tide of bitterness against Alice for Jack's death. It surprised him because he had no cause to think of Alice as in any way responsible for Jack when he was alive. So why for his death? It was Rose who took care of his daily needs and he himself who tried to steer him into the ways of men – or at least, into the ways of one man, his father. So there had been no need for Alice to do anything except agree to the major decisions about the boy's upbringing and to get something thoughtful and appropriate for his birthdays and at Christmas.

The present-giving, Colin reflected, had always been a dismal failure. Alice did not seem to enjoy choosing, wrapping or giving presents. He felt himself a good judge of this failure since his own mother had been quite the opposite. She would seize on any excuse for present-giving. He remembered coming-home presents, going-back-to-school presents, half-term presents and exeat presents, Easter presents, Empire Day presents and gifts for himself on his parents' birthdays. They were all small things, chosen with much thought, and carefully wrapped in tissue paper and then in an outer wrapping in bright colours.

He had them all still – the china horse, the pottery mug with his name engraved on it, the leather book-mark, the tiny compass, the locket with his mother's miniature self-portrait inside, the key-ring with a furry monkey dangling from it, the paper blue-bird on a stick that flapped its wings when you whizzed it round your head.

For Christmas and birthdays the presents were grander and covered in ribbons and bows, sprays of fern or holly, and always a home-made label with a little drawing on it and a loving message.

His father had been just as favoured. He could see his mother clearly in his mind's eye, her bulky body bent over the kitchen table, her ample chest straining the blue material of her painting-smock.

'I've just finished painting this picture for your father,' she said. 'What do you think? Will he like it?'

Colin stared hard at the small oil painting, desperately trying to find the right words. The picture looked rather blotchy to him, with a lot of lumpy bits of green paint sticking out from the canvas like terrible mistakes. Was it a big tree? Or was it the shrubbery at the far end of the lawn?

'How do you make those lumpy bits?' he asked, playing safe.

'That's easy.' She wagged a broad thumb under his nose. 'I use this. Just dip it in the paint and splodge it on. Effective, don't you think?'

'I should jolly well think so, Mama.' He wondered if he sounded insincere and steadied his voice. 'Actually, I think it's a ripping picture. Father will be very pleased.'

His heart sank, however. Father would, he was sure, show as much pleasure in this latest of Mama's gifts as in every other. 'You shouldn't have bothered,' he'd say, narrowing his eyes at it. 'We've got enough pictures in the house. And if that's supposed to be the shrubbery, you've put far too much foliage in it. Even in high summer I can see the south wall through it. You've made it look as if it completely screens the wall.'

His mother would redden and keep a fixed smile on her face, as if his carping left her untouched. But soon she could be heard making her way to the dairy between the kitchen and the glasshouse and emerging a few moments later with a solid-looking bulge under her smock. Then there would be the creak of the sideboard door in the dining-room, the clink of glass against glass and the gentle slurp-gurgle of liquid running from bottle to glass.

No one would go into the dining-room for some time. For his father, there was no interest in doing so. For Colin, there was an invisible barrier keeping him out. He was learning that people had their secret places where it was their right to be alone.

When his mother came out of the dining-room, slightly flushed and with a peaceful, accepting look on her face, everyone pretended that nothing had happened: no present offered and spurned, no hurt given or taken, no mercy dash to the healing sherry. His mother would hang the picture among countless others in a dim corner of some room, hall or stairway and she would try again and go on trying.

Colin wondered now what it was that made his mother push herself repeatedly against his father's churlishness. Was it love? Was she endlessly attempting to raise an answering affection from him? Or was she secretly delighting in these opportunities to show up his father's cold, guarded nature? The consoling drink would seem to be needed in either case, he thought.

Whatever her quest was, Colin had always felt that it left no room in his mother's life for him. She had an easy, chummy way with him and she was certainly a champion at thinking up little presents, but he had never felt that he mattered to her, and even less to his father. And now there was Alice and the well-documented evidence that he did not matter to her either. The important question was, had their son mattered to her? If he had, would he now be dead?

Although Alice had made up her mind not to grieve over Jack's death, she felt some pain at the obvious signs that Colin was somehow blaming her for it. When they were together in the evenings he often came out with a sudden question – 'Where were you exactly when he ... when the boy ... when Jack ... when it happened?' Or 'Rose was soon there, you say? How soon? A few seconds? More like a minute? And you weren't far behind?'

Alice gave him straight answers as well as she could, but would much rather have closed the book altogether on that sad chapter. There had been the years before Jack, the Jack years, and now she was ready to take up the years after Jack. She had no insight into the necessity of mourning. She believed that this tragedy, like Colin's experiences in the war, was best buried out of sight. But Colin seemed to want to ponder on the boy and his death over and over again. She had felt pity for him on this account until an incident in the late summer of 1928 when she was just beginning to think he had got over his bitterness towards her.

Alice had suggested that they ask some neighbours to dinner now and then. Partly this was an attempt to draw Colin out of his melancholy. He was always at his best in company. And partly it was to relieve her own boredom during the times she was at Ballads. These times were even more infrequent than ever, now that she had the taste for foreign travel, but the contrast between her two lives was sometimes almost more than she could bear. So she hit on this idea and suggested it to Colin. Though less than eager, he agreed without protest.

'We might as well,' he had said. 'There are lots of people around here who want to see the inside of Ballads. Why not give them a treat? Only don't ask any of that Deep Ditchling crowd, thank you.'

For their first dinner-party, Alice had invited a married couple from the next valley, together with their two un-married daughters in their twenties. It was a pleasant enough evening, with a lot of impersonal local gossip and some mulling over of public affairs.

The gentlemen had agreed that the country was well over the disastrous general strike of two years before and that there was now a feeling of hope and budding prosperity in the air. Colin's financial affairs were thriving without any undue effort from him, and their guest, a builder, was benefiting hugely from the ribbon development of new homes for the masses in the suburbs of the major cities. It was also a satisfactory state of affairs for Colin and his guest that the ownership of cars, buses, vans and motor-cycles was fast approaching two million, for both of them had shares in Austin and Morris.

Alice was lulled by the two men's expansive, self-congratulatory talk. Otherwise she might have noticed how Colin steered the conversation away from her whenever she tried to bring up the topic of current fashions in clothes, entertainment or society doings. She also missed the acceleration of the tic at his temple and the drumming of his fingers on the arm of his chair. So she was quite unprepared for the force of his hostility when it hit her.

One of the daughters, a pretty, pink, rounded girl with flyaway hands and a dimpling, coy manner, had caught everybody's attention by squeaking repeatedly, 'I say, I say', like a music-hall comedian.

'I say,' she said again when they looked at her expectantly, 'I know a terrific secret about Dr Brown, you know, the one with the house on the hill and all those children. I wonder if I ought to let on?'

She turned to Alice eagerly.

'We've all got to promise to keep it dark, though. Can you promise faithfully not to tell?'

Alice laughed.

'Oh, I don't know about that. Actually, I'm no good at keeping secrets . . .'

Colin's interruption came so quickly and so confidently one might have thought he had prepared it long ago and waited for just this perfect opportunity to voice it.

'Nor sons either,' he said. 'You don't seem able to keep them, do you?'

There was dead silence around the table. Then the girl bursting to tell her secret gasped and twisted round in her seat to stare in puzzlement at Colin. Her sister stared at her plate, her lips twitching and a deep blush creeping up her neck and face. Mr Wallis frowned in Colin's direction and his wife attempted to hide her embarrassment by busily straightening the cutlery nearest to her and muttering in a placatory way.

'Ah well,' she said, almost stumbling over her words, 'secrets, secrets, all of us have some, I'm sure. They're best kept in the dark. Idle gossip is very dangerous, don't you think so, Alice?'

She looked at Alice with compassion, willing her to ignore what Colin had said and put them all out of their misery.

For an instant Alice did feel the wound. She had an impulse to round on Colin and strike him. But it was unthinkable to let him know that he could hurt her. She could not remember his ever having tried before. If, this first time, he were to know how it hurt, that would be putting too much power in his hands.

She looked at him, her face expressionless, and spoke very slowly.

'I expect you're right, darling,' she said and smiled calmly round the table at the others.

They all relaxed and began talking at once, signalling to each other both their horror and their relief.

Colin, however, had stumbled upon a new game called marital warfare and found he had the taste for it. He was not fooled by Alice's calm, though he admired it. It was the 'darling' that alerted him to the wound he'd inflicted. He did not know that she used that term of endearment constantly with her friends and acquaintances. But he did know that she only used it to him when at the extremity of either anger or sexual passion. So he knew he had drawn blood and was half pleased, half sad, but, over all, rather satisfied. He quickly presented a new topic of conversation and the gossip about Dr Brown was never told.

*

The next time she saw Francis, Alice told him about the dinner-table incident. He was in the act of lighting a cigar as they sat over coffee in the Hyde Park Hotel Buttery. He held the still-lit match steady for a moment and raised his eyebrows.

'That must have hurt,' he said, making it sound like a question.

'No, not really . . . watch out, you'll burn your fingers.'

Francis shook the match out and flung it into the ashtray.

'I wish you wouldn't do that,' he said impatiently.

'Do what?'

'Pretend you don't feel things when you do.'

Alice laughed nervously.

'What makes you say I'm pretending? It didn't hurt. I do feel some things, you know that. This time I didn't.'

He drew deeply on his cigar and stared fixedly at its glowing tip.

'Why did you tell me then?'

'Because I thought you liked to hear about Colin, how strange he is and what he thinks about me.'

Francis snorted with laughter and threw back his head as if appealing to the heavens.

'Do I now? My love, he's of the utmost unimportance to me. You're important to me – but only when you're with me. And the other thing that's important is whether that husband of yours is beginning to lose his tolerance for your escapades and travels. The boy's death must have shaken him a lot, you know. Could have loosened a few thinking-habits. Have you been incautious? He sounds damned fidgety and hostile to me. He could be on the war-path, don't you think? I don't want anything rocking the boat, do you savvy?'

His voice was low and kindly, but his eyes were steely. Alice looked at him with her usual passive calm, feeling terribly alone.

'Don't fret,' she said. 'Everything's just the same. There's no danger. I'd love to leave Ballads. But he's not going to kick me out, you can be sure of that, no matter how much he knows or doesn't know. So you won't worry, will you?'

He appeared to have stopped listening and was looking round the room to catch the waiter's eye, meanwhile sucking furiously at his cigar. He patted her shoulder lightly without looking at her.

'That's my girl,' he said absently.

When he turned back he had his hand in his pocket and he drew it out sheepishly with a tooled leather box in his palm.

'Thought you'd like this. Open it later. Just a bit of frippery. It's seven years since we met, did you realize that? I didn't, of course, until Dot reminded me. No, don't thank me. Not here anyway. I don't want to look like a sugar-daddy.'

'You angel,' she said, full of relief that the threatened storm had blown over. 'You spoil me.'

'And I like it,' he said gruffly. 'Now listen, I have a few days spare next week. What about a turn or two at the tables at Monte?'

The waiter came with the bill and Francis, in his usual way, turned away from her before she could answer. When he had dealt with the bill, he seemed to have accepted that she was coming.

'I'll pick you up at the mews at ten o'clock in the morning on the fourteenth. Pack that long, glittery thing with the low neckline. And don't bother to bring any of that house-maid's caution with you. This time we're going all out to win. Come on, now, let's see if there's anything going on at the Glass Slipper.'

Alice followed him out of the restaurant, staring at his broad shoulders and thick, fair hair. I don't know what I'd do without him, she thought. Perhaps I even love him. But I do wish I could like him just a little. And why am I so frightened of him?

Alice saw nothing of Dot, Daisy and their circle of friends for over two years after Jack's death. They had all written polite notes of condolence and then, being quite unable to handle matters of death and bereavement, had remained silent, at least to Alice.

Once or twice, when she was at a theatre, restaurant or ball with Francis, she had caught a distant glimpse of what she was certain was one of Dot's outrageously flaunting hat-plumes or swore she had heard Daisy's distinctive throaty giggle. But she had not the confidence to seek them out and they, if it was indeed they and if they had seen her, evidently could not, like friends of the bereaved everywhere, decide whether to refer to Alice's loss or pretend it had not happened. So they kept their distance.

Nor was Alice any more involved with the twins' lives now that they were her only children. Far from closing the gap between her and her daughters, Jack's death had widened it and she was content to leave their care entirely to the nurse-maid, Rose, and to Cook and the two house-maids. Rose, who had grown thinner and more subdued since the accident, now watched over the twins like an anxious hen. She had moved into their bedroom from the tiny room she used to occupy next to Jack's. It was a move applauded by Colin. He was not at all willing to take any responsibility for the twins, day or night, and certainly not when Alice was on one of her trips to London or any of her increasingly long absences abroad.

He had written in his diary on this point.

'Today Rose announced, not asked, please note, that she's going to sleep in the girls' bedroom from now on. "It will be a proper night nursery then," she told us. "I can see to the fire in the winter, and to Martha's asthma. And in the summer I can sew in there till the light fades. I think they need the company, you see, even when they're asleep." What a homely comforting girl it is!'

'Yes, many of us "need the company",' he wrote. 'Truth to tell, I'm tired of these days and nights alone. Soon it will be Christmas and 1929 will be turning to 1930. But there is naught for my comfort . . .' He had liked the sound of that phrase and had written it three times . . . 'naught for my comfort, naught for my comfort . . . So, at least, the women in the house are all right. Alice has her comfort, Rose presumably has hers, and the twins have theirs.'

He had meant to write more on this theme but he became caught up in thoughts of the twins. He mentally groped for his feelings about them and then waited for a fondness, or some pity perhaps, or even a surge of resentment, to well up in him. But nothing came. Beyond Alice and the shadowy image of Jack, there was blackness. He neither welcomed their presence nor wished for their absence. They simply had no meaning for him. They were like figures in a distant landscape, too far away to be identified as loved ones or strangers.

He forced himself to think about them for a little longer, testing his numbness. The blackness stayed and stretched on and on into infinity. Before he shut his diary for the night and laid down his pen, he wrote in a careless rush, as if he feared the thought might be lost if he paused to shape it, one sentence: 'So they will have to find their own way.'

Rose's increased responsibility for the twins was entirely to Alice's liking too. According to Rose's reports, they were growing into the tiresome habits of catching colds and childish ailments, wetting the bed and waking up in the night with bad dreams. Alice believed that if these annoyances were not under the control of the twins themselves, they were surely amenable to some sort of control by Rose. But whenever Alice was at Ballads the nurse-maid insisted on trying to involve her, and she came to dread the occasions when Rose knocked at the drawing-room door and said firmly, 'I'd like a word with you, please, madam.'

'Martha was coughing a good deal last night,' she complained once, standing stolidly between the door and where Alice was seated by the telephone.

'Oh really? I didn't hear anything. I couldn't sleep at all last night, as a matter of fact. Had a ghastly headache. I would have heard her, I'm sure, if it had been all that bad . . .'

'Well no, madam, not bad exactly. But she does have this wheeze. I'm sure there's something that can be done. She gets very hot and upset.'

Alice's face wore the resistant expression of someone who believes that what is not wholly agreeable will go away.

'I'm sure there's some linctus in the nursery, isn't there? If not, get some from Jordan's in the village. And now . . .'

Alice reached for the telephone. But Rose was now flushed with determination.

'You don't think, madam, that . . . the doctor, perhaps? Shouldn't he have a look at Martha? I've seen other kiddies with that nasty sort of cough and wheezing . . . it does upset them. And it can lead to . . .'

Alice shook her head sharply and looked at her watch.

'Oh come now, Rose. We don't get Dr MacBean out for a child's cough. I shall be seeing him myself this week . . . these bad nights are no good for me. I feel quite exhausted. He'll have to give me something for it. I'll mention Martha to him, if that'll make you happier.'

'It's not me who needs to be made happy . . . it's that little mite.' Rose stopped abruptly, fearing she was bordering on what Madam called cheekiness.

'Well, thank you, madam. That would be nice,' she murmured.

As she left the room she was repeating the conversation to herself in order to recount it to her mother. Her lips moved while she mounted the stairs and she felt quite excited at the prospect of her mother's indignation. 'Her sleepless nights!' she would say. 'Is that all she's concerned about? Really! It seems to be all self, self, self with Madam Whittaker. My goodness, Rose, the sooner you and Arnold make up your minds to marry, the better for everyone . . .'

But not better for the twins, Rose told herself. There was nothing she would have liked more than to settle down with Arnold, who had been courting her so ardently for over a year, and she longed for children of her own. But I'm the only mother they've got, that's the trouble. Mixed with her feeling of pride at this knowledge was a disturbing sense of fear. She thought of Jack and his thin face with its shut-in look. There was no way that child could have had an ordinary long life, not with that strangeness in him. Anyone could tell he was doomed.

She stood outside the day nursery with her hand on the door-knob. She could hear the four-year-old twins chattering together in whispers. What was it about them, she wondered, that gave her a similar feeling? She did not find herself thinking about death or tragedy or anything dramatic like that. It was not that kind of foreboding that hung about the twins. It was something she could not put a name to, a difference in them both when they were together from when they were apart.

With each of them separately there was the normal exchange of hugs and jokes and chatter between the one twin and herself. She could play 'round and round the garden' with either of them, tickling Martha's soft, plump hand or Phoebe's long-fingered, thinner one, and every time end up with a laughing, warm child clinging to her and begging for more.

At those times, they were just like all the children in her own family. But that was only when the other twin was busy with something else or was elsewhere for a short while. When they were together and both occupied with the same thing, whether it was a meal, a game, a story from Rose or the three of them romping in the garden, then it was different. She felt unwanted and somehow cut out.

They constantly exchanged quick glances with each other, whose meaning she couldn't fathom. They touched each other often – a brief pat on the other's arm or shoulder, a quick clasp of the hands, or a gentle swaying towards each other so that their bodies made contact and then, apparently having found what they looked for, slowly drew apart again.

Rose was reminded of a blind man who lived in the village. He used to touch things as he walked along, a lamp-post, a fence, the wrought-iron gates of the houses, the water-trough at the edge of the green. She felt for certain that this was not to check that those things were there, but that he was. She had the same certainty about the twins' touching. It seemed to be that each was saying, 'Ah! You're there. Then so am I.'

Sometimes she wondered if they were still troubled by Jack's death, as she was. There were Martha's nightmares and wheeziness, there was also Phoebe's new terror of the dark and of water. But how could she tell what they felt about it when the whole house seemed to want to forget Jack ever existed and all his things were snatched away?

No one wept openly, or talked about Jack or made anything of it when his birthday came round. She knew Mr Whittaker had suffered but now, two years after the accident, he too was behaving as if Jack had never lived. And, though her kindly soul rebelled at the idea, she supposed that the best thing she could do for the twins was to follow in his footsteps and behave in the same way. So she did not refer to Jack, and nor did the twins – at least, not in her presence. So, if grief there was, it was a silent grief.

In March 1930 the silence that worried Alice most – that of Dot and Daisy and their friends – came to an end at last. Dot telephoned her at Ballads and quickly brushed aside the past two and a half years.

'I know you've been all right, dear. Such a long time – but I hear all about you from Francis. Wasn't I clever to bring you two together? Now listen, darling. Remember Eugene took those photographs in the glasshouse? Clever man, they were ripping studies of your twins. The less said about our piccies, darling, the better – all very waxworks. Several he took of the twins have just been in an exhibition. Great success – really very charming. He wants to take more. He says there's a future for them – and money for you, my dear – in posing for pictures for advertisements and things like that. What do you say?

Alice stifled her impulse to ask, 'Where the hell have you been all this time?' and managed a faint 'Sounds very interesting . . .'

'Right then, we'll come to Ballads for some more pictures and clever Eugene will tell you his plans. How about next Tuesday? I know Francis is in America – without you, such a pity!' – Dot managed to make it sound as if he were with someone else – 'So I know you'll be *chez* Ballads, won't you?'

Alice resented the implication that her life consisted

exclusively of fun with Francis and boredom at Ballads, and then realized it was true.

'Yes, fine,' she said. 'Come in the afternoon, can you?' Then, she thought, there'll be no clashing with Colin.

'No, Alice. It won't be the afternoon. We'll come as before at about noon. Don't you worry about luncheon – we'll bring something.' And she rang off.

At dinner the day before Dot's visit, Alice mentioned it to Colin, truthfully putting it as something that had been forced on her. Colin heard her out with a tolerant smile and then groaned.

'That vampire woman! I thought she'd flown off for good and sunk her teeth in someone else. And she's still got that pansy in tow? Well, you won't see me around tomorrow, sorry. I'll be over at John's with the horses.'

Alice gave a relieved sigh and hoped it sounded like disappointment.

'They will be sorry,' she said. 'Dot thinks you're the tops, you know.'

'Does she now? I wish I could feel flattered by that. But consider the source, consider the source . . .' and he laughed mirthlessly.

'She has her uses . . .'

Colin reached for the wine and smiled at her.

'Don't we all?' he said.

12

THE TWINS ON SHOW

For the twins, the day of Dot's second visit to Ballads was different at the very start from all other days. They were sitting at breakfast with Rose in the day nursery when Alice came in, said, 'Come with me,' and ushered the three of them into the bedroom next door.

She went to the wardrobe in the corner and took out several of the girls' dresses, laid them on the bed and stood looking at them, her hand up to her head.

At length, she picked up two identical tussore dresses with Peter Pan collars and patterned with sprigs of flowers.

'These I think,' she said to Rose. 'Please get them dressed, hair brushed, everything right by a quarter to one. You'd all better have lunch before then and wait upstairs. When I call you, bring them down to the glasshouse. They've got to look their very best. I hope you understand that, Rose, because it's very important. Someone's going to take their photographs. And they might have their pictures in the magazines. Isn't that exciting?'

'Yes, madam,' said Rose dully. 'Though I don't know what they'll think of it . . .'

'That has little to do with it, Rose. And I'll be pleased if you don't even suggest that it's anything but a very enjoyable treat.'

Alice looked at the twins for the first time since she'd come into the day nursery and put on an excited expression.

'Photographs, twins! Pretty pictures! A nice man saying, "Smile, please." Won't that be fun?'

'Why do we have to smile?' Phoebe enunciated the words

very clearly. It had the effect of making Alice's staccato remarks seem comical and patronizing.

'Because it makes you look pretty. And friendly. Which is how Mama wants you to look.'

Phoebe turned to Martha and stretched her mouth into a wide grin.

'You've got to look like this, Mart,' she said through gritted teeth. 'Smile please, smile please.'

Martha also opened her mouth in a forced smile and the twins stood facing each other, smiling ever wider and swaying from side to side.

Alice was unnerved by the way they contrived to cut out the rest of the room and everyone else in it. They were swaying and smiling at each other as if they were in a world of their own. Rose, however, was grinning at them indulgently and thinking thank goodness that, if this was an important day, the twins were in a happy mood.

'Well, I hope they don't carry on like that in the glasshouse,' Alice said mildly. She moved closer to Rose and spoke in a lowered voice. 'I think, Rose, we'll have to do something about this huddling together and day-dreaming. It's not right. They should be listening to us grown-ups, not to each other.'

'I understand, madam. But they don't see anyone much except each other . . . and me.'

Alice brightened and glanced at the twins.

'Oh, that's all going to be different now. Lots of people are going to be seeing them, just you wait and see. They'll be famous and everyone will know them.'

Rose sighed. That's not the same, she thought, as them having anyone really interested in them. It's not being looked at they need. It's being talked with and hugged and being made to feel they matter.

When Alice had left the room, Rose and the twins looked at each other expectantly. Suddenly, they swirled together like separate streams of water joining up in an eddy and danced round in a circle, clapping their hands and chanting, 'Smile please. Smile please.'

Rose's long hair bobbed up and down and her rosy

cheeks grew redder. The children's movements became wilder and faster, their chants reaching a high-pitched screech. Rose sensed a kind of desperation about them – the kind that made her mother predict that 'it would all end in tears'.

She stepped back, broke the circle and clasped Phoebe to her side with one arm, Martha with the other.

'Let's go in the garden. We'll play hide-and-seek, shall we? But we must go down the stairs like little mice. And when we're outside, we'll all be cats. Great, jumping, shouting cats, eh? How about that?'

Once in the garden, they found their mood less abandoned and their game of hide-and-seek began as a rather subdued affair of which Alice could thoroughly approve.

In fact, as she glanced at them through the panes of the glasshouse, Alice was feeling highly satisfied with the one feature of the twins that concerned her for the present, and, indeed, at all other times – their appearance. 'Dainty' was the word that best described them, she decided. Their bodies were neither plump nor thin, they moved gracefully for their age, their faces had regular features and their short, light-brown hair lay close to their heads like silken caps. When they become famous, she mused, people would point to her and say, 'That's the Whittaker twins' mother. Can you believe it? She looks only a girl herself!'

Nevertheless, she decided that there was room for improvement. I'd better get their hair professionally cut – no more of Rose's amateur efforts with a pudding-basin as guide. And perhaps they'd better learn dancing, and a little French, and have elocution lessons.

She caught sight of Rose stumbling towards the silent fountain. Beside its empty bowl, drained soon after the accident and never refilled, Phoebe stood with her eyes tightly shut. Rose's homely face was red with exertion, her plait of mousy hair loose and ragged. She won't do to take the twins around when I'm not here, Alice thought. Not for the first time, she speculated about making a change. What's needed, of course, is someone who can do more than see to their food and clothes – someone who can guide them in their education and manners and suitable behaviour.

The twins were running across the lawn towards the glasshouse, smiling eagerly. Alice waved and smiled back. There was no answering wave, but they continued to smile and then gathered speed towards her. She saw then that they were not looking at her. She glanced out of the panes at her side and saw Rose crouched in between the hollyhocks growing against the glasshouse.

'Seen you, seen you!' the twins shouted as they ran past Alice to Rose's hiding-place and fell on her in a heap, tugging at her arms and burying their faces in her apron.

Alice tapped on the glass. Three flushed faces turned towards the sound. Rose stood up and the children flopped away from her on to the grass.

'Not so much stimulation!' Alice shouted through the glass.

Rose looked puzzled. She came nearer and pressed her stubby nose against the glass.

'Anything wrong?' she asked.

'I don't want them all worked up and difficult.' Alice moved her hand up and down with the palm flat and spread out. 'Calm them down, Rose. Do something quiet now. It'll soon be time for them to change.'

Rose said nothing but turned back to the twins, and all three of them walked in silence past the glasshouse to the back door, keeping their eyes downwards and their arms tightly by their sides.

'Why are we going in, Rose?' Alice could just hear Phoebe's question but she failed to catch Rose's answer.

'Because it's gone cold out here,' Rose said.

Alice was just thinking about going up to get changed too when Colin came into the glasshouse, looking uneasy. For a moment she thought he had decided to stay in and join the lunch-party.

'Not going out after all then?' She tried to sound pleased.

Colin walked across to a pillar and stood with his back against it. He shook his head.

'No, don't worry, I'm on my way out.'

He looked round the glasshouse vaguely and then down at the floor.

'What's the occasion this time? You said something about the girls and some photographs?'

'Yes, it's nothing much. Eugene, Dot's friend, took some pictures of them ages ago. They've been praised. He wants to take some more, that's all. There's some talk of them being used for advertisements. It sounds like a useful idea to me. Something to keep the twins occupied and they'd make some money . . .'

'We don't need to put them to work, you know. They're well provided for.'

'Oh yes, of course. I know that, Col. But they're rather cut off here. They ought to be mixing a bit . . .'

'At five years old? And with the likes of Dot and her friends?'

Alice was beginning to feel irritated at Colin's unusual interest in the twins and at being forced to account for her plans.

'Why not? They'll be going to boarding school in a few years, won't they? They won't get on very well there if they've never mixed with anyone except us and Rose.'

Colin noted that she failed to answer his question about Dot and her friends. He felt scratchy and ill at ease and did not know why. It wasn't as if he at all objected to the twins having some life outside Ballads. But Alice was making her plans sound so reasonable and so beneficial for them that he thought there must be a catch in it somewhere.

'Who'll be shepherding them around to these junkets?' he said.

'Ah, that's something I need your advice about. You see, it will have to be me or Rose. But I'm just not sure that Rose is right for us any longer. What would you say to someone different? Someone with a bit more . . . well, I don't know exactly . . . more . . .'

'Breeding?' Colin's tone was wry.

'Yes, that's it. A better-class kind of person. More of a

governess, say. Less of a nurse-maid. Someone who can start teaching them what they need to know.'

'That being?'

'Oh Col, you know what I mean. Why are you teasing me like this? Is something worrying you? I mean nice manners. And speaking properly. They're catching Rose's broad vowels, hadn't you noticed?'

Colin jerked away from the pillar and turned towards the garden, his back to Alice. She had put her finger on why he felt so uneasy. It was guilt, he thought. Guilt at his immovable lack of interest in the twins. He had tried to shift it by this enquiry into what was happening today. But there was no changing it, he realized now. He hadn't noticed the way they spoke. He hadn't noticed anything about them for the past three years, nor even before that.

'No, I hadn't noticed,' he said. 'But then, I don't hear them speak much, or hear anything of them really, do I? There just doesn't seem to be the opportunity. They're your department, anyway – for the present. Perhaps when they're older . . .'

He paused, wondering just what part he would ever play in their lives and whether they really needed him to play a part at all. His head began to buzz with stabbing reminders of Jack at his side by the desk upstairs, studying the map of Ballads with him, raising his father's rifle to his shoulder with difficulty and squinting down the barrel, banging cricket stumps into the lawn, hurling a ball into the quince tree, walking beside him down the lane to the village.

The twins fitted nowhere into that picture. What could he do for them? And what could they offer him? If Alice had been a bridge to them, that would be different. But she seemed as unattached to them as she had been to Jack, as she was to everyone for that matter. This new plan of hers was obviously going to offer her more of what she wanted most – more people, some vicarious fame, more whizzing about with Dot and her crowd. And if it offered little to the twins themselves, at least it wouldn't harm them.

He spoke over his shoulder, faintly and without interest. 'Do the twins like the idea?'

'Of the photographs and all that?'

'No, of Rose leaving.'

'Oh, Col, you don't think I'm going to ask for their opinion, do you? That would be quite unnecessary – they're much too young to have any feelings about it. Besides, I haven't decided yet. I . . . well, I wanted to know what you thought.'

'Well, I've thought and it's immaterial to me what you decide. You must do what's best for them. And for you, of course. And now I'm off to John's place. We'll very likely go to the King's Head for a pie and a pint. There'll be plenty of local chaps there. Then we'll ride out. He's got a new mare he wants me to try. So don't expect me before dinnertime.'

He came near her as he walked across the glasshouse to the door and looked as if he would touch her. But Alice raised her hand to her mouth and blew him a kiss as if there were some distance between them. He pretended to catch the kiss in his hand and place it on his cheek. He felt glum and happy at the same time. She'd love me if she could, he thought. But why can't she? Why can't anybody?

Dot and Eugene arrived in a flurry of excitement, bearing a hamper of food and drink and exclaiming, with many 'darlings' and 'spiffings', at the changes Alice had made in the glasshouse, at her clothes and her hair, at the twins and at life in general.

Eugene took a few photographs of the wonderfully compliant twins and then pronounced the light all wrong.

'They'll have to come to my studio, darling,' he said to Alice. 'I've got the most splendid lighting there, masses of it. You come too and we'll have a lovely time.'

Dot fastened on to Alice in her old dominating way, promising invitations to parties – 'How we've all missed you!' she said – and engaging herself as agent to act for the twins' forthcoming employment as models.

'They'd make lovely bridesmaids too,' she told Alice. 'A lot of society brides who like a great procession of attendants just don't have enough young relations to go round. I'll shout it about that we've got the perfect pair here. All the clothes would be paid for, it wouldn't cost you a penny. And think of the glory! You see, Alice, it's not so bad having children after all, is it? Everyone will envy you for your precious little jewels. They'll be such a credit to you.'

Alice already saw herself in the foreground of all the attention that was going to be paid to the twins. She gathered them to her side as she waved goodbye to Dot and Eugene, keenly aware of the attractive tableau they made, she and her two little 'jewels', framed in the open doorway of Ballads. She led them back to the glasshouse, ready to be warm and jolly and have some games for a short while.

'Shall we play a game?' she asked them winningly.

The twins were darting round the plates of left-over food, taking little bites out of vol-au-vents, sticks of celery, and tiny, crustless smoked salmon sandwiches, calling to each other 'Try this,' and 'Here's something funny.'

They moved together as Alice spoke, brushing crumbs from their mouths in unison, and looked at each other in surmise. Phoebe nodded to her sister as if she had been asked a question. She turned towards Alice.

'What game?'

Alice's spirits fell.

'I don't know,' she said. 'I don't know any of your games, do I? You tell me what you want to play.'

Martha squeezed her sister's hand and said eagerly, 'Ring-a-ring-a-roses and all fall down. That's what we want to play.'

'And what's that? How do you play it?'

The twins stared at her blankly.

'Rose knows,' Phoebe said, sounding kind.

'Oh, I'm sure she does.' Alice's voice was sharpening. 'But you'll have to tell me. Come on now. Is it a hiding game?'

'No,' they said together.

'What is it then?'

'It's ring-a-ring-a-roses,' Phoebe said. A split second later, Martha echoed her. 'It's ring-a-ring-a-roses.'

Alice saw that the twins were shuffling their feet and very gradually drawing away from her, back to the table with the food on it. But they continued to stare at her in a calm, cool way.

'Oh very well,' she said. 'We won't play a game if you don't want to. I might as well fetch Rose. Then you can have some more of that food if you like.'

She hesitated and then bent her head down and spoke stiffly.

'Listen, dears, I do want you to be happy, you know. Your mummy wants you to be happy little girls . . .' She faltered, wondering what it was she was trying to say. She was planning a new life for them and she had no doubt that this was for their good as well as hers. But surely all children weren't this unyielding and so determined to shut a mother out? Not children this young, at any rate.

She was pulled from her thoughts by the touch of Martha's hand on hers. Both of them were standing close to her, looking up into her face with identical expressions of concern.

Martha tapped Alice's hand and said, 'Phoebe says are you happy?'

Alice was taken aback by the maturity of the question and the strange, second-hand way it was asked. For a moment she felt like responding as she would to an adult – to Daisy, for instance, or to Francis. In some ways I am, she wanted to say, and in some ways I'm not. But I don't know what happiness means. Who does? I was happy here with Colin, at first. But where's it gone? And I was happy with Francis too, and still am when we're out together and having fun. But happy now, right this minute?

She turned from the twins irritably.

'Now that's very precocious of you,' she said. 'I'm going to get Rose.'

The twins looked at each other and smiled with the air of having accomplished something to their satisfaction. They ran to the plates of food and returned to their testing nibbles in comfortable silence.

The day on which Alice and Dot laid their plans in the glasshouse marked the end of the twins' childhood. Their lives were henceforth dictated by Alice's slim leather notebook with the gilt-edged pages. In it she kept a note of all their engagements: the time, the place, the mode of travel, who was to accompany them and what they were to wear.

For the twins, that notebook became a loathed object, the agent of the enormous sea-change in their lives that forced them into adult constraints. There were no more romps in the garden, walks with Rose to the village, or games in the glasshouse and day nursery. Instead, all of the hours of every day were devoted to developing their public personae, preparing for outings or fulfilling the actual engagements.

Anyone concerned enough to probe beneath the surface of the girls' biddable and charming exterior might have concluded that they were suffering from profound shock and bewilderment. But Rose was the only person to be so concerned. She had sufficient perceptiveness to see that their lives were unnatural and unchildlike, but not enough authority to do anything about it.

What she did do was to become depressed. She turned more and more to her own family and to Arnold, her persistent and patient suitor. In her mother's indignation and in Arnold's loving arms she was able to forget the daily pinpricks of being relegated to laundress, sempstress and general dogsbody to the twins, their parents and the rest of the staff at Ballads.

'Rose will do it' was the cry at every turn and she could be seen, at all hours of the day and sometimes far into the night, running to and fro with piles of clothing in her arms, bent over the carpet-sweeper, packing and unpacking the twins' pig-skin suitcases, polishing shoes, ironing frocks or plying a needle by the light of the nursery lamp.

Day by day Rose's spirits fell and her link with the twins was stretched long and thin. Her face became pinched, her manner anxious or surly, and it seemed that the only times she showed any of her old cheerfulness was when Colin gave her a kindly word in passing, when the twins had time for a quick game or a story and when she was about to depart for her half-day off.

There had to be an end to it. It came one day when Rose went shyly to Alice and announced that she was pregnant and would be getting married to Arnold in as quick a time as the arrangements for the wedding and their married home could be made.

Alice greeted the news with unconcealed delight. She had made up her mind to get someone else to take charge of the twins but she was reluctant to dismiss Rose out of hand.

'I'm so glad for you, Rose,' she said. 'You should have children of your own, of course. I've always thought so. And the twins have got past the need . . . I mean they've outgrown you, haven't they? They're so grown-up now and have such busy lives.'

'Yes, madam.' Rose was thinking that they really hadn't grown at all in any way that mattered. They'd become more like little puppets, to her mind, rushing here and there to be shown off and paying for it with their nightmares and bed-wetting and sudden outbursts of tears and tempers, which no one else but she observed or cared a hoot about. Madam knew nothing of that. When she tried to tell her, she didn't listen. And if she had heard, she'd probably think it was all my fault.

'Will I be able to come and see them sometimes?' she asked, without much hope.

'Of course,' said Alice, much too quickly to mean it. 'Or they'll come and see you in your new home. You'll always be friends, I'm sure of that. But we'll just give them a while to settle to their new nanny. Then we'll arrange something. Leave it to me.'

'Thank you, madam. It would mean a lot to me . . . they feel like my own . . .' She stopped abruptly, seeing by Alice's unsmiling face that she had gone too far. She felt the tears pricking her eyes and prayed that she would not blub in front of Madam and perhaps make her feel that it would not be such a good idea if she and the twins remained friends.

Alice looked awkwardly over Rose's shoulder, avoiding her eyes.

'There's one other thing that's important. I think it's best if we don't make too much of your leaving. Why not pack yourself up and move out when we're all out on one of their London visits? It would upset everybody to spin out the goodbyes, isn't that true? It's best if you don't say anything about going, nothing about why or when. It would be awkward to explain about the baby. I mean, they could get confused as you're not married yet. Time enough later for them to learn about these . . . er, these little mistakes. What do you think?'

Rose stared at the ground, feeling lumpen and unbearably sad. The idea of not saying goodbye to the twins, not telling them she was going to be married and to have a dear little baby of her own that they could tickle and hold, not soothing their fears that she would be gone for ever – it all filled her with horror. But perhaps Madam was right. Perhaps they would fare better if she just slipped out of the way.

'Yes, all right,' she said at length with a deep sigh. 'If you think that's best for the twins.'

'I do, Rose, I do. Best for you too, and for everybody. Then I'll tell them on the way back. By the time we get here, they'll be used to the idea that you won't be here, not any more. All right then, I'll let you know a suitable day. I expect it'll be in a week or two. We'll pay you your wages for an extra month, of course. What a happy time for you, Rose, getting married and starting a family. What a lovely life ahead of you, eh?'

She had clearly meant her question to be rhetorical, since she turned away and picked up a magazine from the table by her chair.

Rose, however, still stood there, worriedly rubbing a hand up and down one arm and fighting back the tears.

'I'll miss Ballads,' she said bleakly. 'And Phoebe and Martha.'

Alice did not look up.

'No, no, I'm sure you won't, not with all you'll have to be doing, getting ready for the wedding and knitting for the baby and so forth.'

'They'll miss me. I know they will. I've been here all their lives.'

Alice flipped a page over sharply and bent her head over the pictures.

'Not at all, Rose. Let's not get too sentimental. They have a lot to do now and they've hardly seen you lately. They'll be quite happy to welcome someone new and forget . . . no, not forget all about you, of course not. But they won't be miserable about it, I'm sure.'

Alice raised her head and looked at Rose, willing her to smile or nod or somehow indicate that she agreed, Alice was right, and no one would miss anybody when she left.

Rose said nothing and made no gesture. She walked slowly out of the room and plodded upstairs, looking straight ahead of her with tears misting her eyes. The heartlessness of it, she thought bitterly. They'll miss me more now than they ever would have done before, now that they're little more than Madam's new toys.

It was three weeks later that Alice found a suitable day for Rose to make her secret departure from Ballads. She had instructed Rose accordingly and she and the twins, after a busy session at Eugene's studio, were travelling home in the new Armstrong-Siddeley with Barratt at the wheel.

They were about ten miles from home when Alice turned round from the front passenger seat and checked that the twins had not fallen asleep, as they often did before the end of the journey. They were playing cat's cradles with a length of wool and she had to say, 'Listen, twins,' before she could gain their attention.

'When we get home,' she said, 'you'll have to be very helpful to Edith. She'll be giving you your supper and putting you to bed. Rose won't be there.'

She spoke in a light, airy way as if this was nothing of any importance.

Phoebe and Martha were never fooled by a tone of voice. They dropped the wool and their hands crept together in a tight clasp under the tartan rug on their knees.

'Where's Rose?' they asked in chorus.

'She's at home, her home.'

'But it's not her day off,' Phoebe said sharply. 'She always tells us when it's her day off.'

'No, it isn't. And watch your tongue, Martha . . .'

'No-o-o,' Martha wailed. 'That was Phoebe. She spoke just then. And I nearly did . . .'

'All right, Phoebe then. You must watch your tongue. You could cut a loaf with it.'

Alice had a sudden recall of her mother using this phrase to her once. It struck her as extremely apt for the twin's aggressive tone of voice.

'Why?'

Alice had turned right round to face the twins now, so she knew this was Phoebe again.

'Why what?'

'Why cut a loaf with my tongue? What does that mean?'

Phoebe's head was held at an angle that Alice thought of as pert. She was trying to be reasonable and here was this sharp child winding her up to muddle and a certain headache.

'I mean that you shouldn't speak like that to me, it's very rude and sharp. I'm just telling you that Rose has gone home, that's all.'

Alice turned round to face the front of the car again. She glanced sideways at Barratt to see what effect the twins' behaviour was having on him. She assumed none. His eyes were fixed on the road ahead and his face was impassive as a statue's.

Alice took a small mirror out of her handbag and held it up to examine her face. She tutted at her frowning reflection and then noted that she could see the twins' heads reflected behind her own. They were moving rhythmically, as if in time to music or verse. She put the mirror down and turned to look at them. Like lightning, they both flopped back against the seat and looked out of the car windows on their respective sides.

'Well?' she said, waiting still for some response to the news about Rose.

They both continued to stare at the blur of the passing scenery. Neither moved a muscle.

She shrugged and settled back in her seat.

'Oh well, as long as you understand. About Rose, I mean. She's not going to be there, you see.'

A small quiet voice made itself heard after a long pause. It might have been Martha's. It might have been Phoebe's. Alice had no idea.

'Yes, we know,' it said.

There was not a sound or a movement from the back of the car for the rest of the journey home.

The twins claimed years afterwards to remember that car journey and their arrival home. Both of them could recall every detail as if it were recorded on film for all time. Often they had wanted to forget, but they could not.

As soon as the car drew up at Ballads they leapt out and ran past Edith at the open front door, across the hall and full pelt up the stairs. They ran past the day nursery without a glance and approached their bedroom with slowing steps. They stood outside it for a moment, each with a hand on the knob of the door. Then they walked in and saw at once that Rose had gone, not just for the evening, not just for a half-day or a day, but for ever.

The peg behind the door on which her apron always hung was empty. Her bed was stripped of sheets, pillows and blankets, presenting an ugly black and white striped ticking mattress to the new stark bareness of the room. For the twins there was nothing in the room except the absence of Rose. The walls, the ceiling and the floor seemed to throb with it. They stumbled rather than walked from one side of the room to the other, clutching at each other in disbelief and misery as they saw the mounting evidence that everything that was Rose had disappeared.

Her work-basket, her thick wool dressing-gown with the frayed cord, her bright-red slippers edged with fur, her family photos, the flowered draw-string toilet-bag, the big tortoise-shell comb with two teeth missing, the glass globe with the snowflakes that whirled when you shook it, the funny one-eyed bear that sat on her bedside table, the nightdress case like a pierrot doll, the stout lace-up shoes and the faded cotton dresses – all were gone.

The twins ran to the window as if they would see Rose's beloved form walking up the drive from her day off, waving her carpet-bag and pointing to it, promising presents inside from home – conkers or apples, fudge with raisins in, pink and white squares of coconut icing. The car which had brought them home appeared into view, moving slowly across the big circular space in front of the house. Was it to fetch her back? They watched with bated breath as it hovered at the drive entrance before turning left towards the garage. It was Barratt putting the car away. Strain as they might they could see no sign of Rose walking up the drive in the fading light, smiling towards them at the window as she always did.

They looked again in the cupboards and drawers in the bedroom, in every corner of the day nursery and in the bathroom, for any sign of her. Just one thing of hers left behind would be signal enough that she was coming back. But there was nothing.

The twins sat on their beds, facing each other across the narrow gap between them and tightly holding in some unknown feeling of frightening strength, searching for something to relate it to. But how does one measure loss? The one you are experiencing now is the greatest of all. Their thoughts flicked lightly over Jack's death, over lost toys, over injuries and illnesses and wants denied, and came to rest on the doll's house which had been spirited away in the night to be donated to the local hospital.

Martha looked round the room and said slowly, 'I wish we still had the doll's house.'

'And all the furniture in it,' Phoebe said.

'And Rose.'

'Oh Marty! She didn't say goodbye. Why did she go? What did we do?'

They stared unhappily at each other, weaving their thoughts together, busy and silent.

Simultaneously, their eyes lit up with certainty and they turned suddenly towards the heads of their beds and thrust their hands under the pillows. It was the place where Rose had often left little gifts and drawings, both to say 'hullo' when she came back from a visit home and to say 'goodbye for now' on her days off.

They found and brought gently on to their laps two small bundles wrapped in tissue paper. Inside each was a bright heart-shaped pendant of red glass, set in a silver-coloured mount and hanging from a delicate chain. With it was a simple, childish drawing of a face with tear-drops falling from the round eyes and the line of the mouth curving down at each end in despair. Underneath it were two big Os for hugs and two big crosses for kisses.

The twins sat for a few minutes turning the pendants in their hands and gazing mutely at the drawings. From downstairs came the muffled sound of voices and footsteps. Alice called from the drawing-room – 'Edith! Edith! It's time the girls had their supper. You'd better call them.'

Phoebe leant forward and put her hand on Martha's arm.

'Don't tell. Don't tell about these.'

Martha shook her head vigorously.

'No, we won't tell. It's a secret.'

'Rose is a secret too. She's a secret now.'

'Yes, Fee.'

Thus the pact was made and sealed, the first of many. The presents were a secret, and so was the pain of Rose's going. They had learned well the lessons of Ballads and everyone in it except Rose – that feelings were to be kept hidden and denied.

If they had had the words and the maturity for it, Phoebe and Martha would have described their new roles in the same way as Rose did – they had become Alice's new toys, her pretty puppets. On two or three days or evenings out of every week they were hustled, dressed, polished, groomed, tutored and transported for various forms of public appearances, 'education' and modelling.

They presented flowers to the guests at Masonic Ladies' Nights, curtsied to minor royalty at charity balls and bazaars, and shuffled down the aisle behind society brides. They attended Eugene's studio for hours of posing under bright lights as living proof of the effectiveness of a brand of children's shampoo, mild soap 'for tender skins' or cod liver oil and malt 'for glowing health'. They modelled coats, dresses, hats and shoes. They beamed over expensive toys and made big Os of their mouths at fancy biscuits or malted milk drinks. Whatever they were asked to do, they did, without fuss and in unison, keeping their eyes either on each other, on the camera or on the very important person to whom they offered flowers, curtseys and massive boxes of chocolates.

They seemed unaware of anyone else around them. Commands came from strangers who called them 'the twins' or, individually, just 'twin', and who never seemed to know their names. They were asked to stand here, walk there, sit down now, look this way, smile, say thank you. They obeyed at once, walking straight, curtseying low, speaking politely, sitting gracefully and always smiling. Only a very close observer would have noted that these engaging smiles never reached their eyes.

Fulfilling these engagements was not the whole of it, however. Dot was constantly on the telephone to Alice with suggestions for improvements in the twins' appearance and professionalism. Alice was happily in the swing of the whole venture and readily agreed.

As a result, the twins started on elocution lessons with a strident ex-actress in Pimlico and dancing classes in a Kensington studio run by an elderly noblewoman. Once a month they had their hair cut and crimped with curling-tongs by a 'coiffeur des enfants', otherwise known as Sidney Brown from Putney, in his over-decorated, over-heated hair parlour in Chelsea.

Alice was inclined to think that this was enough in the way of education and improvement, at least until the twins were seven. But Dot persuaded her that spoken French, social graces and general discipline ought now to join the repertoire and that it was time Alice found a governess-cum-nanny to take Rose's place.

In the event it was Dot herself who found the prim young woman of astonishing thinness who came to Ballads shortly after the twins' sixth birthday. Miss Jane Grice cast a long, cold shadow over the twins on the first day of her arrival by standing rigidly before them and demanding in a clipped voice to know *'Comment appelez-vous, mes enfants?'*

'En retard, s'il vous plaît, mademoiselle,' Alice said in a halting aside. 'They've had no French lessons yet, I'm afraid. So you see, there's a lot to do. And I'm sure you'll do it well.'

She felt anxious that this stick of a woman should be on her side. Edith and Peggy were now adequately managing the domestic side of the twins' lives but she hoped that Miss Grice would take over all the duller duties connected with their engagements – the ferrying to and fro, the record of appointments, the choice of clothes, the chaperoning at all but the more glamorous events – and she was pleased to see that the woman had a certain sense of style, spoke well and looked as if she could handle any of the twins' outbursts of weird behaviour or day-dreaming.

One merciful relief, Alice reflected, was that the children did not seem to be missing Rose at all. If anything, they had become even more obliging and unobtrusive at Ballads than while Rose was there.

13

DISAPPOINTMENTS

By the time the twins were seven their popularity as public faces was on the wane. As Eugene remarked in his waspish way, 'The bloom has gone off them.' He said as much to Dot and by agreement they gradually dropped pushing the girls as photographic models, bridesmaids and presenters of flowers and trophies, and simply left it to Miss Grice to arrange engagements when asked for them.

Alice scarcely noticed that the trips to London were getting less frequent. Miss Grice was now doing all the chaperoning for the appearances, the hairdressing and the dancing lessons and Alice herself was just as busy as she ever was with her own trips to the mews house and jaunts with Francis. The visits abroad were getting more frequent and longer, ranging from weekends at Deauville, St Malo and Le Touquet to a fortnight's Mediterranean cruise or several weeks in New York.

To the twins, their mother's life at Ballads seemed to be confined to hours spent on the telephone, evenings entertaining friends to drinks and dinner, and feverish parties in the glasshouse. When there were any visitors to the house, Alice invariably took this opportunity to get the twins down from the day nursery 'to show my friends what you can do'.

What they could do was to entertain the guests with performances of songs and dances. The twins looked back on these private performances with even more shame and loathing than they felt for their public engagements. The public ones did at least mean that they were in another world, among strangers, and could feel that their performances were a form of make-believe which had nothing to do with their real lives or their real selves.

Moreover, there was also a businesslike, matter-of-fact quality about those public occasions that suited them. They knew that the pats on the head and the comments about 'the two little dears' were part and parcel of the job. It fitted with the whole bogus, meaningless nature of things, like the patter of the magician at a children's party. They could take it or leave it, and giggle together about it afterwards to show it did not matter.

But their hearts sank when Miss Grice came to tell them that 'your mother would like to see you downstairs, and she says to put on your best dresses and clean white socks'. For there, in the glasshouse, where some of their rare moments with their father were spent, and where memories of Jack still lingered, and where Rose had sunk laughingly with them on to the roomy settee, there it seemed a kind of torture to disguise themselves with doll-like submissiveness and go through their 'party pieces'.

Alice would be sitting in one of the wide cane chairs beside a tall palm, her eyes flicking over their dresses and shoes and hair, checking that all was suitable. The twins, in turn, quickly took in the number of guests who were there, whether strangers or people they'd seen before, whether young, old, male or female, and afterwards they would compare notes in that clipped, knowing way that had become their custom.

'Let's have "The Keys of the Kingdom",' their mother would say, and they would obediently take up their positions opposite each other and launch into a reedy treble, accompanying the words of the song with stilted gestures indicating the turning of a key, a heart gripped by love or a request to 'walk and talk with me'.

Whatever the guests thought of this somewhat trite performance, they always had the good sense to burst out clapping at the end and 'ooh' and 'ah' to Alice's complete satisfaction. One or two of them would feel that more appreciation was demanded and would try to get talking with one of the twins, though this always ended with talking to both of them. For if anyone addressed Phoebe, Martha would instantly be close at her side. And if anyone turned to Martha, his or her mouth would scarcely open to speak before Martha had sent a lightning glance to her sister and summoned her to come and support her.

Nobody, the twins noticed, bothered to find out which twin was which or to remember, even if they were told. In any case, they had small chance of discovering the truth since, when asked, Phoebe would often say she was Martha and vice versa.

They had an instinct for knowing whether people were really interested or not. After Rose, there didn't seem to be anyone who was. So they sang their songs and danced the Sailor's Hornpipe or recited 'There once was a dear little doll, dears' because they had no idea that it was possible to refuse. But all the time, unawares, they were collectively searching for an ally, for someone who would strike the same warm, concerned chord that Rose had struck and, individually, they were looking, as all siblings do – and twins more than anyone – for any little deed or word that could be interpreted as favouritism shown to the other.

Back upstairs again they dropped their cowed, agreeable behaviour at once. Phoebe always pulled her dress off as if it were a live, loathsome creature that was clinging to her. She flung it away from her on the floor and swiped at it with her foot.

'That old man with the moustache,' she said. 'He kissed you. What was it like? Why didn't he kiss me?'

'It was prickly.' Martha tried to make it sound as if it was well worth missing. 'I was the nearest to him. That's why I got kissed.'

'He could have said, "Come nearer, Phoebe. I'd like to kiss you too."'

'Yes, he could have. Anyway, he called me Phoebe. So he thought he was kissing you.'

'So you didn't really get his kiss then?'

'No, I didn't.' Martha sounded pleased and contented. Making things all right for Phoebe was, indeed, her main pleasure.

'Is that all right now?' she asked hesitantly.

'Yes,' said Phoebe curtly, and then softened and said, 'Thanks, Mart. Shall we play running away?'

This was a game that took place entirely in their heads. They changed into their night-clothes quickly and went meticulously through the routines of washing, cleaning their teeth and brushing their hair. Then, wriggling excitedly in their single beds, they began the ritual.

'This time,' said Martha, 'we'll go to Rose's house first, if we can find it, and then get her to send us to Spain.'

Getting sleepier, they went through every step of the journey, the train-ride, the sea voyage, the possessions they'd take, the life and colour and music waiting for them at journey's end, the confusion and upset they would leave behind them at Ballads.

The pauses between speech grew longer and eventually Martha spoke in a far-away voice on the brink of sleep.

'If you don't mind, Fee, I think it's my turn to be the man in "The Keys of the Kingdom". I'm sick of being the woman.'

'Yes, all right, you can. That's if we ever do it again. We might say no next time and never do it again.'

'Yes,' said Martha drowsily. 'We might. But after I've had my turn as the man . . . And it has to be when Papa's there to see me.'

Phoebe made a last effort to drag her voice from approaching sleep. When she spoke it sounded in her own ears as if it came from someone else in another room.

'In that case,' she heard the distant voice say, 'you'll have to wait for years and years.'

It was true that Colin was seldom at the parties that Alice held. Only when she invited local people to visit would he bring his company and his charm to join them. But at those times the twins were not asked along to show off for Alice. In fact, they hardly saw their father at all and it was only when some guilt or tension in Colin made him seek them out that they had any of the attention from him that they longed for.

At these rare times Colin would suddenly dart from his

study when he heard them pass from their lessons with Miss Grice to a spell in the garden. Or he would stride into the glasshouse as they sat there alone, reading or doing a jigsaw puzzle.

'Isn't it time you girls told me about some of the things you've been doing?' he would say in a would-be jolly tone of voice. Their spirits always rose at these invitations and they would imagine that this dark-eyed man who seemed to crackle inside like a firework was at last going to move close to them and hug them and read to them and perhaps swing them round as they remembered he used to with Jack.

But he would always sit in the canvas and wood chair that had his name on the back and looked as if it belonged outside. The narrowness of its seat left no room for anyone to squeeze in beside him or sit on his knee, let alone two seven-year-olds. So the twins slumped to the floor at his feet, as near as they could get, and waited to be touched.

He always had something in his hands, however – a book, a screwdriver, a walking-stick, a letter to be posted, a box of shotgun ammunition – apparently halfway towards some other task or errand. They never felt that he was there especially to talk with them but merely filling in time on his way somewhere else.

So he did not touch them. Instead, he turned whatever he held over and over in his hands, alternately staring at his hands and darting quick glances at the twins which told them nothing. But the very tension in him was a magnet. They kept their eyes on him steadfastly and strove for words that would bring out a light in his eyes or one of his dazzling smiles. It took no time at all for them thus to develop the characteristic that dogged all their relations with men, the sense of responsibility for their happiness and the feeling of guilt if they failed.

Later on, they were to learn otherwise – that everyone's happiness or despair is of their own making. But that lesson took much longer to learn.

'Anything to tell me?' Colin would ask.

The open-ended nature of his question completely floored them. It produced too many choices. Should they tell him about Miss Grice having to make a frantic dash for the lavatory during an arithmetic lesson, bent double and with the agonized grimace of someone who had sucked on a lemon? Is that what he'd like to hear? Or would he like to know about Martha's tooth falling into the middle of her plate of tapioca, or the frog they found by the pond in the beech-wood, or the funny sight of Cook's long grey drawers prancing on the washing-line? Could they ask him why Alice went to London so often and for so long, or what he did in his study all day or whether they could come to the stables with him or what he'd do if they ran away?

Nothing seemed right. It was all too big or too small. So Phoebe would look at Martha, and then at Colin, and answer him in a semi-whisper.

'We don't know really. What shall we tell you?'

Colin would give one of his heavy, deep sighs.

'Well then, what about your lessons?'

'They're all right,' Martha said.

'And Miss Grice? Any worries there?'

'She smells of peppermint all the time.' Phoebe wrinkled her nose in disgust.

Colin tried hard to show interest in this one positive statement so far. He leant forward and smiled.

'Oh, does she? Does she wear peppermint scent, do you suppose? Or does she eat mints all day?'

The twins looked at each other and shrugged.

'She doesn't eat sweets,' Phoebe said. 'We don't either. We're not allowed to.'

'Quite right too,' said Colin, gazing over their heads to the garden. 'Got to look after our teeth, haven't we?'

The twins turned their heads and followed his gaze. Barratt was plodding round the rose-beds with a wheelbarrow, forking big loads of steaming manure on to the soil. Colin's eyes narrowed.

'I'd better have a word with him. I wonder how many loads he's using this year . . .' He stood up and seemed about to shake hands with the twins, and then he let his hand fall to his side.

'Time to get going,' he said briskly. 'Glad everything's all right . . . just come and tell me if it isn't, won't you?'

The twins' hands slid together limply and their heads turned back to Colin's empty chair as he walked to the garden door.

'Goodbye,' they said in unison. It seemed to be to the chair rather than to Colin. In any case, he did not hear it or wait for an answer to his question. As he walked up to Barratt there was only a shred left in his mind of the encounter with the twins, and that was a vague, half-formed doubt about whether they were 'all there'. Not a spark of intelligence in them at all, he reflected. And no apparent feeling for him. Completely wrapped up in themselves – just like Alice. What a bitter thought that Ballads and everything in it would be all theirs one day and that it would mean nothing to them!

1936.

Miss Grice's role had now switched to housekeeper and she was much in evidence at all hours of the day in every room of the house, picking things up or putting them down, arranging fresh flowers in a vase or carrying dead ones at arm's length on their way to the compost heap, rallying the ageing servants to efficiency and time-keeping, forever checking her watch and the calendar and the slates in the kitchen which carried neat chalked reminders of items needed to keep the household stocks complete.

She covered the ground by gliding rather than walking and used every part of her body so economically that it was difficult to detect her movements at all. One minute she would be just inside the door of the drawing-room and the next, without any noticeable effort or movement, she would be over by the window, her hands raised to draw the curtains together.

'She's a right creeper,' Phoebe commented to Martha. 'What I wouldn't give to see her fall over or jump in the air or do something big or surprising.'

She treated the twins with a secret kind of hostility. It reminded them of the attitude of most of the teachers at school. They seemed to resent the presence of the pupils for making their task more difficult, as if the school existed for their benefit and not for the children.

Phoebe kept wanting to say to them and to Miss Grice 'What are you complaining about? You wouldn't be here if it weren't for us.'

Miss Grice had, however, won Colin's respect by showing an idolatrous love of Ballads and its surroundings. In Colin's presence, she never failed to produce a fulsome compliment – 'Oh the grace of these wonderfully proportioned rooms!' – or some observation designed to display her own impeccable taste as well as her appreciation – 'I've always had a fondness for conservatories, you know, so very uplifting of the spirit. But your glasshouse is the *crème de la crème*, Mr Whittaker.'

To the twins, it all seemed a rather sickening attempt to butter up their father. When Miss Grice glided to the window in the drawing-room and put her hand on her heart and declared, 'Just look at the sun setting over there behind the hill! What a beautiful setting for this superb home! How could anyone fail to rejoice?', they looked at each other with silent imitations of heaving and retching.

Colin rose from his chair and went over to the window.

'There's nothing like it, is there? And this is what other countries want to take away from us – all this beauty and peace.'

For Colin was deeply worried. The world seemed to him to be full of tensions about to snap. Everything told him that chaos was about to come again. There had been the American financial crashes in 1929 and 1930 with the collapse of 13,000 US banks; in Russia communism was putting down its roots; the Spanish monarchy toppled in 1931; the sun of Japan was rising in the Pacific and the swastika in Germany; and Great Britain, bereft of much of its once great imperial power, and heavily in debt to foreign rentiers, teetered precariously on the Gold Standard and eventually lurched off it.

More worrying than any of this, as far as Colin was concerned, were the signals that mankind everywhere was becoming more greedy and violent and that the concept of honour was dying. The Lindbergh kidnapping, which had kept the world on tenterhooks and in tears, ended with the gratuitous killing of the child. For Colin, it symbolized the breakdown of decent restraints against man's piratical, murderous tendencies.

Then there was the suicide of Ivan Kreuger, the Swedish 'golden boy' of high finance, which lifted the lid on his long history of swindle and forgery. Like so many in the financial world, Colin had seen the brilliant young man as the white hope of the new-style capitalism, and he felt personally betrayed by his death and dishonour. He had similar feelings during the abdication crisis in 1936. How could a king, and a British king at that, give up all for love, he thought bitterly, when lesser citizens like Colin himself had to sacrifice their hopes of love in order to follow the dutiful path of responsibility and loyalty?

His dearly held values of honour, peaceful co-existence and fair dealing were rocked by these events and undercurrents. He had not felt so threatened since he was at the front line. This time, however, it was not life and limb that were at risk but, as he saw it, his home, his country and the way of life enjoyed by his family, his neighbours, his few friends, his staff at Ballads and his colleagues in the City – his whole world, in fact. There was no question in his mind but that a holocaust was coming. The tension in him, and the increasing conflicts in the outer world, demanded some such global blood-letting. He listened to no one as concentratedly as he listened to his wireless and he spoke to no one as despairingly as he confided in his diary.

So it was no surprise to Colin Whittaker when Britain and, a few hours later, France, declared war on Germany on 3 September 1939. He had long before taken his old uniform out of mothballs, tried it on and found no little consolation in the fact that it still fitted him like a glove.

The twins were home from boarding school for the winter holidays of 1940. It was a bitterly cold day, with all the paraffin stoves and electric fires that Ballads could muster alight in the downstairs rooms. Shortly before school broke up they had had one of their mother's postcards, which had now become almost her only communication with them.

'Am in Toronto,' it said. 'Plenty of lemons and onions here, of course. Will bring some back for you. What about you two coming out here for the duration? We'll talk about it. Keep warm. Love, Mother.'

'Lemons and onions!' Phoebe had exploded. 'Does she want us to be cooks or something? What about Canada, though, Mart? Are we willing?'

'It might be all right. We'd probably learn to skate . . .'

'But what about Papa? And Ballads?'

'They've got each other,' Martha said.

At home, with Miss Grice always on the move as if on little wheels and Colin striding about moodily in thick, polo-necked sweaters with his gas-mask constantly slung over his shoulder, Canada seemed rather attractive. Phoebe raised the subject when he joined them round an inadequate bowl-shaped electric fire at one end of the drawing-room.

'Alice said we might go to Canada, just while the war's on. Are we going?'

'If she says so,' Colin said wearily. 'I believe the Cotter children have gone. You know, the family at the old rectory. I know their father. A good man. He thought it best.'

The three of them sat in silence for a while.

Colin suddenly stood up and strolled over to peer into a bookcase with his back to the twins.

'I suppose you know that the army won't take me?' he said, his voice contriving so hard to be casual that it sounded as if he were choking.

The twins looked at his back and then at each other in surprise. It was utterly out of character for him to confide in them anything so personal.

They were both about to speak, their faces brightly sympathetic, when he turned round. His grim expression silenced them.

'It doesn't matter though,' he said. 'It's of no importance. In any case your mother needs me here.'

Phoebe could not stop herself exclaiming, 'Does she, Papa? How? She's hardly ever here.'

'Yes, precisely. That's why. When she is here, she needs me to be here too. And this house, it needs me. I have to make sure . . . I hold it in trust, you understand. It must be allowed to live out its life.'

The twins looked at each other in confusion. Their father was rambling in that far-away voice of his, something he was apt to do more and more these days.

He sat down, his hands dangling between his knees and his shoulders hunched. Martha noticed that his hands were trembling and she shot Phoebe a warning frown. Phoebe caught it and looked kindly at Colin.

'Well,' she said, in a low voice, 'Ballads will go on all right, won't it, whatever you do?'

Colin shook his head.

'No, nothing does that. Everything dies, you know, if you don't take care of it. If things, people too, are untended, unloved . . .'

His voice tailed away and the twins, seated on either side of him but at some distance from him, looked at each other over the top of his bowed head. His hair was still full and dark, with only the slightest greying here and there. Martha felt she would have liked to put her hand on it soothingly. Phoebe, as if sensing her longing, shook her head slowly from side to side.

'I expect,' Martha said encouragingly, 'that you could join the Home Guard?'

'Christ!' Colin turned to her almost angrily. 'Yes, of course. I could join Barratt and Rose's father and the youth who helps out at the grocer's. Fine! Fine! We could all stand shoulder to shoulder and protect our womenfolk and the Town Hall. If you don't mind, I think I'll get my fiddle. It should be here somewhere . . .'

He stood up and swung his head frantically in all directions, his mouth held tightly and his hands clenching and unclenching.

'God! Oh God! If things were only left where one puts them down . . .'

Martha jumped up.

'I'll find it. It may be in the glasshouse . . .'

'No, child. It's freezing in there. No one would have put it there. Besides, you can't go in there. It's not blacked-out.'

'Well, then,' Phoebe said. 'Perhaps it's in your study . . .' and she ran towards the door.

Colin was there before her.

'No, no. If that's where it is, I'll get it. Nobody's going in there. You know that . . .' and then, seeing Phoebe's downcast expression '. . . not even to help me find my fiddle.'

His gloom now seemed to have been ousted by his eagerness to find his violin and play it. He ran across the hall and bounded up the stairs.

They heard the key turn in the lock of his study door, the floorboards shake as he walked across the room. The twins waited, craning their necks upwards and scarcely breathing.

'He won't come down again,' Martha whispered, 'not once he's up there in his beloved study . . .'

'With his beloved violin,' Phoebe added.

Sure enough, after a short silence, there was the gentle sound of the study door closing and the lock clicking shut, then the muffled, thin strains of a rambling 'Humoresque'.

'He's all right now,' their nods and smiles told each other.

They knew nothing of what their father did up there in his retreat, except play the violin. They only knew that, whatever it was, it brought him peace. The whole house seemed to settle down with a sigh of relief when he was locked behind that panelled door or playing his violin anywhere. It was strange, they thought, what a sad, damp hand he put on everything and yet how electrifying he could be in his positive moods.

'Have you noticed,' Martha said once, 'how he and Alice hardly ever talk to each other? But they're always looking and noticing and sort of waiting for the other one to do something or say something?'

'Yes, and sometimes they look quite longingly, as if they were in love.' At fifteen the twins were much concerned with questions of love between adult men and women. 'But they never kiss or anything, do they? Anyway, she's got a man in London, that's obvious. But Papa hasn't got anyone else.'

'How do we know that?' Martha asked in a practical tone of voice.

Phoebe had an equally practical answer.

'Because if he had, he'd be a lot happier, wouldn't he?'

Like all daughters, they saw themselves moving into the space left by their mother's neglect. Now, while she was in Canada, it did seem that there was the opportunity to get closer to this sad, mysterious man. Even the hovering presence of Miss Grice could, they felt, be overcome if they were to get him out of the house for walks or engage him in conversation after dinner while she was busy 'putting the house to bed'.

So they took to approaching him after breakfast, before he could either bury himself in his study or go out on his own for the morning, or the whole day.

'Could you possibly take us to the stables?' they would ask diffidently. Or, 'Would you mind helping us with our holiday prep? It's a project on trees and Miss Grice doesn't seem to know much about them.' Or, 'Do you need any help in the garden? We're in the Land Army at school. We know how to dig.'

'Why?' was his reaction the first time they asked. 'Aren't you enough company for each other? It's a bit of luck, being twins, you know. I never had anyone for company.' And he hurried off, with the air of someone intruded on.

They persisted, however, and on one occasion Martha spoke in a rush before he could make his usual protests.

'We do have each other, yes, but . . . but . . . but we'd like to be with you.'

'Yes, with you,' Phoebe echoed.

He smiled at them, surprised and pleased.

'Funny girls,' he said. 'Come on then, this once. I'm off to the stables.'

As they walked down the drive and along the uneven track to the village road, no one spoke. Phoebe and Martha walked either side of him, matching their steps to his.

'Put your shoulders back,' was all he said. 'Don't forget you're a soldier's daughters.'

He cut them each a stick from the brushwood beside the track and carved their initials at the top. After a while he tucked his own stick under one arm and offered his elbows to the twins to link arms. With their gloved hands nestling between his arms and his tweed-coated sides, striding in rhythm down the lane, the twins were in seventh heaven and Colin felt proud of his dutiful attention to their needs.

It was not in his nature, however, to feel such an uncomplicated, sunny emotion for long. The notion that he was now doing 'something about the girls' brought back all his old guilt about how little he did with them at other times. He began to doubt the wisdom of changing the established order. What if they expected more? He was not talking with them even now, and he realized that he did not want to. He liked the silence when he was on his own, but not this accompanied silence which seemed to make demands on him.

'We can't do this often,' he said gruffly.

'Why not?' As usual, it was Phoebe who questioned. Martha merely nodded her head in agreement.

Colin dropped his arms to his sides suddenly, so that the twins' hands fell away from the grip of his elbows.

'Because you'll soon be back at school, won't you?'

The moment of closeness had evaporated. Colin walked a little ahead of them for the rest of the way to the stables. They closed ranks behind him, fighting against their disappointment at the way the atmosphere had suddenly changed, like the threat of rain at a picnic.

When they reached the farm Colin led them straight to the stables, where the owner was mucking out. While the two men talked together the twins moved from one loose-box to another, peering over the half-doors excitedly and stroking whatever part of the occupant was in reach. Some of the horses were hanging their heads over the doors. The girls took their gloves off to cup their hands over the soft muzzles and offer them wisps of hay. They stroked the animals' warm, silky necks and laid their heads against their withers, breathing in the comforting smells of sweat and straw.

'Don't they look kind?' said Martha dreamily. 'Look at those huge, dark eyes. Do you wish you could ride one?'

'I think I'd be scared.'

'Even if Papa helped you?'

'He wouldn't, would he?'

'Shall we ask him?' Martha looked towards their father doubtfully.

The trouble was that you just did not know which way he would jump. He might say, 'Righto, I'll lead you round on this quiet old mare.' Or he might say, 'No, horse-riding is not for you,' and hustle them off home.

So they stood there, yearning and undecided, until Colin ended his conversation with John and came towards them.

He seemed relaxed and leant across Phoebe to run his hand down the horse's neck. Phoebe had her hand under the horse's muzzle, wriggling her fingers against its soft skin.

Suddenly, he snatched Phoebe's hand away from the horse and held it firmly in his.

'What's this? This lump on your thumb? Tell me!'

Phoebe tried to pull her hand away but he tightened his fingers round her wrist.

'It's nothing, nothing,' she shouted. 'It's going down, honestly. It's much smaller. I've stopped ... I don't ... I don't do it now ...'

She looked at Martha wildly and then down at the ground. Her eyes started to brim with tears.

'That's from sucking your thumb, isn't it?' Colin was trying to sound understanding but his own mixed emotions were churning him into anger.

'Do you suck your thumb? At thirteen years old?'

We're fifteen,' said Martha glumly.

'If you've stopped,' Colin went on, 'it must only have been yesterday. Look at that lump! Why do you do it? What on earth reason could there be for such infantile behaviour?'

He knew the reason. Deep inside, he was no stranger to the longings for comfort and safety that had driven him so many times to call out silently for an answer and press his face into the pillow, or take the corner of a sheet into his mouth and draw sleep and sweet dreams from it. These insights were only conscious enough to rouse his anger and self-doubt, and he stared at Phoebe's hand as if it were an accuser.

Phoebe succeeded in loosening his grip and thrust her hands behind her back. Martha stepped forward with both her hands before her.

'Fee doesn't suck her thumb nearly as much as I bite my nails. Look!' She spoke as if she expected some kind of approval, if not for biting her nails, then for her championship of her sister.

Colin looked at her stumpy nails and ragged cuticles.

'Yes, you seem to have made a good job of it,' he said. 'Why have you kept this from me? You always look so neat and tidy. Lots of good clothes. You're well looked after, aren't you? Why these childish habits?'

'That's not all,' Phoebe said sullenly. 'Miss Grice says Martha's wheezing is a bad habit. And sometimes, mostly at school, we wet the bed, don't we Martha? Matron puts our pyjamas to dry on the bathroom radiator where everyone can see them. And if it happens on the dormitory floor, before you can reach the lav, then you have to mop it up yourself.'

'I expect,' says Martha, 'you didn't know because you haven't asked us. You don't get much time for chats, do you? Our mother knows but she doesn't like to talk about it.'

Colin turned and pressed his head against the wall of the stable block. The twins stared at each other uneasily, partly defiant and partly tearful.

'Does it matter so much?' Phoebe's voice was low and shaky.

Colin raised his hands and beat them on the wall beside his head.

'Of course it matters if you're not happy. Happy children don't suck their thumbs or bite their nails, or wet the bed, or keep wheezing.'

'But we are happy,' Martha said unconvincingly. 'We were

liking it here, with you, at the stables, weren't we, Fee?' She wanted to add, 'Only you've spoilt it all now,' but she felt this would be cruel.

Colin swung round and looked across the yard. There was a red mark on his forehead where it had pressed against the brickwork. He straightened his cap and picked up the three walking-sticks propped against the loose-box door.

'Come on,' he said. 'Let's go home. And there's no need to talk any more about ... about ... all this.'

As they walked home Colin reassured himself with the thought that they had each other. It wasn't as if either of them was an only child, as he was. Perhaps they didn't need adults to be so concerned with them when they could support each other. And if they were somewhat insecure, they would grow out of it, surely?

He regretted that he had raised the subject of their happiness or unhappiness. There was nothing he could do about it. It was perhaps a mistake for them to have had this walk together. It had been upsetting and made him feel helpless. He would put it all down in his diary and then it would be all right. Getting it down on paper would put everything into perspective – that always worked. He heard the twins chattering cheerfully behind him and told himself, 'There, I've no need to worry. They're quite ordinary children really. No parents are ever completely adequate. They'll soon accept that.'

14

COLIN'S SOLUTION

By 1942 the country had settled down to a restricted, grey, wartime existence. But this meant little change at Ballads. Peggy, the junior housemaid, had left to work in an aircraft factory, but Cook and Ethel stayed on, doing their bit for the war effort by knitting balaclavas, keeping cheerful and working wonders in the kitchen. Barratt bent his ageing bones over spade, fork and wheelbarrow more determinedly than ever and supervised the conversion of much of the walled garden to 'dig for victory' allotments for landless villagers.

Miss Grice's duties in the house were now limited to the early morning and a short period in the evening. For the rest of the time during the week she was busily engaged as general clerk and dogsbody at a 'comforts for the troops' depot a short cycle-ride away from Ballads.

For Alice, nothing changed. There seemed to be no shortage of any of the things that made her life worth living. She was somehow able to get unlimited supplies of petrol for her frequent drives to London. Once there, meals with Francis at restaurants and hotels, or in the privacy of her mews house, more than made up for the meagre rations of meat, butter, fresh fruit and real eggs at Ballads.

The theatres, night clubs and entire social life of London, far from being drained of colour and vitality by the war, were being whipped up into a frenzy of gaiety by the transfusion of new blood in the shape of visiting foreign servicemen and émigrés – French, Polish, Dutch, Norwegian, Belgian and, later, American.

Francis was as mobile as ever between his home near Dover, his London house and North America. He was having a good war. He always greeted Alice with an armful of nylon stockings, whisky, perfume and other goodies. When he was detained at home or on his travels, Alice found that there were plenty of attractive companions at the social clubs where she and Daisy and their friends acted as hostesses to Allied officers and, in a ladylike way, helped them to spend their leaves happily and their money quickly.

Moreover, Ballads in wartime had become more peaceful. When she did put in an appearance there, Alice found Colin so dispirited that there was little of the sparring of former times. They hardly talked together at all. When they did, Alice would muse on the shortcomings of life at Ballads and Colin would sigh and agree, his eyes fixed on some far-away point beyond Alice's head.

He felt he had one thing to be thankful for. The war made it unlikely that Alice would just up and go. All her plans, like everyone else's, hinged on 'when the war's over'. She had given up the idea of sending the twins to Canada for the duration. That had somehow just fizzled out. It was now her aim to send them to Europe to finish their education 'when the war's over'. She no longer enlisted Colin's agreement for any of her plans, but she frequently quoted the views of Daisy, the now elderly Dot or 'a friend in London'.

He would sit with his head thrown back against the chair, occasionally passing a hand over his forehead as if to still his troublesome thoughts, and would listen to Alice's pleasing, gentle voice saying the most unpleasing, harsh things and wonder over and over where he had taken a wrong turning and why his life was turning out to be so futile and joyless.

He attended the drills and meetings of the Home Guard punctiliously, with his gas-mask and his tin helmet and wearing an ill-fitting battledress outfit. But he hated it. The smell of real war was still in his nostrils and these smells – the dust in the drill-hall, the sickly, rubbery smell of the gas-masks, the fishy odour from the paste that held the strips of paper on the windows, the mustiness of the black cloth that preserved the black-out – struck him as bogus and underlined his feeling that all this activity was footling and pointless.

The sounds too – they were all wrong. War had meant the continual, earth-shattering pounding of big guns, the sound of heavy gun-carriages grinding against stony roads or making sucking noises in the deep mud. It meant huge, heart-rending cries from men in agony or on the point of death, horses screaming in pain, the piercing, defiant songs of birds fleeing from a treeless wilderness and, in the better moments, the wild rush of crudeness and laughter from men at ease after battle.

Here instead, all around him, were the whinges and whines of people deprived of life's frills and luxuries, the phoney bonhomie of his self-styled 'comrades in arms' on Home Guard nights, and the tinny clatter of the bucket and wheeze of the stirrup-pump as they practised fire-drill. It was all as far from his soldier's memories as it was possible to get. He was glad in a way that he had no sons to see off to the war. Jack would have been nineteen at the start of it, old enough to join up straight away. But the house and the village and everywhere he looked seemed to be full of women. He had never before missed the comradeship of the army. He missed it now. The thought that other men were locked together in a common purpose, that they had a point to their lives and could put aside all the confusions and disappointments of everyday life and relationships, filled him with such over-whelming envy and longing that he could scarcely bear it. He found that, once he was safe in his study, the tears came more easily now.

It was early September and the summer holidays were coming to an end. Phoebe and Martha spent most mornings in the garden or, if it were raining, in the glasshouse. On this par-ticular morning it was raining heavily. They were sprawled on separate settees facing each other in the glasshouse, each with a pile of their mother's magazines beside them.

Phoebe yawned several times, gaping widely and not bother-ing to cover her mouth with her hand.

'I wish you wouldn't,' Martha said crossly. 'It's catching – your yawning.'

'Don't look then.'

'I don't have to look. I can hear you. They can probably hear you in the village. You make such a huge groaning noise when you yawn.'

'Why don't you shut up? It's bad enough with all this rain.' Phoebe turned to look out of the glass walls to the garden. 'At any rate, Alice will get soaked in London.' She sounded pleased.

'No, she won't. She'll be in taxis all the time and doormen will rush out with huge umbrellas. She'll be all right.'

'Yes, have you noticed? She's always all right. Gricey said the other day, "Your mother always lands on her feet." It's true. I've never seen her put out or upset, have you?'

'No, come to think of it, I haven't. Do you wish you were like that?'

Phoebe went on staring out into the garden, not answering. But then Martha didn't need an answer. If Phoebe had disagreed she would have said so. The twins used silence in this way, for agreement or assent or 'I'm with you'. A lot of their communication wasn't verbal at all but a different kind of mental bridging.

Martha tapped the pile of magazines beside her.

'I wouldn't mind all this either. Ascot and Henley and Wimbledon and dressing up. I expect she'll make us do the season, won't she? She says that after the war they'll go back to presenting girls at court, debs' balls and everything. I wouldn't mind all that.'

Phoebe looked at her sister scornfully.

'I'd hate it,' she said. 'It's only a cattle-market, you know. Just to get you married off to some pimply youth. The sort of man I'm going to marry won't go to things like that. He'll be flying an aeroplane or writing poetry or playing a violin . . .'

Phoebe looked sheepish as she said this. She realized that Martha might think she meant someone like Colin. She felt they had to be careful not to seem to be too fond of him. One of the girls at school whose father was a psychiatrist said that it was neurotic to be too fond of your father. Girls who did that ended up marrying old men. The girl had said they were quite unable to love anyone else, anyone young.

'Not that I like violins particularly,' Phoebe added hastily. 'He seems to use his the way our mother uses aspirin – to calm himself or get rid of a headache.'

As she finished speaking their father appeared on the far side of the door to the garden. The rain was streaming off his heavy mackintosh and crumpled deerstalker. He shook himself like a dog and came into the glasshouse. The twins straightened themselves on their settees and looked sympathetic. They exchanged glances when they noticed how drawn and dejected he looked. It couldn't be accounted for by the rain. He liked the outdoors, no matter what the weather was like. In fact, a good storm or a foul day was quite a comfort to him, confirming the universal bloodiness of life.

'Anything up?' Phoebe so far forgot the usual inhibitions of the family as to express curiosity.

Her father stared in her direction for a moment, apparently not seeing her. The girls felt a tug of alarm as they watched him slowly take off his mackintosh and let it fall to the ground. He did it with such a degree of pain in his expression that he might have been sloughing his own skin. He did the same with his hat. It fell to the floor with a soggy thump, scattering little drops of water over the quarry tiles. He stared at the floor for a moment and then turned away from the twins to face the garden. He spoke slowly and as if something was choking him.

'I didn't think you'd be here. I thought you were going to London with your mother.'

'No such luck,' said Martha cheerfully. Then, realizing that her tone was completely out of tune with his mood, she added kindly, 'Shall we go away then? Did you want to be alone here?'

'Yes, I did,' he said bleakly. 'I have a reason.' He shivered and placed one hand flat on one of the panes of the garden door, as if to steady himself. He was shaking. The twins, round-eyed and anxious, walked slowly out of the glasshouse and could not look back.

They went into the drawing-room, where Phoebe kicked on the switch of a single-element electric fire and they huddled over its inadequate heat, rubbing their hands and staring into the slowly reddening coil of wire.

'There's something wrong, very wrong,' Phoebe said, shaking her head. 'He seems depressed in a different way, d'you think?'

'Yes, rock bottom, I'd say.'

'Perhaps we shouldn't leave him . . .'

Just then they heard Colin's footsteps coming through the hall. They both sprang from their crouching position over the fire and ran to the door.

Colin was at the foot of the stairs, staring at the portrait of Jack on the wall to his left. He gave no sign that he knew they were close by, but said firmly and clearly, 'Your mother doesn't know, she just doesn't know . . .'

Martha moved towards him, stopping beyond touching distance.

'Doesn't know what?'

'Yes,' Phoebe added. 'What doesn't she know?'

'She knows nothing. Nothing about the effects of what she is and does. This house, this family. It could have been paradise – for me, and her and all of you. But it's a kind of hell, isn't it?'

Phoebe glanced at her twin in alarm.

'I don't know,' she said. 'It's all right really, isn't it? It's not so bad. Some girls at school live in terrible places, houses on main roads with travelling salesmen knocking on the door every day. And their fathers have to go and sit in an office all day long and they never see them. Or they have dumpy mothers who wear frumpy clothes and their hair all frizzled.'

Phoebe was warming to the task of what she saw as encouraging her father out of his black mood.

'You don't have to feel like that, do you? Mother's very nice-looking and I've never heard her nag, have you, Martha? And you can go and ride or walk in the woods or have a bit of shooting whenever you feel like it, or play your violin or sit in your study.'

She stopped abruptly as Colin turned round to face her. He attempted a wry smile.

'I'm not a child,' he said. 'You really don't have to wheedle me like that ... You are the children. I'm not your responsibility. You're my responsibility.'

He looked at them unseeingly for a moment, his eyes blank. When he spoke again it was with such coldness and deliberation that the twins stepped back as if struck.

'That's if I'm your father, of course ...'

His words hovered in the air and would not settle. Phoebe and Martha stared speechlessly at each other and then at Colin. He still stood at the foot of the stairs, his brown, long-fingered hands clutching at the banister. He seemed unaware of the effect on the twins of what he had said and looked up without a trace of interest when Phoebe gasped.

'What do you mean? If? If you're our father ...?'

He smiled at her vaguely.

'You're the one who asks questions, aren't you? Well, there aren't always answers. You don't really need answers. It's not part of the deal. You must accept that. I have.'

The twins felt reason and truth slipping away. They began to wonder if they had heard aright, or if those alarming words had even been spoken.

'But, Papa, you said "if". You must remember,' Martha pleaded. 'Can't you answer that? It's so important. Please, Papa. We heard you say "if". You did, didn't you? Why?'

He smiled wearily again and moved slowly on to the next step up the stairs.

'I'm on my way up,' he said. 'You shouldn't try to stop me ...'

Martha clutched desperately at the only way she knew that might reach him, with an attempt at some kind of comfort.

'Perhaps it's a bit lonely up there in your study ...' She glanced upwards towards the locked door, trying as always to visualize Colin in that room, but doing what? Striding around wringing his hands? Sitting dejectedly in a chair staring at the wall? Reading, writing, playing his violin, cleaning his firearms, staring out of the window at the drive or the orchard or at Alice stepping into her car dressed up to the nines? Whatever he did up there, she felt it was always in a sad, despairing mood. Even the music that wafted down the stairs, though it might have been written to accompany some merry dancing, always seemed to emerge from his playing as a lament for something missing or lost.

Colin shrugged and turned back towards the stairs.

'Oh no,' he said. 'That's the only place where I'm not lonely. That's why I'm going up there now, if you'll excuse me.'

The twins gazed after him as he took the stairs slowly, two steps at a time in big, deliberate strides. The door clicked as he unlocked it and clicked again as he re-locked it on the inside. Then there was dead silence and the twins knew that until Miss Grice returned from work and Alice reappeared from wherever she was, they virtually had the house to themselves. They also felt sure that Colin would not be seen again until dinnertime.

But in that prediction they were quite wrong. They had helped themselves to some cold left-over macaroni cheese in the kitchen and taken an apple apiece from the larder and decided to go back to the glasshouse for a spell when they heard sounds from the study like furniture being shifted. There were noises of scraping and sliding and sudden thumps as of books or boxes being cast carelessly on the floor. They ran to stand in the hall and stare upwards towards the study. Occasionally the floorboards above them shook and groaned.

'What's he doing?' Martha whispered.

'Search me. I don't like it though. We can't stand here listening. He wouldn't like it. Let's go out . . .'

With some relief they snatched their outdoor clothes from the pegs by the kitchen and went through the glasshouse into the garden. There was no perceptible change in the ambient temperature as they stepped outside. The glasshouse was unheated and the rain that still fell outside was of the chilling, wintry kind that seems to pass through clothes and walls and windows. They walked towards the quince tree and stood under the meagre shelter of its leaves. They stared towards the house, shuffling their feet in the sodden grass.

'It's a good house,' Martha said. 'I don't see why he thinks it's so awful.'

'Oh no, it's not the house that gets him down. I think it's people. Alice, and Jack being dead, and us being, well, not quite what he wants.'

'But Fee, what does he want? Do you know? Do you think he wants our mother to be here all the time?'

It wasn't until years later that the twins noticed that it was always 'our mother' or 'Alice' when they spoke of her, never just 'Mother' or even 'Mummy', which was how all the girls at school referred to their mothers.

Phoebe laughed scornfully and rounded on Martha.

'You're so silly sometimes,' she shouted. Martha drew back from the naked look of anger on her face and then suddenly put her hand out to touch her sister's arm.

'He couldn't have meant it, you know, when he said "if" . . . if he's our father . . .'

'Oh that!' Phoebe winced and screwed her eyes tight shut. 'I'm not at all worried about that. You ought to have known. It was just one of the mad things he says. No, it was rotten of him to say what he did about me wheedling him. And then about me always asking questions.'

'But he didn't mean that either.'

'Yes, he did. He did. He's never liked me. He always looks at me as if I'd done something awful to him. Oh Mart, what did I do? Why do I make him so unhappy?'

'If you do, I do too. I get just the same looks . . .'

'No, you don't. I've watched closely and you don't.' Phoebe shook Martha's hand off angrily. 'Why do you try and pretend it's the same for you? Everyone likes you. If it weren't for you I wouldn't have any friends at school. Mary and Caroline wouldn't hang around if it were just me on my own. Still, I don't care. You know that, don't you?'

She swiped petulantly at a low-hanging branch and a shower of rain-drops fell on their heads and shoulders. Then she waved her hands above her head, laughing in a forced way, and vigorously shook the branches in reach. She began to chant hysterically, 'No, you don't care and I don't care. And we'll get all wet and rat's-tailed under the quince tree. Chase you to the iron gate, you don't-care girl . . .' And she launched herself out from under the shelter of the tree and started to run across the garden, looking backwards at Martha and waving her arms round and round like a windmill.

Martha brightened immediately and was just starting to follow her when there was a sharp explosive sound from the direction of the house. They both stopped in their tracks and looked at each other in surmise.

'Barratt's not here today, is he?' Martha's question was full of anxiety.

'No, he's not.' Phoebe turned to face the house and searched the façade for some explanation of the noise.

Without conviction she said, 'Papa could be shooting in the orchard.'

Martha didn't reply, knowing there was no need.

Slowly they started walking towards the house. They moved along shoulder to shoulder, each of them with an arm across the other's back. They fell into step easily, from daily habit, and kept their eyes fixed ahead of them, straining to anticipate answers to their fears. The rain had stopped but the ground was still sodden and their shiny-wet lace-up shoes swished through the grass as they walked. When they were near the glasshouse, their pace slackened and their arms fell to their sides.

'We'd better look into the glasshouse first,' Phoebe said.

Martha nodded and put her hand to her mouth.

'Only I don't want to. You can . . .'

Phoebe stepped up to the cold glass and leant forward to peer in. The dullness of the day made it difficult to see inside. She could make out most of the furniture, at least in the part of the room that was nearest to the garden end where the twins were standing, bent over in arcs like question marks.

'I can't see the far end at all. It all looks quiet and empty, though. I expect Cook's back and has done something daft in the kitchen . . .'

'Like her exploding jam jars . . .' Martha's voice was all set to sound relieved.

'But hang on! I can just make out Papa's chair . . . Funny, the back of it's turned this way. No, we'll have to go in.'

'But why do you suppose we don't really want to? There's something different, isn't there? What is it?'

'Don't go on so, Mart. I don't know any more than you do. We'll have to go in. And look for Papa and ask him what's happening.'

They had not far to look. But there was no possibility of asking him what was happening.

As they opened the glasshouse door they were assailed by a strong, acrid smell of cordite and a motionless bluey-grey smoke hung in the air. The shabby canvas chair, with Colin written across the back, stood at the far end of the glasshouse, facing the house wall. The twins clutched at each other desperately as they advanced slowly across the room, knowing and yet not knowing what they would find.

At first sight there seemed to be a bundle of Colin's clothes flung across the chair. The shoulders of his tweed jacket could be seen slumped against the chair-back and the sleeve on one side hung over the chair-arm, with a woollen-backed, leather-palmed glove dangling from its cuff. Trouser legs were just visible sprawled out from the seat of the chair and ending splayed on the floor. The clothes did not so much look empty as stuffed with something inanimate, like straw.

'Is it a Guy Fawkes?' Martha had hardly whispered the question before they both saw that it was not. Colin's head had fallen forward on to his chest and as they drew nearer they could see the dark stream of blood covering his neck and shoulder and seeping slowly down his chest and into a pool on the floor.

Mercifully, his head had slumped sideways on to the side at which he had aimed his rifle, so they were spared the sight of the actual wound that had brought Colin his longed-for oblivion. His right arm, his 'shooting arm', as he'd often called it, had dropped into his lap and his favourite light weapon, the ·22 rifle, polished and oiled so lovingly during the long hours alone in his study, had slipped to the ground between his outstretched legs.

The twins seemed to be paralysed. Once they had seen the blood and the gun they moved no nearer but stood still and stiff and silent. They dimly recognized something of the same blankness they had faced eleven years before when they found Rose had gone. They still had no currency with which to express grief or loss or shock. No one had told them what it was or how it could be used. They had been drilled into expressing pleasure and gratitude, polite concern and obedience, but the darker, 'inconvenient' emotions were simply unwelcome, unruly children, not to be let into the room however much they might clamour at the door. So they stood there, searching for some means of understanding what they were feeling, let alone expressing it.

Eventually they walked over to the settee nearest to Colin's chair and sat on the edge of it, gazing towards the back of his head. His hair still looked strangely alive, thick and dark, and as unruly as it usually was.

'What if he's still alive?' Martha said in a whisper. 'Shouldn't we make sure?'

'Call him then.' Phoebe spoke in a matter-of-fact tone of voice, sounding slightly impatient.

'No, it's no use. He never misses.'

They began to be aware of time and their surroundings again and looked about them. Once they had taken their eyes off the slumped figure across the room they found that they could no longer look that way. Their eyes slid over his chair quickly or switched to the opposite end of the glasshouse.

'We should put something over him,' said Phoebe. 'That's what's done when people . . . when they die. You cover their face.'

'Our mother might want to do that. Will she be back soon?'

'Gricey will be along soon. She'll know.'

As they lapsed into silence again they could hear the rain still beating on the glasshouse roof and somehow this released their tears. But it was a suppressed kind of sobbing that rocked them, and all the mystery and shock of their discovery was channelled into a vague, incipient resentment against Colin.

'Why didn't he tell us that was what he was going to do? If we'd known . . .' Martha's shaky voice tailed off into more sobbing.

'It wouldn't have made any difference. We couldn't have stopped him. Perhaps if Alice had been here . . .'

'She might have stopped him, yes.'

Now they had a more worthy object for their resentment, one that removed all their own feelings of responsibility and guilt for their father's unhappiness. It was blindingly clear. If Alice had been more at Ballads, if she had been happy there and joined in with their father's life, if she had given more of her company to the twins, things would surely have been different.

So, in the dreamy, if-only way that always gave them comfort, they fell to speculating what their lives would have been like if they had lived as they imagined other people did who had similar homes and backgrounds.

'It might have stopped him if he and Alice had been like the Mortimers when we stayed there, do you remember? They had a tennis court too but it wasn't all mossy like ours. Libby's parents played on it a lot and they had tennis parties, with lemon barley water in between games.' Martha's sobs had ceased and she gave a contented sigh. 'And they were always teasing each other – the whole family – and making rude jokes about gugging and popping and green smells. It made me go red, but I did like it. Alice and Papa would never do that, though.'

Phoebe had brightened too. She settled herself more comfortably against the back of the settee and closer to Martha's side.

'What I liked were all the funny games at meals – "My cat's an angry cat and my cat's a beautiful cat" and all through the alphabet . . .'

'You were good at those. You like words and English lessons and composition. I don't. But I liked some of the other games, charades and murder and playing tricks on Libby's brother when he was trying to kiss his girlfriend. It's jolly boring here, that's the trouble.'

They rambled on, laying out their fantasies of untroubled family life until Phoebe suddenly exclaimed: 'What do you suppose he was doing in his study? All that bumping about and scraping noise?' She jumped up and pulled Martha to her feet.

'Quick, let's see if it's open before they all get back.'

They skirted the canvas chair, keeping their eyes on the door beyond it. As soon as they were through the door, into the passage and past the kitchen, they speeded up and mounted the stairs in a breathless rush.

At the study door, Martha twisted the knob feverishly and pushed with her knees against the lower panels.

'Locked! Of course. He always locked it. It's no good . . . and I'm not searching through his pockets for the key, are you?'

'No need to, silly. He keeps one with him, yes. But haven't you noticed him reach up after he's locked the door? He always did. Look . . . like this.'

Phoebe stood on tiptoe and brushed her fingers across the narrow lintel above the door. A small brass key clattered to the floor.

'There, I told you,' she said, and pounced on it triumphantly. 'But, here you are, you can open it.'

Martha took the key and turned it over a few times in her hand, staring at it with a doubtful expression.

'Should we?'

'If we want to know anything, we'll have to. Go on, open it.'

Martha put the key in the lock with ease but paused before turning it.

'I'm just not sure,' she said, and looked at Phoebe questioningly.

'It's all right. We'll just have a quick recce. No one will know.'

Phoebe leant across Martha and put an eager hand on top of her sister's fingers clasped round the key.

'I'll do the actual opening, if that's what you're worried about.'

Martha shook her head, turned the key abruptly and swung the door open.

The curtains were drawn, muffling the sound of another shower of rain beating against the windows. In the dim light the twins could see Colin's desk. Its drawers were all closed, its surface completely bare. On either side of it, ranged against the wall, were crates and boxes, apparently filled with papers and books. From some of them, they could see the corner of a thick file or the spine of a book sticking out.

They stared round the room, narrowing their eyes and shuffling slowly forward.

'It couldn't have always been like this – so unused-looking,' Martha whispered. 'It looks as if he were packing ... like getting ready for a journey.'

'Well, in a way he was, wasn't he?'

Phoebe spoke in a whisper too. She walked softly to the middle of the room and stared round at the shelves, many of them still full of books.

'I'd love to have read some of these. Look at them all, Mart. It's not fair. If only he'd let us in ...'

She seemed to be emboldened by a sense of injustice and raised her voice to a louder whisper.

'Anyway, we might as well see what's in the boxes.'

Martha drew back towards the door, looking frightened and guilty.

'No, no! We can't. It's all so secret ...'

'Not now it isn't. Gricey and Alice will soon be ferreting around. I think we should be the first.'

Phoebe's voice was loud and firm now. She strode across to one of the boxes with a confident step and grasped a roll of paper that protruded from it. Quickly, as if afraid her resolve would weaken, she pulled back one of the curtains so that a band of grey, rain-dappled light seeped into the room. She began struggling to unroll the paper across the desk-top.

'You see,' Martha said sullenly. 'You're fumbling. It's not right – what you're doing ...'

'The blessed thing's so tightly rolled, it's like a spring. Come on, Mart, lean on the other end, then I can spread it out.'

Her tone of voice was so matter-of-fact that it soothed Martha's anxiety and she came willingly across the room to the desk. Together they unrolled the large sheet of cartridge paper and Martha, in her usual practical way, took two heavy books from a shelf and laid one at either end to hold the paper down.

It was clearly a map of the grounds surrounding Ballads. A square in the middle marked the house itself and neatly pencilled lines showed the drive, the terraces, the walled garden, the flower-beds and the vegetable patches. A circle marked where the fountain stood. There were myriads of smaller circles, spaced out in the area of lawns and flower-beds but clustered thickly in the orchard and woods. Beside every symbol were closely written blocks of figures and letters, some of them showing signs of having been rubbed out and rewritten.

The twins bent low over the map, their hair falling forward so that it almost touched the paper and swinging from side to side as they turned their heads to peer more closely at one part and then another.

Phoebe stabbed a finger at one of the circles.

'That's the new rose-bush a little way from the fountain,' she said. 'But what are the numbers by it?'

'It's the date, probably.'

'Yes ... 3.9.41. You're right. Barratt planted it last September.'

'So it's a kind of history. He put down things to do with Ballads. Look, all these tiny circles in the orchard. He knew every tree ...'

They raised themselves stiffly from the paper and pushed their hair back, looking at each other in awe. The room suddenly seemed to be full of Colin. They felt his absorbed, happy presence as he leant over the desk, his pencil poised to record every detail of Ballads' grounds and thus give it everlasting life. But why did it have to be such a solitary pleasure?

'He should have told us about it,' Martha said sadly. 'It needn't have been a secret . . . we could have helped.'

'Well, *you* could have,' Phoebe said curtly. 'I can't draw, you know that. And my writing's all over the place. But anyway, this can't be all. There must be something much more secret, something about people, or about himself. Perhaps *we're* here somewhere . . .'

She turned towards the full boxes stacked to the sides of the desk.

'Diaries!' she exclaimed excitedly. 'Mart, I bet he kept diaries!'

She was on the point of plunging her hand into the nearest box when Martha caught hold of her arm with surprising force and tried to pull her away.

'Leave him alone! You're always poking into things. Can't you just stop for once? He's . . . he's down there, alone. He can't stop you nosing into his secrets. But I can. And I have to . . .'

Martha was quivering with rage and tears and on every other word she yanked at Phoebe's arm for emphasis. At first it appeared that Phoebe would resist. She tried to pull away from her sister's grasp and then, suddenly, she went limp. She stepped away from the boxes and stood abjectly facing the desk, her head lowered and her shoulders shaking, and only then did Martha release her and step back slowly towards the door.

'It's enough,' Martha said. 'You know it is. I don't want to come into this room again for ages and ages. It scares me. We've no right here. Leave it all alone, Fee, please. Colin doesn't . . . he never wanted us here, he didn't want anyone here. You're rotten to go on like this . . .'

Phoebe shook herself, turned and joined Martha by the door.

'Yes, I know. I want to get out of here too. It was a silly idea . . .'

By now they were exhausted by shock and confusion. They left the room with dragging feet, locked the door and returned the key to the ledge. The picture of Colin, bent lovingly over the map of his home and his land, gave way to fears of what would happen when the other members of the household came back. They foresaw the cries of horror and the questioning. What time did it happen? Where were you two then? Did you find a note? Did he say anything beforehand? Then, probably, there would be muted expressions of concern – poor girls, what a thing to happen when you were in the house alone. Here, have an aspirin. No ifs or buts . . . you must lie down and try to put it out of your minds.

Standing outside their father's study door and silently imagining the likely course of events, they surrendered to despair and went to their bedroom, where they curled up on their beds and before long they slept.

When they were woken by Miss Grice at half past six, having slept for nearly three hours, they found that the commotion and quizzing was much as they expected. Only Alice and her reactions were missing from the scene. She was still in London and there was no answer from the mews house.

Colin's study stayed locked for a month, until one day the twins observed Alice and Barratt mounting the stairs with serious expressions and heard them go into the room. Phoebe and Martha held their breaths and strained their ears as they hovered at the foot of the stairs. Their mother and Barratt spent only five minutes or so in hushed conversation inside, punctuated now and then by the self-same scraping and bumping noises that the twins had heard on Colin's last day alive.

They grimaced at each other, fighting off the memories. The study door closed and the key was turned in the lock. The twins fled to the glasshouse and looked moodily at each other.

'Anyway,' Phoebe said, 'there wasn't enough time for her to look at anything. She's obviously not interested in reading any of the stuff up there.'

'No, that's one good thing. I don't expect she wants to : . .'

'Do you?'

'No, not now. What about you?'
'No not yet. Not for a long time.'

Several weeks later Alice employed two strong lads from the village to take all the movable contents of Colin's study up to the loft. She had been curious about what he did up there while he was alive, but now her curiosity had died with him. The boxes and the crates, the books and the papers, stayed up under the roof, unseen and undisturbed.

15

THE BEQUEST

The twins were the last to know that Colin had bequeathed Ballads to them. It took several months for the will to be proved. During those months Alice avoided discussing the future with them, pleading grief and complete ignorance of anything to do with wills and probate and inheritance.

'Your Great-uncle Frederick is seeing to it all,' she told them. 'We must leave it to him. But I can't see myself being able to keep up this huge place. We'd better get used to the idea of selling it and finding ourselves a nice, smaller home, perhaps in London . . .'

Uncle Frederick, however, was much more willing to take the twins into his confidence. One of the executors, and now a widower in his late seventies, he came often to stay at Ballads, intending to lend his support and administrative skills to the bereaved family. But Alice would invariably be off to London and elsewhere before he had been in the house a few hours, so he found himself more and more in the company of the twins and eventually, against Alice's wishes, he told them that Colin had left his money to his widow and the home and all its contents to his daughters.

It was a mild spring evening in 1943 and the three of them were sitting in the glasshouse after dinner. The twins found Uncle Frederick warm and approachable. They had grown fond of him and they trusted him. Nevertheless, when he told them the news they both looked at him in disbelief.

'Are you sure?' said Phoebe.

'Yes, is it true?' Martha added.

'Of course it's true. In a few weeks, you'll be able to see

the will for yourself. I would have told you sooner, only your mother . . . well, she thought it best . . .'

'She can't sell it then?' Phoebe jumped up from her chair and plonked herself down beside Frederick on the settee. 'Martha, you go the other side. Oh Uncle, you are a darling! Isn't he, Mart? You don't realize what a relief this is . . .'

'Yes, I believe I do know But steady on, girls, it's not as easy as all that. All the money goes to your mother. Which means that, unless she's willing to stay here, you just won't be able to maintain the place, will you?'

The twins put an arm apiece along the back of the settee behind him and gripped each other excitedly.

'Yes, we will,' Martha said. 'We'll find a way. We've got to. We can't give Ballads up. Never.'

'All the same . . .' Phoebe looked anxiously sideways at Frederick. 'It's a bit of a blow, about the money, isn't it? Didn't he leave us any?'

'Not exactly. A few hundreds each, just as a kind of gift. Not enough to be an income, obviously. But let's not worry about it. I'm sure he meant your mother to see to that side of things. She'll be very well off, you know. Colin was very clever with money and he had a lot to start with, from his father. I'll have a word with her. She could easily afford to keep Ballads if she wanted to.'

Martha stood up and faced the others on the settee.

'But she won't want to. She hates the place. Uncle, what can you do? Can't you make her give us some, just enough to keep us going here? When Fee's finished at college and I've left art school, we'll be able to earn money. Then we can be independent. Isn't there a way of hanging on until then?'

Phoebe sprang up and stood beside Martha.

'I know! Why didn't we think of it before? What about the money we earned when we were doing all that prancing about being photographed? There must be lots of it salted away . . .'

'If it really is salted away,' Martha said ominously. 'How do we know it wasn't all spent years ago?'

Frederick leaned forward interestedly.

'Tell me all about that,' he said. 'It sounds to me as if you might have a solution there.'

As the night darkened outside the glasshouse, the twins related the history of their public appearances, and how Rose left, and about their mother's absences and their father's strange ways, and their love of Ballads and their dreams of the future. Frederick, in his courteous, kindly way, listened with all his attention and with frequent halts to ask for further explanations or details. The twins wallowed in the luxury of being heard. All their resentments and sorrows and fears came tumbling out, filling the glasshouse with the ghosts of past emotions that had never had life. Frederick's conventional, orderly soul was secretly shocked by their fevered account of a family in neurotic disarray. And who would have thought that there could have grown such an enormous gulf between his nephew and the lovely young wife he had thought so suitable when they met, long ago, through his agency? Again and again, while the twins talked, he silently wished he had known more of this before, and that Clarice was alive to share these revelations, and that he was younger. Then he could have taken over the whole shooting-match and put what was left of the family on a straight course.

But he was old and alone now and tired. When, at last, the twins seemed to run down, like unattended clocks, and there was a long pause, he drew their heads to his in a warm embrace and stood up.

'I'll have a word with your mother,' he said. 'We'll straighten this out, never fear. We can't let this lovely glasshouse go out of the family, can we? Come on, now. Let's put out the lights and you can give me your arms upstairs. You're good girls, good girls . . .'

Phoebe and Martha lay wakeful in their beds for hours that night. They were almost as excited about Uncle Frederick's interest and championship as they were about having Ballads as their own.

'Wasn't it marvellous,' Martha said, 'when he called us good girls?'

'Yes. No one's ever done that before.'

'Rose might have . . .' Martha's voice sounded dreamy.

'She probably did. I don't remember. But I suppose it's a bit childish to get so pleased about it at our age. We've got to be more grown-up now, Mart, don't you think? Soon, we won't be together all the time . . .'

'Do dry up, Fee.' Martha sat up and thumped her pillow, then slumped down in her bed, her back to Phoebe. 'You don't have to get all serious about it. Let's not talk about that until tomorrow.'

'Yes, but . . .'

'Oh, you do go on sometimes.' Martha sounded so un-characteristically grumpy that Phoebe knew she was anxious about their approaching separation.

'And you worry too much,' she said gently. 'It'll be all right, Mart. We'll have the holidays. And you'll come up and see me at Cambridge, won't you?'

'Shut up. Just shut up, will you? I want to go to sleep.'

They both lay silent then, their eyes wide open, trying to imagine what it was going to be like to be apart for the first time in their lives. But that was another experience for which they had no preparation, no emotional language and no bench-marks. They strained their imaginations in vain until sleep came to the rescue.

The twins never knew how it was managed, but Uncle Frederick evidently 'had a word' with their mother and reassured them that a monthly sum would be going into their bank accounts for their keep and for the expenses of running Ballads.

'Your mother apparently has . . . er . . . a further source of income,' he had added in some embarrassment. 'Even if she leaves, Ballads will be quite safe, at least for the next three years. But there'll have to be some changes.'

The changes were completely to the twins' liking. Miss Grice left. Ethel was promoted to housekeeper, cook and maid-of-all-work. Cook and Barratt were pensioned off. A jobbing gardener and a cleaning lady from Westknoll were engaged to come to Ballads three days a week. Three of the seven bedrooms were relegated to store-rooms, draped in dust-sheets and kept closed and unused. The dining-room was also closed and meals taken in the breakfast-room, the glasshouse or the kitchen. And Uncle Frederick, by frequent letters from his home in Bath, kept a weather eye on the family's financial affairs.

As everyone had expected, Alice's absences became more and more frequent, so much so that it became the twins' natural habit to refer to her short stays at Ballads as 'visits' and her absences as merely periods in between them. To their relief, she made no attempt to control or oversee their lives and related to them more as a casual friend of the same age than as a parent or guide. On one point, however, she was unusually insistent and, on the rare occasions when the three of them talked together, she kept returning to it.

'If you want to hang on to Ballads,' she said brightly, 'your only hope is a couple of rich husbands. No, don't look so shocked. It's never been easy for women to get along without a man's help, take my word for it. And it's going to be harder when the war's over. Everything's changing. People with money and big houses are going to be tightening their belts. Uncle Francis says the socialists will be in power soon and that's not going to be at all comfortable for people like us. So you keep yourselves looking nice and mixing with the right people, then you'll be all right.'

At the time, the twins had to admit that this approach to life sounded rather practical. It was only later, when Alice tried to manipulate them into meetings with the callow or over-sophisticated sons of her friends in Madam Dot's social circle, that their longings for independence and for romance made them reject both her advice and her match-making and follow their own wayward paths to love.

What they had noticed during these conversations was that Alice referred more often to 'Uncle Francis'. With nothing specifically said about him, she was obviously now willing for it to be known that he was an important part of her life. The twins guessed that Uncle Frederick knew all about him – he must have meant Francis when he awkwardly mentioned

Alice's 'further source of income'. They had had a sheltered upbringing at home but their days at boarding school had rid them of any trace of naivety about what went on between men and women. This unknown Francis was quite clearly her lover, protector and keeper, and had been for years. And, in Phoebe's mocking words, she was his 'mistress, kept woman, demi-mondaine and concubine'.

They had no moral view on this state of affairs. But they had a huge emotional investment in knowing what he was like and how he would react to them. They therefore often speculated on whether their mother's greater openness about him was leading up to a meeting with 'Uncle Francis'.

Later that summer, shortly before the twins were to go their separate ways, Alice brought their speculations to an end.

They had both been working in the garden and came in at dusk to find their mother at the writing-table in the drawing-room, bent over some papers.

'Well,' she said, without looking up, 'had some nice fresh air, have you?'

The twins exchanged glances and shrugged.

'We've been pruning the roses,' Martha said.

Phoebe added sharply, 'Yes, someone's got to do it.'

Alice looked up impatiently and then gasped.

'Perhaps they have. But not you two. Just look at your hands! Scratched to hell! Why don't you wear gloves if you must go grubbing in the garden? This is too bad of you. Tomorrow – I was just going to tell you – is rather a special day. Uncle Francis is coming here. I'd hoped you'd be particularly well turned out . . .'

'Like horses, you mean?' Phoebe laughed and looked at Martha for approval. 'And why do we have to call him 'Uncle Francis'? Is he related to us?'

Alice kept her face blank. She had long ago learned not to rise to Phoebe's bait or get drawn into any battles of wits.

'He wants to meet you,' Alice went on. 'And I'm sure you want to meet him. He's done a lot for you that you don't know about. He's always advised me about your education, for instance. You' – she looked at Phoebe – 'wouldn't be going to Cambridge if he hadn't shown the way long ago and . . .'

'But Mother, how? It was me who chose all my subjects for School Cert. and Matric. Me and Miss Fisher, when I was in the Fifth. I don't see how he had anything to do with it. Anyway, you and I never talked about it so how could he have known what I wanted?'

'I'm not going to argue about it. Just take it from me that since your father died, Francis has been a Rock of Gibraltar, an absolute rock. I don't know how I would have managed without his help. It's not easy, you know, bringing up a family on your own. Especially out here in the sticks.'

'Yes, *we're* stuck out here all right.' Phoebe was struggling to sound straight and logical rather than aggrieved. 'But you're not. We hardly see you at all.'

'And I don't suppose that upsets you much,' Alice said lightly. She turned to Martha. 'Does it, now?'

Martha blushed and fidgeted, a sure sign to Phoebe that she was searching for something kind and placatory to say.

'It would be nice if we could see you more often,' she said, avoiding Alice's eyes. 'We're managing quite well, though, here on our own.'

Alice turned to Phoebe with an air of triumph.

'You see, your sister is quite content with things as they are. And she's obviously keen to meet Francis . . .'

'But I didn't say . . .' Martha thought better of her protest and looked at Phoebe helplessly, fearing she had somehow betrayed her.

Alice turned back to the desk and stabbed her finger on the open page of her engagement book.

'Anyway, there it is,' she said. 'Francis is coming tomorrow and he'll take us all out to lunch. Then you and he can get to know each other. So let's have a bright face on things straight away. You can go up now and sort out what you're going to wear. Your blue suits would be suitable, I think. And better get all that earth from under your nails. A hair-wash wouldn't come amiss, either. You look like haystacks. You'll see, we'll have great fun.'

She glanced at them with a hopeful expression and snapped the engagement book shut.

'Right, we'll do all that,' said Phoebe resignedly. 'But, Mother, must we wear the same things? Martha looks all right in her blue suit but I look terrible in mine. Couldn't I wear my red wool dress? Please?'

Alice waved her hand dismissively.

'Nonsense. You both look very nice in those suits. And, after all, you are twins and there's no reason why you should pretend you're not.'

'But we're quite different,' Phoebe said desperately. 'Haven't you noticed?'

'No, I can't say I have. And I'm sure no one else has. And I think you're getting rather too argumentative. What you wear is only a minor matter . . .'

'In that case, why can't I wear the dress?'

Alice sighed deeply and looked at Martha as if for sympathy.

'Because I want you both to wear the same, that's why. Francis will be expecting it. He's known all about you from the day you were born. Really, I don't see why we have to talk about it any more. You'd better go upstairs now . . .' She reached towards the telephone on the desk and turned her back on the girls. 'Let's see now, where did I put my phone-numbers book . . .?'

'It's here, Mother.' Martha reached across and picked up the book from the back of the desk. She handed it to Alice with an apologetic glance at Phoebe. As they left the room, Phoebe hissed at her sister, 'Creep, creep, crawl, crawl,' and they jostled each other through the door and up the stairs, laughing and staggering like drunks.

Up in their room, the twins shuffled through their clothes in their separate wardrobes, whisking the hangers along the brass rail with loud scraping noises.

Martha's voice came faintly from the depths of her wardrobe.

'I could wear my red wool dress if you like, Fee.'

'That's white of you but it's not the point, is it? When are we going to be treated like two different people instead of just "the twins", like one person, or two stuck together? That's what gets at me. She doesn't even use our names, does she? Not ever.'

Martha looked across at Phoebe with a thoughtful expression.

'You're right,' she said. 'That's true. Do you think she knows which is which?'

'Wouldn't surprise me if she didn't. Except I'm sure she knows yours all right. She's always looking at you in quite a friendly way, really. I've often noticed that.'

'Well I haven't,' Martha said comfortingly. 'You imagine it, Fee. Anyway, it'll all be different when we're leading different lives. We can wear what we like then and people will see that we're not the same. Hadn't we better humour her, just this once? I expect Francis still thinks of us as those appealing kids doing the posing and party-pieces. We might as well keep up the act just for tomorrow. Couldn't we, Fee?'

'Your halo's showing,' Phoebe said grumpily. But she was smiling. Martha grasped at the mood change before it was lost. She snatched her blue suit from the wardrobe and held it up against her.

'We could wear them back to front, perhaps? Or we could wear different blouses with them. Or' – she was warming up to laughter now – 'we could have a plan not to say anything to Francis at all. Act dumb all the time.'

'Or we could come out with all the most disgusting things we can think of,' Phoebe joined in gleefully. 'Like how I could spit the furthest in the school and how we used to have midnight feasts with raspberries and sardines all mixed up together . . .'

'And I could tell how Gricey's knickers fell down in Harrods and how she just stepped out of them and scooped them up as if she'd dropped her handkerchief. It must have happened lots of times before. She was so deft at it, wasn't she?'

Phoebe sat down on her bed and rocked back and forth, hugging her sides.

'Mart, you are a pig. You've made me laugh and I wanted to go on feeling cross. I expect Francis is quite a stuffy sort of person, anyway. Business tycoons have to be, don't they? All poker-faced and ruthless. Alice said once that he was a millionaire. Do you suppose that's true?'

'Why not? She doesn't tell lies.'

'No. She just leaves things out. I mean, she doesn't tell us anything that matters. She never has. Such as . . .' – Phoebe glanced at her sister hesitantly, testing the emotional temperature – '. . . such as why Papa killed himself.'

Martha shivered and came across to sit on her bed, facing Phoebe. They stared silently at each other for a while.

'The trouble is,' Phoebe said at length, 'there's never a moment when anything like that could be talked about. It's only ever clothes and what we look like and what we've been doing that get talked about. Imagine, just now, when we were talking about the rotten blue suits, imagine suddenly saying, "Mother, why did Papa kill himself?" She'd go all wooden and we'd get nowhere.'

'We know anyway, don't we?' Martha said in a distant voice.

'Yes. He'd just had enough. But enough of what, I wonder.'

'We'll know one day,' Martha said placidly.

After a long pause, Phoebe leant forward earnestly.

'There's something just as serious she doesn't say anything about. Something I could never ask her, and nor could you. Which is a bind because she's the only one who knows.'

Martha turned her head sharply and picked at the cover on her bed, her face darkening. When she spoke, it was in a whisper.

'Don't let's, Fee. Don't let's think about that. Colin must be our father, he must. I mean, it feels right, doesn't it? If it had been anyone else, we couldn't have . . . well . . . loved him so much . . .' Martha stumbled on the word 'love' and tears welled up in her eyes.

Phoebe put her hand out as if to stem Martha's pain.

'I know it hurts,' she said. 'But it's no use going on

wondering like this. One day we've got to find out the truth. The point is that if . . . say . . . if Colin wasn't our father, we know who is, don't we? There's only one other person it could possibly be . . .'

'Yes, and we're going to meet him tomorrow.'

Phoebe laughed sourly.

'And what do you suggest we do, Mart? Ask him? Call him "Daddy" and see what happens?'

'We could just be very quiet and keep our eyes and ears peeled. You never know. We might get some clues. And if he's all that rich and wants to keep in with Alice, he might want to help us out with Ballads.'

'Do you think so? I bally well don't. I get the idea that frightfully rich people stay that way by hanging on to their money. They don't give any away unless there's going to be some profit for them in it. Still, I suppose he'd profit by hanging on to Alice. He must be quite ancient by now and she's obviously got lots of other boyfriends.'

Martha's eyes widened.

'How do you know that?' she said.

Phoebe stood up and straightened the bed-cover with a few sharp tugs.

'Easily! I looked in her phone-book. It's full of men's names – hordes of them.'

She turned to face Martha and offered her hands to pull her up from the bed.

'Come on, let's go and put her out of her misery and tell her we'll wear the blue suits. And let's be sure to keep up the "little angels" act tomorrow, OK?'

'Absolutely,' Martha said. 'Butter wouldn't melt . . .'

'And little pitchers have big ears – don't forget that too. Let them do all the talking. And we'll gather the clues.'

The twins were intrigued to note how nervous Alice was as the three of them, dressed, hatted and gloved, mooched about in the hall waiting for Francis to arrive. She looked them over several times and sent Phoebe off to polish her shoes and Martha to take the shine off her nose before she was satisfied with their appearance. She fidgeted with her handbag and made darting glances out of the window by the front door, moved a vase of flowers from one position to another and straightened the mirror over the table.

'Isn't he going to come in for a drink first?' Phoebe asked, logically enough, since Ethel had been hard at work all morning polishing, dusting and vacuum-cleaning downstairs. 'If so, why are we all standing around with our outdoor things on?'

Alice was at the mirror, tweaking the brim of her hat for what seemed the hundredth time. She looked at Phoebe with irritation.

'Now, we're not going to have endless questions from you, are we? Just leave it to me, will you? I'll see if he wants to come back after lunch, perhaps for coffee. If we sit around here first, we'll have this smartening-up to do all over again.'

'Oh yes, I see,' Phoebe said with unaccustomed resignation. Alice seems frightened of him, she thought. She glanced at Martha and saw that she was looking at their mother with the same kind of puzzled sympathy which she herself was feeling.

'You look terribly smart,' Martha said. 'That hat suits you.'

Alice's face brightened as unequivocally as a child's.

'Do you think so? It's a good coat, isn't it? And the hat's my favourite. But you don't think it looks a bit too heavy for a luncheon party, do you? And what about this clasp?' She took a silver spray of leaves off her lapel and held it against the other side. 'Which do you think looks better? On this side? Or where it was before?'

She looked eagerly from one daughter to the other. At once the twins keyed into her uncertainty and responded with warmth.

'The hat's just right,' Phoebe said. 'Not a bit too heavy-looking.'

'And I think the clasp should go where it was before,' Martha said. 'It looks lovely.'

Alice positively glowed. She re-fixed the clasp, took a last satisfied look in the mirror and came towards the twins with a hand out to each.

'That's all right then,' she said happily. 'Francis ought to be as pleased as Punch to be taking three girls out to lunch, shouldn't he? And we're going to make sure we get him into a jolly mood, aren't we?'

Suddenly, the atmosphere between them had changed. The twins sensed that this was what Alice had wanted for a long time – this light, loose, girlish partnership between friends, reassuring each other about their appearance, exchanging criticism and compliments, banding together in a cosy sisterhood the better to understand and manage the curious ways of men. She had never wanted the dull responsibilities and demands of motherhood. While they were young there was no other role she could play instead. She was 'Mother', however distant and inadequate.

Now, however, it was possible for her to give up any pretensions to parental authority or concern. They could be 'all girls together', sometimes allies and, by the same token, sometimes rivals, and even, as the twins came to discover, reverse their roles entirely on occasions, so that it was she who looked for approval, reassurance and understanding from them, as a child might, and they who responded with what she needed, as most parents do.

The twins never discussed this change in their relationship to Alice. But they both perceived quite clearly what had happened in that moment in the hall, waiting for Francis to take them to lunch. For a split second her brittle adult mask had been dropped and they had been given a glimpse of the seventeen-year-old Alice, curled up in a ball in an armchair at the Clarendon Hotel, with her thumb in her mouth and her dreams in shreds. By means of one of their instinctive, unspoken pacts, they had agreed to surrender all their expectations of 'mothering' from Alice, and their resentment at her failure to provide it. They saw, in a flash, that her need was greater than theirs. And she had no twin sister as comforter and companion.

*

When Francis drew up at Ballads in his enormous chauffeur-driven Daimler, it was immediately obvious that there was no question of his coming in for a drink first. He opened the back door, put one foot out on the drive and called out, 'Come on, Alice. Bring the girls. We'll lunch out.'

The twins sat with their backs to the chauffeur's compartment and pressed their knees together politely while trying not to stare at Francis. He was all camel-hair coat and cigar smoke and narrowed eyes in their direction, and for several miles not a word was said. The twins had somehow expected him to put his arm round Alice or murmur endearments to her, or at least ask her how she was. But they both sat there in what passed for comfortable silence and in the end it was Phoebe who broke it.

'How do you do?' she said.

Francis leant forward and shook her hand as if she had only that moment entered his line of vision.

'Which one are you?'

'I'm Phoebe. And this is Martha.' She inclined her head towards her sister.

He laughed and shook Martha's hand, and then sat back again and looked at Alice.

'Nice hat,' he said. 'We're going to the Royal. All right?'

Alice nodded and murmured, 'Lovely, darling.'

Francis grinned at the twins. 'All right, Phoebe? All right, Martha?'

'Yes, thank you,' they said in chorus.

He pulled a briefcase up from the shaggy-carpeted floor of the car and snapped the locks open. He shuffled through the papers inside and brought out a wodge of photographs. He handed them to Alice.

'Here, have a look at these.'

Alice flipped through the pile, looking puzzled.

'It's a boat of some sort . . .' she said warily.

'Not a boat, my dear. A ship! A ship! A regular, sea-going ship. What do you think of it?'

He winked at the twins, inviting them to share in his teasing.

'Well,' Alice said, at a loss. 'It's very big. And – wait a moment – I think I've been on it. One night when it was all lit up and there was a party on board. Wasn't it in Poole Harbour? Before the war?'

Francis was alternately smiling at her and darting little glances at the twins.

'Oh come on, come on!' he said. 'It's Harry Brompton's ship. You know it all right. Everybody knows it. There isn't a finer motor yacht anywhere.'

Alice still looked confused. The twins began to feel sorry for her.

'So? What about it?' she said. 'Why the photos?'

'Because, my dear Alice' – and he slapped her heartily on the knees – 'I've bought it! Brompton's had it laid up for the duration. It'll have to stay there till the war's over. But then! Just wait!'

He winked at the twins again, seeming oblivious of Alice's lukewarm interest.

'You won't see us for spray, not once the war's over and I've had her refitted. A good buy, eh, girls?'

He sank back against the cushions, not expecting an answer, and looked out of the window.

The twins were thinking that he seemed to be rather a show-off. They kept silent and stored their impressions to share with each other later. With the 'father' conundrum in mind, they analysed his features and his colouring and his mannerisms, looking for similarities to themselves. He could not have been more alien, they decided, with his thick, wavy, greying fair hair, his heavy build and blue eyes. They studied his mannerisms and the way he spoke and could find no likenesses there.

Lunchtime was similarly lacking in clues. Alice's whole demeanour was completely strange to them, timid and passive and vague. She made no attempt to draw Francis out, or the twins. She spoke only when one of them asked her a question. Francis spent a lot of time looking round the room, calling the waiter, patting his pockets and quizzing the twins in abrupt, staccato fashion.

'Going up to Cambridge are you, Phoebe?'

Phoebe blushed with pleasure at finding that he had her name right and used it.

'Yes, this October.'

'What are you reading?'

'Modern languages.'

He grunted amiably.

'Not going to be a bluestocking, I hope. And what about you, Martha? What's in store for you?'

'Art. I'm going to art school. Not all the time. Just for three days a week in London. But I'll still live at Ballads. I'd really like to be there all the time, though.'

'Why's that?' He looked interested.

'Because it's home, I suppose. And it's so beautiful and needs looking after.'

He stared at Martha thoughtfully, then turned to Alice.

'All right for money, are they?'

Alice looked embarrassed and frowned slightly, as if to say 'not in front of the children'.

'Not entirely,' she said cryptically.

'We'll see about that later. Remind me, won't you?'

Phoebe slid her foot under the table until it touched Martha's and registered hope.

'I'll do that thing,' Alice said. 'As for now, Francis, I think I'll come back to London with you. Does that suit?'

'Splendid,' he said. 'But get your stuff together quickly. I don't want to wait around. Have to be in London by four.'

As the car halted at the front door of Ballads, Francis donned some heavy horn-rimmed spectacles and dived into his briefcase to pull out some folders. Alice ran into the house while the twins stood by the car, feeling they ought to keep him company until Alice came back.

Phoebe leant into the car towards Francis, who was hunched over his papers on the back seat.

'Wouldn't you like to see the glasshouse?' she asked him.

Without raising his head he muttered quietly, 'Not now, Anthea, not now. Daddy's busy.'

Phoebe clutched at Martha's arm and stared at her in

bewilderment. She lowered her head into the car again.

'What? What did you say?' she shouted excitedly. 'It's me, Phoebe. I thought you might like to see the glasshouse.'

Francis looked up with a startled expression and pushed his spectacles up on to his forehead.

'Good God!' he said. 'What a strange thing! You sounded just like my daughter when she was your age. I was miles away. No, no, I can't do any sight-seeing now. Go and fetch your mother – we must be off.' And he turned back to his papers.

The twins hurried into the hall and called up the stairs to Alice. Phoebe was still gripping Martha's arm and they both stood stiffly at the bottom of the stairs, as if holding something weighty between them, while Alice hurried past them, waving goodbye and sending the gravel flying as she ran to the car.

They heard the car-door slam, the motor start up and the receding crunch of the tyres on the drive. They relaxed and let their breath out in a long, wondering sigh.

'Well!' Phoebe said. 'That was a clue all right.'

'Just like his daughter . . .'

'He said that, he definitely said that, didn't he? Just like his daughter. Oh Mart! Do you think it means that . . . well . . . there's a family likeness?'

'I don't know. I just don't know. But we'd better remember that. When we really get down to sorting it out, that's going to be important . . .'

'But what about him, Mart? What did you think? Would you like him to be our father?'

Martha rubbed her forehead and screwed up her eyes.

'Honestly, Fee, I can't think straight about it. He's all right, I suppose. It sounds as if he might help out with Ballads. But "father". I don't think so. I just want it to be Colin. Not anyone else.'

Phoebe turned away and looked out of the window at the drive.

'Let's leave it at that, then. We'll find out more one day. For now, it's Colin.'

'Yes, for now.'

16

1965 TOGETHER AGAIN

Martha had set up her easel just outside the glasshouse so that she had a good view of the whole southern sweep of the garden. She was painting her twenty-second picture of the fountain. They all differed according to her mood at the time of painting them. This one was bold and confident and joyous and she intended to have it finished before Phoebe arrived.

She had not been sure whether her present mood of happy anticipation would be better met by an hour or so at the piano or in the garden. Because the sun was out she had settled for outdoors. She was beginning to regret her choice, however. As she narrowed her eyes at the view ahead, she noticed the unweeded rose-bed on the left and the pile of hedge-clippings far away in the middle distance.

For a moment she felt drawn to doing something about these omissions before Phoebe came. But she resisted the impulse. Phoebe wouldn't notice anyway. Her up-and-down life had never had room for any domestic or horticultural details. After nearly two years' absence from Ballads and England she was certain to pitch straight away into a deep discussion of feelings – her favourite topic. Martha felt a twinge of apprehension as she pictured Phoebe pressing her for details of how Donald had left, and why, and what was to become of the boys. But it will be all right in the end, she thought. When she sees I'm not despondent about it, she'll start talking about herself.

She was filling in a detail of the fountain and feeling at peace when something made her straighten up and shut her eyes. She had a mild feeling of irritation, nothing more, and glanced round the garden to see if there was any immediate cause of it. There was not a sound or a movement anywhere near. She had an impulse to bend down and touch the calf of her right leg. It felt sore and sensitive.

So that was it, she thought. It's Phoebe. She's been hurt and she's going to be late. She did not question the message that had reached her. It had happened too many times before to be doubted. So she continued painting for another half-hour and then placidly gathered her things together and went into the house.

She was upstairs in the main bedroom, looking idly out of the window, when she saw Phoebe's ramshackle Mini nosing into the entrance to the drive where the stone pillars had once stood. The back of the car was full to the roof with her luggage and the rack on top was loaded with boxes and bundles, criss-crossed with an assortment of ropes. What a gypsy, she thought affectionately. I wonder how she can bear not to have anywhere to call home. But she has now. Ballads is home for both of us again. She saw her sister bend low over the steering-wheel and peer up at the window, smiling broadly. Martha waved, turned on her heel and ran down to the front door.

Phoebe stepped out of the car gingerly, rubbing her right leg.

'What did you do to it?' Martha said.

'The wretched door – it shut itself on my leg when I was leaving the petrol station. I had to stop there for a while and have a cup of coffee. That's why I'm latish. Sorry, Mart. But I expect you knew?'

'Yes, I knew. It felt as if it hurt quite a bit.'

Phoebe laughed and wrenched open the back doors of the car.

'Yes, not funny. But not half as bad as when you were having Tim and I had your labour pains. Remember? And Mark too. Only it wasn't so bad the second time, was it?'

She reached into the back of the car and spoke teasingly over her shoulder.

'Not thinking of having any more children, I hope. I don't want to go through all that again with nothing to show for it.'

'Oh God, Fee. You can be really tactless sometimes. Fat chance of that with Donald gone. Anyway it's a bit late now, isn't it?'

Phoebe straightened up and pushed a camera-case and a hold-all into her sister's hand.

'You look all right,' she said. 'But are you? Was it terribly fraught, you and Donald falling out? I couldn't tell, not from your letters.'

Martha reached impatiently into the car and pulled out one of the suitcases with her spare hand.

'Don't let's start on the emotional bit yet. We'll have all the post-mortems later. You can see I'm all right, can't you? I haven't sorted myself out yet, actually. I held back in the letters . . .'

'That was obvious, darling.'

'Come on, let's get all this clobber in. OK for you in our old room? I've got Alice's. It seemed daft to leave it empty.'

Up in the room that used to be the night nursery, Phoebe sat on the bed with all her worldly goods in heaps around her and tested her feelings, like a tongue on an aching tooth.

Firstly, there was the deep contentment of being with Martha. Throughout her wanderings and all the hectic changes of jobs, partners and life-styles she had always felt there was something missing. At Cambridge, the first time they had ever been apart, her twin's absence had been a constant ache. It took the bloom off every adventure and achievement in love, learning or self-awareness.

The vacations at Ballads, where Martha was settling more deeply year by year, assuaged the ache a little but even those times, Phoebe discovered, could not take them back to the days when every event, every piece of interaction with the people around them, every meeting with someone new, every response to the world outside, was experienced by them both simultaneously. Then, there had been no need for post-mortems or reports, or catching up or closing the gaps in their knowledge and understanding of each other. Everything was mutual and shared. Now there were gaps that could never be closed. There could never be enough time now to share everything they had individually felt and experienced during their long separations over the past twenty years.

Nevertheless, Phoebe often distrusted the notion that being one of a twin solely accounted for her unsettling feeling of incompleteness. She had sometimes wondered if perhaps it was not her twin's presence she lacked but something else, some quality in herself which made her less than whole. Why, for example, had no one else been able to take Martha's place? Why had she never felt close to anyone else, not even to the men she had loved beyond all reason, or the women who had been 'best friends' and who had poured out their hearts to her? And why had she never poured her heart out to them, or to anyone? What was the barrier?

Martha, meanwhile, was sitting in the glasshouse, staring at the finished canvas of the fountain propped up against a chair opposite her. She too was content that she and Phoebe were together at Ballads after so long.

Like Phoebe, however, she found her contentment mixed with self-doubt. If I hadn't missed and needed Fee so much, she was thinking, I might never have married Donald and made him so unhappy. I never trusted him or confided in him the way I do with Fee. I was never close to him. Even when our sons were born it was Fee I cried out for, both with fear and also with joy when it was all over. Whenever I felt sad I wanted Fee to be here and comfort me. No wonder he felt left out and would now and again accuse me of being utterly dependent on 'that bally sister of yours'. Is it true? she wondered. Will we ever be free of each other, free to get close to anyone else?

Martha roused herself from her unaccustomed mood of introspection and went into the kitchen. A cup of tea, she told herself, for me and for Phoebe, that's what's needed. And then there are weeks, months, perhaps years ahead to be here at Ballads and find the answers to all our questions. She felt immeasurably happy as she filled the kettle and took two mugs down from their hooks on the wall.

When she took the mugs of tea upstairs she found Phoebe busily stowing her possessions away in cupboards and drawers. She sat on the window-seat, sipping her tea silently and watching Phoebe fling cases open and unzip her numerous bags and dart from one side of the room to the other with piles of books, clothes and ornaments.

'It's going to be a job getting all my things in here,' Phoebe said, looking ruefully at the filled cupboards and shelves and then at the remaining heaps on the floor and the bed. She grinned at Martha. 'Your room's much bigger, of course. Jammy cow!'

Martha waved her hand round her sister's belongings.

'You can put all this wherever you like, you know. There are five other bedrooms, for goodness sake. The boys' things are all going to Donald's new place in a few weeks.'

'Aren't any of them living here any more then?' Phoebe tried to keep her face non-committal and then saw it didn't matter since Martha had turned to look out of the window.

Martha didn't speak for several seconds and when she did her voice was strained.

'They'll come to Ballads for part of the holidays,' she said. 'They love it here. But they need Donald. He's a wonderful father. And I suppose he needs them too. We didn't have to argue about it.' She turned back to the room and faced Phoebe with a bright expression. 'So you see, everyone's happy.'

'You too?'

'Why ask?' Martha said, laughing now. 'You're here. Enough said.'

Phoebe dropped a pile of books on the bed and came to stand by the window with her back to the wall. She looked down at the floor, deep in thought.

'That's what worries me rather,' she said.

'About us?'

'Yes, being twins. What it's done to us. What it means now . . .'

Martha sighed theatrically.

'Wow!' she said. 'A big subject. But, yes, all right. It's important. After all, I suppose it's what wrecked my marriage. Yes, it does worry me too.'

'How exactly?'

'Oh, you know. Wondering if it's OK to be this much bound . . . this much tied up with you. I call to you often. Whenever I'm frightened or low or just, well, needy . . .'

'Yes, and I hear you, Mart.'

'But do you lean on me in the same way? Be honest, Fee. Do you?'

'Yes, I think so. But not out loud. Not consciously . . .'

'What does that mean? If it's some of your psychological jargon, you know I don't get the hang of it. So don't . . .'

'No, I won't. But I can't unknow what I know, now can I? And it's hard to explain things that go on inside without using a few words of more than one syllable . . .'

'All right. All right.' Martha shrugged and turned to look out of the window. 'Only don't make it a bloody lecture.'

Phoebe walked over to the bed and stretched out on it.

'Well, I'll say what it feels like for me. And then you say how it is for you. Right?'

'Yeah – go on.'

'Most people would think that being twins, feeling so close to each other all the time, it must be like being in love, so much in love that the two people feel like one, as if they were joined into one, melting into each other. Right?'

'Yes, I guess that's what other people think. A few have said as much. But I haven't talked about it a lot. People aren't all that interested – except Donald, of course. He really did think that as I loved you so much, I couldn't possibly love him at all . . .'

'Poor Donald,' Phoebe said sadly. 'Well, I don't think it's like that. It's much more like one person split into two. For me, at any rate. All that time at Cambridge and later, when I was so miserable and somehow couldn't start living as me, it really did feel as if I'd had an enormous amputation. A great big part of me had just been sliced away.'

Martha was leaning forward eagerly from her seat at the window.

'Yes, yes,' she said. 'Like an amputation. But I don't think it was as bad for me. I was still here at Ballads, where we'd always been together. In some way or other, you were still here too.'

'I don't know whether that's really worse or better, Mart. Maybe it means your amputation still has to be done.'

Martha grimaced and attempted a laugh.

'You think so? What's it like then? This amputation?'

Phoebe leant back against the bed-head and closed her eyes.

'The thing is, Mart, that I've read lots of times about how people who've had amputations feel.' She opened her eyes for a second and smiled. 'They're called amputees, aren't they? Maybe that's what we are – amputees.'

She closed her eyes again.

'Apparently, long after the leg or arm or whatever it was has gone, they go on feeling it as if it were still there – you know, it gets cold or itchy or hot or numb just like the rest of them does. It's a kind of ghost limb, with sensations just the same as if it were still attached . . .'

'Yes, I've heard that too.'

'That's how it's been, on and off, ever since Cambridge and all the time when I haven't been with you. I'm aware of your absence and can't get rid of that awareness. I've often tried but I don't know how. Everywhere I've been – all the places abroad, for instance – the one thing that's always there is the fact that you're not there. Do you see what I mean?'

'And I'm not seeing what you're seeing, or hearing what you're hearing. Nor meeting and knowing the people you meet. And never will . . .'

'Yes. And maybe that's why I always have this feeling, wherever I am and whatever I'm doing, that I'm not completely there. I'm only half there. I need you, it seems, to fill the hole, to make me whole. To complement me. You whole me, Mart, that's what it is.'

She opened her eyes and looked at Martha.

'I say, Mart, that's rather neat, isn't it? I can make more of that. How about this? To be wholed you must have someone to hold you. Did anyone ever hold us?'

'Rose did,' Martha said quickly, as if not wanting to linger on the thought of those warm, loving arms.

'Yes, she held us. But perhaps not long enough or not frequently enough or not confidently enough or something. So I guess we hold each other, and whole each other . . .'

Martha was doing her best not to laugh, but eventually spluttered and came across to put her hand on Phoebe's forehead with exaggerated concern.

'You are a clot,' she said. 'You're getting quite feverish with all these puns . . .'

Phoebe took Martha's hand from her forehead and held it tightly. She swung her legs off the bed and sat up.

'Ah, dem words, dem words, I do love 'em. But what do you make of it? How is it for you, this twins business?'

Martha gently shook her hand free of Phoebe's grasp and sat down on the bed beside her.

'Much the same, really. But I can't talk about it the way you do. Maybe I could paint it or play it on the piano. But no, I shan't try. I certainly do miss you when you're not around. Especially when you're abroad and I can't even ring you when I'm worried or ill or anything. And it can be quite painful at times, getting these weird messages when something's up with you. That car crash, remember? I woke up suddenly with the feeling that my head was splitting open . . .'

'And mine really was!' Phoebe instinctively rubbed her forehead where she still bore the scar.

'But I can't say I feel amputated exactly. It's more like groping in the dark, or teetering about on shaky ground.'

'That's insecurity,' Phoebe said crisply.

'Oh yes, I'm quite sure we're full of that. But why?'

Phoebe stood up, sighed, and strolled to the window.

'That was Alice's job, and Colin's, to give us that safe feeling that some other people seem to have. They made a pig's ear of it, that's the trouble. But how could they do any better? They were walking on eggs themselves, don't you reckon? And Alice probably still is.'

'I suppose so.' Martha stretched and yawned. 'Look here, Fee, I'm getting fed up with all this deep talk. You haven't seen the glasshouse yet – it looks quite different. And what about a drink? A celebration? I got hold of a lobster for dinner.'

'Scrummy! My favourite. Trust you to think of that.'

They walked to the door, arms linked.

'And what about Alice?' Phoebe said. 'Does she ever come here now? Or will I have to go to the mews to see her?'

'She never comes. She still hates it. The mews is her home now, all the time. But you won't find her there much either. She's always away somewhere. She seems to be terribly restless . . .'

'So am I, wouldn't you say?'

'Not for the same reason, though,' Martha said. 'She adores being looked after and waited on – so hotels and shipboard life are ideal. Also I'm sure she's afraid of losing her looks. She still looks as young as ever, thanks to all the beauty treatments and massaging and whatnot. Plus never having to lift a finger or worry about anything except herself. And, of course, she always has to have a man in tow. It's not easy to find them, just sitting at home in London.'

'She still has Francis though?'

'Oh yes. But he's . . . what? . . . maybe fifteen years older than her so he'd be getting on for eighty now. They're still together, if you can call it that. He's richer than ever and gives her everything she wants. They sometimes go abroad together or on a cruise and I gather they dine out in London in a genteel sort of way and totter to the races and what-have-you.'

'Sounds the full, rich life,' Phoebe said, stifling a giggle.

'But I think she still wants new faces, people who don't know her background or how old she is or anything. She wants a helluva lot of admiration, chaps falling in love with her – which they still do, apparently – all that kind of thing.'

They were in the glasshouse now and Martha went to the drinks cupboard and reached in for bottles and glasses. Phoebe sat down on one of the settees and breathed in the earthy, winy scent of the vine.

'This place looks good,' she said. 'All your stuff around

makes it much more cosy and friendly. It all sounds rather sad, though, about Alice.'

'Not for her,' Martha said brusquely. 'It's sad for me, for us, though. Francis hasn't put any money into Ballads for ages and she doesn't give any help either, not since I got married. Donald did all he could but he reckoned it was a right albatross. He spent hundreds on keeping it in good nick and yet you can hardly see now where it all went.'

'Oh, but I hadn't noticed any terrible dilapidation or anything.' Phoebe attempted reassurance but realized that she had not looked at her surroundings since she arrived.

Martha laughed grimly.

'Well, just don't look beyond the vine, that's all. Then you'll miss the cracked panes. But they're not important. Donald used to tear his hair out over them, and the heating bills. He thought we – you and I – should sell it. Alice has always wanted that too. But of course that's ridiculous. Now you're here, it's even more ridiculous, isn't it? Here, Fee, sink this.'

She handed Phoebe a full glass and went back to pour her own drink.

Phoebe took a large gulp, trying to swallow a rising sense of alarm. Oh my God! she thought. Martha thinks of me as Ballads' saviour. How idiotic of me not to have made it clear long ago that what I earn, I spend. I suppose she thinks the life of a travel writer is all flesh-pots and big money. But why not? I've done nothing to disabuse her. In fact, I've encouraged that very illusion. Always boasted about my assignments, sent lashings of photos of exotic places for her to copy on canvas, flammed it all up no end in my letters to her. How could she know that the first-class travel and the four-star hotels were all on expenses, or a free publicity exercise? And that the actual fees I get are pitiful? She probably imagines that I'm wallowing in money and, with no family or domestic ties, I'm just waiting for some way of putting it all to good use.

But there was no nest-egg of any useful size. All Phoebe had was the money from the sale of her tiny flat in a Chelsea block for transients, a 'home' that she'd never been in for more than a total of a couple of months in the year and then only for a night here and there. That sum, Phoebe supposed glumly, would just about cover her keep here at Ballads for a year. Or maybe two if she tightened her belt a bit and stopped buying camera equipment and books, and stuck to wine instead of outsize brandies, and remained content with the clothes she already had, and grew out of her addiction to shellfish, foreign films and custom-made shoes.

For a moment she considered telling Martha the truth. Then she saw how happy and relaxed her sister was, sitting opposite her under the vine, against the evening light shimmering through the glass. I just can't say, 'Hard cheese, Mart. I'm as skint as you are. There's nothing I can do about Ballads.' I'll leave it a while, she decided. Get settled in first and let her see for herself the way things are. Let her dream a little longer about having Ballads for ever.

She raised her glass towards Martha.

'Here's to us!' she said loudly and cheerfully.

'And to Ballads,' Martha added, her face suffused with such glowing happiness that Phoebe felt well pleased with her decision. Now was certainly not the moment to tell her that putting Ballads up for sale, far from being a ridiculous idea, was going to be the only answer.

BOOK THREE

17

THE SEARCH

The day after Charles and Sue Endicott had come to view Ballads, Mr Coleherne, the estate agent, telephoned the twins in some excitement.

'I'm pleased to say,' he said, 'that Mr Endicott is very interested in your property, extremely interested.'

It was Phoebe who had answered the phone and she was not slow to notice that Mr Coleherne had not said that Mrs Endicott was interested too.

'And his wife?' she said. 'Is she equally interested?'

'I wouldn't say that, no. She needs a little more – er – reassurance . . .'

'Arm-twisting, you mean. She wasn't exactly passionate about the place.'

Mr Coleherne hesitated and could be heard clearing his throat nervously.

'Well,' he said at length. 'Let's not worry about that. I take it I'm speaking to Miss Whittaker? Yes? I'll remind you, Miss Whittaker, that it's Mr Endicott who's the potential purchaser, not his wife. He says he's not making an offer straight away. He'd like to think about it for a few days. Then, if you're agreeable, he'll come along for another look-see. Shall I give him your phone number so that he can contact you direct?'

'Yes, I should do that.'

'And you'll let me know when he comes again for another . . .'

'Look-see, yes. Or he will, after he's been. Meanwhile, is anyone else showing any interest?'

'There are some other nibbles, as a matter of fact. It looks as if Mr Endicott's interest has started the ball rolling. It often works like that in the property business.' He guffawed breathily and Phoebe was aware that he was winding himself up to a joke. 'We've got our grape-vine too, you know,' he added and gave a loud bray of laughter.

Martha pulled a face when Phoebe told her about the phone call.

'I half hoped he wouldn't want it, didn't you? Still, if anyone's to have it, I'd rather like it to be him. Do you think we'd better tart the place up a bit before he comes again?'

'No fear, Mart. Too much slog. Besides, anything we could do now would just be a drop in the ocean. He knows what it's like. A bit of spit and polish isn't going to make any difference to whether he really wants it or not. Not to the price either. I reckon his chilly wife is going to have the final yes or no, in any case.'

'Agreed then,' said Martha, with relief. 'Let's start searching the attic right away.'

'Not right away, Mart, please. Let's save it until this evening. I don't want to miss the sun and the garden all day, do you? Today, for instance, I was going to take some pictures of the place. I've still got bags of film I haven't used.'

'And I'll do a water-colour of the glasshouse.'

'OK. Lunch at one?'

'Just a salad and ham – all right?'

They were both so eagerly looking forward to their search among the papers in the attic that the day passed quickly and at six o'clock they made their way along the first-floor corridor to the upper staircase at the eastern end which led to two small bedrooms and the large attic in the roof-space.

This staircase, unlike the main one, had a hairpin turn in it and was carpeted in coarse hessian. Phoebe, as always, led the way and pushed open the green baize-covered door at the top. The only light in the windowless attic came from two bare bulbs hanging on long flexes from the roof-beams, with cone-shaped shades which restricted their light to two small circles below. As the door opened the rush of air from the depths of the house set the two bulbs swinging on their cables and sweeping, like the beams of a lighthouse, round the contents of the room. Furniture, military chests, cabin trunks, hampers, crates and cardboard boxes were briefly illuminated and then plunged into darkness as the arcs of light swung away. A rocking-horse had its moment in the spotlight, then a tailor's dummy, an old horned gramophone, some over-stuffed, bursting armchairs and sofas, an empty glass dome on a round wooden stand, baskets overflowing with china and glass, and stacks of pictures, their faces to the wall.

'My God,' Martha said. 'Didn't anyone ever throw anything away?'

'It seems not. Look, there are even piles of old newspapers and magazines over there, by the gramophone. And, no, I don't believe it – a glass jar, a sweetie jar, full of lengths of old string!'

They stood silently in the clear space in the middle for a while, looking round and wondering where to begin their search. The roof-tiles creaked as they settled into the cool of the evening after hours in the sun, and they could hear the frantic flutterings and scratchings of birds jostling each other for territory under the eaves.

'It's funny, isn't it?' Martha whispered. 'It doesn't seem a dead place at all . . .'

'No, it feels full of life – sort of breathing. Look, there are our cots. And isn't that Colin's violin-case?'

'And his guns, look, and walking-sticks and cricket bat. Jack's too – that smaller one.'

Martha was pointing to the far corner of the attic just beyond one of the two neat circles of light thrown by the now motionless bulbs.

'If that's where all Colin's stuff is, that's where we ought to start looking.'

They walked slowly across the pool of light to its edge, their eyes lingering on all the reminders of their childhood that lay about them.

'Those tea-chests,' Martha said, still in a whisper. 'They're the ones we saw in his study. The day it happened. And those boxes. They're all his papers and books. They must be. Come on.'

Together they pulled the sheets of yellowing newspaper from the top of one of the tea-chests and manhandled it into the circle of light. It was packed with rolls of cartridge paper and books of all shapes and sizes, small notebooks, large ones, paper-covered exercise books and slim ledgers. They unrolled some of the cylinders of paper, opened a few of the books, laid some on the floor, handed items to each other, puzzled and wondering.

'Here's the map we looked at,' Martha said, half to herself. 'Every stick and stone of Ballads is on it.'

Phoebe was bent over one of the small notebooks, flicking its pages. She gasped and raised her head.

'It wasn't just the sticks and stones,' she said. 'Look, this one is all about just one room – the dining-room. He's put down its size and the kind of wallpaper – and when it was changed – and every bit of furniture. He's even written down what pictures were in it, and the ornaments – absolutely everything. But why this room? Unless . . .'

She reached into the crate of books and shuffled through them, peering at the labels on their spines. She sighed heavily as she drew one out.

'I knew it . . . there's one for every room. This one's for the glasshouse.' She turned the pages slowly, pushing the book nearer to the light and narrowing her eyes.

'Mart, for goodness sake, he's listed everything. Here's a category called "Furniture", and a little way below a sub-category called "Seating". Talk about obsessive. Here's where Alice threw out the old chairs and bought new ones. It's all recorded – what they cost, where the old ones went to. They're in one of the garages, apparently . . .' Her voice trailed off on a despairing note and she raised her head.

Martha was gazing into the distance beyond the pool of light, a look of compassion on her face.

'All the rooms, you say?'

'It looks like it.'

'And I suppose they're all the same, with every detail of their decoration and the furniture and everything.'

'I expect so. Do you want to look?'

Martha shook her head vigorously.

'No, no. That's not what Ballads means to me – all those boring details. I don't want to see them. But Fee . . . why? Why did he do it? It seems so monstrous, so . . . so pointless.'

'It seems there was a point for him, though. He must have enjoyed it hugely. It wasn't a chore, after all. Do you remember how he used to dash up to his study? Like a lover to a tryst. And he certainly did love Ballads. All this . . .' – Phoebe waved vaguely towards the crate of books – '. . . it's all a kind of worship, an act of devotion. Makes me think of the monks toiling for hours over copying the Scriptures.'

Martha started to speak, then stopped, then began again haltingly.

'Do you think . . . was he perhaps . . . you know . . .?'

'Mad? Really mad?'

Martha gave a long sigh of relief that Phoebe had uttered the thought for her.

'Yes,' she said. 'Was he?'

'I don't think so. Pushed to the brink maybe, but not actually over the edge. Perhaps all this is what held him back. He made some order out of what was maybe complete chaos for him. If he hadn't had this he might have gone right over the top. But let's see what's in this other crate.'

The second tea-chest was full to the brim with what appeared to be ledgers covered in marbled binding.

'It just looks like household accounts or something,' Martha said, sounding disappointed. 'Or it could be stuff from his work, to do with money.'

They each pulled a volume out of the box and began to flick through the pages. Simultaneously they gave whoops of joy, like prospectors who had struck gold.

'Eureka! They're diaries!' Phoebe shouted.

'Diaries, thank heaven!' Martha exclaimed. 'Mine's for 1941. When's yours?'

'This is 1940. Much too late. Let's dig down and get to the

earlier ones. Do you suppose he kept a diary all the time?'

'I bet he did, Fee. It would be just like him, wouldn't it?'

They quickly took the volumes out, stacking them on the floor beside the box, now and again glancing at the neat labels on the spine where Colin had written the date. Sometimes one year had taken up more than one volume, sometimes only one, but all were closely covered, page by page, and filled to the very end.

'Look, if we actually read them now,' Phoebe said, 'we'll be here all night. Why don't we just pick out the important years and take them downstairs? This light's awful and I can't take much more of this dust.'

Martha had not noticed the dust. She was sitting cross-legged on the floor, bent low over the open book on her lap.

'Good idea,' she said without looking up. 'We'll take this one. It's 1927, the year that Jack died.'

'I'll get some earlier ones. We must find 1925, for when we were born. And 1924, for when we were conceived.' Phoebe was enjoying getting some planned order into the search and almost missed Martha's quiet sob.

'What now?' she said impatiently.

Martha looked up and her eyes were moist.

'Listen, Fee, you must listen.' Her voice was loaded with pity and horror. 'This is just after Jack's death. The date's 22 July 1927. There's a lot about gathering up all Jack's things and putting them in his study. He makes it sound like an army exercise. Then he goes all lyrical. I didn't know that about him, did you? Listen.' She began reading in a shaky voice.

'"You don't know, my dear Alice, how cruelly you stamp over my sorrow. How I've longed for you to help soothe my grief or simply show me some tears to match my own. How wonderful it would be if we could sit together, our heads and hearts close as they used to be when you first came to Ballads, and I could feel, without the need for words, that you shared the darkness inside me and were willing to stay at my side until the light comes again."'

Martha broke off and looked up at Phoebe, her face distraught.

302

'All that emotion! Why didn't he ever show it to anyone? Had you any idea that he felt so much?'

'No, of course not. No one could have. And certainly not Alice. If only he'd spoken out. The waste of it . . . Go on. Go on. Read more.' Phoebe sounded angry, but Martha knew it was not anger against her.

'"Just now,"' she read on, '"I heard you running upstairs to our room – that shrine to my hopes of our love – and I could scarcely believe what I also heard, that you were humming. The door shut and no doubt you prepared for one of your trips to London. You may wonder, if you ever think of me, why I don't come out on these occasions to say goodbye. It would hurt me more than I could bear, knowing that you are going, I believe, to someone else who loves you."'

Martha stopped and peered more closely at the page.

'First of all he wrote "professes to love you". Then he crossed out "professes to" and left just "who loves you". Strange, that. He means Francis Bourne, of course. He obviously knew all about him. But how? And why was it better for him to believe Francis loved her?'

'Well, it would have been a lot worse for him, I suppose, if it were only a physical thing and Alice was being, well, just used.'

'That sounds a bit tortuous. Still, I'll read a bit more . . .'

'"I will never hurt you in return by allowing you to know how often you drive a knife into my heart. If you have any conscience, it could not survive knowing what you are doing to me. For your sake, I shall keep silent, for ever and for ever."'

Neither of the twins spoke for several minutes. Martha let the book fall from her lap on to the floor. It make a skid-mark in the dust before it came to rest and she stared at it, her face drooping with sadness. Phoebe stood with her back against one of the heavy wooden posts supporting the roof. She pulled herself upright, then leant back again and forward again, rocking like someone in a trance.

'She broke his heart,' she said at length.

'Yes . . .'

'But someone must have broken hers first.'

Martha jerked her head up in astonishment.

'What makes you say that?'

Phoebe shook herself as if she had been asleep.

'Oh that's just the way it goes. People are cruel because others have been cruel to them. They can't love because they weren't loved. Or thought they weren't, which amounts to the same thing. It just goes on in a great long chain, from one generation to the next.'

'But, Fee, that's so defeatist. Do you mean that no one can break out of it? What about us then? We must be part of that chain.'

'Not necessarily. At least we know what may be missing. Alice doesn't. She probably thinks she's quite a loving sort of person. Anyway, we probably got something from Colin. He could love. It's all there, in his diary, isn't it? And much good it did him.'

'Well, we must be all right, Fee. We love each other.'

Phoebe looked at Martha testingly, hesitated and then drew in her breath sharply.

'Do we?' she said. 'Or is it just that you're my life-line and I'm yours? And we're clinging to each other for survival?'

Martha jumped to her feet and brushed the dust from her skirt.

'You can be really brutal sometimes,' she said, not looking at Phoebe. 'I think it's time we went downstairs.' She bent down and picked up the diary she'd been reading aloud. 'I'll bring this one and a few others. You find 1924 and 1925.'

'I didn't mean . . .' Phoebe looked apologetically at her sister and put her hand out across the top of the tea-chest which stood between them. 'It's only playing with words. You know that, Mart. Of course we got something from Colin. It was love. It is love. And even if he isn't our father . . .'

'There you go again!' Martha interrupted angrily. 'If, if, if. Why do you have to twist the knife? If he isn't our father, there's no hope. Francis Bourne has about much as love in him as a pound note.'

'That's not fair. You don't know that.'

'Oh, I see. You're rather hoping he's our father, aren't you? That'd suit you down to the ground, having a millionaire tycoon for a father. Success and money and fame – it's all you think about. You're just like her. You make me sick.'

Martha gave the tea-chest a strong shove towards Phoebe. The top of it swayed a little and then it tipped back again on an even keel with a soft thud. Martha glared at the chest as if it had betrayed her. She held the diaries in a pile under her chin and walked to the door. Phoebe rummaged in the chest until she found what she wanted and joined Martha in the doorway. Please make it Colin, she was thinking. It has to be Colin. Mart's going to hate me and hate herself if it turns out to be Francis.

She patted Martha on the shoulder as they left the attic and went down the stairs.

'Don't mind me,' she said. 'I'm all mouth.'

Martha laughed. 'That doesn't come from Colin, that's for sure.'

They were at ease again when they reached the glasshouse, put their piles of books on one of the settees and sat down beside each other. They started with the earliest volume, hoping to find out how Colin and Alice had met. At the top of the first page of this diary was a short entry dated 28 November 1917. 'I'm engaged to Alice,' it read. 'Next time I'm at home I'll write about her.' There was nothing for the rest of the year, nor for the whole of 1918. The diary proper began in March 1919 when Colin noted, on 5 March that 'today was my wedding-day and I have brought to Ballads the most beautiful, the sweetest and the kindest girl in the world'.

'It sounds as if he were offering her to Ballads,' Phoebe said. 'Like a gift to the house. He must have terribly wanted her to love the place too.'

'But there's nothing about how they met.' Martha was flipping over the pages. 'I'd love to have known that, wouldn't you? Where do you think she came from? Who were her parents?'

'And our grandparents? I'd have liked one or two of them around. Still, at least we know she's our mother. There's no mystery about that.'

Phoebe took the diary from Martha and turned some more of the pages.

'Let's get on to after Jack was born. Things obviously changed around that time.'

She held a page open which was dated 10 December 1919.

'Listen, this is while Alice was pregnant. He sounds beside himself with joy. "Alice looks even more beautiful carrying our child. We were in the drawing-room after dinner and she listened while I played. It was exactly as I'd dreamed during the war. The firelight, the slender, loving arms waiting to wrap themselves around me, the music, the feeling of safety. I have few nightmares now – perhaps my troubled thoughts have gone for ever. And now there is the happiness of knowing that Ballads will have an heir, and can stay in the family for another generation at least. I had worried that Alice was lonely here. She had lost that young gentleness I loved so much. But all's well. Motherhood will keep her happy and the child will bring us closer together."'

'Gosh,' Martha said. 'He did idealize everything, didn't he? He seems to have got Alice completely wrong. How couldn't he see that she wanted company and excitement, not a cosy family life? And not cooped up here all the time.'

'Strange, isn't it? But he wasn't at all perceptive. Not many men are, have you found that?'

'Sort of,' Martha murmured, and turned a few more pages.

'Here's where she started going out – October 1920 – he's writing about someone called Daisy coming to stay here . . . "Daisy, who's a delightful girl, if a little frivolous, seems to bring Alice to life in a way that I'm unable to, at least since Jack was born. Barratt tells me that they called on Madam Dot at Deep Ditchling. It was disturbing that Alice gave me a completely different picture of the visit, describing that notorious woman as a benevolent old lady interested in good works. I said nothing. If Alice wants secrets, I'm not going to spoil it by facing her with what I know. Only they won't be

secret from me. I can read her like a book. And that's something else she'll never know."'

'He was starting to be suspicious,' Phoebe said. 'He must
have watched her like a hawk from then on. Probably made
all sorts of checks, with Barratt and whoever else he could
get things out of without showing he suspected anything. But
I get the feeling that he never confronted her or tried to
understand or work things out. Why not, I wonder?'

'Too much the gentleman, I expect. Anyway, let's get on
to 1924 and around the summertime, when she started us.'

Martha shuffled through the volumes until she came to the
one for 1924 and opened it slowly, seemingly half reluctant
to know what was inside. She put her hand flat on the open
page and looked at Phoebe seriously.

'Are you sure?'

'Yes. I want to know. Don't you?'

Martha sighed heavily and looked across the glasshouse to
the darkening garden.

'I want to know if it's Colin. But if it's Francis, I don't
want to know, that's the trouble, Fee.'

Phoebe hugged her briefly.

'Don't fret. We probably won't find out anything for certain anyway. You'll still be able to think whatever you want
to.'

She leaned across Martha's shoulder and peered at the
page.

'Look. His writing's much bigger and darker. It looks kind
of angry. Shall I read it? "You take me for a fool, my dear
Alice, with your feeble deceptions. I saw a photo of you
yesterday. 'Mr Francis Bourne and Mrs Colin Whittaker
enjoy the final day at Ascot.' You looked happy and beautiful,
standing there in a big white hat that I've never seen, and
smiling up into the face of a man I have no desire to see or to
know. I suppose you imagine that I never see these trivial
society journals that you're so fond of? Did you think you
were safe when you stopped keeping them at Ballads? Didn't
it occur to you that I might come across them at my club?
You have turned my whole life into a fortress against

disclosure. I am constantly on my guard lest I reveal what I know. And everyone around me is on their guard lest they reveal what they know. I met Mrs Dacre in the bank today. 'Is your wife well?' she said. 'We hardly ever see her in the village.' These prying people would like to bring me to my knees and see me openly admit to being betrayed. But they never will. In the eyes of the world, you shall be my beloved, loyal wife until death do us part. Honour demands it."'

'So that's it,' Phoebe said. 'Honour. The honour of an officer and a gentleman.'

She read on. '"How clever you thought you were when you told me you were going to stay with Daisy because Julian was away. How can you stay so beautiful and so calm when lies are pouring out of your lovely mouth like poisonous fumes?"'

'Phew!' Phoebe leant back against the cushions and gazed at the book on her lap. 'He saw it all like some sort of play they were acting in, didn't he? Don't you get that feeling? There's something very contrived about it. It's as if he wasn't part of it, more that he was watching himself grappling with Alice – his beloved enemy – and pulling out all the appropriate emotions. Undying love and loyalty, honour, treachery tolerated for the sake of what people might think of him. And the idea that everyone knew and was trying to catch him out. What a battle! He kind of made himself another war to fight in, didn't he? What a sad, strange man . . .'

Martha was not inclined to speculate on Colin's complex nature and merely said, 'Yes, a strange man.' She seized hold of the diary and moved it from Phoebe's lap to her own.

'Come on, let's get to the summer . . .'

She turned the pages quickly until she was half-way through.

'Several times he mentions "union with Alice" – have you come across that? Do you think that means making love? God, Fee, I'm beginning to feel like a voyeur.'

'Yes, me too. But I suppose it must mean that. And that's what we're trying to find out, isn't it? Whether or not they "had union" at the vital time? Go on, Mart, don't start getting qualms now.'

Martha bent over the diary again.

'Here we are, the beginning of June. He seems to have stopped addressing Alice directly. He refers to her as "she". He writes: "She has just been away for three days and led me to believe that she had been in London for dress-fittings and staying with Daisy. But I noticed that a hotel's label had been removed with difficulty from her case and there was a programme from a Parisian theatre among the shoes in her wardrobe. So I have no doubt that she has been abroad with 'F'. I gave no hint of this, of course. But we began a pointless argument about Jack's education – why do we so often find ourselves ensnarled in these? – and it ended in union. As always, I felt more alone afterwards. And I wondered if I had pleased her. I can never tell."'

Martha flung the book away from her and turned to Phoebe with a look of triumph.

'That was it, then. Exactly the right time. It's him!'

Phoebe stood up and strode to the far end of the glasshouse.

'It tells us nothing, nothing,' she said wearily.

'I don't see why not. It's there in black and white. It clinches it.' Martha was on her feet now, walking towards her sister determinedly. 'You can hardly argue with that.'

'Clinch nothing,' Phoebe shouted. 'What do you suppose Francis and Alice did in Paris? Hold hands all the time? There must have been "union" there too. Don't you see? The conception could just as well have been there, in some hotel bedroom. We've still no way of knowing which was actually ... biologically ...'

'... the father.' Martha, for all her disappointment, was trying as usual to be helpful. 'So what do we do now?'

'Back to square one, I'm afraid,' Phoebe said gently.

'We could ask Alice?'

'We could. But she won't know either. If you sleep with two different men within about 24 hours, or even a few days, and you find you're pregnant afterwards, how could you ever know which one was the father?'

'Can't there be blood tests or something?'

'For that you need blood from both men who could be the father, and from the mother, and from the children. One man's dead. The other is not likely to want it proved one way or another. Nor is the mother. Which knocks down the whole idea. No, we'll just have to hope that Alice has some thoughts on the subject.'

'I doubt it somehow,' said Martha resignedly. 'She hates looking backwards.'

Slowly they collected up the diaries and put them on one of the tables.

'One thing that might help,' Martha said, 'is to go and see Rose. I can soon find out where she's living. One of her daughters is still in the village. I'd like to see her anyway.'

'So would I.' Phoebe had small hope that this would get them any further forward in clearing up the mystery, but she saw it as the means of some nostalgic comfort for Martha. 'Let's go and visit her as soon as we can fix it up. This week, say? Then Alice next, when she gets back to England.'

The following day Martha called on Rose's daughter in the village and obtained from her the telephone number of the other daughter in Norfolk who had Rose living with her. At once Martha rang the Norfolk number and arranged for the twins to visit their old nurse-maid in two days' time.

Later that day Charles Endicott's secretary rang and an appointment was made for his second visit to Ballads, the day after their Norfolk trip.

'Things are moving,' Phoebe commented as they marked the arrangements on the calendar in the kitchen. 'Thank heavens for that. Aren't you fed up with all this uncertainty?'

It was true that the twins experienced this period as a kind of limbo and were unusually edgy with each other. Their friction always seemed to come to a head in the kitchen, over some trivial item in the day-to-day routine of their lives. On this day Martha was preparing their lunch when Phoebe wandered in from the garden, her camera slung on a piece of webbing round her neck. She stood leaning back against the sink and watched Martha take the salad ingredients from the refrigerator.

'That looks like the remains of yesterday's lettuce,' she said jokingly. 'Is that what we're having for lunch?'

Martha glanced up with a cross expression as she thumped the china bowl on to the table.

'Yes. Why?'

'I bought a nice, fresh Webbs this morning. It's in the fridge. Can't we have that?'

'Not while we've still got this one to finish up.' Martha was at her most confident when dealing with household matters, secure in the knowledge that Phoebe had little experience of them and even less liking for them.

'Why not?' Phoebe was still trying to sound jokey. But she felt her own and Martha's growing tension.

'Because it would be a waste,' Martha said.

'A waste of what?'

'For heaven's sake, Fee, why the inquisition? It would be a waste of this lettuce' – and she slapped the side of the bowl – 'wouldn't it? You can see the logic in that, surely, with your famously keen brain . . .'

'No, I don't get it. If we have the old lettuce today, we'll have to leave the Webbs until that's old and then that'll be wasted.'

'No, we'll eat that tomorrow – or most of it.' Martha began transferring the leaves to a wooden bowl with sullen deliberation.

'I see,' said Phoebe, with a sarcastic edge to her voice. 'So we never get to eat today's lettuce. Always yesterday's. Are you mad?'

'No, I'm not. I've always done it like that.'

'Yeah, that's what's so crazy. Buying fresh lettuce and eating old lettuce. What could be madder?'

'I didn't ask you to buy the Webbs,' Martha said accusingly. 'That was your choice.'

'I bought it because I like fresh lettuce. I thought you did too. Look, Mart. Why don't we try it the other way round this time? Throw out yesterday's stuff and eat today's? How does that strike you?'

Martha made a small gesture of surrender with one hand and shrugged.

'All right, if you like. But I don't see the point.'

Phoebe, always magnanimous in victory, laughed and fetched the Webbs lettuce from the refrigerator. She shook it out of its paper bag, exposed its heart and tore off a few tiny curled leaves.

'Here,' she said, 'have a taste of real crispness. Isn't that good?'

Martha chewed on the fragments of lettuce cautiously while Phoebe scooped up the contents of the wooden bowl and slid them into the waste-bin.

'Mmm, very good, I have to admit. But that's a shillings-worth of lettuce you've just chucked away . . .'

'Better than down your throat, if it's not fresh.'

They stood smiling at each other, feeling for their old, familiar sparring positions, remembering how all the past conflicts had begun and ended much as this one had. There was something reassuring for them both in the speed with which they had advanced from their corners, mentally raised their fists and fought for points.

'My scratching-post, that's you,' said Phoebe fondly. 'Still the same. I've missed that. People do so want to agree with me all the time, trying to please.'

'Oh come off it, Fee. It's not that they want to please you. They're probably scared of you, the way I am sometimes.'

Phoebe did not seem displeased at this.

'No need for that,' she said airily. 'It's quite easy for you to stop me being so bossy. You're the only one who can.' She walked across to the table and began pulling the outer leaves from the lettuce. 'Who's going to do the driving on Thursday? Your car or mine?'

'You hate being a passenger. I couldn't bear to have you beside me working your legs on phantom brakes and clutch all the time. You can be driver. And, if you don't mind, I'll see to the lettuce before you mangle it to a pulp. OK?'

*

That evening they went up to the attic again at six o'clock. This time Martha, mindful of the previous supperless night while they pored over Colin's diaries, had put a casserole in the oven to cook while they searched, and its rich smell followed them up the stairs to the top floor.

'What are we looking for now?' Phoebe said as they stood again by the tea-chest in the circle of light.

'What about some of the later ones? After Jack died and up until he . . . up until Colin's death. There might be some more about us, and perhaps about the big "if".'

'Yes, that was strange about that "if". I mean, it was strange because of when he said it. You'd have thought that if he had doubts about being our father he'd have done something about it before. Why did he say something then, when he was just going to make it impossible for us, or anyone, to ask him anything more? Within an hour, he was gone. It was cruel, really. And not like him.'

'Oh, I don't know.' Martha was losing interest and had begun to lift books out of the tea-chest. 'It was *in extremis*, obviously. He must have been in a terrible state of mind.'

Martha held out one of the volumes towards Phoebe.

'This is the one we looked at a bit yesterday: 1927, and about how Alice reacted, or rather didn't react, to Jack's death. Shall we skim through that one?'

'Yes, that one. And let's take 1928, and 1930, when Rose left, and then the wartime ones, up until they finish altogether. That would be in 1942.'

'I know, Fee, I know.'

'We'll take them down, like yesterday. It's so gloomy up here. I say, Mart, would you mind if I took this box camera down? I'd rather like to handle it.'

'In that case, is it OK if I take his violin? I could see if it's still playable.'

Armed with the diaries and their trophies, they went downstairs to the glasshouse. Martha put the violin case on the canvas chair marked Colin and looked slightly sheepish as she caught Phoebe's eye.

'His chair, his fiddle,' she said. 'Sort of symbolic, isn't it? I'll have a go at playing it another time, not now.'

Phoebe nodded in understanding. She took up the diary for 1927 and began to read it to herself. Martha sat beside her with the volume for 1930 and silently turned the pages.

Suddenly Phoebe nudged her sister and pushed the diary she was reading across to her.

'Look at this. Not long after Jack's death, past the stuff about Alice, there's a lot about Rose, how she tried to comfort him. "What a sweet girl, what a tender heart!" he keeps saying. They must have talked together a lot. She was like that, wasn't she? Really warm. And she noticed and listened. I'm so glad she comforted him . . .'

'Perhaps she did more than that,' Martha said excitedly. 'Here, I've got the year she left. I can remember how terrible it was for us. It seems it was terrible for Colin too. Look – he keeps sort of calling out to her.'

They both bent their heads over the diary and Martha began to read aloud.

'"Rose! Rose! If only you could hear me. Are you happy there with your adoring husband and your child-to-be, in your cottage by the church? Rose, you did well to leave this house with all its sad memories. But the twins are not the only ones who miss you. We shall never speak again, except perhaps to say "good-day" if we should pass each other in the village. But I shall always remember your gentle voice and those strong brown arms and your kind heart. I shall never know their like again. And it's too late now to try to conjure from others the wonderful things I took from you, though you didn't know that you gave, or what you gave. Rose, Rose, my comforter, you understood so much without words. I didn't have to tell you about the horror that night after night sits grinning on my pillow . . ."'

'That's a quote, I'm sure of it,' Phoebe exclaimed. 'I've heard it before. But I can't remember the rest. I don't know what the "horror" was. I think, though, that it was something to do with love . . . Anyway, sorry to interrupt. Read on.'

'"You heard my despair, even though I never spoke of it. I

hated the way you just slipped away – you were terribly wronged by the manner of your going. I couldn't even say goodbye . . ."'

Martha faltered. 'The writing here goes all thin and scrawly. He must have been tired, or weeping perhaps. It tails off in a jumble of words – "Rose, Rose, how much longer can I go on like this? Hear me, hear me, I shall go on speaking to you, don't shut your ears to me. Please Rose, dear mother-to-be, when you're a mother, listen to me, dear, sweet mother, mother . . ."'

'It stops there, the entry for that day,' Martha said. 'He thinks of her as a mother, obviously. As a mother to him, I mean.'

'And she was motherly, wasn't she? Even before she really was a mother. I felt that, didn't you?'

They stared at each other, eyes brimming.

'Poor Colin!' Martha murmured, but what they each read in the eyes of the other was, 'Poor us.'

Phoebe blinked several times and turned away.

'Better not get drowned in self-pity,' she said in a shaky voice. 'One thing that sticks out a mile is that it's even more important that we see Rose. She must have reached him in some way. She might know much more than we realize.'

'Right.' Martha snapped the diary shut and stood up. 'I don't think I can bear any more of this melancholy either. Let's call it a day until we've seen Rose and Alice. There's so little about us in any of these. I don't honestly believe he thought about us much at all. He just didn't have the space for it. He was full up with his own sadness and horrors.'

Phoebe nodded and stood up.

'Talking of horrors,' she said, with a broad grin, 'there's a terrible smell of well-cooked casserole – I hesitate to say burnt, but what do you think?'

Martha made a dash for the kitchen with Phoebe in pursuit, and for the rest of the evening they managed to shake off the ghosts of Colin's sorrows and spoke only of the happy times with Rose more than thirty years before.

18

SUNDRY VISITS

The twins set off in happy mood on the journey to Norfolk. Phoebe, who rated herself a driver of advanced proficiency and panache, but whom Martha considered to be far too inclined to take flashy risks, set up a cracking pace through Berkshire, Hertfordshire, Cambridgeshire and Suffolk, refusing to stop for a meal until they were approaching Bury St Edmunds. Over their picnic lunch at the side of a field of corn they speculated on what kind of welcome they would get from Rose.

'All her daughter said on the phone,' Martha reported, 'was that she was well and would be pleased to see us. I guess she's over sixty now, only a couple of years younger than Alice. She might not remember much. A lot of water under the bridge and all that.'

'True. Besides, she might have wanted to forget quite a lot. From some of the things that Cook and Ethel used to hint at, I gather she wasn't treated too well. The way she left sounded rather grisly. Do you remember? One morning she was there, and when we came back in the afternoon she was gone.'

'Yes. Not a trace of her. I remember all right. It was horrid. I rather hope that's something she's definitely forgotten.' Martha flung a crust into the hedge and reached into the hamper for an apple.

'Well, we obviously haven't forgotten it,' Phoebe said. 'And that's your second apple. Where's mine?'

'Whoops!' Martha quickly took a large bite out of the apple, making it unarguably hers. 'There's a plum for you there. It's only got one mouldy patch on it . . .' She smiled innocently and chewed on the apple with exaggerated lip-smacking pleasure.

'Oh thanks.' Phoebe lay back on the rug, her arms above her head, and looked up at the sky. 'Anyway, it's worth a try. It's a nice day and this is good grub and I like this flat countryside. If we were at home we'd only be sitting around wondering if Charles Endicott really was going to buy Ballads.'

By two o'clock they were travelling along the long, empty, straight roads which link the numerous small hamlets inland of Sheringham and Cromer, and soon they were drawing up at a trio of terraced cottages standing in isolation at the edge of farmland. As they climbed stiffly out of the car, a short, grey-haired woman came out of one of the end cottages and hurried towards them, her face wreathed in smiles.

She was instantly recognizable as Rose, still russet-cheeked and strong of arm. The twins clutched at each other, as if needing support against the sudden onslaught of memories. Then they stepped apart, allowing Rose to draw to a halt between them and gather them to her sides as if they were small children. Although they topped her by several inches, they found themselves nestling against her comfortable, cushiony body just as in the old days.

'Rose, Rose,' they said, over and over again, their eyes meeting over the top of her head, signalling thankfulness and joy.

'My dear twins, my dear Phoebe and Martha, oh my dear twins!' Rose murmured repeatedly. 'What a terrible long time it's been! Come on now, let's go in . . .'

They pulled apart and stared at each other.

'We're all crying!' Martha said, laughing.

'Can you wonder at that, when it's been so long?' Rose said in her remembered matter-of-fact way. 'Oh, I did miss you girls . . . Here we are, this is my home. This part of the house is all mine. We can be on our own here, just like in the nursery.'

She led them into a sunny living-room, sat them down and went through a curtain into what was obviously a small kitchen beyond it. They heard her fill the kettle and light the gas. A strange sense of peace and home-coming stole over them and they sat in silence, gazing round the room and drinking in all the signs of a busy, happy life. There were children's toys and picture books here and there, knitting and newspapers, wellington boots at the ready by the door, a pile of ironing in a basket in one corner, goldfish pouting and lazily swishing their tails in a bowl by the window, and everywhere plants, flowers, cushions and family photos.

'Mrs Tiggy-Winkle!' Martha whispered, waving her arm to indicate all the cosiness.

'To the life,' Phoebe said.

As soon as Rose came back into the room, the twins fired questions at her.

'You have grandchildren? How many? How long have you been here? Is that your knitting? Do you garden? Are you happy?'

Rose put her hands over her ears and laughingly shook her head.

'No, no, twins. Not both at once. Just give Rose a chance. Well, then, now you're good and quiet I'll tell you. I have four grandchildren living here – next door, in the rest of the house. My daughter Joan is married to the farm manager here, so it's a tied house. There's a grandchild in Westknoll and another two in Yorkshire. You just wait until you're grandmothers! It's marvellous. And, yes, I'm happy because I'm busy and that seems to be the same thing, as far as I'm concerned.'

'And your husband, Arnold, where's ... when ...?' Martha looked hesitantly at Phoebe, checking that she was not being insensitive.

'Dead,' said Rose simply. 'He died ten years ago. That's why I came up here, to be with the family. I couldn't live on my own. Never. That's his photo, on the mantelpiece.'

She pointed to a silver-framed portrait of a florid, jolly-looking man with a beard.

'The very best, he was,' said Rose.

'And when you left Ballads,' Phoebe rushed on, 'we heard ages afterwards that you were going to have a baby. Was that your daughter who lives at Westknoll? I wished we could have gone on seeing you after you went. Do you know why we didn't?'

Rose stiffened as much as her soft plumpness would let her.

'Your mother thought it best, dear. She had her reasons, I suppose.'

'Did you like her?' Phoebe surprised herself with her blunt question.

Rose looked from one to the other, no longer smiling.

'I tried to,' she said.

She went out to the kitchen where the kettle could be heard whistling and bubbling. When she came back she carried a tray of tea-things and set it down carefully on a low table between the twins.

'I must hear about all your doings,' she said as she sat down.

'But first,' Phoebe said, 'what about that baby you were having when you left Ballads?'

'Oh yes. You pour the tea, Phoebe. You're the oldest. You see, I know which one is which! No, the daughter in Westknoll is not my oldest. That was a boy, a fine lad, in looks and every other way. He was killed on his motor-bike. That was fifteen years ago. He was twenty.'

'Oh, Rose. That's dreadful.' Martha looked round at the photographs displayed all over the room. 'Which is him?'

'No, it's not here. I don't keep it out. It upsets my daughter to see it. They were very close. It doesn't upset me. He gave us all great joy while he was alive. I'm not going to spoil it all by filling my mind with his death. I lost a young brother, too, you know, so I know what it's all about. I tried to tell your father not to grieve so long and so bitterly. He took Jack's death very hard. You wouldn't know that. You were too young. It was a terrible tragedy for him.'

'And for our mother?' Martha asked.

Rose stared into her tea-cup thoughtfully.

'No, I don't think so. Like a greyhound, dear, your mother was. I hope you don't mind me saying that. She always put me in mind of a greyhound. Have you ever known one?'

The twins shook their heads.

'Well, they keep themselves to themselves. They don't like being touched. They're worse than cats for going their own way and shutting you out. You never know what they're feeling, or if they're feeling at all. It was my mother who first put me on to the likeness. And she never met your mother. It was just from all I'd told her about your mother and Mr Colin, and you children and the whole goings-on at Ballads. But there, I've said enough. She's your mother, after all.'

Phoebe leant forward and gripped the arms of her chair.

'Yes, she is. But, Rose, what worries us is who our father was. You see, he said something just before he died – I expect you heard how that happened . . .?'

Rose nodded, her expression quite blank.

'Just before he . . . before it happened . . . he was talking to us and he said, "If I'm your father". He seemed not to be sure. It's worried us because, as I expect you also know, our mother had . . . she wasn't faithful to him, hadn't been for a long time and when she became pregnant with us – well, she wasn't faithful then. There was another man who might have been our father . . . Did you know that, Rose?'

Rose was blushing like a young girl. She looked awkwardly towards the door, as if seeking escape.

'This is very embarrassing,' she said. 'Your mother's still alive, of course. I'm not sure any of us should be talking about her like this.'

'She'll never know, Rose,' said Martha encouragingly. 'This is just between us, like it used to be in the nursery.'

'Well, dear, I don't know all that much about your mother. I just knew she was away a lot.'

'And she was away for a long time – three days – in the summer of 1924, the year before we were born. Does that ring any bells? Jack would have been about four. Can you remember anything, absolutely anything about that time?'

'Oh dear, Phoebe, I do remember that you were always such a one for questions. Nobody seemed to like that habit of yours very much. But I always thought it was a good thing, to be so eager to learn and find things out. I was always very proud of your curiosity. Anyway, let me think. 1924 you say? The summertime and Jack was four?'

Rose put her hand up to her head, as if she could thus turn a key into her thoughts, and stared up at the ceiling.

'No, it's all just a blur of your mother's comings and goings One thing I can say is that your mother and father ... well, I know all children like to think that their own parents don't do such things but they did used to sleep together, of course. Making love or having sex is what they call it now, isn't that right?'

'Yes, that's right, Rose.' Martha struggled to keep a straight face. 'Yes, we can believe that. When they were together, which wasn't often, they were close somehow. But we're not sure it was love. More like some kind of need. But what we wondered was whether you knew for certain if it was her lover she went away with for those three days, like Colin says it was in his diary ...'

Martha stopped apologetically as Rose gasped and put her hands up to her face. When she brought them down again she was blushing a deep red and there was a look of horror on her kindly face.

'His diaries, my dears? I thought they would all be gone long ago. Have you seen them? Have you read any of them?'

Rose was clearly agitated and the twins looked at each other with concern and mystification. Phoebe was now consumed with curiosity and a sense of having stumbled on something important.

'You know about his diaries then? Did you ever see them? Did you read any of them?'

The twins were immediately aware that Rose was experiencing a struggle between her natural, honest openness and some other pull towards concealment.

'It's all right,' Martha said softly. 'We've seen them. And we've read a lot of them. They give nothing away.'

Rose looked from one to the other tensely.

'Did you ever see them? Or read them?' Phoebe leant forward eagerly.

'Oh do shut up, Fee. You sound like a lawyer.' Martha sat

back in a relaxed position, as if to show that there was no pressure on Rose to answer. 'In any case,' she added, 'it doesn't matter if Rose read the diaries or not. What we're looking for, Rose, is anything, any real information, that he didn't write in his diary.'

'About your mother?' Rose said cautiously.

'Well, yes, and about her lover. And whether you know anything about who our father was.'

'Oh no, I'm sorry. I know nothing about any of that.' Rose seemed relieved, as if the talking had moved on to safer ground, which pleased Martha but made Phoebe frown thoughtfully.

'I can tell you,' she said, speaking more easily, 'that he did let me into his study – his holy of holies I used to call it. And I knew he wrote a diary there, and lots of other things. Maps and goodness knows what else. I was afraid for his sanity when I saw all that writing and drawing. I never knew anyone so driven to watch and listen and write things down. But it was because of the war, wasn't it? Lots of men came back like that – all at sixes and sevens.'

'Yes,' Martha said. 'It was the war – and other things. We've seen all those papers too. All the diaries show is that either he or Francis Bourne could have been our father. But did he ever say anything to you about any suspicions? Any doubts that he was really our father?'

'Oh no, he didn't. And he wouldn't have. He wasn't a man to say much, as you know. Not about anyone else, anyway. He would talk about himself often, the terrible time in the war, his strict father, Jack's death, that kind of thing. He did seem to want a great deal of comforting. He was on his own such a lot, wasn't he?'

'So he did talk to you?' Phoebe said gently.

'Oh yes, dear. About his troubles ... but I shouldn't be saying this. I was only a servant. I don't know why he trusted me. He just did.'

'We know why,' Martha said in a rush. 'Because you're so like a mother. Everyone's idea of a real mother. That's how you were with us. And you loved him, didn't you, like we did?'

For a moment it looked as if Rose would deny Martha's suggestion. Then she smiled broadly and the twins noted again her air of having been relieved of a burden.

'Yes, of course I did. No one with a heart could help loving him ... such a good man, and so needy ...'

Phoebe glanced at Martha, drew some sort of permission from her answering smile, and spoke to Rose in a quiet, matter-of-fact voice.

'And he loved you,' she said, as if there were no argument about it.

'Oh no, dear. I wouldn't have expected that. He loved your mother, you see. Loved her to distraction. Though I don't think she knew it. But he gave me what he could. That's all that matters.'

She braced herself, reached for the tea-tray, took a firm hold of the tea-pot and stood up.

'I'll just freshen this,' she said and walked unsteadily into her tiny kitchen.

'So!' Martha said, with a questioning look at Phoebe. 'Where are we now?'

'Nowhere any further about the father mystery. Still, we didn't expect to be. But ...' – Phoebe leant forward and lowered her voice – '... the photo of the son who died – ask her if we can see it. I rather think she wants us to ...'

Martha nodded. Rose came back into the room. She poured out more tea and slopped some of it into Martha's saucer.

'Oh dear,' she said. 'You girls have got me all rattled. I don't think of those days at Ballads very often, you know. So much has happened since, such a lot of happiness for me. They were dark days, most of them. But some were all right. We had some good games and cuddles, didn't we?'

'Dear Rose,' Martha said. 'You were the one nice, ordinary person ...'

'Ordinary, eh?' Rose giggled and glanced at Phoebe. 'Hark at her, the cheeky girl!'

Martha seized on the warmth of the moment.

'That photo of your son, your first-born? Could we see it? We've seen all the rest of your family ...' – she waved her hand round the photographs on the mantelpiece, tables and walls – '. . . it would be lovely to see what he looked like too.'

There was a movement on the other side of the wall which separated Rose's cottage from the rest of the house. Rose looked anxiously towards the connecting door.

'My daughter's back,' she said. 'If I get the photo out, I don't want her to know. It would worry her. Just a moment . . .'

She went to the door and opened it a crack.

'The twins are still here, Joan. We'll be out in a while and then you can meet them.'

'All right, Mum. Take your time,' came a cheerful response from the other side of the door, followed by the rustling of paper.

'Been shopping,' Rose said, nodding towards the next room. 'But she specially asked to meet you. I'm glad she's back in time.'

She went across to a small chest of drawers in the corner of the room. She pulled open the bottom drawer and took out a slim cardboard box. She held it close to her as she walked slowly towards the twins.

'Just a quick look then,' she said. She was trembling as she took the lid off the box and lifted out a glass-covered photograph. Its plain wooden frame was so highly polished that it gleamed brightly in the sunshine and made little bars of light on Rose's face as she held the picture in both hands in front of her and gazed at it proudly.

'You take it, Martha, and hold it carefully. Only I want you both to look at it at the same time. You go over to your sister, Phoebe. Get close now. That's how I remember you always were. There you are. You can have it now.'

She passed the picture to Martha. Her hands slid away from it slowly, as if she could hardly bear to let it go.

The twins were tense with a half-formed idea to which they did not dare give full substance. Phoebe stood behind Martha's chair with one hand on her sister's shoulder. She tightened her grip as Martha turned the picture round, so that the young man was looking directly at them from out of his portrait. The look was eager and natural, as if someone had just called his name and he had turned to answer, his face open and expectant, his head inclined a little, his mouth and eyes ready to smile.

'Yes,' the twins said in unison, so quietly it was more like a sigh.

It was just as they had known it would be. The face that looked out at them, with the dark, thoughtful eyes and the thick, unruly hair and the eyebrows as straight as ruled lines, was Colin's face, as close in likeness as if they too had been twins.

They looked at it and smiled at Rose and looked at it again, but said nothing. Eventually, Martha handed it back to Rose, who slipped it into the box, closed the lid and returned it to the chest of drawers.

When she sat down again she smoothed her skirt and said, 'There we are then,' in a contented tone of voice.

'Did our father know?' Phoebe asked.

Rose shook her head.

'Did anyone? Does anyone?'

'Only you.'

'Not even your husband?' Phoebe persisted.

'He might have guessed,' Rose said calmly. 'I don't know. We never spoke of it. But he was a wonderful father to him, to all our children. The boy had a lovely life. Far happier than if he had known the truth. Or if anyone else had. He was spared the hand of Ballads.'

The hand of Ballads. It sounded, Martha thought, like the toll of a giant bell, warning of Gothic horrors. What, indeed, would Ballads have done to him, if he had ever had to claim it as home? What could knowledge of his real father have given him in return for what it took away? She found herself envying him his secure, uncomplicated life with the accepting Arnold and the loving Rose. Spared the hand of Ballads – lucky child!

She stood up. Immediately Phoebe was on her feet too.

'We must go now,' Martha said. 'Can we hug again, like the olden days?'

Rose embraced them both, reaching upwards to clasp their heads against her neck, one on each side.

As they drew apart, Phoebe took Rose's hand in hers.

'One more thing, Rose. You didn't tell us his name. But I think we know what it is . . .'

Rose squeezed her hand and laughed.

'Get on with you, Miss Needle-Nose. That's the last, the very last of your pryings. Yes, of course, it was Jack. His name was Jack. Now let's be moving. Come and meet our Joan. She knows all about my twins. And now,' she added, putting a finger to her lips to signal a secret, 'my twins know all about me.'

As the twins headed southward for home in the dusk they kept up a comfortable silence for several miles, each occupied with her own thoughts.

After a while Martha stretched and yawned and turned to Phoebe.

'Are you glad?' she asked.

'Very glad.'

'He did have some comfort, then.'

'And some love.'

Martha threw her head back and shouted at the car-roof.

'Hooray for Rose! Marvellous Rose!'

It was dark as they drove away from refuelling at Baldock.

'I like it in the car at night,' Phoebe said. 'It's a little world hurrying through the darkness. I say, I'm really pleased we found out about all this before Ballads goes. I feel much more settled now, ready to let Ballads go. Do you?'

'Yes. It doesn't seem to matter so much, losing Ballads. But I hope it goes to the charming Charles, all the same.'

'And our father?'

'Oh yes, Fee, that still matters. But, it's funny, I feel quite different now about tackling Alice. Quite looking forward to it, in fact.'

The trouble was, the twins agreed on their way to London, that they always set out on their rare visits to Alice with high hopes that, somehow, things would be different. They taxed each other frequently on exactly what differences they could reasonably expect, but neither had a firm answer.

'She might suddenly show a real interest in us,' Martha had occasionally suggested. 'Ask about Donald and the boys. Or want to know about your travels . . .'

'Or about your painting. Or Ballads.'

'She'll probe about men,' Martha added glumly. 'She always does that. But she might even open up about her own travels. Give us the really interesting stuff, instead of what she ate and what's in the shops and who paid court to her.'

As Phoebe rang the bell at Alice's mews house they both settled to the inevitable spirit-lowering wait before she answered the door. Inevitably, too, they felt that stab of doubt – that they had come on the right day and at the right time – which overcomes anyone deprived of an instant welcome.

'If it were my children coming to see me, I'd be waiting at the window,' Martha said. 'And I'd leave the door open. But still,' she made an effort to be charitable, 'you can't do that in London – leave your door open.'

'You could be at the window, though.'

As Phoebe spoke, the door opened and Alice stood there in a silky blue house-coat with a miniature collie-type dog in her arms. She had to strain across the dog's body in order to proffer her cheek to the twins. Her eyes were closed, but it was impossible to tell whether this was through pleasure or distaste.

'A dog, Alice?' Phoebe said. 'How come?'

'Follow me and I'll tell all. Here, we'll go in the sitting-room. Don't expect perfection though. I've hardly had time to turn round since I got back.'

Nevertheless, her house was in its usual pristine state, with the ornaments in the same places at the same angles, the furniture and cushions looking as if they had never borne the imprint of a human body, and not an open book, a discarded newspaper or a used cup or glass to be seen. In spite of the warmth of the day, the heating was full on. Phoebe fanned herself discreetly.

'Phew!' she said. 'It's very . . . er . . . very cosy in here.'

Alice sat down with the dog in her lap. It began to struggle and make little yapping noises, but soon gave up under pressure of Alice's hand and slumped somewhat dejectedly with its head on its front paws and its back legs dangling down beside Alice's knees.

'Francis gave it to me,' Alice said. 'Isn't it a beauty? Hair a bit like mine, don't you agree? Francis worries that I might get lonely. He doesn't come up so often now – old age creeping on, you know. And his wife's very poorly. He thought the dog would be good company for me.'

She bent her head down and kissed the dog's twitching ear. 'And so you are, my lover-boy, aren't you?'

'What's he called?' Martha asked in a bright, interested voice.

'Disraeli. It was my idea. It suddenly came to me in the bath. I wondered about calling him Benjamin at first. Then I found myself saying "Benjamin Disraeli" and I thought, that's it! Why not Disraeli? I tried it out on him. I spoke to him directly, like this ' – she twisted the dog's head round to face her and addressed it in a stern voice – 'Hullo Disraeli! Mother's speaking to you, Disraeli. And do you know, he seemed to understand straight away, didn't you, my darling? He's always answered to it ever since. I've only to call "Disraeli", suitably clearly, and he comes running.'

The twins were sinking slowly into a state of lethargy, lulled by the heat and the stream of trivia, almost forgetting their visit had an important purpose. Martha roused herself and began wriggling out of her denim jacket.

Alice looked in the twins' direction for the first time since they had arrived, though still not directly at either of them.

'That's a remarkable garment you're wearing, Martha. Is that one of the latest fashions for people your age?'

Phoebe saw Martha's face crumple. She gritted her teeth against the impulse to glower at Alice. Martha took the jacket off very slowly and laid it over the arm of her chair.

'Outside, on the peg, Martha, if you wouldn't mind . . .' Alice said. She was bent over the dog again and seemed oblivious to the fact that she had expertly hit on Martha's

Achilles' heel. She had no confidence in her choice of clothes, but today she had thought, after long consultation with Phoebe, that she had settled for a combination of good taste and imagination that would not arouse any comment from Alice. She gave Phoebe a pained grin as she walked out to the hall.

'Well, I expect you'd like to hear all about my trip.' Alice leant back in her chair as Martha came back into the room and sat down, hugging her knees tightly like someone trying to be inconspicuous. The dog, freed from Alice's embrace, leapt from her knees and squirmed under a low table at the other side of the room. Alice waved at the dog dismissively. 'It's because you two are here,' she said. 'He doesn't like company. Not women, at any rate.'

'Yes, of course. We're longing to hear about the trip. But first, Alice, there are a few things we'd rather like to know.' Phoebe shifted nearer to Martha, feeling ashamed of the wheedling note in her voice.

'About Ballads?' Alice said without interest. 'Have you sold it yet?'

'No. But almost . . .'

'Who's buying it? Anyone I know?'

'You might know him,' Martha said. 'A man called Charles Endicott, but he hasn't made up his . . .'

'A nice man, is he? Our kind? What sort of age?'

'He's around our age, it's hard to tell. About fortyish, we guessed.' Martha turned to Phoebe. 'And he's definitely nice . . .'

'Good-looking, you mean?' Alice was always relentless with her questions about people, though never seeming to want to know more than what they looked like and what their social status was.

'Not good-looking, no, but a very pleasant face, kind and sensitive. We liked him a lot.' Phoebe realized at once that she had spoken rashly. Alice showed a glimmer of keen interest and leant forward.

'Ah, did you¨ she said. 'Anything there for you, Phoebe? Is he married?'

329

'Yes, very much so. He brought his wife with him.'

'That's neither here nor there, in this day and age, is it? He must be well-off, that's certain, if he's thinking of buying Ballads. Endicott? Endicott? I think I know the name. Did he give a hint of what he does for a living?'

'No, Alice. He didn't . . . but let's not . . .'

'Where does he live?'

'London, I think. No idea whereabouts. But, the point is, he hasn't said he definitely wants it yet. He's coming tomorrow evening for another look.'

'In the evening, eh? To me, that points to a more than passing interest, a social interest, in one of you.' She gazed at the twins thoughtfully, her head on one side. 'Of course, Martha, you're somewhat committed to Donald. Or are you? Is he still about?'

'Yes and no,' Martha said in a shaky voice. 'He's got his own house now and the boys are with him. He wants me to go and live there too . . . all of us together again.'

'Oh well, that seems the best answer to me. Why don't you?'

'I probably will, once Ballads has gone. It's just that I've never been ready before – to leave Ballads, I mean. I say, Fee,' Martha turned to Phoebe with a look of discovery on her face, 'I didn't know that until I heard myself say it. It's true though. It's only at Ballads that Donald and I have any problems.'

'I know, Mart. It's true . . .'

'That doesn't surprise me in the least,' Alice said with a laugh. 'Ballads has always done that to people, given them problems. And what about you Phoebe? Anyone in mind at all?'

'Not really. No one you know anyway . . . but, Alice, please, we must ask you about our father . . .'

Alice glanced at the clock on the table by her chair.

'Yes? Only let's not forget the passage of time. I'm due for a massage at noon. Then Disraeli and I will have our usual walkies. You weren't thinking of staying up for lunch, I take it?'

'No, Alice. Don't worry,' Martha said soothingly. 'We know how busy you are. It needn't take long.'

'Mysteries, mysteries,' Alice said nervously. 'Come on then. What's on your minds?'

Phoebe spoke with assurance, as if she had rehearsed over and over again what she wanted to say. She was not diverted by Martha's anxious fidgeting beside her, nor by Alice's finger-clicking and wheedling noises in the direction of the dog, which still cowered under the table, its small, coal-black eyes looking accusingly at the company.

'When Colin spoke to us before he died, he said something that showed he had some doubts about whether he was our father. We didn't know much then about your life at Ballads, nor outside it. But we know more now. And we've seen his diaries. We've also seen Rose . . .' – Alice raised her eyebrows and made as if to speak, but Phoebe pressed on – '. . . Yes, we went yesterday . . . we'll tell you more about that later. For now, let's stick to the question that worries us. Are you certain that Colin is our father? Do you think that anyone else might be? Francis, for instance? This may seem like prying into your privacy. But we don't mean it like that. It's just that it's terribly important to us. We really need to know who our father was. So, please, can you help?'

If anyone had been present who knew Alice better than her daughters did, they might have said that she was considerably moved by Phoebe's plea. She twisted her ring round and round on her finger. She smoothed her hand over her hair. She looked across the room. She called the dog softly and was then silent when he remained motionless. But to the twins it seemed that she was searching for a way of not answering the question and was completely unmoved by it.

At length, she looked distantly at the space between the twins and shrugged.

'It's all water under the bridge. I really can't think why it matters. If the truth be known, I was extremely surprised to be pregnant with you in the first place. I thought I had taken precautions to make any more children very unlikely, if not impossible. You weren't at all welcome, believe me . . .'

The twins gasped in unison.

'But of course you were welcome when you were here. Certainly . . .' Alice seemed to be racking her mind for proof of the truth of this statement. Her face brightened. 'Colin was very pleased to be a father again. He never showed anything else, did he? It was only after Jack was gone that he was rather, well, rather distant. And that was with everybody.'

'So he was our father then?' Phoebe said in a would-be casual voice.

'If you like, yes.' Alice drew her house-coat closer round her throat and began stroking her neck with the palms of both hands. 'It's one's neck that shows one's age first, you know. You girls ought to start quite early to make sure all stays firm in that area, like I have.'

'Thanks, we'll watch that,' Phoebe said. 'But what do you mean by "if we like"? Does that mean either of them could be?'

'Got it!' Alice clapped her hands as if Phoebe had made a lucky winning move in a game of chance. 'That's exactly it. And there you have it, so we don't need to brood over the past any longer, do we? Now, you said you'd seen Rose. She must be sixty or more now. What does she look like?'

The twins looked confusedly at each other for a moment, unable to make an immediate leap from their sense of disappointment to more small talk. They both shrugged as if to say, 'It's as we thought,' and stood up.

'We'd better go,' Martha said. 'Rose was very well. She looks just the same really – motherly.'

'Yes, she was always rather a homely girl.' Alice looked pleased, evidently equating motherliness with dullness. 'Does she look her age?'

Martha knew what Alice was asking.

'You look much younger than her,' she said.

'And did I come into your cosy conversation?'

'Yes, of course,' Phoebe said, with a touch of irony. 'She remembers you well. But she said nothing that we didn't know already.'

'That's all right then,' Alice said with satisfaction. 'It never really helps to look back at the past, does it? I always find it quite gruesome.'

She stood up and shook out the folds of her housecoat.

'Well, I must get myself together for the masseuse. And you have to get Ballads ready for the nice Mr Endicott. We must get weaving, all of us. Did I tell you? I'm going to the Canaries in two weeks – lucky me! I'll send you a card, of course. And we'll meet up when I get back. I shall want to hear more about your plans then, when you've got rid of Ballads.'

As the three of them went into the narrow hall, the dog shot out from under the table and made a dash for the front door, pawing excitedly at the mat and yelping frantically.

Alice scooped him up in her arms and backed into the sitting-room.

'Not walkies time yet, my angel,' she said soothingly. 'Come on now, calm down. Sit here with mother until the visitors have gone . . .'

'Visitors!' Phoebe hissed at Martha, jerking her head towards the sitting-room. 'Ever get that unwanted feeling?'

'Better see yourselves off,' Alice called out. 'Disraeli's all upset.'

'Right then, we're away. Have a good trip. Bye . . .' The twins hesitated for a moment, waiting for an answering goodbye. But all they heard were Alice's fond, cooing reassurances to the dog.

Charles Endicott came to Ballads in the early evening, bearing wine and flowers.

Martha looked at the label on the bottle as she took it from him.

'Goody!' she said. 'It's much better than the bottle we've got ready. Let's drink yours instead.'

'May we talk in the glasshouse?' Charles looked from one twin to the other with his urbane smile. 'I've thought about it so much.'

'Of course. We were going to anyway. We saw you loved it.'

In the glasshouse Charles stood silently in the middle for a while, looking up at the vine. He had a habit of putting his finger-tips to his mouth and lightly stroking his lips. Phoebe and Martha smiled at each other, sharing their perception that here was a sensuous man who pleased them. Charles walked to the far end and looked out at the garden.

'You don't keep the fountain going then? Why's that?'

Martha was wrestling with a corkscrew and answered without looking up and without hesitation.

'We had an older brother who was drowned there. It's never been used since.'

'Aah, I thought so. This place is full of resonances. You know that, don't you?' He turned round and strolled across the glasshouse to Colin's chair. He stroked the back where Colin's name was written. 'This, for instance. Colin was your father's name?'

Phoebe, normally so guarded, dropped all her defences in the face of his interest. It was a completely novel experience, this feeling of instant intimacy between the three of them. After exchanging a quick confirming glance with Martha, she relaxed on to a settee and smiled warmly at Charles.

'Are you sure you want to know?' she said. 'It's a bit of a Pandora's box.'

'I do want to know, yes. This house intrigues me. And so do its owners. I've never come across twins before. But do I seem to pry?'

Martha handed him a glass of wine with a slight, mocking bow.

'If that's what you're doing, we like it,' she said. 'We've been doing a lot of prying ourselves lately, as a matter of fact. And you've incidentally touched on the subject of it.'

'Your father? Go on.'

As Phoebe and Martha took it in turns to tell of Colin's doubts and their search for the truth, of Alice's double life and of Rose and her son, they both sank gratefully into that self-indulgent state they remembered from long ago, when they had talked into the night with their Uncle Frederick after their father's death. As it was then, the light faded outside while they talked and the glasshouse became a mysterious place of shadows and hushed voices. The vine seemed to listen too, rustling its leaves now and then or creaking with the weight of its nearly ripe fruit. Another bottle of wine was opened, and a third. Pauses grew longer and speech was slower. Laughter was quick to bubble up at things that were not funny, and deep thought given to remarks that were not profound.

'You're just like an old friend,' Martha said at one point. 'It's really incredible. Do you always get close to people like this? And so quickly? It's not the wine, you know. And it's not us. We don't ever get close to people, do we, Fee?'

'Only each other,' Phoebe said and turned towards the circle of pale light that was Charles's face. 'Before I get too drunk to care, what about Ballads? Are you going to buy it?'

'Oh, Fee, not business . . .' Martha protested. 'We don't know anything about him yet. Why should all the confidences come from us?'

Charles gave a low laugh and stood up.

'There's little to tell,' he said, 'and certainly nothing to match what's happened in this house over the years. But I'll be honest with you about one thing . . .' – the twins drew breath expectantly – '. . . I'm ravenously hungry. Shall we explore your kitchen?'

Martha plunged into flustered apologies. 'How awful of me! I just wasn't thinking about food. Charles, I'm so sorry. Look, you two stay here a bit longer. I'll go and get something ready, pâté, French bread – that all right? – and then we'll scoff it in the kitchen.' She hurried out and could soon be heard opening and shutting drawers and cupboards.

A shaft of light from the passage shone on to the glasshouse floor between Charles and Phoebe. He stepped across it carefully, as if it were a solid hazard, and stood in front of her.

'Shall we meet another time? In London perhaps?' he asked softly.

'Yes.'

'All right to ring you here?' He looked questioningly towards the kitchen.

'Yes. Mart would know anyway, even if I didn't tell her.'

'She would, yes. It's strange, you and her . . .'

'But not to us. And you? I don't expect I can ring you?'

'No, it's best not.'

He put his arm along the back of her neck and Phoebe leant her head against his. She felt his facial muscles flex suddenly.

'I couldn't say in front of Martha,' he said, 'but . . . there's a hitch . . .'

'You can't have Ballads. Isn't that it?'

'I don't think I can. But I'm still trying. And hoping.'

'That's sad for you. I'm so sorry. When will you know?'

'In a few days. I'll tell you straight away. You mustn't worry. Someone else will want it.'

'We're not worried about that. But you wanted it badly . . .'

'Yes.'

He turned and took her face in his hands. It was night now and the glasshouse was so dark that not even the shaft of light revealed their expressions to each other. Thus sightless, they kissed and confirmed their mutual longing and hope.

'Soon, soon,' he said, as they drew apart and turned to leave the glasshouse.

In the kitchen all was bright and warm and they sat round the table in attitudes of unbuttoned ease, cutting slices for themselves off the loaf, helping themselves to pâté and cheese and curling their hands round steaming mugs of coffee. After the confidences in the glasshouse, all three had switched to a more matter-of-fact, light-hearted mood.

'About your father,' Charles said, reaching across for the butter, 'as I see it, you've just got to face the fact that you may never know which it is. Does that bother you? What about you, Martha?'

'I don't think it bothers me all that much. Not as much as it did, anyway. But the sticking-point is that I hope terribly that it was Colin. Whereas my dear sister here, I'm pretty certain that she'd rather it was Francis. Am I right, Fee?'

'I suppose so. Though it's not quite as black and white as that.' Phoebe caught a warning glance from Martha and interpreted it as a plea not to darken the happy mood around the table. She lightened her voice and ended lamely, 'Of course, the ideal solution would be if we had different fathers. It's being so bound up with each other, like one person, that's most of the trouble. But, unfortunately, that's impossible. So . . .'

Charles suddenly thumped his hand flat on the table, making the plates rattle and the bread-knife skitter off the edge to the floor.

'No, no,' he shouted, half rising from his chair. 'It's not impossible. I'm absolutely certain it isn't.' He wrenched at his tie as if loosening the knot would somehow liberate his thoughts. 'God, let me think! I know there was something in the papers once, a court case or something similar. Maybe it was something to do with inheritance, or a crime, I can't remember. But it concerned twins . . .'

Martha stared at him in bewilderment.

'You mean, we could have different fathers? Are you serious?'

'Yes, Martha. It's a fact. And, what's more, I'd think that any respectable book on genes or heredity would have something about it. Would you like me to find out? I can get to a decent library, better than you've got around here, that's for sure.'

'Yes, yes!' Phoebe was on her feet. 'Please do that. When? When can you get to a library?'

'Tomorrow, if I can. And if I can't, I'll get someone else to do it.'

'And will you ring us straight away?'

'You'll be rung,' Charles said, with a businesslike air. 'And now, forgive me, it's a case of eat and run. I must start on the drive back.'

He tightened his tie and put on his jacket. Suddenly, he had the air of a businessman again, a visitor interested in buying a property, and the twins found themselves making formal, polite noises of regret at his going and thanks for his coming.

At the front door he exchanged a brief embrace with them both and hurried to his car. As the tail-lights disappeared down the lane, the twins looked at each other with beaming faces.

'We'll have to be patient,' Martha said. 'But oh, Fee. If it's really possible, well, it's the answer, isn't it?'

'Good enough for me,' Phoebe said cheerfully. 'But I'm not too sure he's going to be able to buy Ballads.'

'Oh never mind. I mean, that's bad news for him. But there'll be someone else. I'm resigned to leaving here anyway. I really am. I've pretty well made up my mind to make a go of it with Donald and the boys. What will you do, though?'

'I'll find somewhere. Perhaps a cottage by the sea. Or a flat bang in the centre of London. Either will do. What I don't want is anything in between – a semi in suburbia, or a villa in Clapham . . .'

'No. They're not you.' She took Phoebe's arm as they walked back to the kitchen. 'You wouldn't be able to see much of Charles, though, if you chose the cottage by the sea . . .'

'You could tell, could you? Yes, I shall be seeing him. But it doesn't have to be often. He's not going to be my whole life, just a bonus. And I won't be all his. It doesn't have the feel of permanence or marriage, or anything heavy. He has his wife. It'll be the usual under-cover thing, I suppose. Funny how I always end up loving married men.'

Martha paused between the table and the sink, a pile of dishes in her hand. She looked at Phoebe searchingly.

'Perhaps that's something to do with being a twin. You just can't get out of the habit of sharing. I mean, you've had to share me with Donald. We both had to share our parents right from the start – neither of us ever had them to ourselves. Or had them at all really. Rose too – we shared her.'

Phoebe put her hands over her ears and shook her head vigorously.

'Enough, Mart, enough! Let's sleep on it all. Here, I'll take those.' She took the pile of dishes from Martha and placed them haphazardly in the sink. 'Let's have "pax" until we hear from him about Ballads, and about the father problem. All right?'

'All right, no more said. Are the lights out in the glass-house?'

'Yes. I'm certain of that. They were never put on – not tonight.'

Phoebe thought for a moment of telling Martha about the conversation and the closeness, there in the wine-scented dark, she and Charles, and the touching and the kiss. Then she thought, no, it's about time we stopped sharing everything.

19

THE PARTING

The twins rose early next day and resolved to be both busy and patient, so that the unanswered questions would not preoccupy them. But by nine o'clock they had begun listening for the ring of the telephone and hovering in the drawing-room in order to be nearby to answer it.

'I've never felt so beastly unsettled,' Martha said. 'Shall we go for a walk? Or go up in the attic again? Or what?'

'I don't feel like doing either of those. But it's crazy hanging about the house. Charles can't possibly come up with any answers before lunchtime at the earliest. To tell the truth, Mart, I feel like being alone. Does that suit you?'

'Perfectly,' Martha said with obvious relief. 'Anything to avoid more fights over the lettuce or some other niggly domestic detail.'

She laughed and thumbed her nose at Phoebe.

'What I really feel like doing,' she added, 'is nipping over to see Donald and the boys. Donald has an idea for us all to go away abroad somewhere for a couple of weeks. He and I need to talk about that. So you can hold the fort here and receive all the news.'

They stood looking at each other, both uncertain that separation, on this day of all days, was acceptable.

'Can you bear it, though?' Phoebe asked anxiously. 'Not knowing about anything until you get back?'

'I'll be home by teatime. That's not so long. And you mightn't even have heard anything by then. I don't expect Charles is making it a number-one priority, somehow. Or do you think so?'

'Hardly. All right, then, Mart. Go soon and come back

soon. I'll probably write some letters. It's about time I did something about getting some more work, anyway. I'll do a bit of brushing-up on my contacts . . .'

Phoebe turned to go upstairs and Martha put out a hand to restrain her.

'What do you think about me and Donald? Should I go back?'

'Do you want to?'

'Yes, I do. I really do. There was a hurdle, a kind of barrier, but I think it's gone.'

'And if it isn't, you could bust it down, couldn't you? I mean, it's all different now. Don't you feel somehow changed?'

'Yes. And you too?'

'That's what's different . . . that you have to ask me.'

Charles rang just before one o'clock.

'Oh good, I'm glad it's you,' he said. 'I was wondering how to put it to Martha.'

'You can't have Ballads then?'

'No, it hasn't worked out. I'm so sorry. But, look, I've spoken to your estate agent down there – thought I'd better do that straight away. He says there are two other interested bodies. They're both keen, apparently, and prepared to try and outbid each other. So it'll go all right '

'What sort of bodies? Did he say?'

'You might not like this, but they're both organizations. Not individuals who feel like I do about it . . .'

'You fell in love with it, didn't you?'

He sighed and paused.

'Well, yes, I did. Especially the glasshouse. We'll talk about that one day. But, listen, if you want to know – one of the bodies is a charity. It runs homes for maladjusted children . . .'

'Oh, very apt,' Phoebe interrupted with a mocking laugh. 'Just right to follow Martha and me. Maladjusted children, that's us . . .'

'You idiot,' he said affectionately. 'That's not how you strike me. But more of that anon also.'

'And the other interested party?'

'That's some commercial outfit. Medical insurance, I think. They want it as their new headquarters. Lots of businesses are moving out of London these days, snapping up country manors and mansions. They'll pay a good price. Don't worry, Phoebe. One of them will take it.'

'There we are then. I won't worry, I promise. And I'll take care that Mart doesn't, either. But what about the twins thing? Did you find anything?'

'Yes. It's clear as daylight. Got paper and pencil handy? It's from an American book on heredity — lots of stuff on identical twins and then, about fraternal twins, it says, "These are two-egg twins, products of two different eggs and two different sperms" — I say, my secretary is having fits. We're not used to such clinical explicitness here.' He laughed and Phoebe heard a feminine giggle in the background. I wonder if she's pretty, she thought. And if he fancies her. 'There's more here about fraternal twins, how they can be no more alike than other non-twin children of the family, etc., etc. Do you want all that?'

'No. I'll read it up later. Let's have the seminal part — if you'll pardon the expression . . .'

'Witty too! All right . . . here we are. I quote again: "Fraternal twins just happen to be conceived about the same time, when a mother produces two eggs instead of the usual one, and each egg is fertilized by a different sperm . . ."'

'At about the same time? Oh dear, that doesn't sound too hopeful . . .'

'Hang on. I'm coming to the crunch. "In rare instances one of a pair of fraternal twins may be conceived several days, or even a week or more, after the other." So how's that?'

'But, Charles, that's fine as far as timing goes. But it doesn't say anything about different fathers.'

'It doesn't have to, does it? How much explicitness do you want, for goodness sake? If twins can result from two different sexual acts — I put it no more baldly than that, Phoebe' — she heard another feminine giggle in the background — 'then it follows that it can be two different men participating in those acts. So there you are. I rest my case . . .'

'Yes, Charles, that's clear. So you were right. I can't thank you enough. It means a lot to us, you know . . .'

'Think nothing of it. But kindly stay in my debt. I shall take advantage of that in due course . . . All right if I ring off now? I'd better get along to my lunch appointment. See you soon.'

'Goodbye. And thanks again.'

Phoebe put the phone down with a contented sigh, reflecting happily on the sound of Charles's voice as much as on what he had said. How easily and dependably he had strolled into their lives and thrown light into the dark corners. The longer she thought about this ease and dependability of his, and the bland, unthreatening 'ordinariness' – she could think of no better word for his apparent lack of any neurotic urge to play games – the harder it was to think of him as the owner of Ballads. It was sad, but right, that he had lost it. There had been little ease here for any of its inhabitants. And it was not a place for dependability or everyday human kindness. 'The hand of Ballads' – Rose's menacing phrase – would have put its mark on him before long.

When Martha came back her face fell at the news that Charles was not going to buy Ballads, and fell still further when Phoebe told her who was interested in buying the house instead.

'You mean it'll be offices? Desks and filing cabinets here in the drawing-room? And in all the bedrooms too, no doubt.'

Martha had come back full of satisfaction with the visit to her husband and sons. This latest news was so far from her fantasy of Ballads being restored and treasured by the appreciative Charles that it completely wiped out her feeling of well-being. In its place was anger at the contrariness of life which gave with one hand and took with the other.

'It's monstrous,' she said angrily. 'Are we going to allow it?'

'We'll have to, Mart. We're selling it, and that's that. Who it goes to, provided we get the price we want – or more – just doesn't have to matter.'

'Well, it does matter to me . . .'

'Only if you keep looking backwards. Don't, Mart. Let's look ahead.'

'Christ! One of your auntie homilies. You can trot one out for every occasion, can't you? What about the glasshouse? Had you thought about that?'

'What do you mean?'

'Well, a bunch of bloody clerks isn't likely to look after it, that's for certain. They won't want the vine, for a start. Not if they're going to stick their desks and typing chairs and nasty little plastic baskets in there as well as everywhere else.'

'We don't know that. They might want to keep it up as it is. Why don't we wait and see?'

Martha's anger had now turned to frustration at Phoebe's calm acceptance. She paced the floor of the drawing-room, darting distracted looks at the corner of the glasshouse just visible through the windows. Phoebe watched her helplessly, dreading the inevitable moment when Martha's anger would surrender to tears.

But that moment did not come. Instead, with big, angry strides, Martha walked across to the bookcase and, with both hands, wrenched a volume from one of the shelves, whirled round on her heel and pitched the book forcefully in Phoebe's direction. From her red, contorted face, in a voice utterly unlike hers, came a series of staccato shouts.

'You rotten bitch! You bitch. You always spoil things. Always. You cold, rotten bitch. I'm fed up with the sight of you.'

The book came hurtling past Phoebe's head and landed behind her on the floor. It was spread open, its spine uppermost, and as Phoebe went to pick it up she could not resist glancing at the title.

'Oh, it's *Rogue Herries*,' she said in a matter-of-fact voice. 'It's ages since I read any of the Herries books. Do you know this one?'

Martha's anger collapsed like a pierced bubble. She walked slowly towards Phoebe, half contrite, half indignant.

'Is that all you can do, start reading? You really are very

odd sometimes. It almost hit you . . . I'm sorry. I don't know what came over me.'

Phoebe looked up from the book and smiled forgivingly.

'You were angry,' she said. 'And had good reason. But at least it was out instead of in. I bet you feel better now.'

'Therapy time, is it?' Martha was laughing now, and came to take the book from Phoebe. 'Yes, I feel a lot better. But I don't altogether understand why. Still, it doesn't matter. You're not a bitch, of course . . .'

'Oh yes, I sometimes am!'

'OK. OK.' Martha raised her hand to silence Phoebe. 'If you say so. But you'll never get me to feel any differently about the glasshouse. Maybe it will end up in the hands of people who don't give a button for it. But don't expect me to like it.'

'I don't. And I won't like it either. But let's cross that bridge . . . For now, the important thing is what Charles has dug up about twins. I take it you'd like to know.'

Martha nodded. 'But only the gist, Fee. Not a great treatise on it.'

Phoebe reached for the piece of paper on which she had noted the telephone conversation with Charles.

'It's just as he said, actually. With two-egg twins, like us, one could be conceived several days or even a week or more after the other.'

'No, I can't believe it. It sounds so weird.'

'It's true, Mart, honestly. It came from an American book by some expert on genetics. Charles read it out and I took it down. Mind you, it does say that this is rare. But the main point is that it's possible and that's all we needed to know.'

'That's right. It's enough. But it's confusing too. Let me get it straight.' Martha looked seriously at Phoebe and began to count off the possible variations on her fingers. 'One is that Colin could be the father of both of us. Two is that Francis could be the father of both of us. And three is that Colin could be my father and Francis could be yours. Right?'

'You're forgetting a fourth possibility – that Colin could be my father and Francis could be yours.'

'No, I didn't forget. That's a possibility that doesn't appeal to me. But, Fee, the marvellous thing is that these are all possibilities; none of them is a certainty. So we can decide what we like. Same father, or different ones.'

'And you don't mind not knowing for sure?'

Martha shook her head.

'No, not a bit. I've got used to that now. After the diaries, and the talk with Rose, and seeing Alice, I know we can't expect anything else. What I couldn't have borne was to find that Francis was definitely our father. Or that Colin definitely wasn't. And there's always been this longing for some explanation of why we're so different. I mean, in our natures. Because we are, aren't we?'

'Yes. But it's been hard to make that stick. Being lumped together as "the twins" didn't help. And all that strange telepathy business, knowing what you're thinking and what's happening to you when I'm not there . . . it does make you think of mirror images and sameness and, well, almost as if we were two halves of one person . . .'

'That's it,' Martha sounded jubilant. 'And now it's sort of up to us. We've got some control over it. You can believe whatever you like about who your father was. And I can believe whatever I like.'

'Choice! What a luxury!' Phoebe spread her arms wide. 'But I'm not going to choose here and now.'

'Nor me. I'm going to take my time.'

'And bags we don't help each other. It's got to be independent.'

'Of course . . .'

After a short silence, Phoebe said, 'I want to know how things went with Donald.'

'Oh, that's all falling into place,' Martha said, cheerfully dismissive. 'I shall go on the holiday and then, yes, back with them. Not because I can't have Ballads any more. It's because I want to be with them. I guess I need them – and I love them. And Donald is good for me.'

Phoebe searched her sister's face for any sign of doubt, found none and nodded happily.

Without another word the twins rose and strolled into the glasshouse, where they sat in silence, easing themselves into the novel sensation of separateness. Once more, and for the last time, they darkness watched as the sun set beyond the western garden wall and slowly fell on the lawns, the fountain and the quince tree.

Mr Coleherne the estate agent strode into the hall at Ballads with far more assurance than on his previous visit with the Endicotts. He wore a pork-pie hat at a jaunty angle and, once inside, removed it with a theatrical sweep of his arm. As he grasped Martha's hand in greeting, she had the feeling that he was about to raise it to his lips and give it a courtly kiss.

She drew her hand back. 'What, no clip-board?' she said.

'Not necessary,' Mr Coleherne said breezily. 'It's in the bag, dear ladies. Mr Hardy, the purchaser – and I can safely call him that – is close behind me in his own chariot. All he wants is a rapid, a very rapid, look at the inside of the house. He's already seen the outside and pronounced himself satisfied.'

Mr Coleherne was himself positively glowing with satisfaction. He had vastly enjoyed having two would-be purchasers in contention and seeing his commission pleasurably rise as they plied him with bids and counter-bids. All his misgivings about the saleability of Ballads had been scotched. And there was no Mrs Hardy to queer the deal. It was a glorious day for Mr Coleherne and he even found himself feeling genuinely friendly towards the vendors.

'You mean he definitely wants it? Before he even sees inside?' Martha asked incredulously.

'Oh yes. And his money's good – I've checked on that.'

'And which one is he? The charity or the insurance firm?'

Mr Coleherne drew himself up proudly.

'He's none other than the chief accountant for the most rapidly growing firm in his field.'

'And his field is . . .?' Phoebe asked.

'Ours not to question,' Mr Coleherne said, looking a little uncomfortable. 'Insurance he says, so insurance it is.'

'An accountant, you said. What on earth does he know about property? And why would a commercial outfit want Ballads?'

Mr Coleherne felt his friendliness draining away and stiffened his smile.

'Now, Miss Whittaker, let's not look a gift horse in the mouth, eh? It's the position he's after most, I gather. And, of course, let's not kid ourselves, there's cheap labour to be drawn on around here. Those are good selling-points, you know. I made the most of them and they paid off.'

He paused, inviting their praise for his acumen. The twins were silent, however, and he continued in the same breezy tone.

'Better if you leave all the talking to me. I understand these money johnnies very well. A word out of place and he might seize the chance of lowering the price. Get my meaning?'

He tapped the side of his nose and winked at Martha.

'All right then . . .' Phoebe was prevented from making any further grudging comments by the sound of a car drawing up in the drive. There was a throaty roar from the engine just before it came to a stop. It sounded as if the silencer was missing. Either he's an aggressive type who likes to make a din, Phoebe thought, or he's the sort to run his car into the ground before getting a new one. Either way, it wasn't her idea of an appropriate owner for Ballads. She looked at Martha with foreboding.

Mr Coleherne darted out of the front door and came back with a man at his side who uncomfortably upset the twins' notions of what an accountant should look like. He was enormously fat, sported side-burns, a full beard and a walrus moustache, and wore a loose-cut suit with built-up shoulders of such an astonishing width that it gave the impression of a clothes-hanger, or possibly several, having been left inside.

His handshake was more in the nature of a tug at a pump-handle, leaving the twins clasping their wrists as if to check that their hands were still attached. He nodded at Mr Coleherne and strode to the drawing-room door with as much panting and puffing as if he were climbing a hill.

348

'This the lounge?' he said, with the hint of an accent that Phoebe tried, and failed, to place. He walked into the room.

Martha hovered by the doorway, anxious to go through the motions of a good hostess.

In a polite, interested voice she said, 'So you're in insurance, is that right, Mr Hardy?'

Mr Coleherne placed himself quickly between Martha and the drawing-room door and put his finger to his lips.

'No questions,' he hissed. 'Leave it to me.'

From inside came a loud laugh and, 'Yeah, that's right,' then the sound of Mr Hardy's lumbering steps towards the windows and back again. When he came into the hall he was holding one of the handles from the glass-fronted bookcase.

'This fell off,' he said and thrust it into Mr Coleherne's hand. 'What's that great glass thing at the back?'

'Ah, yes, the glasshouse. Quite a feature . . . shall we take a look?'

Mr Hardy edged the estate agent towards the stairs.

'Not now. I'll have a quick butcher's upstairs. Then the kitchen and the gubbins at the back.'

The twins stood in the hall on the verge of hysteria.

'Accountant, my foot,' Martha said, stifling a guffaw.

'Likewise insurance. I just don't believe it, Mart, do you? Those spivvy clothes! And all that hair round his face. I've never seen anything so bizarre. What do you think he's really into? And that accent — I can't put my finger on it. Is it American?'

Martha shrugged.

'Could be. Or perhaps Australian. Or Cockney. But what gets me is the offhandedness of it all. He acts like someone handling stolen goods. So does Mr Coleherne. No questions asked and if the money's good, cut and run — that kind of thing. Perhaps he's a crook. Or a member of the Mafia. Or he's going to run something illegal here. A gambling den. Or a brothel. Or one of those cults that brain-wash people and turn them into zombies . . . what's up with you?'

Phoebe was almost bent double with laughter.

'You and your fevered imagination,' she said, struggling

for breath and a straight face. 'He could simply be an accountant who eats too much. And has an appalling clothes-sense.'

'And no access to a razor. And a clapped-out car . . .'

They heard the men's footsteps come back along the first-floor corridor towards the head of the stairs. Phoebe grasped Martha's hand.

'Let's get out of the way. Come on. I don't care what he thinks about the rest of the house. But when he gets to the glasshouse, I want to be there.'

Mr Hardy could have done no more than glance at the downstairs rooms, for the twins scarcely had time to subdue their mirth and take up casual attitudes in the glasshouse before he came puffing down the shallow step with Mr Coleherne close behind him. The estate agent looked pleased but wary, as if he feared a fall at the last hurdle.

To the twins' amazement, Mr Hardy looked neither to left nor right, nor up at the vine, nor out at the garden. He came straight towards them, rubbing his hands and smiling amiably.

'Very nice, very nice,' he said. 'That's it then. We have ourselves a deal. Mr Coldtrain can take it from here. Solicitors' names, draft contracts, all that business, get the ball rolling. Completion a-s-a-p will suit me. Should be all over in a few weeks.'

'But . . . but . . .' Martha looked at him in bewilderment. 'What about this? The glasshouse. You haven't really looked at it . . .'

Mr Coleherne was signalling frantically behind him, his hands making closing gestures, his mouth a firm 'no' and his eyes imploring the twins to keep silent.

Phoebe frowned at him and went to Martha's side, facing Mr Hardy with an encouraging smile.

'Yes. You haven't said anything about it. We'd so like to know what you think of it. How do you imagine you might use it?'

He appeared to be not in the least put out by the twins' insistence and merely glanced quickly round him and above him.

'Nice bit of ivy up there,' he said. 'Should be out of doors, shouldn't it? But no. I shan't have any use for a greenhouse this size. The devil to keep warm, isn't it? No, this'll come down. Cost a fortune to replace all those cracked panes anyway.'

'Too right,' said Mr Coleherne treacherously, beaming with relief.

Mr Hardy thumped the floor with his foot.

'The foundations seem quite solid. I'll probably have an extension here of some sort. How's that?' He smiled affably, as if he had now made amends. 'Righto then. That's all up to me now. What's the name of this place, by the way?'

He was turning for the door and looking at Mr Coleherne impatiently.

'Ballads,' Martha said faintly.

'I might keep that,' he said, with the air of offering a final redeeming favour.

Mr Coleherne scurried out of the glasshouse after him, turning at the door to give a thumbs-up sign.

The twins looked at each other, knowing they had cause for celebration yet feeling strangely downcast.

'Ivy?' said Martha contemptuously. 'He didn't even realize it was a vine.'

'He didn't seem to realize anything. It was just an outsize greenhouse to him. A greenhouse! I ask you! What a berk . . .'

'Slightly anti-climax department, isn't it? But at least it's sold, that's the main thing. I just wish I could feel all joyful about it, but I don't.'

Martha looked questioningly at Phoebe, wanting a lead.

'Not joyful, no,' Phoebe said. 'But I do feel sort of ready now to start packing and sorting things out. There isn't a lot of time.'

'We can have big bonfires.'

'And put things in a sale . . .'

'Donald and the boys will come and help.'

'And I'll get on with looking for a home. I'll go by the sea, that's what I've decided. I've always wanted to live by the sea.'

The glasshouse seemed warm again now. The twins relaxed and sat down, Phoebe on a settee, Martha in Colin's chair. They looked up at the vine. Its gnarled, twisted trunk and branches, more like weathered rope than living plant, seemed to them as immovable and solid as the house itself. Phoebe stood and reached up and tucked a wayward tendril behind another. The nearby clusters of grapes shook and swung at the disturbance. She smiled at Martha and sat down again. In both their minds were images of past times – of Colin on a ladder, snipping at the ripe fruit and lowering the bunches gently into their outstretched hands, of hours spent plucking the grapes from their stems, of the buckets and bins and bowls holding the juice at various stages of its trans-formation into wine, of Alice taking a testing sip from a glass and saying, 'Ummm. Not bad this year,' of Colin rolling the liquid round and round in his mouth, a measuring look in his dark eyes, and delivering his judgement – 'Too sweet,' he would sometimes say, or, 'Passable, considering we had no summer.' Last of all were the images of row upon row of bottles in the dairy, full of the pale, clear, rose-tinted golden liquid, each with a label in Colin's hand saying simply 'Bal-lads' and the year.

'Some years it was pretty awful,' Martha said dreamily. 'Remember the year it was so cold and wet that they never ripened at all? This year's look pretty good to me. A bumper crop, as they say. What shall we do with it?'

'There won't be enough time to do anything much with it. Why don't we just cut the fruit? We could eat some. You could take some to Donald. We could hand it around the village. And some to Alice.'

'Charles must have some . . .'

'Yes. Oh Mart, I do wish he could have enjoyed himself here for a while.'

'Especially in the glasshouse . . .'

'The thing is . . . I do just wonder if . . .' Phoebe jerked upright and began to speak forcefully. 'I just can't visualize leaving it like this, waiting for people to come along and end its life. I keep seeing a gang of swarthies coming with pick-axes and laying into it, sawing through the vine and maybe even using dynamite. I don't want that. It's not right.'

'Colin wouldn't have allowed it,' Martha said indignantly. 'So we shouldn't, should we?'

'Maybe not. But we have to. We can't take it with us.'

Phoebe's thoughtful expression slowly changed to an exultant smile.

'In a way, Mart, we could.'

Martha studied her sister's face for a moment and then she too broke into a smile.

'Yes, I see,' she said. 'There *is* a way. You're right. Shall we save it for the last day, just before we go?'

The mental bridge was there again, joining them to each other and to their unspoken plan. Phoebe nodded in agreement.

'Yes, on the last day,' she said.

It was the last day and it was nearly autumn. What little furniture remained, after the series of sales and auctions, had disappeared down the drive an hour before in a large van, on its way to storage. The windows of Ballads were curtainless, the floors bare. Scattered here and there were cardboard boxes of miscellaneous household items, destined either for Martha's new home with her family or for Phoebe's cottage within sight of the sea.

Stripped of all the trappings of life, Ballads was not a home any longer. It seemed to have swelled into a vast, empty public building waiting for some new, alien purpose. Where pictures had been taken down from the walls there were squares and oblongs and ovals of darker wallpaper, kept guarded for years against the light, the colours fresh and unfaded. In every room there were similar patches where pieces of furniture had stood against the walls and left their imprint behind them like giant stencils.

As the twins walked from room to room, checking that nothing had been forgotten, their footsteps echoed in their wake and their voices were bounced from wall to wall, sounding harsh and intrusive. The usual creaks and groans of the woodwork were magnified by space. 'It's protesting,' Martha had whispered. 'We're not wanted here any more.'

They lingered in the room where Colin had poured his emotions into his diary and charted every stick and stone of his beloved home, and they murmured of mundane things like the keys of the house, and whether the outbuildings were cleared, and which of them was to have the pride of the house-plants. In spite of their desultory talk, both appeared to be repressing some kind of anticipation and excitement. They were waiting, it seemed, for the right moment to do something they longed for but also dreaded.

At length, after a long silence, they turned their backs on the room, as if on a given command, and walked slowly out and down the stairs. As they passed through the empty glasshouse Martha took Phoebe's arm, a gesture that started as encouragement to her sister but ended as the means of steadying herself.

The air in the garden was chill, with a slight wind to urge it. It made them quicken their steps as they walked to the quince tree and sat down on the bench circling its trunk. They turned their faces towards the glasshouse.

'How shall we do it?' Martha looked down at the ground and began rubbing at the moss on the wooden slats beside her.

'There's still that pile of logs on the terrace,' Phoebe said in a matter-of-fact voice. 'Not too big to lift . . .'

'And we'll never come back?'

'No.'

'Are you sure?'

'I'm sure.' With a touch of her old bossiness Phoebe added, 'I'm sure for you too. Are you getting cold feet?'

' 'Course not.'

Still they sat, savouring their resolve and their fear. A pale sun shone rosily on the topmost panes of the glasshouse and lit up the spindly brown branches of the cropped vine inside.

'There's one thing,' Martha said. 'I don't know what

you've decided but Colin is my father. That's what I want. He's here. And I want to leave him here.'

'Good. I don't know yet. I haven't decided. I'm not sure I ever will, or want to. It doesn't seem to matter so much now. I'm who I am, not who made me. But,' she sighed long and deeply, 'I do wish life was a bit slower. I wish one had time to learn how to live it . . .'

'Never mind. You can do both, you know, at the same time. Learning and living. Shall we move? It's damp here.'

They stood up and walked briskly towards the terrace alongside the glasshouse, stopping at the pile of split logs, then surveyed the garden for a moment, as if making sure there were no uninvited spectators.

They each picked up a log and, leaning back to get a good momentum, they swung them in a graceful arc towards the glasshouse. They had aimed high and the logs crashed simultaneously through the uppermost panes with a sharp crack, followed by two thuds as they fell to the floor inside, one shortly after the other, and then by the gentler sound of falling glass. This first throw, and the sounds that followed, seemed to release the twins' pent-up energy. They bent quickly for the next logs and whooped and shouted as they threw. Log followed log in quick succession, flying ever faster through the air and thudding ever more loudly against steel and wood and glass.

The falling glass shimmered in the sun and fell in shining waterfalls to the ground. Wood splintered and groaned under the onslaught. The iron framework juddered occasionally but stood its ground as it was gradually denuded of all its covering. Some of the wooden frames were left with spikes of glass clinging to their inner sides. Others were cleanly robbed of every bit of glazing. Many of them were so badly rotted that when they were struck by one of the missiles they crumbled into splinters and fell with the showers of glass to the ground.

Several branches of the vine, formerly trapped by the glass roof into unnatural curves, were set free to sway in the open air. Smaller twigs and shredded leaves mingled with the timber and glass on the floor inside the glasshouse and in a wide crescent outside it. The noise echoed across the garden and over the house to the woods beyond, so that it seemed that a second glasshouse was being shattered a short distance away, and that the entire hill-top and surrounding valleys were being laid waste in an orgy of destruction.

The twins did not pause to see where the logs landed. They moved like over-charged robots, bending to pick up a log, straightening for the throw, leaning forward as the missile was released and stooping down again for another. Their hair flew around their flushed faces and their skirts whirled round their legs as they bent, twisted and turned. They had the fevered air of drug-induced dancers in a primitive ritual of revenge.

'Enough?' shouted Martha at length.

'No, look!' Phoebe pointed to where several panes at the top had escaped the onslaught. They glittered in the pale sun, solitary signals of distress as if from a fast-sinking ship.

'I'll get them,' Martha shouted excitedly.

'And me.'

They stooped and threw for the last time and the rogue panes fell to the ground in defeat. All that was left was the white-coated steel skeleton of the glasshouse, with here and there slivers of wood and glass clinging to the wreckage. The floor of the glasshouse was now part of the garden and was covered with shattered glass, logs, fragments of vine and scraps of timber. The twins stared at it with deep satisfaction. They were both aware that they were standing some distance apart from each other and not hurrying to touch or link arms as they always used to. They felt a strange satisfaction about that too.

They skirted the debris and headed for the French windows to the drawing-room.

'Have you packed?' Phoebe spoke slowly, as if coming out of a trance.

'Yes,' said Martha. 'It's all done.'

FOR THE BEST IN PAPERBACKS, LOOK FOR THE

In every corner of the world, on every subject under the sun, Penguin represents quality and variety – the very best in publishing today.

For complete information about books available from Penguin – including Pelicans, Puffins, Peregrines and Penguin Classics – and how to order them, write to us at the appropriate address below. Please note that for copyright reasons the selection of books varies from country to country.

In the United Kingdom: Please write to *Dept E.P., Penguin Books Ltd, Harmondsworth, Middlesex, UB7 0DA*

If you have any difficulty in obtaining a title, please send your order with the correct money, plus ten per cent for postage and packaging, to *PO Box No 11, West Drayton, Middlesex*

In the United States: Please write to *Dept BA, Penguin, 299 Murray Hill Parkway, East Rutherford, New Jersey 07073*

In Canada: Please write to *Penguin Books Canada Ltd, 2801 John Street, Markham, Ontario L3R 1B4*

In Australia: Please write to the *Marketing Department, Penguin Books Australia Ltd, P.O. Box 257, Ringwood, Victoria 3134*

In New Zealand: Please write to the *Marketing Department, Penguin Books (NZ) Ltd, Private Bag, Takapuna, Auckland 9*

In India: Please write to *Penguin Overseas Ltd, 706 Eros Apartments, 56 Nehru Place, New Delhi, 110019*

In Holland: Please write to *Penguin Books Nederland B.V., Postbus 195, NL–1380AD Weesp, Netherlands*

In Germany: Please write to *Penguin Books Ltd, Friedrichstrasse 10–12, D–6000 Frankfurt Main 1, Federal Republic of Germany*

In Spain: Please write to *Longman Penguin España, Calle San Nicolas 15, E–28013 Madrid, Spain*

In France: Please write to *Penguin Books Ltd, 39 Rue de Montmorency, F-75003, Paris, France*

In Japan: Please write to *Longman Penguin Japan Co Ltd, Yamaguchi Building, 2–12–9 Kanda Jimbocho, Chiyoda-Ku, Tokyo 101, Japan*

A CHOICE OF PENGUIN FICTION

Maia   Richard Adams

The heroic romance of love and war in an ancient empire from one of our greatest storytellers. 'Enormous and powerful' – *Financial Times*

The Warning Bell   Lynne Reid Banks

A wonderfully involving, truthful novel about the choices a woman must make in her life – and the price she must pay for ignoring the counsel of her own heart. 'Lynne Reid Banks knows how to get to her reader: this novel grips like Super Glue' – *Observer*

Doctor Slaughter   Paul Theroux

Provocative and menacing – a brilliant dissection of lust, ambition and betrayal in 'civilized' London. 'Witty, chilly, exuberant, graphic' – *The Times Literary Supplement*

Wise Virgin   A. N. Wilson

Giles Fox's work on the Pottle manuscript, a little-known thirteenth-century tract on virginity, leads him to some innovative research on the subject that takes even his breath away. 'A most elegant and chilling comedy' – *Observer* Books of the Year

Gone to Soldiers   Marge Piercy

Until now, the passions, brutality and devastation of the Second World War have only been written about by men. Here for the first time, one of America's major writers brings a woman's depth and intensity to the panorama of world war. 'A victory' – *Newsweek*

Trade Wind   M. M. Kaye

An enthralling blend of history, adventure and romance from the author of the bestselling *The Far Pavilions*

A CHOICE OF PENGUIN FICTION

The Ghost Writer   Philip Roth

Philip Roth's celebrated novel about a young writer who meets and falls in love with Anne Frank in New England – or so he thinks. 'Brilliant, witty and extremely elegant' – *Guardian*

Small World   David Lodge

Shortlisted for the 1984 Booker Prize, *Small World* brings back Philip Swallow and Maurice Zapp for a jet-propelled journey into hilarity. 'The most brilliant and also the funniest novel that he has written' – *London Review of Books*

Moon Tiger   Penelope Lively

Winner of the 1987 Booker Prize, *Moon Tiger* is Penelope Lively's 'most ambitious book to date' – *The Times* 'A complex tapestry of great subtlety . . . Penelope Lively writes so well, savouring the words as she goes' – *Daily Telegraph* 'A very clever book: it is evocative, thought-provoking and hangs curiously on the edges of the mind long after it is finished' – *Literary Review*

Absolute Beginners   Colin MacInnes

The first 'teenage' novel, the classic of youth and disenchantment, *Absolute Beginners* is part of MacInnes's famous London trilogy – and now a brilliant film. 'MacInnes caught it first – and best' – *Harpers and Queen*

July's People   Nadine Gordimer

Set in South Africa, this novel gives us an unforgettable look at the terrifying, tacit understandings and misunderstandings between blacks and whites. 'This is the best novel that Miss Gordimer has ever written' – Alan Paton in the *Saturday Review*

The Ice Age   Margaret Drabble

'A continuously readable, continuously surprising book . . . here is a novelist who is not only popular and successful but formidably growing towards real stature' – *Observer*

A CHOICE OF PENGUIN FICTION

The Dearest and the Best Leslie Thomas

In the spring of 1940 the spectre of war turned into grim reality – and for all the inhabitants of the historic villages of the New Forest it was the beginning of the most bizarre, funny and tragic episode of their lives. 'Excellent' – *Sunday Times*

Only Children Alison Lurie

When the Hubbards and the Zimmerns go to visit Anna on her idyllic farm, it becomes increasingly difficult to tell which are the adults, and which the children. 'It demands to be read' – *Financial Times* 'There quite simply is no better living writer' – John Braine

My Family and Other Animals Gerald Durrell

Gerald Durrell's wonderfully comic account of his childhood years on Corfu and his development as a naturalist and zoologist is a true delight. Soaked in Greek sunshine, it is a 'bewitching book' – *Sunday Times*

Getting it Right Elizabeth Jane Howard

A hairdresser in the West End, Gavin is sensitive, shy, into the arts, prone to spots and, at thirty-one, a virgin. He's a classic late developer – and maybe it's getting too late to develop at all? 'Crammed with incidental pleasures . . . sometimes sad but more frequently hilarious . . . *Getting it Right* gets it, comically, right' – Paul Bailey in the *London Standard*

The Vivisector Patrick White

In this prodigious novel about the life and death of a great painter, Patrick White, winner of the Nobel Prize for Literature, illuminates creative experience with unique truthfulness. 'One of the most interesting and absorbing novelists writing English today' – Angus Wilson in the *Observer*

The Echoing Grove Rosamund Lehmann

'No English writer has told of the pains of women in love more truly or more movingly than Rosamund Lehmann' – Marghanita Laski. 'She uses words with the enjoyment and mastery with which Renoir used paint' – Rebecca West in the *Sunday Times* 'A magnificent achievement' – John Connell in the *Evening News*

A CHOICE OF PENGUIN FICTION

Other Women   Lisa Alther

From the bestselling author of *Kinflicks* comes this compelling novel of today's woman – and a heroine with whom millions of women will identify.

Your Lover Just Called   John Updike

Stories of Joan and Richard Maple – a couple multiplied by love and divided by lovers. Here is the portrait of a modern American marriage in all its mundane moments and highs and lows of love as only John Updike could draw it.

Mr Love and Justice   Colin MacInnes

Frankie Love took up his career as a ponce at about the same time as Edward Justice became vice-squad detective. Except that neither man was particularly suited for his job, all they had in common was an interest in crime. Provocative and honest and acidly funny, *Mr Love and Justice* is the final volume of Colin MacInnes's famous London trilogy.

An Ice-Cream War   William Boyd

As millions are slaughtered on the Western Front, a ridiculous and little-reported campaign is being waged in East Africa – a war they continued after the Armistice because no one told them to stop. 'A towering achievement' – John Carey, Chairman of the Judges of the 1982 Booker Prize, for which this novel was shortlisted.

Fool's Sanctuary   Jennifer Johnston

Set in Ireland in the 1920s, Jennifer Johnston's beautiful novel tells of Miranda's growing up into political awareness. Loyalty, romance and friendship are fractured by betrayal and the gunman's flight for freedom, honour and pride. 'Her novels . . . are near perfect literary jewels' – *Cosmopolitan*

The Big Sleep   Raymond Chandler

'I was neat, clean, shaved and sober, and I didn't care who knew it. I was everything the well-dressed private detective ought to be. I was calling on four million dollars'. 'A book to be read at a sitting' – *Sunday Times*

10H9F